Abduction

Abduction

Anouar Benmalek

Translated by Simon Pare

ARABIA BOOKS

Copyright © Anouar Benmalek 2011

First Published in France as *Le Rapte* by Editions Fayard
Copyright © Editions Fayard 2009

First published in Great Britain in 2011 by
Arabia Books, 70 Cadogan Place, London SW1X 9AH

Ouvrage publié avec le soutien du Centre national du livre.
Published with the support of the Centre National du Livre.

English translation copyright © Simon Pare 2011

The moral rights of the author have been asserted

A CIP catalogue record for this book is available from the British Library

ISBN 978-1-906697-33-4

Typeset in Minion by MacGuru Ltd
info@macguru.org.uk

Printed and bound by CPI Group (UK) Ltd, Croydon, CR0 4YY

This novel was inspired by actual events.

I condemn no one, I absolve no one.
Chekhov

Why did things happen thus and not otherwise?
Because they did so happen.
Tolstoy

Part I

"It's far too fine for a winter morning. God keeps His books in good order and He never does anything without reason; if it carries on like this, we can expect one hell of a drought this summer. Bloody global warming!" he whispered, his face pale.

I burst out laughing at this non sequitur and the acting Zoo Director's offended tone. He seethed through clenched teeth, probably some insult about people who'd be better off with their balls grafted onto their brains rather than dangling uselessly between their legs. That was his favourite insult, but he only used it when he was in a *good* bad mood, as he put it. Unless, that is, disgusted by the two males coupling in front of us, he had shouted, "May Satan burn your arseholes until the end of time, you damned replicas of the sons of Adam!"

I thought, "You old relic, just admit that you'd love to swap places with these two monkeys! Butt-hole bliss at least once in your life, eh?" The prudish administrator gave me a nasty look as if he'd read my thoughts. I tried to arrange my face into a more serious expression, and we continued our tour of inspection.

I was carrying a spiral-bound notebook and conscientiously writing down my boss's comments (he was acting Director because the incumbent had just been hospitalized with an upset prostate due to the Algerian sun), unaware that by the end of the day I would be in a state worse than death. Or, more precisely, that my agony would commence only a few hours later – a little bit around 9 p.m. and a lot more towards 10 p.m. After that… well, I would envy the imperturbable serenity of those lucky enough to be safely dead and buried.

The day had started well enough, even if, from time to time, an unpleasant pinching in my stomach reminded me that Meriem, the woman I had loved for the last fifteen years, had mentioned divorce for the first time the week before. I had made the mistake of reacting to her recriminations with a joke. And that had really got her angry. She'd slammed our bedroom door and slept on the couch. The next morning we hadn't mentioned our argument, but that day and the following ones she refused to let me give her my usual quick kiss before we parted for the day, me heading off to my bread-and-butter job as a biologist at Algiers Zoo, and she to her foreign language institute. I had left earlier than her this particular morning; we had only one car, which we used alternately, and it was my turn to take the bus.

She had caught me on the doorstep – after once more rejecting my kiss – and told me in a concerned tone of voice, "Our girl's having trouble at school. I've looked through her exercise books – they're a right mess. We're going to have to crack down on her."

"Can you really see me lecturing her on her birthday?"

"Her birthday's no excuse."

She gave me what I call her 'responsible mother' look (which meant: look out, you little pervert, this has got nothing to do with any of our kiss-and-make-up stuff or our more and more frequent arguments. It's about something more serious, sacred even – *the-fate-of-our-daughter*!)

"I think she's got a boyfriend…"

I didn't like the way those three suspension points had virtually materialised in the air between us. I grumbled, pretending that I didn't understand.

"She's got several boyfriends, and some girlfriends too, hasn't she?"

"Don't act the fool, Aziz! You know what I'm talking about. I found a note from some little shit in with her things. He arranged to meet her at the cinema in the Ryadh el-Feth shopping centre. And guess how he signed it?"

She threw her arms up.

"'*I luv you, darlin*', with 'love' spelt wrong and no 'g' on the end of 'darling'. The kid's an ignoramus too."

A look of dumb protest must have appeared on my face, something like: *Come on, she's too young for stuff like that!* I went bright red. I must have blushed (to judge by my wife's mocking expression) as badly as when she had told me six months earlier in a normal, chatty tone of voice that our daughter – whom I still called *my baby* far too often – had had her first period.

"At the cinema? The day before yesterday? But she was at school…"

The same suspension points, but this time it was I who had uttered them.

"Yes, she skived off. Your beloved daughter is a liar. Girls often lie at her age, and later on too. Didn't you know that?" she added with that little condescending laugh that really got under my skin.

A worry line quickly creased her brow.

"Remember the kind of neighbourhood we live in. The woman next-door whispered to me that the imam's wife is spreading nasty gossip about our daughter."

"Well, you know where those yokels the imam and his wife can stick their gossip?"

"Gossiping yokels wearing hijabs and beards can be dangerous in this crazy country!" she hissed. "Half of our neighbours in the City of Joy would sell their souls if the Islamists told them to, remember?"

Bloody City of Joy! Of course I remembered, just as I remembered the overjoyed looks on the faces of some of our neighbours the day after the first attacks on intellectuals and journalists thought to be anti-Islamists. After the sordid murder of a writer in front of his wife and daughter, even the pretty young widow on the sixth floor who made ends meet by trading on her charms had felt obliged to tell me that a new era of justice, free of heathens and heathenism, was nigh.

This bloody City of Joy and bloody us too! We had been forced to hide our worry and feign a neutrality that could be taken for approval. Meriem was careful about her appearance now, and we were both sick of the duplicity we imposed on ourselves. We had realised though that this excitability was not just some burst of political hotheadedness and that it might pose a threat to our physical safety. We had never entirely thrown off that tension, that vital obligation to weigh what we said, since. We weren't the only ones, far from it, who drew a veil if not over our bodies, then at least over our words. Many Algerians, maybe even most – who could know with such a silent people! – waited in spineless anxiety to see which way the wind would blow. While fate dithered over whom to make the country's new rulers, it was better not to get one's feet wet. "If you are killed in this godforsaken, lawless country, only your mother will mourn you for more than a day; everyone else, starting with your closest friends, will hasten to dry their tears for fear that their grief will identify them to your enemies!" were the words of wisdom doing the rounds in Algiers.

As for me, after a few years of this exhausting ordeal, I had become a master of the art of charting a course between completely opposing opinions and leaving my interlocutor from the City of Joy – no matter whether he was an Islamist, a policeman or just an 'ordinary' neighbour! – convinced, through a series of knowing expressions and smiles, that I wholeheartedly agreed with him. With one exception: the overly friendly ground-floor tenant, always dressed in the same dark jacket, who said he was a simple postal worker and whom I suspected of being an army or police informer, albeit a lowly one, since he lived in the same trashy block of flats I did.

Fifty-odd and balding, he had an unpleasant way of pressing your fingers while asking his harmless questions. I felt both sullied by the touch of his hand and vaguely uneasy at the feeling of guilt he inspired in me, even when he was asking me what I thought of the weather. "Rat-man!" I had once insulted him under my breath and I had thought, later, that this name suited him well. Rumour had it that he had been involved in the riots of October '88 while officiating in a different part of the Algiers area, and that he had taken advantage of this to rape some teenagers who had been arrested during the troubles. These events had taken place in a police station according to some, and in a paratroopers' barracks according to others. The man didn't seem to have got wind of these grave accusations – or else he couldn't care less – because he didn't think twice about going to the mosque every Friday dressed in a magnificent white burnous.

I had inherited this miserable dwelling after my father died in an accident; my mother had been divorced since I was a teenager and had opted to go and live out her days with my older sister in the village of her birth. Mine and Meriem's salaries didn't allow us to rent a flat in a less seedy area. I had resigned myself to living in this hole infested with bearded men for a few more years while we saved up a few hypothetical wads of dinars.

"OK, OK," I had granted Meriem in my cowardice, "we'll talk about it with Shehera this evening if I don't get home too late. You better believe it; it's going to be a real family council with lots of arguing. And some beatings, if you insist! By then I'll have grown a moustache so that I'm up to the task! And I'll buy a burqa too, just to be on the safe side."

"You never take anything seriously, do you? You always find a way to wriggle out of it," she'd muttered, but broke off because our

6

daughter, barefoot and in her pyjamas, had joined us by the front door. Although her eyes were still sleepy, she already had one Walkman earphone in her right ear, which she claimed was the more 'musical'.

"Hi Mum, hi Dad," she'd called with a lisp that an expensive speech therapist was battling to correct – but which still made me melt with selfish affection.

"You're late getting up, Sheherazade."

I always used the full version of her first name when I was about to tell her off. She didn't like her first name – the cliché of the tacky Oriental princess – and in any case, she said firmly, no man, not even a king, would keep her nattering away for a thousand and one nights.

"My first lesson's at 10 o'clock. The maths teacher's off ill. Lucky really, because I don't understand a thing he says!"

"We need to talk to you, Shehera. I haven't got time now – we've got a rush on. A committee from the ministry is descending on us tomorrow. And take that earphone out – you'll go deaf!"

I had put on a stern voice, but my charming (and lying) daughter took no notice. She pushed me out of the door.

"You'll miss your bus and your animals will die of boredom without you. Don't forget to give Lucette a kiss from me. Tell her I'll be over soon to teach her about DMS."

'DMS' stood for 'Daddy, Mummy, Sweetie', Shehera's first words, and the only ones she had uttered for so long that we had worried that she might be retarded… until, overnight, our daughter had decided to chatter more than a flock of magpies in spring.

I had smiled and Meriem, disheartened by my attitude, had shrugged and reminded me not to forget to invite my vet colleague to Shehera's birthday lunch, which we had put back to the weekend.

As I left the building, I had almost walked straight into the widow from the sixth floor. She'd aged terribly, in her veil and her black gloves. I had said hello to her. Head down, she had mumbled a reply. I had been told that, at the beginning of the troubles, some night-time visitors with sawn-off shotguns had threatened her with the ultimate punishment if she didn't change profession. Ever since then, the too-beautiful bigot, terrified and desperate to make amends for her bad habits of the past, never left the local mosque. From time to time, however, howling children, spurred on by some jealous wife, would fling oaths at her as she passed. Recalling her once eloquently jiggling

7

buttocks, I caught myself thinking, "What a waste! All those dicks in distress while a magnificent backside that Mother Nature and Darwin put so much passion into sculpting grows wrinkly from lack of use…"

I had bought a newspaper and some mints from Moh, the limbless man who spent summer and winter in front of a makeshift shelter halfway between the bus stop and the zoo's ticket office. Torso balancing on a crate mounted on casters, he had called out an offhand "Hello, doctor! Are you doing all right?" to which I had replied, "Yes! And yourself? And may I remind you that I'm not a doctor, unfortunately!"

I never went any further because the man's unfailing good mood made me uncomfortable. It was as if I could hear him saying, *Look on my misfortune, mate, and acknowledge how brave I am, as someone who moans at every opportunity yourself! Reckon there's a place with my name on it in heaven?* He was always ready with a joke, stammering out the punch line amid hoots of laughter. I had dropped the money in a plastic box covered in verses from the Koran standing on a table decorated with the same texts. One day when I voiced my surprise, he told me that he had surrounded himself with sacred scripture to keep swindlers at bay.

"As you can see, I can't run or throw stones! So I make do with appeals to people's piety. But Holy Scripture doesn't make any difference because there are as many thieves in this country as flies on a general's turd!"

He had lowered his voice. "My poor mother slipped a Koran into the inside pocket of my jacket to protect me. She brought it back from Mecca, where she paid a lot of money for it. That's what she says anyway. My mother's extremely stingy, but she must be telling the truth because the cover's decorated with gold thread. But if guys round here found out, they'd strip me down to my underwear and nick it!"

I had grimaced. "But you don't mind telling *me* your story about the golden Koran?" Rubbing his nose with his stump, he had retorted, "You're a doctor, not a thief… Well, until proof of the contrary at least!" before bursting out laughing again.

I had reluctantly shaken the hand of the guard behind the counter of the ticket office. He did have two (sticky) hands – as if he hadn't bothered to wipe them after wanking, one of my female colleagues said with revulsion. A little further on, I had chucked a sweet into my mouth, a paltry substitute for the cigarettes I hadn't smoked for some time now. It took me a few more seconds of pity and disgust for the image of the limbless man to fade and to rid myself of the foolish, but persistent impression that the handicapped man's rotten luck would rub off on me.

I went out of my way to greet Lucette, as I had promised Shehera – and there I met my boss, already out and about, and took out my spiral-bound notebook to make him think that I was already hard at work. Some time previously, my daughter and I had watched a documentary containing virtual images of man's ancestors. The film had made a great impression on Shehera, who had claimed that our little female monkey was the spitting image of the computer-generated Australopithecus on the television. She had made me promise to put pressure on my colleagues to officially call her Lucette – the descendant, all the way from prehistoric times, of the venerable Lucy in the film. Luckily, Lounes, a family friend and our zoo's head vet, had agreed to this with good grace, although he doubted whether the real Lucy had been as wild as the modern cousins of hers we had recently welcomed.

The baby monkey eyed me indifferently before resuming its suckling, while the two hairy rascals went about the business that had so shocked Hajji Sadok. The acting Director conspicuously avoided looking at the primate enclosure. I saw that he was afraid that this morning's visitors would be party to the sight of a large male primate fornicating with an ape of the same sex with unrestrained joy.

Catching an involuntary glimpse of the delighted face of the ape being 'paid' homage by its fellow, Hajji Sadok gave a nervous chuckle, much to my surprise.

"No doubt about it, it's all these bastards ever think about! What did we call them again?"

"Kader and John."

"And is the Arab the one…"

"The Arab? What do you think the other one is, a Texan?"

"Kader the monkey, I mean…"

"Yes, that's Kader mounting his mate right now. The Arab world has shafted America this morning. But I think that geopolitics is, erm, quite democratic in this case; they take it in turns."

9

Hajji Sadok stared me in the eye and his gaze was clearly to remind me of the respect due to a superior, even an acting director. Suddenly he commented irritably, "This habit of giving them human names is ridiculous. What's more, they look so like us… In my opinion, it's verging on blasphemy."

Still worried, he added, "I hope these stupid apes tone things down. Can you imagine if a group of school kids walk past? Not to mention all the beardy weirdies lurking around the zoo to flush out illegitimate couples. They'll accuse us of corrupting youth."

Adopting the neutral tone of a bureaucrat weighing up the pros and cons, I replied, "They're quite capable of chucking a bomb into the monkey cages or sending us a kamikaze in a hurry to swap his ugly wife for a harem of *houris*. But let's not forget the pimps making sure their prostitutes are hard at work in the bushes all over the zoo. They'll be desperate to jump on our bonobos' bandwagon! Men in Algiers are so scared of stray bullets and bombings, they're not as horny as they used to be. Stress is a real downer. Thanks to our bonobos, our hookers soon won't know what's hit them!"

I pretended to look pensive.

"Maybe we should ask the procurers to pay something towards the cost of looking after our animals? These Congolese Casanovas are providing a social service, right? Maybe a political one too, if their fine philandering encourages a few beardies to look for a little tenderness behind a bush rather than poisoning our lives…"

Hajji Sadok stared at me with a mixture of amazement and revulsion. He glanced around to check that no one had overheard me.

"You speak like you spit; you take nothing seriously. You'll live to regret it some day."

My face must have clouded over because a mocking expression lit up the old man's.

"I didn't know you could be so touchy. Got some shame after all, boy?"

"Firstly, I'm not a boy. And secondly, you're only the second person to accuse me of not taking anything seriously today."

He burst out laughing.

"But you take that *seriously*? Well, well, that is progress, *boy*!"

I deflected the conversation by pointing to what we called the monkey enclosure, a small space separated off from the public by wire fencing and a wide ditch with a series of cages at the back that were open during the day. Having just exchanged something more than a few caresses, the two anthropoids were now sharing some fruit. One of them was chewing on his orange with such languidness that it made me think of smoking a cigarette after sex.

"Anyway, great apes fucking each other up the arse isn't the only thing in life!" exclaimed Hajji Sadok with unexpected cheerfulness and crudeness. "God created what He wished and who are we to question His decrees. Come on, Aziz, I'm going to have a nose around at the ministry; you take a look at the Addax antelopes and then think about getting ready for the visit."

He scratched his head and screwed up his face.

"How about slipping a dose of Valium into their grub?"

"Do you really mean that? (I stared at my boss: the old man really did mean it!) The vet will never buy it. He'll point out that we know nothing about the effects of Valium on these animals and that you are mistaking the bonobos for regular conscripts."

"Quit your mocking. With the committee members coming tomorrow, tell the keepers only to let the females out."

I interrupted him.

"But when the females are together they…"

He broke in.

"Yes, but a woman with a woman is much less shocking than a man with a man."

I stared wide-eyed at him; he'd used the words *woman* and *man* instead of *female* and *male*. He realised his mistake. Ashamed, he pretended to absorb himself in reading the plaque that explained, in gold letters, that the seven bonobo chimpanzees (*Pan paniscus*) were a gift from the Republic of Congo to their sister Republic of Algeria as a token of their eternal friendship after the visit of His Excellency the President, waffle waffle waffle…

My prudish boss walked back to his car grumbling that he couldn't bloody figure out why the Congolese dictator had given our president these kind-of-failed humans instead of some decent animals like those funny lions or elephants.

I hung around for a good quarter of an hour watching Lucette and her mother, whom Shehera and I had rechristened, giving her the obvious name of Lucy. While her baby was suckling, snuggling up to its mother in a disturbingly human way, the female bonobo (a little under 15 years old if the Congolese diplomatic service's official papers were to be believed) flashed me a slightly contemptuous look, as if to say: "You lazy git, haven't you got anything better to do than goggle at the misfortunes of an honest mother and her brat?"

Still clutching her load, she put her fingers through the steel fencing and shook it violently, first with one hand, then both, and finally bringing her lower limbs into play. The baby was thrown off-balance and only just managed to cling on to the hairs on its mother's breast. The female's screaming grew to a deafening crescendo before she suddenly broke off, her throat cramped up. Then, with one last exhausted yelp, she crumpled to the floor in the middle of the patio. She examined her chafed thumb. Sucking the battered digit, her eyes wandering, still panting, she scratched the back of the black ball clinging to her breast with her other hand. The newborn baby's mind must have been full of terrified questions about how the order of her world could have been turned so dreadfully upside down.

The mother ape looked round at the two males, Kader and John, who were picking lice off each other. She thought about getting up, then changed her mind, wedged her baby on one side, placed her fingers on her two labia majora and started massaging her clitoris – without any enthusiasm, as if she were merely passing the time.

I gulped, thinking: "Hey, cousin, if you believe in some bonobo god, this would be the moment for him to show up and remind you that you're in an Arab country, girl! Worse: Arab and Berber, the stupidity of one added to the stupidity of the other! No more al fresco sex, no more female superiority over men! You'll soon be entitled to the local holy trilogy – hijab, niqab and idiot imams – from the age of 7 to 77! You and your family would have been better-off if the chief of the Congo had gone gooey over his Swedish counterpart."

It had only been about a month, we had learned, since the monkeys presented to our president had been deported from their equatorial rainforest home, two months at the most counting the time they'd spent waiting to be freighted from Congo to Algeria. Lounes had made me read the email from a primate protection charity recounting how the monkeys had been 'kidnapped' close to a Japanese research station, somewhere between the Congo River to the north and the

Kasai River to the south. Ignoring the scientists' protests, soldiers armed with tranquilliser guns had lured the bonobos by leaving bunches of bananas in the spot where the primatologists usually left dietary supplements. Some groggy monkeys had fallen out of a tree and died. Others had lain in the undergrowth for hours in agony. An old male had succumbed to a heart attack. The surviving anthropoids had discovered the unfortunate consequences of a revival of political affection between African despots.

Thus our new lodgers had never been in captivity before. I was growing quite familiar with the fits of anxiety and rage that seized them at certain times of the day, especially at dawn. Maybe at night they retreated into dreams of tender delousing sessions under the canopy of their native forests and hence found the return to reality when they woke up all the more cruel and unbearable?

These bloody primates were too like real people. And had I, the failed biologist, really dreamed of following in the great Pasteur's footsteps throughout my adolescence only to resign myself to ending up a mere prison guard for near-humans? I sighed, unhappy that I could find nothing to laugh at in my exaggeration.

"Sorry, Lucy. If it were in my power, I would open every cage in this miserable zoo. But, well, firstly I'd be out of a job and, secondly, what good would it do you to escape in this crazy country? You'd either get raped to death in the bowels of some police station or one of those fanatics of religious beheadings would tear you apart alive!"

I tapped on my notebook. The female ape looked up as if she were listening to me.

"You're right not to believe me, my dear: human beings spend a lot of their time lying. It's true – I was laughing at you, and that's not good."

The word 'lying' reminded me of what Meriem had said about our daughter. I had a premonition that our discussion was going to be difficult because my sweet, stubborn daughter would probably tie herself up in knots of denial, and Meriem, then I, would get angry, first of all with Shehera and then with each other.

I was overcome with a faint sense of nostalgia for the time not so long ago when, as young parents, and close to tears, we had bent over the small creature we'd just brought back from the clinic. Curfew, bombings and massacres might well be the only tangible reality in

Algeria, but in our little abode, Meriem, our still-wrinkled baby and I formed the happiest family in the world.

Even then, of course, I had a big hole in my soul – what Meriem called my almost biological cynicism – as well as the touch of craftiness needed to get by in Algiers somehow. In my defence, there was also the blissful love I felt for my wife. The moment I saw her, everything alive within me – my heart, my balls, my brain, my guts – was shaken to the core. I think that Meriem felt the same wonderful pain. In her more sarcastic moments, she would go on about our first meeting: "An unexpected shock in this land of bombings – what could be more normal?"

We sometimes forced a chuckle at how the history of our relationship seemed to mirror the 'political' almanac of Algeria. We first caught sight of each other during the great riots of October 1988; we fucked for the first time the night of the coup after the Islamists had won the December 1991 elections; and six months later we decided on a rushed wedding following the announcement of President Boudiaf's assassination after his return from Moroccan exile to play the role of puppet for a bunch of potbellied generals. Maybe we were scared of having our throats slit or being blown up before either of us could do something with our lives.

We indeed took full advantage of those early years. Our discussions were fierce, but our tenderness turned out to be boundless, and our desire was often fuelled by the ludicrous places and times we endeavoured to satisfy it in. One evening, for example, we were on our way back from a dinner on the outskirts of Algiers. There was very little traffic because the curfew had been only partially lifted. It was raining and the journey was dreary. We couldn't stand it anymore, so we turned off the road and drove down a dirt track along the side of a wheat field. Meriem had already stripped off on the back seat and I was doing likewise when an old 404 with its headlights on full appeared on the track, which the downpour had turned to mud. A whole family was squashed inside, probably local farmers on their way home. Seeing us in the nude, the patriarch in his *chèche* turban, his wife wrapped in her *haik* and their swarm of children were initially stunned, but this quickly changed to indignation.

"How dare you? You're on my land, you dogs!"

The driver had got out of his car brandishing a club. Panicking,

I started the engine while I fumbled with my trousers with my free hand. For a few terrifying seconds, the wheels span in the mud. The 404's driver was banging on the boot of our car like a lunatic while simultaneously damning us, and any swine that might result from our depravity, to drown in the flaming faeces of hell. Meriem, paralysed with fear, made no move to get dressed. Eventually, with a screech of its battered gearbox, the car leapt forwards and we found ourselves driving like lunatics towards Algiers, squawking with laughter and relief, me with my dick out and her stark naked.

"Oh, Meriem…"

Even as I noted down the alterations that needed to be made to the bonobos' shelter, I could feel the questions *Were we still just as much in love or was our love getting bogged down in a pitiful mire of disenchantment?* sticking in my throat like fishbones.

Before… Now…

"Hey Lucy, could you weave me a magic carpet to take me back to those wonderful times before our doubts?"

Lucy turned her back on me.

"You couldn't give a damn about your guards' worries. You've got a tragedy of your own to deal with, haven't you? So who am I supposed to turn to for advice? The only person I've got in Algiers is…"

I stood there stupefied for a few seconds, realising that my intonation had changed and that I was *actually* pleading with an animal for pity.

"Maybe I'll soon be reduced to asking you to read my cards for me, you pancake-faced witch?"

I felt a stab of anguish. Without Meriem and my daughter I was nothing, just one more idiot in a cruel city that was already crawling with them. When I was a kid, I had dreamed of being a knight in shining armour. All I had become, though, was an individual with no particular qualities, a waverer and a fair coward all in all, whose sole success – which was probably undeserved compared to its importance – was to have met Meriem.

I don't know why I started thinking about my wife's family, a strange couple made up of her mother, Latifa, and her stepfather Mathieu, a Frenchman as thin as a prickly pear spine who had lived in Algeria for so long that he spoke Arabic like a native, yet never mentioned the period before independence. He had remained in the country even when the wave of assassinations of foreigners was at its peak, taking only two ridiculous precautions that probably fooled no one: firstly, he put on a farmer's hat every time he went out so as to look as un-European as possible; and secondly he demanded that everyone call him by his chosen Arabic first name, Ali. Once, I thought I could discern the bulge of a pistol beneath his jacket. I had told Meriem, who had muttered that it was just some old handgun with a rusty mechanism and that I shouldn't tell anyone about it. Possessing none of the habitual expansiveness of the European *pied noir* settlers, this man made you ill at ease with his silences and his shy, thin-lipped smiles with their occasional, fleeting flicker of sarcasm. Meriem didn't seem overly keen on her stepfather either and spoke to him in curt, clipped sentences.

I had a burnt taste in my mouth; after several years of marriage, Meriem still held some secrets for me. Everything about her family was obscure to me. It was by a slip of her mother's tongue that I had learned that Meriem's deceased father was a revolutionary hero. He had a street in a town in the Aurès mountains named after him.

I had tried to find out more about the exploits that had earned him this honour. Meriem had quashed my curiosity: "My father died fifteen years ago and it was not easy for any of us, so let's just let him and old stories about the war of independence lie."

I had been stupid enough to push her, asking, "What did your father die of?" Avoiding my gaze, she had sidestepped the issue with a catch-all expression: "A death willed by God." I had been taken aback by this somewhat religious turn of phrase that was so unlike Meriem. After this strange exchange, I had given up all hope of her ever revealing how this Mathieu bloke, having appeared from nowhere, had ended up marrying her mother.

The argument awaiting me at home seemed so inevitable that I felt overwhelmed with sudden hostility towards myself. As I dragged myself off to the Addax antelopes' enclosure, I gave a nervous laugh, trying to fend off the sort of bad mood that I had learned to hide so skilfully from those around me. I was thought of as a constant livewire who even joked the evening he almost died in an ambush dressed up as a checkpoint. The coach bringing us back from Blida had been stopped about twenty miles from Algiers by men in army uniforms.

We had immediately realised from the worn-out shoes some of them were wearing and the hairy beards of others, though, that we were dealing with terrorists.

It was in the middle of the electoral campaign for a referendum to decide on an agreement establishing an amnesty for all the acts of violence committed over the previous decade; "a sponge to wipe away the blood of all the atrocities by people wearing beards and kepis' was how the public summed it up, with resigned dark humour. However, it was acknowledged that many Islamist fighters were refusing to hand in their weapons and were bent on seeking to demonstrate this in the bloodiest way possible. That particular day they lined us up along a ditch and told us to give our papers to the 'brothers' for checking. My identity card showed that I worked at the zoo – and therefore for the government the bearded men held in such contempt. Of course, this wasn't my first 'fake checkpoint', but my stomach was in knots. My neighbour's teeth were chattering. The podgy old man had been rambling on about importing sheep from New Zealand for half the journey. He bitterly deplored the fact that, despite being cheap, these animals had been declared non-halal by extreme religious groups because their tails had been docked level with their hindquarters; and yet, he recounted indignantly as we crossed the Mitidja plain, nothing in the Koran or the Sunnah outlawed the sacrifice of animals with shortened tails. He was even thinking of writing a petition to the president of the Algerian High Islamic Council with a request for this disastrous misunderstanding to be officially cleared up.

Despite his fear, the shady sheep-dealer tried to reassure himself by muttering that he knew the local Islamists and that these particular 'brothers' didn't take it out on civilians. "It's just a routine check, and maybe a small tax while they're at it," he said with a grimace. He had been interrupted by screams – an armed man was viciously laying into a young man, calling him a liar, a heathen and a hellhound. With regard to his papers, he was accusing the smartly dressed lad with his pomaded hair and his impeccably pressed white trousers of being in the army or the police. Another beard had come over to them and put his machine gun to the young man's temple. The latter was protesting that he was an accountant for a private construction company.

"... Private," he beseeched them with a wretched smile of complicity. "A small private company, not state-owned, guys. I hate the state as much as you do, I swear by love of the Prophet and his companions!"

Producing a long knife, one of the terrorists ordered the wretched man to kneel down. The man refused, sobbing and calling out to his mother for help. The beard with the knife muttered that neither his whore of a mother, nor that crony the President of the Republic would save the lives of renegades like him who tortured good Muslims in prison. He grabbed hold of the young man's neck and tried to force it downwards. The prisoner bucked and managed to break free. Dazed, his face streaming with tears, he shouted, "Look, brother, look at my white trousers. I just bought them, they're brand new – you can't expect me to kneel down in the dirt!"

I thought I must have heard wrongly. I saw the eyes of the man with the knife widen in disbelief before creasing in a huge burst of laughter. Still snivelling, the traveller – who had barely turned twenty – had smiled beatifically, relieved to see a man who had almost murdered him suddenly turn cheerful. He called us to witness.

"See, this brother is a good man. He understands what life's about, he does! I'm sure that..."

He didn't have time to finish his sentence. The second maquisard grabbed him roughly by the hair and with a dagger that had, as if by magic, taken the place of the machine gun, he slit his throat from ear to ear, bellowing out a furious "Allah Akbar" as he did so. Blood spurted out and spattered the other terrorist, who hadn't had time to get out of the way.

"See," the cutthroat cried, "you're dead before your trousers could get dirty. Try using your pick-up act in hell, you son of a bitch!" he said, shoving the corpse aside with a kick in the backside.

Then, addressing us: "That's what'll happen to you if you lie to us. Look, he's just shat his pants. So much for boring us about his new clothes! And if he thinks Satan is going to clean his arse for him..."

The young man's bowels had emptied and a dark stain was seeping through the thin fabric of his trousers. The killer looked at his own hand in disgust. Muttering "God curse all heathen! What kind of gel did that bastard put in his hair!" he held his hand in the air, looking around for something to wipe it on.

His irritated 'colleague' shouted, "Stop complaining! My jacket's fucked. You could have warned me you were going to cut his throat standing up!"

That was the only time in my life I have felt both a vile sense of debilitating pity and an uncontrollable desire to burst out laughing.

Just then, one of the terrorists yelled, "They're coming! The soldiers!" The cutthroat shouted in our direction, "Your luck's in, you bunch of ungodly fuckers!" before running off after his fellows and disappearing into the bushes along the verge.

The soldiers were furious at having missed the terrorists and they interrogated us forcefully. An officer dealt the driver an almighty slap around the face when he said he was worried about the delay with night falling. Confiscating his driving licence, the officer ordered him to come and pick it up the next day at their barracks. "He's going to get one hell of a thrashing there, the poor sod…" someone behind me whispered prophetically. The same officer called us all cowards and terrorist cocksuckers who were guilty of allowing a young conscript to be killed who could have been our son. When the coach drove off again, I hazarded a glance at the curled-up body; his shirt and fine trousers had turned a hideous brown colour. As I fought back my nausea, I thought, "Sorry, my boy, I'm not laughing at you… Sorry…" and I guessed that had he been a ghost swirling around me, he would not have forgiven my disrespectfulness one jot. Another fit of laughter was not far off, and I had to breathe deeply and close my eyes for a good minute until I finally got myself back under control.

The journey continued in oppressive, distrustful silence as a passenger had suggested that one of us must have informed the terrorists of the traveller's true identity. A small girl broke into irritating little sobs, joined almost immediately by her mother, and no one made any attempt to stop them. At Algiers bus station, as we were getting out of the vehicle with heavy hearts, the shady dealer, who had suddenly perked up and was now acting as if nothing had happened since we had all emerged unscathed, wanted to resume his conversation about dock-tailed sheep from New Zealand. I cut him short by asking him if his knob had been circumcised in accordance with Sharia law and, if so, suggesting that he write to the High Council to find out whether it would permit him to shag a non-Muslim female sheep from the other side of the planet. The old man looked me up and down as if I'd taken leave of my senses, then spluttered that my soul was drowning in a sea of spit and that the 'brothers' should have slit my throat, not that poor young man's.

I told Meriem about the trousers and the slicked-back hair and then, unable to control myself any longer, I burst out laughing while she stared at me in disbelief. I uttered some scurrilous and stupid remark, then went off to throw up my fear and shame.

Even then, our relationship had already taken a turn for a worse. That night I dreamed a lot of the young soldier: his body had been transformed into an overflowing garbage bag that was slit down the middle with a knife.

Having finished my tour of the cages and enclosures, I now headed for the office. There were quite a few details to sort out if we wanted to elicit a favourable response from the ministerial committee. Our annual budget was at stake, as were two jobs – including my own, as I was only a contract worker. So we had to 'nurse' the inspection visit, both in the field (although here the result could only be mediocre) and at lunch in the zoo's upmarket restaurant. Following the orders from my puritanical but crafty acting Director, I discussed the menu at length with the restaurant manager (foie gras – oh yes… – game, of both fur and feather, a range of sweets) without being able to resolve the tricky issue of alcoholic drinks; thirsty officials plied with fine wines and top-quality whisky always show more indulgence when it comes to writing their final report. On the other hand, if we were unlucky enough to come across some teetotallers or, worse, one of the Islamist hardliners currently teeming at every level of the administration, the consequences could be disastrous. Hajji Sadok and I had already checked: of the three committee members, two were not averse to a little tipple and the older man was even said to be a boozer; the last one had only just been promoted to the ministry and we hadn't been able to find anything out about him.

I left my office late in the evening, well after my colleagues, with my head still full of existential doubts – 'Soft drinks or alcohol?" – and promising myself that I would find some way to sound out the new inspector. Despite my tiredness, I couldn't resist the urge to have another look at our new guests. The monkeys had gone back inside their shelters at nightfall. There was a magnificent starry sky; the silence that had enveloped the huge leisure complex, of which the zoo was only one small part, was occasionally broken by the braying of camels, the muffled roars of lions and the cackling of sacred ibises. I'd forgotten that I didn't have the car today. The thought of the climb from the zoo to the park's main entrance turned my legs to jelly.

"Hey, my African glamour girls!" I chuckled. "Your Algerian guard's dropped by to wish you nightie-night!"

My mobile phone rang. "This old thing still works?" I commented not unhappily. It had fallen on the floor of the bus the day before and the battery had come out of its case. I read Meriem's name on the screen. I took the call and got ready to stammer the customary excuses for my unusual lateness. I anticipated her recriminations. She would no doubt accuse me of coming home at some ungodly hour to avoid the discussion with our daughter.

"Where are you?" she asked brusquely. And without waiting for an answer, she whispered in a strangled voice, "Our daughter hasn't come home from school."

"What? I can't hear you, the reception's really bad here. You know the zoo's in a bowl."

She repeated, in something between a scream and a groan, "Our daughter's hasn't come home. And… it's… it's dark now. Shehera's so young…"

Then, losing all control of herself, she whined (and then, because I had never heard her lamenting so horribly, I felt my bones freeze inside me, along with the flesh that covered them), "Bring back our baby, Aziz… This isn't just her being late… Mathieu and my mother are here with me… Bring her back, I beg you… Mum received a strange phone call quarter of an hour ago… Someone was laughing…"

"That's it?"

"Yes, that's it. They laughed. And then they hung up."

There was a silence, then quite an animated but unintelligible conversation followed by another silence.

"Aziz?"

It was Mathieu's voice – muffled, as though he was making sure that the two women couldn't hear him.

"I think…"

He swallowed.

"I think… it's a kidnapping."

I yelped, "What? Are you crazy?"

He cleared his throat. Then his voice quavered, almost breaking into a sob – as if he too were giving in to the horror of what he had just uttered: "I got the same phone call as your mother-in-law."

I was standing under a street lamp. I had a horrible feeling that my testicles were shrivelling and being sucked up into my stomach. I glanced at my watch without thinking. It was eight twenty-three p.m. and eleven… twelve… thirteen… seconds. I tried to catch my breath and for one moment, for one very long moment in this shitty country of mine, I thought I wouldn't be able to.

There it was. My agony had begun.

From the zoo I made it to the motorway slip-road before I found a taxi that would agree to take me for twice the normal price. The cab driver defended this by saying that it was late and that I lived in a 'dodgy' part of town. I got into the passenger seat, as is usual in Algiers. Even though my brain was gradually coagulating with fear, I remembered another taxi driver's strange, offended comment when he saw me getting into the back of his vehicle: "Get in the front, mate. Who do you think I am – your private chauffeur?" As the old banger stinking of tobacco drove me off towards what might well be total disaster, I thought that only a few minutes earlier the mere thought of the driver's hurt expression would have made be burst out laughing.

I now found myself in almost the same position as someone with both arms amputated looking at a photograph of himself before his mutilation. I bit my lip in a reflex of fearful superstition, thinking about an event as tragic as amputation at a time like this could only call down the worst kind of trouble on my daughter's head.

Even in the dark, the man noticed that my hand was trembling. He mocked me. "Been overdoing it on the drink a bit, have we, brother?" I made no reply for fear that my voice might betray my anxiety. The man muttered something about courtesy being a dying habit, even when you showed weakness and did someone a favour. He lit a cigarette and defiantly turned the music up to full volume.

Throughout that entire drive across the city by way of the Kouba neighbourhood, I clutched my mobile phone so tightly as to break it. I couldn't believe that the damn device could have whispered in my ear such a vile word as 'kidnapping' in connection with my daughter. With all its might, a part of me tried to convince myself that all of this was down to a mother and two senile old people panicking. As for the phone call, well, there were legions of frustrated men in Algiers who dialled numbers at random until they happened upon a female voice with whom they could strike up a flirtatious conversation. That other part of me listened docilely to these arguments, only to discover to its horror that it was more 'convinced' by the quavering fearfulness of old Mathieu, who was usually so reserved. An atrociously mocking thought flashed through my mind: *So, my boy, you really thought you could escape unscathed from the disasters that have plagued this bloody country for so long, did you? Why should everyone else be affected by the murders, the kidnappings and all the other things you no longer dare name and not your own precious little family, eh?*

I paid the taxi driver, adding, after a momentary hesitation, a generous tip – perhaps to earn a friendly comment before I faced the worst. He didn't thank me. Opening the door, I grovelled and begged him, "Hey, wish me luck, brother!"

With immediate repartee he said, "You think your sort really deserves it? Ask God, His hearing's better than mine!"

I was hardly able to stay on my feet after the taxi drove off. The towers on the estate, with their peeling facades and the slashed garbage bags scattered around them, had never looked so sinister. The few street lamps whose bulbs hadn't been smashed lit up ugly buildings studded with satellite dishes, half of which were turned – with the country's customary schizophrenia – towards Europe and half towards the Middle East. Young people hung around the bottom of the staircases in small groups trying to keep boredom at bay. I felt a sudden pang when I caught sight of Meriem on our balcony. She shouted, "Aziz! Aziz! Hurry up!" in such a heartbreaking voice that a teenager sprawling on the stairs looked up at me and said, "Got a problem, mister? Need a hand?"

The local imam's son's eyes contained lazy curiosity, a mixture of distrust and goodwill.

"Nothing thanks, Rachid. Say hello to your dad," I replied in a strangled voice.

Meriem rushed up to me, her face smudged with tears. She was trembling. Scared stiff, like me. I held her tight, patting her softly on the back.

"Stop crying, Meriem, everything'll be OK. Shehera will come home, it's nothing, just a…"

"Don't give me that," she exploded. "She's never stayed out this late, she wouldn't dare. She's scared of the dark, you know that! He… he… How could he? She's only a little girl… I…"

Her whole body was shaking and rebelling. Stiffer than ever, Mathieu whispered, "Aziz, your wife has just had a phone call from the… laughing man."

"*The laughing man*… Coming on all literary now, are you, you old fool?" I was stupid enough to remark to myself despite the terror-stricken atmosphere. Mathieu, whom I had never seen smoking, was holding a cigarette the old-fashioned way, between his forefinger and thumb, with the red-hot end facing in towards his palm. A saucer doubling as an ashtray showed that this was not his first cigarette. His eyelids were twitching, a sign of his extreme effort to remain impassive.

Meriem gasped, "He has… called… every… one. But… but how did he get hold of our mobile phone numbers?"

"How about you, Aziz, did this… this thug phone you?"

My mother-in-law was slumped on the couch, her face puffy from crying, and her tone was resentful, accusing even. It was as if Latifa was criticising me for being the only one not to have been subjected to the mysterious stranger's jeering.

"No… I…" I hesitated, but then anger overcame me when I noticed that I was trying to justify myself. "That's normal," I almost spat out, "I changed network a month ago and no one's got my new number!"

Mathieu gave me a blank stare I'd never seen before. He too was petrified. I was surprised by the intensity of his reaction. "Really," I thought maliciously, "why bother pretending you're worried? You're only Meriem's stepfather and not my daughter's real grandfather!"

I felt like rebuffing them in the crudest terms. *Wake up, you bunch of idiots – we don't know anything for certain yet! What makes you think a family like ours would get caught up in this? The girl's probably hanging around somewhere with her crazy boyfriend. Just wait and see the telling-off I'll give her when she gets back!* But I kept quiet, incapable of warding off my own distress. I embraced my wife, sinking my nose into her hair, before I stammered in a falsetto voice, "We'll… we'll report it to the police…"

My mother-in-law eyed me disdainfully.

"We didn't wait for you to give us the go-ahead. We phoned all your daughter's friends before going to the local police station. They say it's too early to start a search. According to the sergeant, she might just have run away because of some bad marks at school. If not, it's a matter for police headquarters, he said, not the local station. He more or less chased us out of there. We had to stand our ground until the duty policeman took down our telephone number. The bastard was implying that we should keep a better eye on our daughter. Bloody cops," she concluded, "you'd have thought we were there to report the neighbours for making a racket."

She shrugged her shoulders.

"Anyway, in matters like this the Algerian police… Well, what has she ever done to…"

Latifa huddled up against the cushions of the couch and, sobbing violently, buried her face in her hands. I hated her for saying out loud what I was trying not to think in secret. Whether carried out by criminals or terrorists, abductions were not uncommon in Algeria. Most of the time, the police didn't manage to prevent a tragic outcome.

My mother-in-law was referring – all of us knew – to a recent kidnapping that had made the front pages of the Algerian press, perhaps because of the child's angelic looks. The police had undertaken no serious investigations, only bothering to visit the parents three days after the five-year-old's disappearance. Her father and mother had taken things into their own hands, putting up posters of their son all around Algiers. Angry at the police's laziness, some neighbours had eventually decided to call in a dog handler. In two hours, the dog had found the corpse, less than a mile from where the kidnapping had taken place. The child had first been raped, then killed and thrown down a well. Of course the kidnapper had had all the time in the world to disappear. There were furious editorials suggesting that the police's inertia was due to the victim's parents' low social status. The little boy was 'worth nothing' was one columnist's cruel take on the affair.

"What should we do, Aziz?"

"First of all, Meriem, we shouldn't imagine the worst… Maybe…"

I couldn't think of anything more reassuring to say. The old Frenchman growled to no one in particular, "I've made some coffee."

Just then, as I was giving my father-in-law a grateful nod, the telephone rang.

Mine.

The man who was about to turn my life on its head didn't sound like an ogre. He asked me very politely, "Good evening. First of all, *Bismillah*, in the name of God… Am I speaking to *Si* Aziz?" stressing the traditional Algerian Arabic formal *Si*.

"Yes," I replied, letting out a sigh of relief. This voice was too 'normal' to be the one I dreaded. "And you are…?" I added with a hint of irritation. "I'm sorry, it's just that…"

I wagged my finger at the petrified group composed of Meriem, my mother-in-law and Mathieu as I continued talking.

"…I'm expecting an important phone call and…"

He gave a short, almost friendly chuckle.

"No, no, there's been no mistake, my friend. *I* am your important phone call… We need to talk."

I felt my heart skip a beat and then suddenly start pounding again. My saliva had taken on a revolting consistency.

"What about?" I replied softly, pressing my mobile phone hard against my ear as if to absorb the violence of the words the man was about to inflict on me.

"About your daughter, of course. Because you do have a daughter… Shehera, isn't it? She is young and… so pretty… But she doesn't dress decently. Sharia law foresees strict penalties for that… It's all very unfortunate…"

Meriem, her eyes standing out on stalks, had realised. "Is it him?" I nodded, careful not to show the terror that was taking hold of me.

"Hello. Are you still there? (The man once more gave a light, almost jovial chuckle.) Of course you are, my friend!"

I had trouble unclenching my teeth.

"Yes, I'm here… Are you… Is my daughter with you?"

A few seconds' silence. Meriem had brought her ear up close to the mobile. Tears had stuck a strand of hair to her cheek.

The voice resumed, "Yes, your daughter is with me… with us, to be more precise."

I groaned, "What gives you the right to detain my daughter?"

The man guffawed, but still without any aggression. "You're a bit of a jester. Still insisting on your rights in such a crazy country?"

"Do you want money?"

"Ah, my dear Aziz, is it because you spend so much time with monkeys that you come up with such lame jokes? Money – as if you had any! As you can imagine, we've done some prior research. And anyway, we're no heathens; we love God and our intentions are not that mundane."

"Let my daughter go! Or else you'll be sorry, you…"

"No insults, please, or else…"

I heard the sound of a chair, then some quick footsteps, a door being opened, an incomprehensible exclamation, then the smack of a hand…

A *slap!* I immediately realised.

"Help!" squealed a woman's voice. No; a *girl's* voice.

"Stop bawling, will you! See this telephone – your father's on the other end."

"Dad, help me. Save me, dad, he's…"

There was the sound of a second slap, after which the screaming diminished to a sob. I felt like a huge hand was kneading my guts to make me throw up.

"Stop it… Shehera… My girl…"

I bent my knees – to plead with the stranger.

"Please, don't hit her! Please…"

Meriem had raised her fingers to her cheeks and scratched herself.

The man didn't bother replying. I could hear my daughter's moaning through his noisy breathing. There was the same series of noises, but the other way round this time. The stranger must have sat down on the chair again.

"Have you… have you understood?"

His breathing contained a hiss of restrained anger.

"I'm just a good bookkeeper: you insult me, she pays! I hit her with my bare hand. I could have chosen a stick, a metal bar, or a knife, to sharpen it on her soft skin. Will we be a little more polite from now on, my dear sir?

"Yes," I assured him tamely. "Take mercy on her! Sorry…"

I felt a shooting pain in my head, like after an appalling binge: *he'd mentioned a knife!* I felt about as wretchedly 'convincing' as the young soldier begging his killers for mercy! This was no nightmare; my interlocutor was talking quite casually about stabbing my daughter!

"Sorry I lost my temper. It won't happen again, but please don't lay another hand on her."

"That all depends on your goodwill."

Meriem shook my arm, her face distraught. "Ask him what he wants, for the love of God!"

The stranger must have heard this because he asked, "Who else is with you, apart from your wife?"

"My parents-in-law."

"The Frenchman who pretends he's an Arab and his whore, right?"

"Erm… (I felt myself blushing as I lowered my gaze so that my parents-in-law were no longer in my line of sight.) Erm… yes."

"Perfect, perfect… (This news seemed to overjoy him.) Put us on loudspeaker and tell them to come nearer."

I was shaking so much that I could hardly press the button.

"Fine," he started, "you have probably told the police. That's normal – you are good parents. But tomorrow, Aziz, immediately it opens, you will go along to the police station and apologise for the false alarm. You eventually found your daughter at a friend's house and to punish her you're going to send her off to rot for a while with your parents in some *douar* out in the sticks. It's up to you to make it sound plausible. All of you will have to act normally. Most importantly, keep going to work and wait for further instructions there. Any trickery and we won't think twice about cutting your daughter up into bits and dumping them on your doorstep. But before we kill her…"

His mouth simulated an obscene kissing sound, followed by a clicking of his tongue.

"I don't need to spell it out to you. Especially as this pretty thing has what it takes for a few games…"

"Sir… How… how old are you?"

Holding her out-turned palms towards the telephone, Meriem asked this question like a prayer. There was no response, just a 'hum, hum', perhaps of surprise.

"Sir, my daughter's still scared at night. She's moody and there are lots of things she won't eat, even if she's hungry. Sometimes when she's upset, I tell her a story, just like when she was very small. You see, she might seem big for her age, but she's still a child. Don't… don't do anything to her, for the love of all you hold most dear… for the love of God…"

She gripped the back of the armchair and continued.

"We are good Muslims, sir, we observe Ramadan and we have put our names down this year for the pilgrimage to Mecca. If you order us to, I swear on my soul that my husband and I will fast all this year and the following years and that we will offer what little we have to the mosque of your choice. In the name of the God that we all love, both you and ourselves... Look, if you give me back my daughter, and if you so request, I will cut off my arms and legs in exchange..."

The same silence greeted my wife's absurd supplication – untrue, grotesque and heartbreaking for me in its utter sincerity. Two thin scratches ran under the tip of my wife's chin. Her shoulders slumped. I knew then – and I had never known it with such clarity – that I loved this grief-maddened woman more than life itself; that I loved the little girl who found herself in the antechamber of hell with the same strength; and that if I lost either of them, the lowest, mangiest dog on this planet would be worth more than me.

Meriem's voice faltered.

"Why *us*?"

"Hello, madam. You're... the girl's mother, am I right? How are you? All right? Were you trying to trap me with your question about my age? Dangerous that, you know, behaving like... like a slut!"

The perky kidnapper seemed to be hoping for some reaction from Meriem. Then, with false fatalism, he said, "Why you? Call it rotten luck, madam, or better: destiny. My destiny, your destiny. You know full well that God wrote one out for each and every one of us even before poor Adam was born."

He chuckled, delighted with this stroke of inspiration. "And, as with the size of our arseholes, He doesn't ask for our opinion! I know quite a lot about destiny, believe you me. Now goodnight. Try and get some sleep because tomorrow is going to be a long day. Aziz, I'll call you about nine o'clock. Make sure you're at work. And don't forget – your daughter's life depends on your silence. The longer it lasts, the longer she lives. Don't underestimate us; our *brothers* are everywhere, trust me. Even in the police! On the other hand, don't go hoping you can trace us through this telephone number. You know full well that mobile phone chips are as easy to find as oranges in any souk in this country; no identity papers required and no formalities! Till tomorrow then..."

And he added hurriedly, as if he'd almost forgotten, "Allah Akbar... God is great, great is His might and great is His wrath!"

We slept little, if you can call it sleep when you collapse on a bed for an hour at the most because your exhausted body abandons all control over itself. Until morning each of us retreated to a corner when our own fear became incapable of enduring the sight of the others' fear.

Meriem's teeth were chattering and she was making little whining sounds: "Shehera, give me back my little Shehera… Shehera…" I took her in my arms and rocked her, swearing that she had nothing to fear, that our daughter would be returned to us safe and sound, that I promised that from the depths of my heart, all of them fanciful oaths that she can't have believed because she started weeping again and, no longer able to cope with my powerlessness, I followed her example.

I had never felt so incapable of assuming the role that it seemed to me was expected of a father: to protect, come what may, the life of his children and his wife. I was ready to offer up my life to save my daughter, but to whom? The man who had spoken to me on the telephone seemed as ordinary as he was unreal. Sometimes, when tiredness numbed my brain, I managed to persuade myself that no family as normal as our own could be caught up in an event as crazy as a kidnapping. Then a beating drum in my chest reminded me of the crushing density of reality.

We pushed a wardrobe up against the front door. I'm not sure who it was who whispered, "What if they come and get *us as well*?" However, we were gripped by shame ("I don't want to be safe when my daughter isn't!" Meriem screamed) and we immediately put the wardrobe back in its original place. The question of the police bothered us: should we inform them or not? "If this bastard is one of those GIA terrorists, we can't take any chances. Those madmen couldn't give a damn about death, either their own or their hostages. The police doesn't care about hostages either. Any sign of danger and they'll just start shooting!" Mathieu had spoken as if he was almost apologising for offering his opinion.

At one point, as he and I were clearing the table, he whispered to me, "I hope they're just normal crooks and that they'll demand a ransom. If that's the case, maybe there'll be room for negotiation? People are less unpredictable when they're driven by a craving for money rather than for heaven."

Mathieu anticipated my silent objection with a shrug of the shoulders.

"A ransom? The four of us could rustle up a tidy little sum, even if it means selling both our flats. I've got some savings and Latifa has a couple of pieces of jewellery."

"But he told us that wouldn't be enough. What's more, we could pay the ransom and still find ourselves with a…"

I realised with horror that I'd almost said 'corpse'. Luckily, only the Frenchman heard me. He shot me a slightly disdainful glance. I felt a taste of bile in my mouth at the realisation that this funny old man had just suggested selling everything he and his wife owned to save my daughter's life, and she was just the teenage offspring of a daughter-in-law who was not sparing in her coldness towards him! I felt quite ashamed of my prejudices against him. I almost asked him why he was being so generous, but his grim expression put me off.

He curled his lips bitterly, as though he had heard my question.

"Your daughter is my granddaughter… well, almost…"

And then, after an awkward silence that seemed like the old man had a blank: "Her… her real grandfather, Meriem's father, was my friend. If there is such a thing as friends, that is…"

He turned his back on me, bringing the confidences to an abrupt end. Of all of us, he was the only one who had maintained a semblance of calm. Until now at least: in the middle of the night, when Latifa succumbed to a new fit of despair, screaming and weeping, he gave his wife a good shake and ordered her to get a grip on herself at once because the danger was too great, he told her harshly, that the neighbours would call the police and that the girl would pay the price. As soon as he had gagged Latifa with this horrific possibility, the old man left the room and locked himself in the bathroom. A few minutes later, he came out again with red eyes, but close-shaven cheeks and carefully brushed hair.

He spoke to me in a hoarse voice.

"It'll be dawn in less than an hour. Meriem and you should get some sleep. I'll take care of Latifa. No point in wasting our strength when we'll need it in the hours to come. I'll stay by the telephone and, if anything happens, I'll wake you up. Go…"

He pushed me authoritatively towards the bedroom. Just as I was about to close the door, he looked me straight in the eye.

"We'll have a chat a bit later, but if you want my opinion, this guy knows us too well for us not to have bumped into him at some point."

"What makes you say that? The phone numbers?"

"Not only that… even if no one apart from your wife and mine knows my number. Actually, even you don't have it. Of course (he pulled a slightly piqued face), we've had no reason to call each other, eh? And my phone has always been set up to hide my number from the person I'm calling. But that's not what's bugging me."

"What is then?"

"I don't know yet. Just a feeling. Go and get some rest; we'll talk about it again later."

"Do you think we can rescue her?"

"Yes…." he said, looking away too quickly. "Look at your hands, though. You're no help to your daughter by skinning yourself."

I almost asked him what right he thought he had to speak to me in that tone. He wasn't my father, as far as I was aware! Nevertheless, my eyes followed my father-in-law's gaze; red scratches crisscrossed the backs of my hands.

I opened my mouth wide to utter some stupid protest like *I didn't do that!* Mathieu didn't look round at me, probably out of charity.

I arranged my face into a neutral expression before facing the other panic – my wife's. I felt a dual sensation of shame and fear: was I so incapable of keeping my cool in a situation that required so much of it? Could my little girl rely on such a cowardly father to help her?

Maybe I slept for an hour or two? I don't remember having nightmares, but rather floating in a sort of treacle in which I seemed to be unconscious or rather dead to all sensation.

I half-opened one eyelid and half-saw my wife snuggled up tightly against me, something that hadn't happened for donkey's years. A hazy thought, soft and warm, spread through my body, a mixture of an admiring *How beautiful she is!* and a concupiscent *I would love to lick the insides of your thighs, fair lady…*

I groaned when the dagger of Shehera's name appeared from nowhere and stabbed into my wildly imagining heart. I sat up, fizzing with such searing anxiety that it was as if I had just caught sight of a thousand-strong crowd chasing after me to tear me apart.

"My daughter…"

"Yes, Aziz?"

I'd been mistaken; Meriem wasn't asleep. She cradled my head in her hands.

"How is she, Aziz, can you tell me?"

Before I could answer, she reacted strangely: her hands caught my cheeks in a pincer grip. I didn't dare move.

"It's the first night she's spent away from us. And in the meantime, we're sleeping and… and…"

A dry retch, a grating at the back of her throat, prevented her from continuing. She pulled away from me abruptly. It must have been five o'clock in the morning going by the muezzin's loudspeaker calling the faithful to morning prayers.

"Do you hear him?"

She repeated, "Hey? Can you hear the keeper of dawn?"

Her voice had taken on a more pensive, more irascible tone. She cleared her throat, started to speak twice and ended up bent over double, coughing dryly. I thought, "She has no more tears to wet her throat." She turned on the night-light. The faint beam of light emphasised the rings around her wide, staring eyes and the scratches at the base of her chin.

"Where are you going?"

"I don't know, but I can't sit idly by any longer, waiting for someone to rape her, kill her and then dump her in the street somewhere!"

Contemptuous of both herself and me, she hurled, "Get up. No parent can breathe easily while their fourteen-year-old daughter is being murdered."

She got dressed calmly, too calmly, while I watched her, unable to raise a single objection to this fundamental truth. She was right. Anything that happens to a child is its parents' fault; for a child, God is above all mum and dad! I had been a child and I recalled my own unshakeable personal pantheon. Spitefully, I choked back a dry, convulsive sob.

Mathieu was already bustling around the living room. Latifa was on her knees, praying fervently. Meriem waited until the prayers were over to place a kiss on her mother's head.

With ecstasy in her eyes, Latifa cried, "I'm sure He doesn't know about this!"

"Who are you talking about mum?"

My mother-in-law clutched her daughter's arm.

34

"God, for heaven's sake! The Almighty doesn't know about this because, honestly, He'd never have let something this cruel happen!"

As I sniggered silently at the paradox ("If He doesn't know about this, then He isn't God, stupid!"), I could see that Meriem was wondering about her mother's mental state. She stroked the old woman's hand, but refused to show any more emotion than that.

"Get up, mum," she ordered. "Come and have a hot drink and afterwards you can have a rest."

The old woman did as she was told, glad, in her disarray, to have someone to obey. She allowed herself to be led to her chair and she grasped the cup Meriem handed her. As she sipped her tea, she didn't leave off studying her daughter's and husband's faces, afraid of discovering there a sign of some terrible piece of information that had been withheld from her. Her misty eyes blinked constantly, doubtless to strengthen the fragile dam holding back the tears that might burst forth at a single word or intuition.

Meriem bent over her mother. For a few seconds, I could see their two faces side by side, like for like, despite the difference in age, in their beauty and the expressiveness of their grief! Petty, ridiculous rancour welled up inside me at this old lady who was stealing a part of my wife from me by 'daring' to experience the same sorrow as she did.

Oh, how irritating the grief of people we don't like can be! And how terribly, conversely, can our hearts be broken by the grief of those we love when we show ourselves incapable, even when we share it, of offering them the slightest succour!

Meriem accompanied her mother to Shehera's bedroom. Mathieu and I watched each other, making no attempt to disguise the fact that we didn't think much of each other, even if, deep down, we hadn't the faintest idea of why this was. The embarrassed silence lasted for a few seconds before my father-in-law spoke. He looked pensive.

"The kidnapper knows I'm French. If it really is those GIA bastards ..."

Meriem appeared in the corridor and interrupted him.

"I know what we have to do."

She gave us a hostile stare. She never covered her head, but now she had wrapped herself in a broad scarf and an old coat. She had stuck one of her hands in a pocket.

"Where are you off to like that? It's dark outside."

My anxiety went up a notch when – as if this were sufficient explanation – she held up the thing she had stuffed into her pocket: a small, illuminated Koran.

"Where did you dig that out? I didn't know we had one in the house."

She shrugged her shoulders with a defiant expression containing not an ounce of love.

"You assume I'm going to just twiddle my thumbs until my daughter's corpse turns up?"

Her near-exhausted tone contrasted with the sparks of anger glittering in her eyes. I no longer recognised the woman I had been living with for the last fifteen years; first the Koran and now this haunted look…

"I'm going to see the imam. He'll be able to intercede. He's almost one of them, remember?"

I jumped out of my chair.

"You're mad! That's the last thing we should do. He won't lift a finger. Quite the opposite: he always said bad things about Shehera! His wife told you…"

Pushing me violently aside, she made for the front door. I yelled, "You're out of your mind!"

"Don't go, Meriem. Your husband's right, it's very dangerous," Mathieu begged, advancing towards her. "The fact that they bothered to call us means that it could be a matter of negotiating. Stay here; we'll find a solution, I swear! One life is already in danger. Don't make things worse by adding yours."

Momentarily taken aback, Meriem shook her head in revulsion.

"Don't come on all fatherly towards me!" she chastised him from the doorway. "Marrying my mother by betraying my father doesn't give you any rights over me! You're the one who has to stick to his rightful place – that's all we ask of you!"

She slammed the door. Mathieu shouted, "Stop her!" I hesitated for a couple of seconds – I was in my pyjama bottoms and vest – before rushing after her. The imam lived in the tower block on the southern edge of the estate. Although the gravel cut into my feet, I ran towards the building with mounting unease when I didn't catch sight of Meriem. Assuming that she was running too, I should have caught up with her by now. Despite its gentle pinkness, the rising dawn over Algiers couldn't manage to soften the landscape of urban ruins through which I ran like hell – some repair work on the gas pipes that had been dragging on for a year, piles of trash, some sprayed slogans to the glory of the FIS – the Islamic Salvation Front – and its leaders, graffiti calling on people to fuck a certain Hassan's mother, a burnt-out car. As I panted along like a madman, a part of me, a tiny one admittedly but one that would retain, I suppose, its sense of sarcasm even if the devil was flipping me over and over like a cutlet in his pan, remarked: *We were meant to be the descendants of the sublime Andalusians and Harun al-Rashid the Magnificent, and we have become the bastards of a trashcan country that aspires to disappear up the anus of al-Qaida!*

A neighbour on his way back from some place or other called out to me with a mixture of amusement and reproach: "Hey, sports star, training for the Olympics in our bare feet and pyjamas now, are we?"

I had already made it to the second floor of the imam's building when, like a wasp sting, I suddenly recalled the strange comment Meriem had made during the call to prayers: "Do you hear him?"

"Shit…"

'He' was obviously at the mosque! Quite logically, Meriem had decided to go to where the muezzin was leading the service. I ran back down the stairs four at a time and crossed the estate in the opposite direction until I reached the building site of the mosque – which had been deliberately left unfinished so that it didn't come under the control of the Ministry of Religious Affairs. A few latecomers were hurrying towards the entrance. Breathless and streaming with sweat, I searched for Meriem's face.

I felt like my chest had gone hollow when I caught sight of her half-hidden behind a digger, slight inside her coat and disfigured by the scarf covering her beautiful hair.

"Meriem, please, wait for me, I'm nothing without you…" I whispered to myself like a prayer.

I remembered how she would laugh in delight at the moment of orgasm and how, if I started holding forth in front of supposedly important guests, she was quite capable of sliding a mischievous hand under the table and guiding it towards my genitals…

My passionate, happy wife. My wife and mother of my child. My wife, broken by grief. And I couldn't do a thing, neither for her, nor for my child.

"Meriem, listen to me…"

I was just behind her now. She carried on walking, not looking round and mumbling, "I'm going to do what I have to do."

"And what do you have to do?"

She ignored my question. I grabbed her by the arm. She tried to break free. Her large pupils, faded from crying, stared at me as if I were a stranger.

"He knows some of the people who took my daughter."

"How can you be sure?"

"After the elections were cancelled, the imam spent four months in jail. It's common knowledge. They even say he was tortured. That's some kind of proof, isn't it?"

"He *only* did four months. Four short months. If he'd belonged…"

I lowered my voice because we were being closely watched from the mosque entrance.

"… to the GIA or that kind of group, do you think the police or the army would have let him off so lightly? They'd have found him tied up on the edge of the estate with a bullet in his head. If he can carry on waking us up every morning since he got out of jail with that bloody loudspeaker of his, it's because the authorities back him."

This argument hit home. Meriem's eyes, which had been almost malicious up till now, reflected her bewilderment. I drove home my advantage, ready to damn a man whose son I sometimes gave a lift home to and whom I actually barely knew.

"Quid pro quo, I guess. In any case, that's the rumour. If he doesn't preach, the leader of the mosque is just one more unemployed in this shit-hole neighbourhood. They must have offered him a deal: his freedom and a chance to make a living selling sermons in return for some information about troublemakers on the estate. Maybe he even grasses on both sides: one day to the cops, the next to their sworn enemies… Look at where it leaves us: if you talk to the imam, every-one will find out, the cops and the terrorists. That kidnapper swine insisted we…"

I didn't continue. Meriem's drawn face paled a little more.

"I wanted to suggest an exchange to the kidnapper – an adult for a child."

"And then what?"

"I would've killed myself. I've brought along what I'd need."

She half-opened her coat. The handle of a kitchen knife was poking out of the inside pocket. A chill wave swept through me. I tried to clear my throat, but nothing, not a sound, came out of my gullet.

Meriem hung her head, beaten once and for all. A little liquid ball, then another, rolled down her nose. I caught myself smiling stupidly as some snot flowed out of her nostrils and linked the two streams of tears. I felt like yelling: *You locals, save us. You think we're alive because we're still standing and speaking, but we're drowning before your very eyes!*

I stretched out my arms to embrace my wife.

"Hey, you two, aren't you ashamed of yourselves, arguing in front of a mosque this early in the morning?"

The man guarding the entrance ran up to us. He was 'Afghan' in appearance, with his unkempt beard and the small dimple above his eyebrows typical of devotees reputed to pray so fervently that their mat leaves an imprint on their forehead.

"As for you, you ass, don't you have an ounce of modesty, showing yourself in public in your pyjamas with a woman within the confines of God's house? Get out of here before I call the faithful!"

"Come on," I said simply, "let's go home."

We walked away in silence, infinitely sad, leaving the cleric to his imprecations. We were only a few yards from our building when Meriem murmured, "Your feet are covered in blood."

Her voice was so gentle, so like how it *used* to be, that a breath of gratitude for the council workers' negligence filled my lungs.

"It's nothing… just the stones from the building work."

We started with the police. Meriem wanted to come to the police station with me, but I insisted she wait for me in the car. A duty policeman blocked my path. I announced that I wanted to withdraw a complaint. With a cigarette dangling from his mouth and his cap pushed back, the man joked, "Good idea! At last someone sensible, who doesn't come and heap us with every misfortune that has afflicted him since birth!"

I grimaced.

"One can get carried away sometimes. Then, after a good night's sleep…"

Inside, the man at the desk asked me to wait, muttering that there was no panic and that he had an urgent report to fill in for his boss. I waited a good twenty minutes for the officer to return. People came in and sat down tamely next to me on the bench. A man and his son were arguing fiercely about the burglary they had suffered the night before. The father accused the son of not having checked the padlocks on the grocer's shop; the son defended himself by claiming that it was the father who had done the checks. The two individuals looked strikingly like each other: the same thick, short-sighted glasses, paunchy and bald apart from a tuft around the edge. I mused bitterly: "How about your respective harpies? Are their arses as big as yours?" Their argument was welcome: I focused on the two of them chatting away to try and calm my shaking. Sensing my gaze on him, the father greeted me, then commented, with friendly concern, "You ought to wrap up warm. Your teeth are chattering."

"I don't know where my mind was this morning."

"Nothing serious, I hope?"

I saw in his eyes that he thought that he was due the story of my trials since he had entertained me with his own. The officer's return created a diversion. I stood up, dizzy to the point of collapse. I wiped my moist hands on my jacket, silently cursing myself: "Hey, yellow-belly, now's not the time to have a heart attack!" The policeman was putting on the arrogant airs of someone who's just been torn off a strip by a superior and is bent on taking it out on everyone under him.

"Officer…"

He gave a groan and continued to pay no attention to me. I had prepared a little speech with Meriem that we felt was more or less convincing. I had polished it while I was waiting. And then just as my hand gripped the desk, I suddenly felt like throwing myself at the guy's feet, yelling that a murderer and rapist had abducted my daughter and calling on every last cop in the world to help me bring my child back safe and sound. Otherwise my wife would die of sorrow and, without my little girl and my wife, I was fit for the asylum…

A telephone rang. It took me a couple of seconds to realise that it was my own. I got it out of my pocket under the policeman's irritated gaze. The screen read 'Caller unknown'. I knew straightaway that it was *him*.

"Where are you? Have you finished at the police station?"

The voice was more guttural than the day before. I shuddered with horror.

"I..."

A few scattered neurones did actually send the order to my tongue to articulate the words *I'm still at the police station...* But nothing happened. I stood there dumb, caught between two opposing urges to obey and to disobey the man who was planning to wreck my life. The officer leaned forward to pick up a few snatches of our conversation.

"Listen to me," the stranger continued, "I'm going to kill your daughter right now, but not before I've fucked her. You hear me? And I'll give everyone here a turn... It won't be a vagina she's got – it'll be a pipeline! And I won't mention her arsehole. So stop trying to be clever and answer me now!"

My tongue forgot all rebellion, as if it had been whipped. Gathering the little will I had left to offer the irked policeman a contrite smile, I stammered, "Everything's fine, don't worry... Really... But I can't talk to you right now. I'm with them... Call me back in ten minutes... But please don't do anything..."

I hung up. I must have been white as a sheet. I prayed that my hands wouldn't shake.

"That was... that was my mother. You know what mothers are like..."

I gave a little cough to regain my composure. The monster's words were still ringing in my head.

"So... I want to cancel a complaint (*I'm going to kill her right now*)... My wife was here yesterday (*fucked... You hear me?*) to report that my daughter hadn't come home. In fact, my daughter (*I'll give everyone here a turn*) was at her aunt's, but she hadn't told us..."

"You think it's our job to sort out problems with your children's upbringing?"

The officer looked me up and down with the stony and slightly threatening haughtiness Algerian policeman adopt when they intend to remind you that you are in enemy territory in a police station and, as such, are potentially guilty of any crime they might care to accuse you of. The subliminal message emitted by this den, painted 'administrative green', is extremely clear: you who enter here, do not imagine that we are here to serve you; should you persist in this delusion, remember that only a dozen steps separate the grotty normality of our offices from the sordid jails in the cellar below!

As a teenager in Constantine, I had been introduced to this cast-iron truth after making a salacious jibe about a traffic policeman. Unfortunately, I hadn't noticed one of his colleagues on duty a few yards away. The two cops had handcuffed me and led me down into the basement, where the offended man had pulled out an erect penis and threatened to sodomize me unless I made up by giving him a blowjob. I think he would have raped me if my screams hadn't put the wind up his colleague. The policeman then tucked his dick away and proceeded to beat me with his truncheon. That evening my father was summoned and informed by the officer on watch that I was liable to imprisonment for having insulted a policeman in the discharge of his duties. However, he added, if my father promised to punish me severely for my misdemeanours, the police would forget all about it. My poor old man thanked them profusely and gave me a second volley of blows at home. Naturally, I didn't dare tell him about the rape I had almost suffered. Furthermore, having first choked on his indignation, he might actually have given me my third thrashing of the day and called me a queer incapable of defending his honour…

A servile chuckle escaped me at this memory.

"My wife panics easily. You know, with everything that's going on. It's in a woman's nature to be more anxious than a rabbit. As for my daughter, don't you worry, I… (I brandished an imaginary stick) as she deserved. I hope we didn't bother you too much with these stupid matters."

The man made a strangled sound that could just as well have been a life-saving *yes* or a fatal *no*. I felt a pain in my belly: *This twat doesn't believe you… Try something else, quick! Your daughter… your daughter!*

I mustered all my remaining strength to assume the attitude of a citizen worried about the detrimental consequences for the police of a blunder he has made.

"It would really cap it off if you've already started investigations just because of some silly woman! Might we have to pay a fine?"

My heart was beating so fast that my thoughts suddenly became confused. To regain my footing, I sucked in the sickly, contaminated air of the police station hard. I tried another smile but just stopped myself in time, as this last masquerade threatened to turn into a fiasco.

The cop was busy trying to extract a scrap of food that was stuck in his teeth with his tongue and didn't bother reacting to my tone of complicity. He was probably wondering which mental drawer to file me away in. I reckoned from the face he pulled that he'd opted for the category 'standard bootlicker who blubs at the thought of losing some dosh'. Grabbing a register, he asked me for my name and telephone number before scribbling 'Cancelled' opposite some writing I couldn't decipher. Then he went back to reading some of the documents lying around on his desk.

I ran back to the car. Meriem opened the door for me. She had been crying.

"What took you so long?"

Her hair was totally dishevelled. Grief and worry had made her ugly overnight. My throat tight, I had a kind of dark, hare-brained revelation of the boundless love I felt for this woman: "It doesn't matter whether you're beautiful or ugly, Meriem, it'll take a whole lot more than that for me to tire of your love-bites!"

Inside that sorrow-laden car, I wanted to confess this epiphany to her – that it was vital that together we form a wall of steel against the disaster that was threatening to engulf our family. But immediately the words had formed in my mind, they seemed ridiculous and with an aching heart, I stifled the urge.

She was twisting her handkerchief around her fingers.

"He… He rang me again. He said he'd kill her if… What are we going to do, Aziz?"

Meriem interpreted my silence as a reproach. She averted her eyes towards the windscreen.

"I've been trying to tell myself since this morning that I'm going to be no use to my daughter if I keep crying. I stop crying, I think I've summoned up enough courage, and then… this bastard calls and whispers into my ear that he'll cut Shehera's head off if he feels like it…"

I made no move to console her: I was too scared that my body might disintegrate if our two despairs should touch.

She jumped as if she'd just been bitten by a poisonous animal.

"Oh no… not again… the phone! *Your* phone!"

I read the inevitable 'Caller unknown' message on the screen before raising it cautiously to my ear. With dark irony, I thought that I would have handled radioactive material the same way.

"Where are you?"

"In the car with my wife."

"Did you convince the police?"

"Yes… I think so."

"All right, let's move on to more serious matters. Get out of your car now. If you're driving, pull over."

I did as he said, asking Meriem to wait for me inside the vehicle. The tension was exhausting me; for a second I felt like an athlete sentenced to run the hundred metres over and over again under pain of death. The memory of a cigarette tickled my tongue. With an intense feeling of nostalgia, I thought, "Ah, a drag of some nice pungent grey tobacco and I'd cope with this better…" It'd been ten years since I'd stubbed out my last fag butt. I promised myself that I would treat myself to a packet of unfiltered cigarettes before the morning was out. A second train of thoughts, just as out of place as the first, had wormed its way into my brain.

The voice, terribly familiar now, brought me back to my surroundings. I tensed my muscles to ward off goose pimples. I also recognised, somewhere in the background of my sensations, an urge to vomit after another fit of panic.

"What I'm about to ask you is strictly between the two of us. Even your wife mustn't suspect anything. There's no one next to you? No cheating – that would have disastrous consequences for you know who!"

"No, there's nobody. My wife's in the car. How is my daughter?"

"Fine. Now, our deal is simple, Aziz: she will be fine *as long as* you obey me. Any pranks and – she croaks! Now, open your ears wide and keep calm. Are you calm?"

The man's inflexion had changed: more excited, with a hint of – how would you say? – *childish* enjoyment. It was this cheerfulness that made me feel with awful certainty that the worst was yet to come.

"I'm calm."

"Do you have enough imagination, Aziz?"

"What's imagination got to do with it?"

"You'll need some, because you're going to have to kill someone for me."

"**K**ill someone for you? Are you mad?"

There followed a few seconds of silence – enough time for me to bite my lip at my own stupidity: I had mentioned madness to a madman! Something slimy slithered into my mind: *Hey! Don't act so surprised. Everything's been mad since yesterday. Why would what this guy's asking you to do be any less mad?* I raised my eyes to the skies in search of help; the blanket of cloud, impassive as ever, looked like a badly cleaned zinc bar counter.

The voice articulated its words slowly. "'Mad', eh? You're going to pay a heavy price for that insult. The generous time limit of forty-eight hours I was going to offer you is reduced to twenty-four, meaning by 8 o'clock tomorrow morning."

"I…"

"Every time you protest, the time limit will be halved. You don't have to obey me, Aziz. But if you don't, your daughter will die in a very unpleasant fashion when time runs out. Unlike many people in this country, I'm honest – I always keep my word."

The crackpot was deadly serious – *he really did want me to kill someone for him.*

"And who am I supposed to…" I said, taken aback.

Meriem was watching me through the windscreen. Quite obviously, my gestures were not sufficient to keep her still any longer.

"Go to work," the kidnapper ordered. "I shall call the zoo in the morning to check you're following my instructions. I shall give you the name of the person. I shall also make sure that you have no reason to doubt the seriousness of my demands. I repeat: no one must know about our little agreement. Your safety depends on that too, you nitwit; by tomorrow, God willing, you will be a murderer. Dear Lord, grant long life to those who revere You even at the cost of their own lives… and the lives of unbelievers!"

And he ended his prayer with a burst of laughter that sounded almost like a bark. He had hung up by the time my stunned mind had finally succeeded in formulating a question: *But how can you order me, you fucking terrorist devil, to do something that I will never do?*

I got back into the car in a daze. I had already turned the key in the ignition when I felt Meriem's mouth right by my ear.

"… So what did he say to you, for God's sake?"

I managed to shake myself out of my mindless state. I decided not to hide anything from her (how could I keep *that* to myself!) and I whispered (because of course it was impossible to inflict *such* horror on her!), "He spoke of… (I took a big gulp of air, too big, scrabbling desperately for a credible lie.) Erm, nothing specific… He'll phone me later with instructions. He insists I go to work first."

"So what does he want? A ransom?"

"Maybe that's what he'd like… but I'm not sure, Meriem."

"And our daughter… Is she OK?"

I ventured a smile.

"He assured me she was."

The careworn face studied me suspiciously, ready to detect any attempt to deceive her on compassionate grounds.

"If he demands a ransom, tell him we're ready to sell the house, the car, everything we own. So are my mother and her husband. We'll borrow if need be. Do you think the bank will lend us money?"

"Of course, Meriem."

"Who is this man? Why us? We're not rich…"

Her voice was so wretched that I leaned over and kissed her lightly on the mouth.

"I've no idea, but we'll find a solution. And we'll get our daughter back safe and sound, I promise you."

"Are you sure?"

To avoid answering – and what would I have answered? – I placed another kiss on the corner of her lips, which were moist with tears. I felt defiled by sharing a secret with the kidnapper and concealing it from the woman I was kissing.

A man with a nasty expression on his face tapped on the car window.

"Go and snog your bird somewhere else, mate, or I'll call the police. This isn't Pigalle. This is a respectable neighbourhood."

The well-dressed sixty-year-old who was eyeing us with disgust displayed none of the presumed attributes of an Islamic fundamentalist. I drove off without even giving him the satisfaction of reacting to his provocation. Inside my head, a multitude of frightened voices were screaming at the same time, each vying to offer an opinion, some of them trying over and over again to convince me that the man on the telephone was only making fun of me, since the GIA's men had amply demonstrated that they had the necessary clout to murder whoever and whenever they wanted without resorting to such a tortuous mechanism!

I took Meriem to her secondary school. The thing she was most afraid of, she confessed to me, was going in to teach as though nothing was wrong, even as her daughter's life was hanging by a thread. I reminded her that we hardly had any choice since the kidnapper had made this a specific condition.

"He'll probably ring your administration under some pretext or other to check. But we'll stay in touch all day, you and I. As soon as one of us hears something, they should tell the other straight away."

I double-parked in front of the gates of her school. Before leaving she had one last doubt.

"What if we were wrong not to tell the police? What if we were condemning Shehera by keeping quiet?"

I held her gaze.

"I don't know. All I can tell you is that I sense he'll kill her if we put a foot wrong... Even though I think..."

I broke off, shocked at my own discovery (I was thinking: "... though I think he'll drag out this game for as long as possible. This sadist is toying with our lives. That's right; he's laughing his head off and he's in no hurry to let go of his new playthings!") I leaned over to her side to open the car door.

"Yes? You think...?"

She looked me up and down with mistrust. I must have blushed. As I leant over, I'd touched her thighs. She pushed me away unkindly and repeated, "Yes?"

"No, nothing. Quick, we're going to be late."

"Are you hiding something from me? You wouldn't dare hide anything to do with this from me, would you? He talked to you on the phone for a long time..."

I protested a bit too fiercely. The window of the passenger door was open. A passer-by looked round. He smiled, the unwitting witness, he imagined, to just another domestic quarrel in this city whose inhabitants were permanently on edge.

"What are you leading up to?"

Meriem got out without kissing me. She walked away quickly. Her figure, sorrowful and resentful towards me, soon disappeared behind the heavy iron gates that were like a barracks' and had been installed two years earlier after a failed assassination attempt on the previous headmaster. I drove on through the Algiers traffic jams, still in shock at my wife's attitude as she proclaimed, with the staggering dishonesty of a suffering mother: "*My daughter's been kidnapped and, look, the only way my wimp of a husband can think of to free her is to toe the line drawn by the man who took her from us!*"

At a crossroads a driver swore at me with a vicious smile. "Hey, when did you get your driving licence? When you came out of your aunt's vagina?" I had a searing, almost paralysing pang of nostalgia for that wonderful time – less than twenty-four hours previously – when I would have felt gravely offended and when my only concern would have been to come up with a retort worthy of the driver's wholly paradoxical obscenity. I realised that heaven did indeed exist – even though its irremissible drawback was that it existed only in the past. The previous morning Meriem, Shehera and I still led a 'normal' life, our sole cares those of a 'normal' life: bad marks, relationship problems, petty rivalries at work. We had been living in heaven because no member of our little family was threatened with death, rape, or both of those things at once.

But we didn't know that then! However, what we had learnt to our cost in the space of one short night was that, although heaven's delights often pass our ungrateful senses by, hell is immediately recognisable. Our bodies do not generally burn there, as holy scripture would have it; but our souls do. And far more cruelly.

Walking past the bonobo enclosure, I realised that I'd forgotten to pass on my boss's orders to the zoo employees. All the apes, both male and female, were outdoors, trying to keep themselves warm under the grey sky. I greeted Lucy and her baby, poor Shehera's favourite. The mother came over to the wire fence making a sort of yapping noise that I chose to interpret as meaning "Hello. How are you doing?" I whispered back, "Badly, friend, worse than you could possibly imagine... A kidnapping, but then you know what that's like..."

Right then I could easily have stepped into the enclosure and curled up against the bosom of the female bonobo, snuggled up to her baby and begged for a little consolation. Yet maybe she would have 'said' to me – or at least 'thought' – with biting sarcasm, "*Hang on, since when have bloody jailers taken to seeking solace from their prisoners?*"

With a heavy step I reached the zoo's administrative building. There was an unusual bustle in the staircases. The Director, Hajji Sadok, was waiting for me in the doorway to his office with a morose look on his face.

"It can't be said that you're the king of punctuality, Aziz."

"It wasn't me who invented Algiers' traffic jams," I retorted curtly.

I saw my acting Director's eyes harden in surprise. He looked round to check that no one had heard me.

"You should have taken precautions and left home earlier on a day like this!" he hissed through his teeth as he turned back into his office. "Fine, fine... Let's talk about the visit by the delegation. For my part, I've been in touch with a few people. How about you?"

I cleared my throat, hoping to find a less aggressive tone of voice. The acting Director studied me closely.

"Tell me, Aziz, do you feel all right? Has something... happened to you? You don't seem... too well... You look... (he hesitated over the word) shattered."

I tried to smile.

"No, you're exaggerating... It's just that... that I've had a stomach ache since yesterday, a bit of trouble digesting some food."

Not very convinced, Hajji Sadok shrugged his shoulders.

"Well, whatever your problem, make an effort to be friendly until the end of the visit. Otherwise neither you nor I will be in a job for much longer. Especially you, by the way... It's not so bad for me. I'm the incumbent. At the worst, I'll find myself in a different department, but that's not the case for a contract worker like you. Is that clear?"

I had understood the threat perfectly. He signalled with a gesture that the conversation was over.

"Ask the driver to prepare the minibus for the visit, then make sure that everything is ready: the press kits, the prospectuses, a Thermos of coffee, mineral water, lunch at the restaurant. And tidy your hair, Aziz."

I returned to my office, already exhausted by the docile act I was going to have put on all day long. I checked that the phone was working, before trying to concentrate on the visit by the apparatchiks from the ministry. I made a few phone calls to the relevant colleagues, using my mobile so as to leave the landline free. The accountant was amazed I was calling when his office was at the other end of the corridor. I kept the conversation short, before skimming through the extravagant and fairly false argument that old Hajji Sadok and I had drawn up.

All of a sudden my brain rebelled, refusing point blank to take any further interest in the visit, which just a day earlier had seemed absolutely vital to my future and to my family's. I held my head in my hands like someone grappling with a foreign body. Inside that ball of bone, blood and soft, grey flesh, thoughts were fighting like rabid dogs that would have me screaming in pain if I removed their muzzles. I shut my eyes, waiting for the call from the stranger who had become, to me, the most important human being since our nasty species' appearance on earth.

It was in this mental state that I saw the Director walk into my office.

"Feeling up to the visit?"

"Erm, yes… Sure."

"Doesn't look like it," said Hajji Sadok, raising an eyebrow. "You could have chosen a different day to fall ill. Come on, get a move on, they'll be here in quarter of an hour."

Suddenly the landline phone rang.

"Well, pick it up," grumbled the Director, noticing my hesitation. And as it lasted too long for his taste, Hajji Sadok picked up the phone. He listened without a word, then handed me the receiver.

"Private, it would seem."

A malicious smile playing on his lips, he remarked loud enough for my correspondent not to miss a word, "Remind your friend that private calls are not to go through office reception. I want you downstairs in five minutes, with the press kits."

"Your boss is a tough cookie… and not very polite, is he? Remind your boss that I've become crucial to you, and maybe to him, if I felt like it. Hey, are you listening?"

The voice tut-tuted, as though reprimanding a child.

"Not answering me, Aziz? Weren't you looking forward to my call?"

"Yes… I…"

"You are at the office and I appreciate the fact that you obeyed me. Anyway, here are some details about my request: *Anyone you like!*"

"What do you mean?"

"I repeat: *'Anyone you like!'* Didn't you get that?"

I replied, quite honestly, "No… not really…"

"Don't act more stupid than you are. Here's my proposal. Kill anyone you like, but I want a nice fresh corpse by tomorrow morning. By way of proof, you will take a photo of the corpse with your mobile phone and send it to the number I'll give you. Don't get any ideas. The chip for the number will only be used once, so there's no point in trying to trace it back. You'd better get a telephone with a camera as soon as possible. And…"

He continued in the same tone, half cordial, half technical.

"…I'll ring you on your mobile in a few minutes so you've got time to think it over. You'll tell me your decision next time we speak. Should you refuse, I will be forced to cut off your daughter's fingers one by one until you give me a total and unreserved *yes*. Goodbye, my friend."

I clung to the banister as I walked down the stairs. On the bottom step I almost fell over Lounes, the vet. His smile faded when he saw my face.

"If you're drunk, Aziz, then you're very unwise to declare your fondness for a tipple on the day of the ministerial inspection. (He shamelessly held his nose up to my mouth.) No, you're not. Are you ill, Aziz? You're very pale…"

"My stomach," I managed to mumble. "I…"

"I thought your wife was a pretty good cook. Maybe she's trying to get rid of an ancient relic like you, old boy?"

I tried to regain some of my composure.

"Excuse me, I was on my way to the toilet."

"I don't like it when you lose your sense of humour, Aziz. It's a very serious sign with you. Go home, man, and let yourself be pampered. The Director will understand."

I was already in the toilets, bent over the wash basin, when Lounes,

51

who hadn't laid off mocking me, called through the door to me: "I know a radical treatment if you've got stomach ache. I did a rectal examination on one of the lions the other day. Can you imagine sticking your finger up the king of the jungle's arse? The fellow was asleep, of course. I can offer you the same examination, but without anaesthetic if you insist. What do you reckon, Aziz?"

"I think you're a degenerate," I groaned. Then as I washed my face, I started crying.

I went back up to my office to fetch the pile of press kits and prospectuses. Lounes stood in the doorway, signalling that the party from the ministry had arrived. I rushed out, almost tripping over Hajji Sadok in the process. I deduced from his overly broad smile that the old man was hopping mad and that he would be sure to make me pay for my attitude once the delegation had left. He was flanked by a group of men, all of them wearing the kind of solemn mask that senior officials are given when their appointment is announced.

The youngest of them had a beard that was trimmed in the 'ambiguous' fashion that was more and more common among pen-pushers taking care not to put all their eggs in one basket: thick enough whiskers on the chin as a signal to the Islamists, the country's potential future leaders, that their heart was with them, yet smartly combed so as not to antagonize the current bosses, the sole dispensers – perhaps for some time yet – of rich administrative emoluments. My boss introduced me as his colleague 'in charge of forecasting'. Even given my state, I was momentarily taken aback by this pompous title for my humble position. Taking the opportunity as the members of the delegation piled into the minibus, Hajji Sadok whispered furiously in my ear, "At least arrange your tie and your hair!"

No sooner had the director got into the minibus and made the customary greetings than he presented the zoo as if he'd swallowed one of the advertising prospectuses I had just handed out: 750 acres of land, a 10-mile perimeter, a miniature 'Far West' train to get around it, a safari park and a theme park, a collection of antelopes, addax, oryx, Barbary stags, birds of prey, wildcats, etc.

The man with the beard interrupted Hajji Sadok's spiel with exaggerated politeness. Feigning embarrassment, he asked to see the new monkeys the press had written about. "It seems they have some… strange customs, ahem…"

"After a general tour of the facilities?"

"No, the monkeys first… unless my colleagues think differently."

The bearded man's tone had sharpened. His 'colleagues' remained impassive. Going bright red at this reprimand, the director called to me, "Here is our specialist on the subject. He will be delighted to say a few words about it."

Having completely ignored me up to this point, the three members of the delegation turned to me as one, with the slightly faraway look one puts on for flunkeys.

"Aziz?"

I considered the group of officials squashed into the three front seats of the minibus. Ever since the phone call from the kidnapper, I had been watching myself move as though some hidden pilot had taken over the controls and was carrying out, in my stead, the basic gestures that made it possible to simulate active presence. The 'real' captain had sought refuge in the darkest corner of an inner cave, shivering with indescribable terror. I showed no more reaction when my boss, beside himself, insisted, "Aziz, tell them about this precious gift we received from the Republic of Congo – rare creatures that few zoos can profess to house!"

The automatic pilot was unable to relax my lips. Interpreting my silence as a confession of a breach of administrative rules, the official with the thin beard went back on the attack.

"You see, we in central management have received letters from citizens complaining about the… (He searched for his words before pronouncing them with a subtly disgusted grimace.) hardly respectable behaviour of your new residents."

"But how have they had time to complain? We've only had these animals a few days!"

The official made do with a tap on his briefcase as if it contained some proof of our turpitude. Hajji Sadok once more went red at what was increasingly turning into an indictment. He rolled his eyes at me, his incomprehension of my unbelievable inertia switching to panic.

"Aziz, can you bring yourself to speak?"

And, turning to the others in bad-tempered justification, he said, "Please excuse him. He has not been feeling well since yesterday."

With a forced snigger, he added, "His wife cooked him something that didn't agree with him. Too much chilli, perhaps."

The members of the delegation let out a little chuckle, which was nonetheless too polite to relax the atmosphere. I thrust my hand into my pocket the moment the phone rang.

"Yes?"

"It's me, dear friend. Hold on, I'll pass you someone dear to you."

"Aziz," Hajji Sadok castigated me in my free ear, "you'll wait until the break to telephone. Turn off your mobile!"

I pushed him brusquely aside. He squawked, "Are you going mad? Being disrespectful to your superior in front of...? Well... what..." I don't know how the other passengers reacted to this because I completely lost touch with what was going on inside the minibus when I heard my daughter's voice. I believe I simply jumped out of the vehicle after the driver had already put it in gear.

"Dad, I'm scared..."

"No, my baby, don't be scared. I'm here, nothing can happen to you!" I answered Shehera stupidly.

My daughter screamed, "Dad, he wants to cut off my fingers... I'm tied up... Dad, save me, please... Help, Mum... He..."

I heard a muffled sound like a punch and then a cry of pain.

"There you go. Now you know I'm not joking. I'm holding a dagger, an unbelievably sharp one. If you don't answer "Yes, I am ready to fulfil my part of the bargain right now, then..."

He sniggered.

"I'm not nasty – I always start with the least useful finger of the less important hand. Your daughter is right-handed, right?"

"..."

"Do you confirm that?"

"Yes," I spluttered.

"Tell me, I can hear all sorts of noise again. What's going on?"

"Hey? What are you talking about?"

"Someone's shouting next to you. That's your boss, isn't it? I'm sorry to put you in a spot of bother. But let me remind you: total secrecy or else..."

I looked up. The scene might have been taking place on a different planet. A middle-aged man was standing by the door of a minibus yelling at me. Meaningless snatches of word-noises reached my ears: "Suspended... warning... You're crazy..."

The voice on the telephone started talking again cheerfully. "Make sure you're well away from any people. When you're sure nobody else can hear you, you will repeat clearly the words I dictate to you. Clearly, my friend, for I shall be recording you. Do you agree?"

The delegation minibus had driven off without me. A walker and two children were coming towards me. Without any hesitation, I plunged into the vegetation by the side of the path. A bendy branch covered in thorns lashed my neck.

"I'm ready."

The kidnapper took a deep breath.

"OK, listen. '*I, Aziz Merad, declare that I am going to commit the murder of an innocent person. I do not yet know the identity of my victim, but I am intent on taking his life before 8 o'clock tomorrow. I am of sound mind, I am speaking calmly and I am ready to assume every consequence of this premeditated assassination...*'"

Changing intonation:

"... Now, give the date, your address and your identity card number... which you have on you, I hope?"

I hazarded one last plea, adopting, without realising it, the inflexion of a parent reasoning with a temperamental child.

"You can't be serious about this... This is impossible... How am I to kill someone I don't know? There must be a less absurd way of dealing with this... Islamists don't do this kind of thing... Religion doesn't permit..."

"Ah," was all he replied in a sincerely surprised voice, "you still don't take me seriously... *But I'm not joking...*"

There was a brief silence, followed by a series of noises, then a terrified "What... what... what's going on? Please, sir..." from my daughter.

Then I heard a scream that was such an adult expression of pain that at first my ears refused to believe that it came from the mouth of a fourteen-year-old girl.

I too screamed, "What's going on? What's he done? Shehera? Shehera?"

"Be quiet," the man's voice ordered, quavering. "No one must hear you or else it's her throat I'll cut, right here and now."

With one fist thrust into my mouth, I was weeping uncontrollably when I spoke to Shehera again. She too was choking on her sobs.

"Daddy, it... it hurts... it hurts... cut off my finger... My finger...

There's blood everywhere... Daddy, I'm scared... my... my finger... finger... Mummy... it hurts... Daddy please... Daddy... da...

Her speech was disrupted by the chattering of her teeth. She didn't manage to finish her sentence. Her flawed pronunciation, which she could usually more or less control, made it even harder to understand her.

"... Daddy... he's got a die... a die... knife... Do... to..."

She let out another scream, every bit as heart-wrenching as the first.

"Daddy, he's about to... help... to cut off another finger... Daddy, if you love me, to... do what he says..."

I couldn't stop myself asking her, "You know what he wants me to do?"

"Yes, Daddy... I heard... but I'm too scared... and it hurts too much... Daddy, I don't want to die... for pity's sake, Daddy..."

I leaned against a tree trunk. I heard an elephant trumpeting in strange modulations in the distance. A stupid corner of my drifting mind had the cheek to speculate: "That poor animal must have diarrhoea. Let's hope the vet's there..."

"My beloved girl, tell him I agree, tell him not to hurt you anymore... I'll get you out of there, I promise... Tell him I accept..."

"Yes, Daddy... yes, Daddy... I'll tell him... Daddy, Daddy, what do I do with my finger?... The finger on the floor?"

I didn't have time to reply. The kidnapper's sugary voice continued, "Well, now you've seen sense. Don't worry about your daughter; they're tough at that age. I'll put a bandage with some tincture of iodine on it and everything will be just fine... Just don't make me angry again, that's all. OK... let's record... I'll count to five, then you start..."

I ended my proclamation with the date, my address and my identity card number. Around me the sky had not changed, there had been no eclipse of the sun, the park had not been swept away by a storm. On the other end of the phone there was a muffled click, the button of a recording device maybe, then a satisfied "hmm hmm".

"Those aren't the exact words I dictated to you, but it'll do. I'm not one to quibble."

"Listen..."

"Yes?"

"If I do what you told me to, what guarantee do I have that you'll release my daughter... unharmed?"

"None... Except that I've got some reasons for you to be satisfied with that *none*; I can even count them. Ten... er, no, nine now... Have you changed your mind?"

"No, no... But why... why *us*? Did you choose us *by chance*?"

"Chance, chance... You're going a bit far if you think I'd go to such lengths by chance! On the other hand, what is chance, my friend, if not necessity disguised as incomprehension? Only the innocent and the feeble-minded talk of chance. And, quite honestly, very few creatures turn out to be truly innocent on this earth. Even the child who whistles as he walks along a path, watched for years by an old tree that chooses to fall *specifically* on him..."

The voice gave an almost embarrassed sigh.

"The universe, God, the whole lot of it – don't you think that we're victims of a whole bundle of mysteries anyway? But knowing that is of no consolation to either you or me. So then, tomorrow, eight o'clock sharp. Prepare some persuasive photos of your feat. You'll give me the name and address of your corpse so I can check. If I have the slightest doubt, I will send you a photo of your decapitated daughter. Most importantly, don't forget..."

The mad beast allowed a pregnant silence to expand slowly through my ear – to the point where I thought the call had been cut off.

"...Amazing as it may sound, my lad, don't forget that *I exist*!"

The kidnapper repeated solemnly, with a touch of vanity, "I exist. And I have just proved that by making you my slave. Don't be startled: the Arab world, the whole fucking Arab world, is made up of masters and slaves. Think hard: have you ever been free, *truly* free, in this country? You'd be lying if you answered yes. So don't lie! If you are an Arab, you are already something of a slave. Don't worry: everyone's turn comes round in this shit-hole world of ours. Formerly, I used to be – how should I put this? – enslaved for life by certain events, and it lasted a long time, believe you me!"

He coughed, as if he'd been overcome by sudden emotion.

"One last thing: avoid being caught by the police. If your incompetence lands you in prison, your daughter is lost. But before that she'll go through hell on earth. And so will you, by the way; our cops aren't particularly gentle souls and they'll beat you till you can't take it anymore. The judges will back them up by giving you life at least, and your cellmates, frustrated yokels who could make a goat pregnant, will be happy to enlarge your arsehole until you can shit watermelons. Listen to your beloved daughter…"

He must have held the microphone closer to Shehera because I heard, for a short while and very clearly, her moans of pain that sounded like a tortured puppy's. Then the line went dead and I stood frozen to the spot, with my ear stuck to the phone for several long seconds trying to plumb the futile mystery of the tone. I put the mobile back in my pocket, slipped my identity card into my wallet, and ran my hand over my face, maybe to check whether the life of an individual like me fell within the bounds of possibility – *a father who had just listened to his daughter being tortured over the telephone!*

Suddenly I vomited; my breakfast first, followed by a liquid that was milky to begin with and then a yellowy colour. I carried on vomiting even when there was no more liquid left to throw up.

I only stopped because cramp had sunk its teeth into my oesophagus, forcing me to my knees with pain. While I was struggling to my feet, a corkscrew of an idea bored its way into my skull: Why hadn't I dared to ask my daughter if she was blindfolded? Did she see her kidnapper as he was cutting off her finger?

An inner sentinel whispered that this question wasn't a mere detail, of course, but that it would be better not to go into it for the time being, since too detailed a reply would have crucified me on the spot.

Shehera… My little Shehera…

I shut my eyelids, then opened them again immediately: I still had the *impossible* image of that bit of finger lying in a pool of blood on the floor in my mind's unseeing eye.

In an additional blow to my reason, I remembered the delight that had filled my soul when, so few years ago, I would bend over my daughter's cot and play with her little fingers in mine.

Once more, I felt my fear spreading like an awful disease through every organ in my body.

"How do Arabs kill?"

The words had slipped out, but I could hardly believe they were mine. I put my hand to my mouth as if the words might have left a wound. I didn't move, unable to tear myself away from the flimsy cover of the bushes. An insect dropped off a branch above me onto my jacket. It immediately took to crawling laboriously up the sleeve. I contemplated its uncomfortable progress across the checked fabric in a sort of waking unconsciousness.

"You are going to kill someone."

My mouth had once more pronounced these words without asking my leave. I moaned in the horrified certainty that the kidnapper had just cast me into hell. I dreamed: "And this time, it's *real* hell, not an image or a turn of phrase."

In stupefied admiration, I also noted: God really is economical in his means. No need for any ridiculous special effects or afterlife to create a place for destroying souls at a knockdown price.

I wanted to call for help. And did nothing – *Shehera's little fingers.*

"Meriem, yes, phone Meriem…"

"Then what? What are you going to tell her?"

That the madman has cut off one of our daughter's fingers and that I have to murder someone before dawn?

I pulled a handkerchief out of my pocket and wiped my face; there was a little blood on the material from the scratches. I emerged from the bushes, scaring a passer-by. The person looked at me with accusing eyes before walking on. I made for the car park. The man thought I was following him and speeded up. A thought crossed my mind, sharp as an arrow: *If I killed you, someone I don't know, perhaps my daughter's suffering would be over, all it would take…*

"…would be for me to… what – strangle you, stab you, drown you?… And where would I throw your corpse, you bastard?"

The man had disappeared out of sight. Maybe he'd started running just around the corner? I laughed. And I shuddered because I'd laughed.

I flexed the muscles of my soul – because soon I would have to make a decision.

And I realised that I loved my daughter too much to refuse the awful proposition.

A guardian angel inside me knelt down and silently implored me: *You cannot even consider killing a human being, Aziz! If you destroy a human being in cold blood, you leave the community of honourable men. Every stranger is like you: he has flesh as fragile as yours, an arse-hole that hurts him when he is constipated and a woolly-minded head on his torso that's as full of hopes and wild ideas as your own. No, you have no right to, Aziz...*

Wait, listen to me, it insisted – and its supplications were now punctuated by tears – *think of your wife... Meriem... could you look her in the eye when you've murdered some poor guy who's as attached to his wretched life as you are to yours?*

I stood rooted to the spot in the middle of the road, hardly breathing. The mention of Meriem was heartrending, but I did not react. Staring at a landscape whose every detail was indistinguishable to me, I 'listened' to myself. The terror-stricken voice tried a different tack.

What about Shehera... could you bear her to despise you...

"You're wrong, you old fogey!" I replied, chilled by self-contempt. "That's exactly the wrong argument. You say nothing about my child's delicate body and her right to live longer than us, her parents. If I do not kill, Shehera will be killed. And what will I do with my daughter's respect if some madman slices her up?"

I went back into the bushes, this time to urinate. My vanquished organism must have thought it was better to piss than to cry. While my kidneys emptied themselves of their impure water, my head filled with filth: I had just aged by several decades and the old man who had taken my place had decided to capitulate to the demon on the telephone.

But *whom* should I kill? And *how* should I kill?

I realised that the second question was the more difficult one in the short term. If all I'd had to do was press a button to eliminate an unknown person and recover my daughter, I don't think I would have hesitated. But grappling with someone who would give me a first unsuspecting glance before screaming in fear when he discovered my true intentions; who would defend himself with every last drop of strength to stay alive, blood spreading, intestines perhaps voiding themselves of their shit – that was something else.

Of course I had seen a terrorist slit a man's throat without it seeming to affect him in the slightest. That gesture to snatch life away had been so extraordinarily simple: a simple back-and-forth of the blade across a neck that didn't expect it. But by his complete indifference the bearded killer's had seemed to belong to a different species.

Feeling nauseous, I headed towards my car. I don't know why, but I felt I had to make a detour via the bonobos' shelter. Miraculously, there were no visitors hanging around nearby – and, most importantly, no little tie-wearing runts from the ministry. For the first time since the phone call, I thought back to the incident with my boss and his guests. It felt as if it had happened ever so long ago, back in prehistoric times, and that the foreseeable consequences (a reprimand, suspension, maybe even sacking) had nothing more to do with me, for I had left the human race.

Two males were fighting over a branch without any real conviction. A female was scratching her equally morose neighbour while chewing on a piece of fruit. The others were warming themselves in the weak morning sunlight. I looked in vain for Lucy and Lucette. I was almost overwhelmed by a sob when I realised that I was standing there in front of some monkeys, hoping – yes, indeed! – for one final sign of humanity before I plunged into ignominy.

I shrugged my shoulders. I guessed, however, that I would have given up everything – not least the ridiculous slop filling my skull – to change places not with the bonobos (they seemed to me to be too perspicacious to be still unaware of the wretchedness of their captivity), but with even the stupidest animal in all creation, the earthworm for example, and never have to worry again about trading one life for another.

From afar I saw Lounes, the vet, approaching – the mere sight of my friend in a previous life had become unbearable to me. Although he waved energetically at me, I drove off before he could reach me. I shot out onto the slip-road leading to the motorway.

It was only ten in the morning. It was already past ten in the morning. The crowded and untidy stream of vehicles on the sloping carriageway looked like a horde of animals fleeing from a raging fire. I had never felt more alone or more desperate. I had never felt this abandoned, other than in a nightmare that had haunted me when the first wave of assassinations of intellectuals began; I writhed in slow and painful agony surrounded by smiling people who pretended not to hear my calls for help. But I quickly decided that this comparison was inappropriate; the terror then was as nothing compared to the merciless humiliation and the soiling of my deepest self and, by contagion, of the entire universe that I felt as my brain started to scratch around for a way to satisfy the abductor's demands.

I realised that the word *soul* kept cropping up in my inner ramblings. What was the meaning of the word *soul* inside my skull that kept coming up with every thought of love, death and of the memories I would leave behind (I was going to say *for my family*, but I realised that what I really meant was *for myself*), even though I was fairly dubious about the notion of eternal life.

I honked my horn at a driver who had overtaken me on the hard shoulder. I then edged into the same lane, accelerating for no reason and twice changing lanes suddenly. This earned me a chorus of horns accompanied, I presume, by a stream of insults. One driver shook his fist at me.

I shouted, "Pull over, mate, if you dare and my soul will come and box yours until it's out for the count for good!"

I spluttered angrily as the car disappeared in my rear-view mirror, "And I've got a right son of a bitch of a soul, just so you know what you're up against, mate!"

I realised from the sound of the engine that I was still accelerating. For a few seconds, I felt the thrill of imminent deliverance. Boundless joy flooded through me. I sensed that such exultation was disgraceful, but it was so pleasant that I decided I would shut my eyes as soon as the pedal hit the floor.

A little more pressure on the accelerator (keeping it *secret* from the rest of me so as not to change my mind…) and everything would become as insignificant as the consequences of the disappearance of a tiny worm on the future orbit of the planets…

… Insignificant… Your daughter is insignificant?

I let out a shrill "Ah" as I braked a few inches from a huge articulated lorry loaded with sacks of cement. The car skidded; I braced myself, hoping for, and simultaneously dreading, the fatal impact with the car behind.

The miracle came to pass: no crash of crumpled metal, no lancing pain as the steel frame and the plastic of the dashboard pierced my flesh. Just a high-pitched screeching of brakes and horns trumpeting the panic of a herd of clockwork animals!

I sat up, my eyes bleary with sweat, both feet cramped up, one on the brake pedal, the other on the accelerator. I turned the engine off, laid both my hands flat on the dashboard and waited for my body to stop shaking and the scraps of thought surging and bursting through my head like angry bubbles to settle. My empty gaze wandered across the traffic and on to a sheet of newspaper caught on a bush on the central reservation. I bent down to read the headlines: 'Boumerdes teacher told to wear hijab by pupils' and, in bigger letters: 'The president opens a...' I wasn't brave enough to get out of the vehicle to find out what it was the president had inaugurated – an automatic laundry, the civil war or a rest centre for amnestied terrorists.

The car still reeked of burnt rubber. I drummed my fingers on the dashboard. I realised that I loved my daughter and my wife with the weight of all the oceans on earth and that my only mission in this world was to protect them, whatever curses it might bring down upon me. One day, at the second coming of the messiah of one of our world's many religions, a kindly angel would perhaps dare to forgive me or, at least, take account of mitigating circumstances.

Even before I had finished counting my fingers (five on the first hand and five on the second), I had accepted my fate.

All I had to do now was to find the victim, the weapon and the moment to kill.

And almost immediately I sensed that I was well beyond that, that my reptilian brain, the archaic part of the nerve matter that is the source of our species' survival instinct, had been much quicker and had already ensnared its prey.

Yes, I was a coward. Yes, I had spontaneously resorted to the most spineless kind of reasoning: if you kill for killing's sake, you might as well kill the man with the least value in the eyes of the world, including his own. You might as well kill – and this argument complements the previous one – someone who has no means of defending himself...

The old prehistoric beast within me had at once identified the weakest animal in the flock: Moh, the armless, legless newspaper-seller.

I mused: "If you had also been mute and blind, my friend Moh, you'd have served my purpose well…" I gave a surprised gasp at my 'pragmatic' reaction, a little bile rising deep in my throat. I shivered at the thought of this 'new' side to a subject I was supposed to know more intimately than anyone else alive: myself. I felt a mixture of disgust and a strange feeling that I dared not identify as a sort of dismayed fascination: was the real *me* so different from the basically normal *me* I had been presenting in total ignorance since my birth? Might this everyday identity have been merely the handmaiden of another less unsavoury identity waiting patiently to surface?

"Oh shit!"

I forbade myself to go any further with this introspection, suspecting that it would destroy what little willpower I had been able to summon up. I had opened the boot to rummage through the toolbox I always carried with me to deal with my car's frequent breakdowns. I hesitated between a monkey wrench and a hammer I had already used once to beat a bit of metal back into shape after a crash at a red light.

The wrench was too light and the hammer too bulky. But out of the mess of washers and bolts emerged a long, sharp, flat-ended screwdriver.

"Need some help?"

Holding my breath, I turned towards the van driver who was beaming at me out of his open window.

"What?" I stammered, imagining for a horrible instant that he could read my murderous plans on my face.

"Broken down, have you? Because I know a thing or two about cars."

I forced myself to smile back at him as I hurriedly tossed the tools back into the boot.

"No… thanks… Erm… I was just checking something."

"Sure you don't need any help? I can tow you. I've got a towbar in the back and I know a garage nearby."

"No," I interrupted him brusquely, "I haven't broken down."

The man in the van's friendly expression had vanished.

"Hey, calm down, cousin, calm down! I just wanted to give you a hand. Strange times when you offer your neighbour some help and he throws it back in your face!"

Then, seeking to have the final word in revenge for my rudeness, he said mockingly, "Anyway, you won't get far in that heap of junk. And then you'll be left high and dry, with that useless hammer and poofy monkey wrench of yours!"

A gust of wind blew the smoke from the exhaust pipe into my nostrils as the van sped off towards the Kouba hills. I followed the vehicle with my eyes, overcome by a new fear – of being arrested for the crime I was condemned to commit.

You'd better not get caught by the police, think of your daughter was, in substance, the kidnapper's warning.

"Meriem…"

I wanted to take refuge in her arms, put my head between her breasts, tell her everything, share the tragedy of the ignominious deed I was about to perpetrate.

I moaned, suffocated by the coming solitude.

I got into the car and huddled up on my seat. A good quarter of an hour passed. All that time I had the impression that a huge foot was pressing down on me and crushing me under its weight.

At last I started the engine and checked that there weren't any policemen around. I drove about a dozen yards, then suddenly cut across the yellow line and took the motorway in the opposite direction, towards the park.

I stuffed the screwdriver and then, after a moment's thought, the hammer into an old bag that was lying around in the car. With a pang of anguish, I crossed the road that separated me from the limbless man's shop before I suddenly felt all my determination leave me.

I must have staggered because a passer-by muttered reproachfully, "Well well, getting in a state like that so early in the day… May God curse Satan and his scheming mind!" I rushed into a little café. The waiter served me coffee in a dirty-looking cup. I drank it down in one and ordered another. The waiter laughed.

"A nice cup of coffee tastes good even if you're carrying all of Algeria's problems on your shoulders. Don't forget to sweeten it with lots of sugar if you're in a bitter frame of mind! If I were president, I'd put a spoonful of sugar in every Algerian's head!"

I responded to the waiter's cheerful chatter with a mutter that discouraged all further conversation. All the same, I followed his advice. I forced myself to sip the thick, sugary liquid. The feeling of having had my legs amputated gradually faded. The telephone rang. The icon announcing a text message blinked on the screen.

I opened the message. I stared at the two lines on the tiny screen, first in incomprehension, then in horror:

```
10 - 1 = 9
9 - 1 = ?
```

I sat up with a start, knocking my cup over. I paid the waiter, who was now grumbling, "I told you not to overdo it with the coffee. Everyone's so highly strung in this country – no one listens to anyone!"

As if in a nightmare, I reached the booth, a garishly painted breezeblock cube with a corrugated iron roof. The limbless man was resting in an old wickerwork armchair like some enormous cucumber wrapped in a sleeveless coat. The crate on wheels was standing by one of the walls. He was listening to the radio with his head hanging to one side. I vaguely heard that the management of Al-Jazeera had just removed the results of a poll of thirty thousand Arab Internet users from its website. "Fifty-five per cent of them," the journalist exclaimed, "support the recent kamikaze attacks in Algeria!"

The handicapped man was surprised to see me, but he greeted me with his unfailing smile.

"Did you hear that, doctor? No one wants to see Arabs die more than other Arabs, it seems! Nice timing – I'm dying for a drop of coffee after all that twaddle! Would you mind pouring me some?"

He gestured with his eyes towards the Thermos under his table decorated with their 'anti-theft' Koranic verses.

"Go on, have a cup with me, doctor."

"I'm not…"

"…*not a doctor*, I know, doctor. But you deserve to be," he added with a guffaw. "You know, you work too hard for a civil servant. You've gone all pale and you're sweating even though it's cool. You should go and see…"

"A *real* doctor, right?"

"I don't have to spell things out to you!"

I had trouble swallowing. *No, dear old Moh, if the brain in that elongated head of yours could only fathom one-thousandth of my intentions towards you, legs would sprout miraculously from your backside and you would scarper as fast as your legs could carry you away from this screwdriver-carrying doctor.* Without further thought, without being able to utter the slightest riposte, I held out the cup to him. *My task now is to manage to hate you so much in the next few seconds that I can then slit your throat.*

I didn't understand what caused his smile, at once patient and sarcastic.

"I… Sorry… sorry… I'm an idiot, I forgot your… I mean…"

Even my ears must have gone red, for I was holding out a cup to a man with no arms. Moh's eyes twinkled as if he'd just watched a comedy sketch.

"Got you there, doctor! You're not the only one, though. If you only knew the number of people who try to shake my hand or hand me a banknote before they realise that they have to look after the till themselves. Anyway, for the cup, look down here to my right, there's something my son made for me… There, that's it."

He had a son. A lump of icy dirt had formed in my stomach. *And I, bastard son of a bastard, have a daughter. And she's worth more than anything you could possibly raise in your defence!*

The device was made out of bits and bobs, a metal bar with a board on the end with two holes in it, one bigger than the other.

"It's not complicated. You fit the cup into the first one; the other's for a bowl. Hold the thingummy-gob – that's what my son calls it – up to me, then stick the straw between my lips."

He sucked in the coffee with visible relish. I poured myself a cup too. I grimaced as I swallowed the bitter brew. My grimace didn't escape the cigarette-seller's beady eye.

"I can't offer you any sugar because of diabetes."

The straw in his mouth made him mash his words.

"Because you've got…"

"No, no! When you're in my situation, it's better to know when to stop! But who knows – maybe I'll get that diabetes thing one day or another! I'm scared of God when He tries to show a bit of humour. So let's pray He keeps his sense of moderation."

"Do you think Allah has shown moderation towards you?"

"Yes, because I could've been blind, dumb and deaf as well. I can find any number of creatures whose fate is far uglier than mine. From that point of view, I'm privileged. And maybe, in return for my submissiveness, Allah is planning to offer me a prime position next to His throne with all the conveniences you can imagine: as many *houris* as I can handle, milk, honey, wine and all the rest… Unless…"

He dropped his straw. After wiping it with his paper tissue, he put it back in his mouth. I thought: "What if I smothered you? You couldn't even put up a fight…"

"Thank you…"

"You were saying, a prime position?"

"Unless he forgets me, like a craftsman chucking a reject part on the scrapheap. The only thing I ask myself about what will happen to me after death, is this: will I have a full set of legs and arms? Let's change the subject, brother, because we are flirting dangerously with blasphemy. I don't want to risk losing my heavenly couch because of a word out of place!"

I felt the screwdriver through my bag. This man was chatty, his head waggling from side to side in time with his words, not allowing me to gather my thoughts. Anyway, there was no chance of doing anything for the moment; there were too many people walking between the bus stop and the nearby buildings. A teenager walked up and asked for a packet of Marlboros.

"Real or fake?" the shopkeeper asked good-naturedly.

"The fake ones from Niger?"

"That's right, my friend," Moh agreed. "But take the real ones from Hong Kong. They're a little more expensive, but worth it – they're guaranteed against lung disease, friend. Those Chinese have invented machines that take out the cancer grains, one by one. The Niger cigarettes are made illegally by uneducated Blacks; they're a total disaster."

With a wink, Moh asked me to fetch a packet of cigarettes out of the cardboard box stashed under the table. I did as he said, regretting bitterly the trap of familiarity I had fallen into.

The radio was now playing the whining quavering of a Middle Eastern female singer about the joys of living by the Nile. When the teenager had gone, I said, as much to pad out the conversation as to contain the storm inside me, "Did you make that up, that stuff about fake and real cigarettes?"

"Yes, of course I did. Both of them have been smuggled in from some African country, but my customers feel better if they think they've chosen the right ones.

"That's a…"

He chuckled. "Of course it's a lie, but you're not really going to demand honesty from me. For lack of arms and legs, I've had to develop my tongue. May God forgive me for exaggerating a little! On the other hand, He didn't have to make me this way. Tell me…"

He hesitated, trying to make his cunning look seem complicit.

"Aren't you working today or did you sneak out of the office?"

"What makes you think that?"

My tone was too snappy. He shook his head.

"Excuse me for saying so, but you look harassed. And… have you seen your jacket?… Next to the left pocket?"

A big greasy stain flecked my jacket where it had touched the bag. I was seized by sudden irritation at the handicapped man's prying eyes. I bent my nose over my cup of coffee before mumbling, "My boss gave me the day off. He doesn't think I look good either. A stomach bug probably."

"My son'll be round soon, after school. If you want, you can ask him to go and get you some medicine from the pharmacy. If you're not in too much of a hurry, that is…"

"You have a son?"

He sniggered – but it was no longer the same cheerful laugh.

"You're wondering how this sausage-man managed to find himself a son? And how low did a woman have to stoop to tie her life to his?"

"No, I…"

His wrinkled face with its thin crop of hair lit up.

"I'm not lying this time. Want me to tell you a secret?"

I didn't answer. My face closed. *There's no way I'm listening to you, no way you're going to save your skin and my daughter lose hers – I can see right through this sob story!*

Moh sighed and the straw fell out of his mouth. I pretended I hadn't seen anything. But the man obviously wanted to talk; he seized the opportunity – a rare one for him – of having a supposedly benevolent ear available.

"My son is the most wonderful thing that's ever happened to me. He's a little over 14 and he's the one who takes care of me. Well, washing, brushing my teeth and… all the other stuff… I'd be unable to manage by myself… Think of the number of erm, personal things for which hands are essential. I don't have to draw you a picture for you to understand, with all due respect of course… It's a terrible chore and yet my young son carries it out morning and evening with no complaints and without showing any disgust. He even joked about the colour of my shit one day when I'd eaten too much beetroot!"

The man looked down.

"As for my wife, that's something different. I should probably say my ex-wife. When I was younger, my father was a well-to-do shopkeeper, whereas my future wife's family was poor and heavily in debt to him. It was a good deal for everyone when my in-laws gave us their daughter: for my old man, who'd been dreaming of getting rid of me since my birth; for the young woman's parents, who wiped off their debts in one go and even received an allowance for looking after me; and for me, the nearly-nothing, the less-than-dwarf, who gained a nurse and a wife at the same time. Everyone was delighted, apart from the beautiful young girl whose opinion no one had asked. That wasn't common practice in the country in my day! Since then, my father has gone bankrupt and had the unfortunate idea to kick the bucket as a result. I've even had time to have two children by my wife, a girl and a boy. But my wife couldn't stand me any more. She insulted me, she kept saying…"

He went off on another round of giggles. (I thought cruelly that, if he'd had hands, he would have slapped his thighs.)

"She kept saying, with all due respect, that a cock stuck to a sub-monkey doesn't make a husband. She isn't wrong, I must confess. She wanted to remarry a man who was, let's say, all there. My daughter very quickly took her mother's side. At school she told them I was dead. My son, though, carried on loving me. I don't know why, actually – I didn't rock him, I didn't play football with him, I didn't help him with his homework, all those little things that fathers are supposed to do with their kids, not to mention spanking them when they get in trouble."

He was interrupted by a brief sigh.

"My kid is a little drop of heavenly mint poured into my life potion at the very last moment, maybe a little sign of regret from the Almighty."

He cleared his throat, overcome with emotion.

"The funny thing is that the new husband, a good lad, pulled some strings to get me this breezeblock box to sleep in and trade from."

He motioned with his head towards the metal sheet that served as a roof.

"Can you guess what my beautiful store used to be?"

"Er, no."

"Take a closer look. Forget the paint and the little sign, take the roof off and cover the lot with some dirty thatch... Never seen one before? Maybe even at the foot of your block of flats?"

Irritated, I almost replied that I hated riddles before I started in embarrassment, gripped by a nervous desire to laugh.

"You've really squatted a rubbish tip? And no one objected?"

"A rubbish tip, spring-cleaned and with added roof and door. My ex-wife's new husband wanted to get rid of me as fast as he could. All the same, I think he felt a bit ashamed about kicking out someone like me. In return for a few banknotes, he persuaded the council worker to 'forget' this rubbish tip. Anything goes in this crazy country, you know that, as long as you pay the right price."

Moh turned his head to the right and, using it like an index finger, pointed with his tongue.

"You see those bin bags over there by the car park? They're piled up around a construction just like mine. It's the new tip but, as you can see, it's not really any use. People prefer to chuck their rubbish any old place; it's as if having cleaner surroundings would annoy them! At least I use mine as a villa. All right, it's true there aren't any windows, nothing but a badly made door, but I only shut myself in at night. I don't take up much room, as you can see; I can live in next to nothing."

His head was still nodding furiously (*Ha ha ha, don't forget he's a Mediterranean, he gesticulates with his head for want of hands.*) Once more his mouth produced a shrill laugh, too cheerful by half.

"When I say I come in... what I mean is that my son puts me inside in the evening and shuts the door until the next day, except for Friday when it's the people from the mosque who take care of me, pamper me and feed me before they help me pray. The imam has threatened any locals who try to steal from me or do me any harm with reprisals. He dreamed that I was sent by heaven to test the believers in the neighbourhood. According to him, I am of indubitable social and religious usefulness."

His eyes shone with mocking pride.

"What time does your son come?"

"He always comes in the morning to open the door, wash me and help me set out my goods. In the evening, he's here around 7 o'clock to count the till and feed me. When he hasn't got school, he sometimes drops in at lunchtime."

"And you sleep alone?"

"Yes, until (as he laughed, he clicked his tongue against his palate) the imam or some accommodating Muslim comes up with a new wife for me."

"How old are you, Moh?"

"Forty-four and a few months. Do you want my star sign too?"

Something evil had moved within me, like a venomous snake raising its head to put an end to this idiotic dialogue with its prey. *Time you shut up, you dwarf. Your smile is forced, you feign cheerfulness because you're scared that people will be put off by your appearance and shrink from talking to you. But I'm sure you spend your nights weeping over the injustice of your fate. This evening I will come and put an end to your mother's blunder and we won't even need to bury you in the rubbish because you'll already be there.*

I felt a kind of dizziness at such a hideous emotion. I blinked with the violence of this discovery: a part of me about the size of a hazelnut had just murmured gleefully at the thought of taking another person's life.

The handicapped man had fixed me with eyes brimming with anxiety.

"Ah, I'm boring you with my chatter…"

And as if he were afraid that I might flee, he hurriedly added, completely out of context with what had gone before, "Please wait. I have to tell you what my son's called."

He contemplated me with a disturbingly fierce glint of defiance.

"My son's called Yacine. When I gave him that name, I didn't know that he would deserve it far more than I bargained for. You know the Surah *Ya-sin* from the holy Koran, which is called that because it begins with two separate letters – the letters *Ya* and *Sin*. No one knows why God chose to put them all on their own. We will find out, it seems, at the end of time when we are born again to be judged. Long time to wait, don't you think?"

The limbless man was interrupted by a long and whistling cough. He smiled awkwardly by way of apology. Some saliva dribbled from the corners of his mouth. For a second, I thought about getting up and wiping it away.

"You see, doctor, my son is a real mystery. How, at his age, can he be so considerate towards his runt of a father and never lose patience? Everything has a heart, and it is claimed that the heart of the Koran is this mysterious Surah *Yasin*. As you can imagine, I am too ignorant to dare to express an opinion about God's plans..."

The cigarette seller had tears in his eyes. The trap had just sprung shut on me: I had let him talk too long about his cursed offspring.

"...But it's simple as far as I'm concerned – my boy Yacine is my heart of hearts!"

I stood up, overcome with anger at my clear defeat. I would never have the courage to seize this man by the throat, plunge the point of my screwdriver into it and hold it there until the death rattle came. I hated the miraculous teenager whose mere existence had just saved his father's life.

My hands were itching. With shame, with despair.

So you don't want to do away with an innocent person? A big word that! Look at them, all these people around you, so profoundly, so spectacularly innocent, *as if by vocation; examine their* innocent *gestures, listen to their* innocent *conversations and their* innocent *arguments! You'd think that no one had ever killed anyone in Algeria in all these long years, that no one had denounced a neighbour who talked too much, that no one was getting ready to kill people in an attack or a fake roadblock tomorrow! And see how, still armoured with the same* innocence, *they throw themselves at today's amnestied prisoners and yesterday's mass murderers, how seductive they find them with their hennaed beards, their big, melancholy eyes and their rhetoric about the Eden of promiscuity that awaits the Obedient!*

The mastiff careering around in my mind interjected: *Aziz, you are a downright chicken. Where are you going to find someone this easy to eliminate now? You want to stay clean? Well, stay clean, but it's your daughter who'll be sullied! First blood, then sperm, and finally decapitation...*

Without another glance at Moh, I looked at my watch. I had wasted half an hour of the scarce time the kidnapper had granted me. Hastily I walked off, my jaws clenched, incapable of responding to the shopkeeper's invitation to have another cup of coffee, this time with some extra-special cardamom someone had brought him back from Morocco.

I mumbled, "Sip your shitty coffee with some poison instead!"

I immediately felt like gulping down a few swigs of that merciful drink and dying right there, on this spit-spattered pavement – because I couldn't see how I might save my child.

I got back in my car and put my useless bag down beside me. I looked at it in amazement. And, having not once invoked the heavens since my childhood, I started praying, like a coward, like a villain. "Dear God, forgive me, free my daughter, but do not ask me to kill an innocent. I do not have Abraham's mad obedience; I am only the basest kind of man. Have mercy, have mercy!"

This prayer did nothing to diminish my terror. Worse: I felt as ridiculous as a chicken destined for the dinner table begging the farmer to spare it.

I took out my phone. I realised that the back cover had moved slightly and that the battery had come out of its housing. The telephone had therefore been off, probably ever since I'd put it back in my pocket. I pushed the battery back inside in a panic, cursing my negligence; I should have either changed phone or put a strip of sticky tape on the lid to stop it slipping.

The screen showed some waiting messages. I checked my voicemail. The first was from Meriem. In a strangled voice, she asked me whether the… (she didn't dare name him) had rung and if I had any news about Shehera. The second was also from my wife. "Why aren't you answering, Aziz? Call me… I'm dying of fright… Call me, please…"

Her voice was exasperated and at the same time on the verge of tears.

My soul melted with shame. I almost interrupted the succession of messages.

"…So you think not answering your dearest friend on earth is funny, eh? Why are you doing this? …"

I stiffened when I heard the third message.

"…I am extremely disappointed in you, Aziz, extremely disappointed. I shall call again in nine minutes. If you do not pick up in nine minutes' time, then nine will only be eight, and eight will only be seven… Speak to you soon. Hey, my boy, don't try and be clever, and most importantly don't tell you-know-who about our plans."

The menu came up again. I looked at my watch in horror. I was shaking so hard I couldn't work out how to get back to find out when the message had been recorded.

"Aziz… (Meriem was sobbing) What have you done? … The man rang me… He said that you had disappointed him a lot… that his disappointment always has a price… What does he mean? … Aziz, I called your office… Your colleague said you'd left the zoo (A hiccup interrupted her moaning)… Come home… My daughter, I want my daughter…"

I hung up again. I stood there, not moving, taking short gulps of air, refusing to grasp what my ears had heard. *Nine minutes, one finger; eight minutes, another finger… How many minutes would it take until she lost all her fingers?* It was like the relentless teacher during my childhood dictating a mathematical problem about taps that kept on running, trying desperately to fill up bathtubs riddled with holes. But in this case the water was replaced by my daughter's blood. I shook my head to break off this obscene calculation, but to no avail.

The telephone rang. I held my mobile up to my ear, my senses all at sea. The man tutted a dissatisfied *no no no.*

"Why did you turn your phone off?"

"I had a problem with the battery," I stammered. "Please…"

"You understood my warning? The stuff about deadlines? It's very annoying, to tell you the truth. Deep down, I don't wish you any harm."

His tone was so normal that I misunderstood him. I let out a sigh of relief. I heard an irritated snigger.

"Hey, don't get ahead of yourself! I told you I found it annoying, but not enough to forget my promises. Exactly fifteen minutes have elapsed since my warning. A first period of nine minutes and a second of eight. You've studied, so go ahead and calculate, given that the second period doesn't merit any punishment because it hasn't finished yet and because you're chatting away with me right now."

I didn't react, my horrified mind refusing to bend to the madman's reasoning.

"Anyway, Aziz, it's not so bad! I've only removed one more finger, her left ring finger. Come on, no need to make a diplomatic incident of it! It'd be better if you kept your mind on our agreement if you want her to keep the most important part."

His tone of voice was that of a doctor explaining learnedly to his patient that he has had to proceed with two or three unavoidable operations that were apparently unpleasant but had benign consequences.

My mouth uttered some garbled words.

"Pass… Pass me my daughter…"

"Why? Don't you believe me? And you're giving me orders now?"

His tone was puzzled, with just a hint of amusement – the cat taken aback by a rebellious mouse.

"No… no. Please let me talk to my daughter."

"And will you do as you promised?"

I answered "Yes, yes!" and every nook of my soul was sincere.

"I'll see what I can do. Don't cut us off," he said, then burst out laughing at his pun.

I was left standing there with my ear glued to the phone for a good minute. Then I picked up some moans that appalled me more than any scream.

"Is that you, Shehera?"

A feeble "Yes, Dad' answered me, and it was so painful that I knew the kidnapper wasn't bluffing.

I murmured, "Did he hurt you again, my girl?"

"Yes… It's bleeding… Dad, it… hurts so much… He gave me some pills, but they don't help one bit…"

Tears welled up in my eyes. *My baby, my tiny, tiny baby.* I had asked to be there when Shehera was born. The midwife had scowled at my request, muttering that it was a *haram* custom that invaded a woman's privacy. I objected that my wife had agreed. Surprised by my stupidity, the midwife retorted that she was talking about her own privacy and that she refused to touch a woman's private parts in the presence of a man! Nonetheless, the birth had taken place in my presence and my daughter had emerged from her mother's sex like some strange astronaut visiting the Earthmen. Beside myself with joy, I had seen the infant smile at me as I stroked its head.

And now my mischievous astronaut was gulping down pills because a demented man from a different and evil planet had cut off two of her fingers! The black bile of pity rose in my throat.

"I'm sorry… I love you, my girl… I'm sorry… so sorry…"

"Dad, he's definitely going to kill me… Just now, I begged him… Oh Dad, how I begged him… But he wouldn't listen…"

She added in utter amazement, "Is there really nothing anyone can do for me, Dad?"

She had formulated her supplication in a tone that said "*You are my father, after all. It's up to you to protect me!*" It was her heart-rending pre-adolescent voice, from back when she still thought me the most powerful man on earth.

It hit me with more glaring certainty than the sun – nothing, not even debasement through the worst kind of ignominy, was worth a jot compared to my daughter's suffering!

"I swear on my own life, Shehera, that I will set you free!"

I didn't hear her reaction. Instead I was rewarded with the kidnapper's approval.

"Not a moment too soon. Now there's a resolution I can second!"

He clicked his tongue.

"Now… A little patience while I leave your daughter's room… We need to talk."

I could tell by the screeching and rattling of metal that he was locking a door. He was out of breath when he next spoke.

"Yes, we need to have a little chat…"

Once more, his words were interrupted by a wheezing cough.

"He's ill… or rather, old… The bastard's old!" I thought and this realisation, along with its simplistic conclusion (*an old man's got less to lose*) paralysed me.

"Pardon me, let's call it… the emotion… Believe me – I'm just as overcome as you are. You've made up your mind?"

"Yes."

"Really? You won't hold back at the last moment?"

"No, but you have to give me some assurance that you won't hurt my daughter and that you'll free her tomorrow… *afterwards.*"

"If you behave, tomorrow your daughter will be free."

"That's not good enough. How do I know you'll keep your word?"

"You don't, sonny. Here in Algeria not even the president has to keep his word. Why should I give you any guarantees? This matter is between the two of us; *I* decide and *you* accept my decisions. Otherwise, *your* daughter suffers the consequences. You've seen so far that I haven't been joking. Is our contract clearer now?"

I managed to articulate an indeterminate *yes*. And almost without my realising it my lips stammered, "Why… me? Why… my family?"

"Let's just say the story goes back a long, long way. Maybe one day, when you and I have become friends, I will tell you everything and you will understand, if you have the heart."

He had spoken this last sentence without the slightest hint of mockery.

"Tell me, have you already chosen?"

"Erm, yes… I mean… no…"

He let out a strange, understanding laugh.

"Let me guess. You chose some unpleasant so-and-so and you hesitated at the last moment… You weren't brave enough. Your weapon's a knife? Or something similar, am I right? You're not the kind of guy who could dig up a pistol. I bet you've never slit a throat, not even a sheep's for Eid. You're gentle by nature; the war that is sending this country to the dogs is nothing to do with you. At least that's what you thought until today. Am I wrong?"

The bile rose into my mouth again.

"You see, the secret is to choose someone you can unleash your own hate mechanism against. You've had one since you were born, hidden away deep down in your guts. All you have to do, somehow or other, is to find the 'on' switch."

His tone had grown passionate.

"I'm sure there are people you know whom you would hate if you really wanted to. But hating is a fulltime job; I know from experience. On the other hand, there's no lack of potential prey in this country of ours: the corrupt, the cheaters, the thieves, the child rapists, people who murder entire families…

He stopped to catch his breath. It was obvious, in spite of the wickedness of his crime, that he didn't include himself in the category of rapists and murderers.

"All right, those crooks are so much part of the scenery that it doesn't even offend honest people to rub shoulders with them anymore. Often, in fact, they envy them for being richer and more powerful. Nobody ever got rich from being honest in our wonderful Algeria, just as having a virgin arse has never fed a girl's stomach. But in this particular case, be more moral than you are normally: seek out the scum, even if they're well dressed. You'll know you've chosen your victim well if your reaction to someone else killing him were something like 'Serves the bastard right!'"

You're not just any old terrorist – you're too articulate for that. You're not some ordinary bearded, filthy 'Afghan' who can just about manage to mumble a couple of surahs before blowing himself up in the street! You're probably middle-aged, educated, maybe even one of the dignitaries you've just portrayed?

"Think about what I've told you, Aziz, and sniff the air: vermin smells! Rapier-sharp hate and contempt; those are your weapons."

"But what good does it do you if I kill an innocent person?"

"For the time being that's none of your business. Keep to the terms of our agreement: you kill, I free; you don't kill, I kill. Understood? While we're on the subject, don't ever turn off your mobile – I shall ring you several times today. I don't want to miss any of our hunt; I want to savour every minute of it."

He had stressed the words *our hunt*.

"To sum up: do you love your daughter *more than your own life*?

"Yes, of course. That's exactly what a parent is for: to love his children more than his own life. That's what your religion proclaims, isn't it?"

I could have kicked myself for making such a scathing remark. But there was no trace of irritation in the stranger's reply, just impatience verging on bitterness.

"You're mistaken: I know that as well as you. And what's more, I've known it for far longer."

He concluded in a husky voice, "So everything's very simple for you, Aziz. You agree with me that there is always a price to pay for fine sentiments. It's payback time. Fair journey, brother!"

Immediately I thought of my wife, of the complex yet simple love I felt for her and of the lie I must now invent to protect her. At the same time, I readied myself for the awful possibility that Meriem might not love me by the same time tomorrow, when my soul had been sucked down into the mire of premeditated murder.

I rang Meriem. She answered immediately.

"Why did you put your phone on voicemail?"

And leaving me no time to explain myself: "At the office they told me that you left straight after you arrived, even though there was a delegation from the ministry… Why did you turn your mobile off?"

In her reproach bristling with anger there was still the same crazed grief that had not left her since the day before. I was tempted to confess everything to her, to share with her the burden of our daughter's torture, but I had a premonition that my wife's suffering, however strong and courageous she might appear, would be like a bottomless void, and that what she had endured up till now was nothing compared to what awaited her.

The only side I knew of Meriem was her ability to create happiness in a country that revered misery. I was now discovering the reverse of this skill: her utter fragility, like an immune deficiency, in the face of the cruelty enacted upon her family.

A rush of almost physical hatred for the author of this devastation swept up through my lungs. I had trouble swallowing the oxygen as it resisted my attempts.

Then, sick with compassion for Meriem, I began to lie.

"I'm sorry about the telephone. Battery problems. I managed to talk to the terrorist... Shehera... Shehera's fine..."

"Oh," she gasped.

"He's going to free her soon."

"Did he say that? Huh, did he?"

I detected in her question a battle between the scolding of her reason (*You stupid goose, why would this sadist free her without anything in return?*) and her desire to believe that she would soon hold her daughter safe and sound in her arms. I ran my tongue over my lips to wet them and realised that I had no saliva left.

"Yes. He sounded sincere... and... and..."

I couldn't think of anything to add. I finished off miserably, "That's it..."

"That's all? *Sincere?* That's all you can think of to tell me? But the guy's a GIA madman! He's going to... He's going to... Everyone knows what they do to their prisoners..."

She didn't burst into tears; she just produced a muffled gasp. It sounded as if an axe had come crashing down on her lungs.

I heard a crackling on the line as if someone was handling the mobile carelessly. Then another voice took over.

"Aziz, it's me, Mathieu. Can I have a word with you?"

His voice was curt, almost commanding, unlike the shy, polite tone my father-in-law usually adopted with me, but he carried on before I could tell him to get lost.

"I'm in the kitchen, the women can't hear us. The kidnapper contacted me. He inferred that he knew me well."

"What difference does it make? Everyone in the neighbourhood knows you're my father-in-law!"

"Let me finish. That he'd known me for *a long time*. You hear: a *very* long time. He called me Mathieu, son of Bernard."

"Bernard?"

"That's my father's name. No one knows my father's name."

"Did he give you any other details like that?"

"No, except that he would refresh my memory when the time came."

"What difference does it make to… to our situation?"

"I've no idea."

Then, continuing a little more uncertainly: "Probably none."

I looked at my free hand; it was shaking. I stopped myself from calling my father-in-law an impostor, for his voice contradicted his words.

"You haven't told Meriem all of that, have you? What are his *real* demands?"

And without leaving me any time to invent a plausible answer, he demanded, in his newfound imperious tone, "We've got to talk about all of this, the two of us. Very soon. Where are you, Aziz?"

I sensed that my determination not to tell Meriem anything would melt like snow in the sun as soon as I met her anxious gaze. I knew my wife's powers of persuasion, her ability to untangle the threads of my thoughts perhaps more effectively than I could myself. Yet I still went home, on the pretext to myself that I had to recharge the battery and repair the casing of my phone. During the whole drive, I considered which person I should sacrifice.

I double-parked the car at the foot of our block of flats. A kid selling peanuts smiled at me. I didn't smile back – I didn't feel I had the right to anymore. My father-in-law was waiting for me in the entrance. He wanted to talk straight away. I flatly refused.

"In a minute! I want to see Meriem first."

Checking his anger, Mathieu's face bore a senile expression of guilt. I watched my father-in-law out of the corner of my eye as we climbed the stairs. His tic was striking: one eyelid shut and opened so totally independently of the other that they no longer seemed to belong to the same person.

My wife was sitting staring at the window. She wasn't crying. In front of her was a box of aspirin. When I came in she turned her head towards me and stared at me indifferently, as if I was no longer one of those who shared her pain. "Have I already lost you, my beloved?" I wondered, with a feeling that my heart was crumbling. Laying my hand on her shoulder, I murmured, "I spoke to the kidnapper. He promised me that…"

"Oh, he promised you… And you believed him?"

Her voice wasn't even sarcastic. *Meriem, my love, I don't want to argue with you; these are perhaps the last moments of innocence that I'll spend with you. Help me gather enough strength…*

"And you believed him?"

… to cross over to the soul-killers…

"Why won't you answer me, Aziz?"

"I have no choice. If I don't believe the bastard, my only choice is to bury my daughter alive."

Without meaning to I had raised my voice. Meriem's mother glared at me before returning to her prayers. My wife stared at me wide-eyed. Shadowed by dark rings of exhaustion, her eyes hovered on the verge of anger before misting up. She took my hand, seemed to examine it with interest and then sighed in a defeated voice, "I'll never cope. Find her, Aziz, I beseech you."

"I will find her, Meriem, I promise you, I… whatever the cost."

In my lying mind circled a black hawk, impassively observing the rabbit I had become as I ran back and forth in search of a non-existent hiding-place. My voice cracked. I broke off my oath just before I uttered the unutterable: *I shall obey him, I shall kill not just one but a thousand strangers for you and for Shehera. I swear to you by… by I don't know whom… but I swear to you!*

I leaned towards Meriem's ear and whispered the motto from our small family's imaginary coat of arms: "The three of us form a solar system, and each of our celestial bodies stands united with its two companions."

I had pronounced a different version of this maxim the first time we made love: "You are my sun and I am your planet. Together we form the beginning of a solar system!" Exhaling both her own fragrance, our intermingled sweat and the sperm between her legs, she retorted impishly, "The sun only exists because it is consumed by a perpetual fire. Watch out that you don't get burned, you horny stargazer!"

The motto had changed when our little girl was born. Shehera became our sun and we, the planets, orbited around her! When we made love, I would sometimes nibble Meriem's ear and whisper that I was no ordinary planet, I was a wild satellite that would forever spin around her so as not to miss a single curve of her buttocks, her breasts and her miraculous cavities.

Meriem looked up. For the first time since her our daughter had been kidnapped, a miserable smile flickered across her lips.

"Make sure, Aziz, that our little sun doesn't die. A planet and its satellite cannot survive the death of their star."

I had trouble choking back a sob. She accepted my allusion to our nights of joy even as we floundered in the deepest misery. Maybe, I tried to persuade myself, she meant that she still loved me despite the gangrene around us? I shook my wife's hand in gratitude, but my throat was so tight I was incapable of returning a single sound.

"Aziz, let's go and do some shopping, just you and me. Some vegetables, some coffee."

I jumped. Mathieu was standing in front of me with his ridiculous peasant's hat on his head and a basket in his hand. I would have burst out laughing if I hadn't felt so sad. "Let's go, you old fool. Let's go off arm in arm to get some carrots and tomatoes, and you can give me your brilliant thoughts on my daughter's kidnapping."

"How about if you went on your own?" I tried, making no attempt to hide my loathing. "Perhaps I'd be more useful here?"

The face paled, the eyes hardened.

"I really need your help," the old man insisted.

I was already in the doorway when Meriem called me back.

"You're sure we shouldn't call the police? What if we're wrong about this?"

Overwhelmed, I held out my empty palms in a sign of ignorance. I looked down to avoid her gaze. I shut the door behind me like a robber while my mother-in-law carried on reciting the prayer against the whispering devil that concludes the Koran: "...*Against the mischief of the stealthily withdrawing whisperer, who whispers in man's breast against djinn and men.*"

At the local grocer's shop, Mathieu selected, almost at random, some fruit and vegetables, bread, coffee and a kilo of frozen meat. Each time the old man asked for an item in Arabic, the shopkeeper answered him brazenly in French. "It's really working, eh, your genuine Aurès peasant's hat?" I whispered maliciously, picking up a packet of rice. At the till, Mathieu held out two thousand-dinar notes, but I brushed his money aside.

"Let's go to your car," he said, basket in hand, as I made for the block of flats.

"OK," I mumbled, "but make it quick."

We jumped into the car. He pushed aside the bag that I had forgotten to put back in the boot and then put the basket between his feet. Running his tongue over his lips, he stared anxiously at me, then his eyes left mine and roamed aimlessly for a few seconds.

"Well?"

"The man on the telephone..."

"Yes?"

"I don't think he's a terrorist, an Islamist from the GIA or some other group. His language, the jokes he cracks... It's true that he spoke like an Islamist at first, lots of *Allahs* and *Sidna Mohammads* all over the place. But then he changed register. He sounded like he was making fun of himself and of religion, as if he were taunting us with the idea that maybe he wasn't the crazy terrorist we thought he was. I might be wrong though..."

"Oh really? And what difference does it make to us, Mathieu? Whether he's an Islamist or not, whether he's acting in the name of God or of the devil, the result is the same: he's still taken my daughter!"

I don't know. I told you he gave my father's name."

"Maybe he works for the civil service or at the public records office? You must have had to give some details about your family – father, mother, things like that – when you filled out your naturalization forms."

He remained silent. I heard him swallow down his saliva. I sensed that he hadn't yet told me the most important thing. He got out a cigarette, but didn't light it.

"Actually, he said something else just before her hung up. "Do you remember M'sila?'"

"What's this about M'sila?"

"It's up on the High Plateaux…"

"Because now you're going to explain to me where M'sila is?" I said with a vulgar snigger.

"No, but it's where I did my military service."

I gave a start.

"What do any of your veteran's stories have to do with us?"

"Nothing, probably."

He blinked, then looked away, too quickly, leaving me with the unpleasant feeling that he was lying.

"Say what you've got to say, Mathieu."

"He also said something about Tahar."

"Tahar?"

"Yes, Latifa's first husband."

"Meriem's father?"

He wagged his chin to say yes.

"That's all common knowledge," I protested, "especially as Meriem's father's a war hero. There's even a road named after him in a town up in the Aurès mountains!"

Mathieu's eyebrows arched helplessly.

"Of course, but he also mentioned the place where I arrested Tahar."

"You arrested Meriem's father?"

"Yes, when I was in the French army. You won't have forgotten that I'm a good old Breton and that, at the time, a guy my age from my country had no choice but to enlist under the French flag and do his bloody military service fighting your people. The *fellagha* and their kind, if you see what I mean, son…"

His voice was full of dark humour. I didn't pick him up on either the scornful 'son' or '*fellagha*', which sounded even more contemptuous when spoken by a Frenchman to an Algerian.

"And what was the place called?"

"It happened not far from a *douar* called Mechta Kasbah."

"Doesn't ring any bells. Should it?"

A sarcastic twinkle glittered in his eyes.

"I see that you really know your country's history *well*, like all Algerians."

I reached for the door handle, exasperated by his condescension. I had more urgent things to do than to subject myself to the barbs of some stupid old fool, even if he was my father-in-law. The French-man's gaze, both evasive and beseeching at the same time, made me break off my gesture. The man decided to light the cigarette he had been abusing for some time.

"There's probably no link. I don't think so, anyway."

He took a first nervous drag and then a second before throwing the cigarette out of the window.

"I've been smoking non-stop since yesterday. I feel like there's tar in my mouth," he said, justifying himself.

"Mathieu, what exactly are you hiding from me?"

The vertical wrinkles that had formed between his eyebrows were now so pronounced that they reminded me of gashes with a scalpel.

"This man knows me too well to be a simple criminal."

"What is this crap? So there's some link between you and this bastard?"

"Or… between him and Meriem's father?"

"But he's been dead for ages…"

I looked at him in disbelief.

"That's it?"

"Yes, that's it. But it's incredible, all of this."

His evasive attitude fuelled my exasperation. I tapped on the steering wheel with my index finger.

"Sorry to rush you, but I've got things to do. Go home, and I'll catch up with you later."

"Where are you going?"

"Urgent errand."

"What errand can be that urgent on the day your daughter was kidnapped? Your wife needs you."

My voice shook with impatience.

"I don't need any lessons from you, Mathieu. I know better than you how I should behave towards my wife. Hurry up, please!"

My father-in-law did as he was told with bad grace. The basket was heavy, but I didn't help him. Just as he was about to slam the door, he called out slightly breathlessly, "He didn't make any particular demands?"

I hesitated, my cheeks burning.

"Er, no… He got in touch with me just to tell me that Shehera was in his hands. He didn't make any demands, apart from keeping everything quiet from the police. Let's wait for a ransom request, either today or tomorrow."

The Breton put down his basket. He arranged the baguettes, all the time peering strangely at me.

"You're not fobbing me off?"

"What is this little game, eh? Accusing one another of keeping secrets?"

The suspicious look hadn't left his face. I thought: "Go screw yourself!" as I replied as calmly as possible, "Why would I fob you off? Aren't we both on the same side, our family's side?"

A sordid observer inside me burst out laughing: *There you go, pretending to be such a good boy! You'll need an alibi later on and you can't afford to let this nitwit suspect anything!*

Mathieu picked up the basket again, his face twisting with the effort. He took two paces towards the block of flats before suddenly turning round.

"You know, whatever you may think, Tahar was a very good friend of mine."

He seemed to be weighing up the pros and cons of the confession he was about to make.

"Might even be the only friend I ever had in life. I married his wife, but that's got nothing to do with it. I fell in love with her by accident. She's one of the only things I still love in Algeria – along with Meriem and your daughter."

His eyes glinted with a sudden sparkle and I caught myself thinking that this apparently timid man, diminished by the humiliations of age, must have been an awkward customer in his youth – and the image of a merciless tracker of maquisards flashed through my mind. He paused slightly, as if stunned by his own candour, before concluding, in a panting, almost furious outburst, "And I love them more than you could ever imagine!"

Standing there in front of the entrance to the tower block, he looked even thinner than usual. "You'll snap soon like a dried-out reed, Mathieu. Whatever made you stay in a country that dislikes you? I don't know what you did for them, but you were well and truly wrong to trust in the fraternity and gratitude of a people intent on forgetting!"

I toyed with this idea for a couple of seconds before deciding that

I would postpone a critical examination of my father-in-law's tiny shavings of revelation till later. I checked my mobile's battery and screen; the kidnapper hadn't tried to reach me. My relief was almost immediately transformed into its polar opposite: there was always a chance I'd receive some news about my daughter as long as this nutter got a kick out of threatening me over the phone!

...Are you going to finally make up your mind, you blathering coward!

I felt the foetus of fear in my belly kick out brutally. My God, how could my brain talk to me as if it were lodged in someone else's skull? *He'll cut her to pieces if you don't make up your mind fast! Choose the fine human lamb you'll offer up to this telephone devil quickly, you two-bit Abraham! Right now, he is your all-powerful God! Do you really think old Abraham was any better off than you? If he hadn't resigned himself to killing his beloved son, he and his whole family would have been punished and his son with them, in the cruellest fashion imaginable too, if you want my opinion.*

"I don't want your opinion," I whined.

My voice echoed eerily around the inside of the car. By some absurd reflex, I looked round to check that there was no one in the back.

I didn't have much time left. I had to commit a crime within the next few hours and I didn't have the faintest idea of which 'procedure' I should follow. I pushed down hard on my bladder with both fists, as my terror was not only giving me a splitting headache but also a constant urge to urinate. Closing my eyes, I tried to regain a semblance of control over my limbs and my bowels – to no avail, of course.

I sighed – and the *efffff* sounded like a groan. I started the car without a clue where I was heading, depressing the clutch with an absent-minded glance in the rear-view mirror. It was just at that moment that he came out of the block of flats – striding ahead, with a broad, toothy grin, engaged in animated conversation with a neighbour.

A great lump of coldness condensed my panic into a sort of ice-axe about to drive a hole through my stomach.

How come I hadn't thought of him?

Is he the one?

"Yes, he's the one," I answered myself.

How can you be so sure? If I understand correctly, you've just decided the fate of a human being in the time it took to depress the clutch?

I refused to listen any further. Gritting my teeth, I pulled on the handbrake. The man, now alone, was still in sight.

I massaged my temples vigorously. I got out of my vehicle after pushing the damned bag under the front seat. I blinked. The weather was wonderful. I chuckled through my teeth: "It's a very fine day for killing, my friend Aziz..." and, after some thought, "It's a wonderful day to get killed, my stupid friend."

I didn't take anything with me as I realised that the murder couldn't take place until after dark. I walked towards the man with the intuition that spontaneity would be my best decoy.

He was buying some peanuts in the local café. For a second, like someone taking a lungful of oxygen before diving deep underwater, I thought of my daughter. Then, extinguishing all lights of humanity in my head, I saw myself only as an animal lying in wait, all its faculties trained on one overriding instinct – to defend its offspring.

I approached the man locals suspected of 'working' as an informer for shady police or army agencies with a fittingly shy smile, the 'submissive' smile any beggar in the human horde adopts when the person he is approaching is socially superior to him. And, as normal convention willed it, my interlocutor reacted with a distrustful expression containing a slight trace of smugness that justified my obsequious attitude.

"Hello, *Si* Abdou."

"Ah, hello *Si* Aziz... How is our chief biologist?" he replied in an almost familiar tone of voice.

I couldn't remember ever having talked about my job in his presence. I immediately stiffened, as though my interlocutor had just confirmed everyone's suspicions. He noticed my confusion and it seemed to amuse him.

We exchanged the usual meaningless phrases about the health of our respective families, the weather and the incompetence of the council departments who weren't getting round to filling in the potholes.

"Well?…" he suddenly interrupted me with a meaningful arching of the eyebrow, "let's get to the point."

"*Si* Abdou, I need a bit of advice."

"Oh?" he replied. His inquisitive eyes studied me with the attention of an entomologist hesitating as to whether a new species is dangerous or not.

"I've got a slight administrative… problem."

"And?"

"And they say you know a lot of people…"

"You know people talk a lot of nonsense."

The man's face remained impassive. I swallowed hard, making it up as I went along.

"I'm looking to sell a building plot… in a very good location. I inherited it… But I'm having some trouble with certain civil servants at the land and property office. You know, things involving the repeal of the agrarian revolution, land being nationalised and then handed back to its owners. My late father was lucky enough… I mean, if we can really call it luck because the land was only restored after his death. The plot's huge, it's worth a fortune and I desperately need money… A wife and child, our flat's too small… I'm sure you can help me out, *Si* Abdou."

I looked at him with a deliberately fearful expression to show that it hadn't escaped me that he worked in the upper echelons of the 'office' and that he must have – it went without saying in such cases – some influence in just about every council department.

"I know how to show my gratitude, believe me. I'm a man of my word."

This phrase was so bombastic and out-of-place that he blinked in surprise. He stood there, dumbfounded, his teeth nibbling at his lower lip. He had ordinary features that could either have been those of a good family father or the worst kind of criminal. He had put down his newspaper on a bench to open his packet of peanuts. Wordlessly, he motioned for me to dig into the packet of peanuts. I thanked him with a smile, though I was afraid it might twist into a grimace.

To stiffen my courage, I thought of all the gossip about my neighbour, particularly stories about him being guilty of raping teenagers during the riots.

"Don't give me your answer just yet. We'll talk about it later, if you agree, when you get back from work."

I took his hand and shook it gratefully. At that precise moment, my gesture was completely heartfelt but for reasons that would have horrified my interlocutor: I thought that I had detected in his eyes the glint of greed that any hunter looks for when he has laid his trap. The informer let me clasp his flaccid hands without any resistance.

Bending my head, I whispered, "I shall be waiting for you in my car at about seven this evening. We'll go and have a look at the plot of land and you'll see how good a location it is. It's a real bargain, trust me. You'll come, I hope?"

He studied me with his expressionless pupils. He put his packet of peanuts in his pocket and walked off with a curt nod by way of goodbye. To judge by his impassiveness, the man I imagined to be an expert in dirty tricks must have sensed a trap!

I collapsed on a bench under the shock of this new onslaught of despair. I leaned back on the bench and put my arm over my face. For a few seconds of dizzying abjection, I gleefully considered the thought of publicly drowning myself in a pool of tears.

"Ooh, what a face! Is it that trouble with your land that's put you in this state?"

I was aghast. The man was bending over me, examining me without any decency, just intense curiosity. Straightening up, he wagged his chin in satisfaction.

"I forgot this," he said at last grabbing his newspaper, before adding, as if it was of no importance, "Seven o'clock, right? And don't keep me waiting."

I watched the hunched man as he strode off. I began to feel myself breathing again. A stranger had slowly stretched out his body within mine, knocking aside everything that got in his way; the snarl he had sketched did not appear on my face, but its bitter cheer spread almost voluptuously through the ruins of my blood.

I looked around for a place to spit – I felt, in fact, as if my mouth was flooded with blood.

Initially I had thought of asking Mathieu and his wife to go home, but meeting Abdou had changed everything; there was no longer any question of Meriem staying in the flat on her own. That afternoon I'd got a call from Hajji Sadok. I didn't feel up to arguing with him. I allowed my voicemail to record a message in which he ordered me to explain my incomprehensible behaviour that morning; "hysterical" he called it. But right now, he scolded me, that wasn't the most urgent matter; the delegation had been extremely put out by the fornicating monkeys. For reasons of public morality, it had advised the relevant ministry to give them to an Algerian university as soon as possible or, even better, to sell them for a high price to a foreign pharmaceutical company. To spare the Congolese president's feelings, the zoo would find a way of replacing the bonobos with some ordinary chimpanzees that were less keen on petting. There were two endings to my boss's message: first, a threatening "Come back quickly, you knucklehead, or I'll be forced to file a report to the ministry!", before he thought better of it and said, in a beseeching tone I'd never heard him use before: "Hurry up, Aziz, I… I don't want those fucking monkeys put down or turned into laboratory sausages. Shit… It's *haram* – they're almost human!"

For a brief moment, in the depths of my Sahara-like sorrow, I felt like laughing. So, despite his prudery my director had finally taken a liking to our new lodgers! Immediately afterwards, the tiny part of me with any generosity left judged that I deserved a good slap for my sarcasm. "The coming days will lap up your blood, my dear Lucy, and you won't have a clue how to save your own skin or your baby girl!" I thought disconsolately.

Time was running out unbearably slowly, as if every second now had to squeeze through far too small a hole. Mathieu and I frequently caught each other checking our phones were on properly. I didn't speak to him, as I was scared that I would arouse his suspicions. I felt his eyes on my back the whole time. My mother-in-law was slumped on the sofa like a heap of rags, crying.

As for Meriem, she was beyond tears. She flicked endlessly through the family photo album, repeatedly shutting it and opening it with stifled groans. Her hand furtively stroked a portrait of our daughter. Her suffering gradually filled the whole room like a liquid. With a heavy heart, I watched my wife's lacerated face. Somehow or other, I was certain that she would refuse to carry on living if our daughter were not returned to us.

"Do you think he's treating her well," she asked me suddenly as she examined a photograph of Shehera on her first day at school.

I coughed before explaining, with as much conviction as I could muster, "It's not in his interest to harm her. His sort only have one so-called political objective. The hostages are in no danger as long as everyone does what they're told to. They must just have got the wrong person with us."

She stared eagerly at me.

"Are you sure?"

"I'm sure. We'll have her back by tomorrow at the latest."

She studied every line of my face in search of arguments to back up the idiotic phrase I'd just pronounced. She finally shrugged her shoulders.

"Aziz, I don't need lying to. Especially now."

I laid one hand on her hair. She pulled her head away, leaving me with my hand hanging there and my useless love.

"I'm not lying to you, Meriem. It's just what I believe deep down."

Mathieu, who was bringing us an umpteenth cup of tea, gave me an inquisitorial glance. I sought refuge in the kitchen and my father-in-law soon joined me there. As he put the cups in the sink, he whispered, "How come you're so sure, Aziz?"

I lost my cool.

"What do you want me to do? Break her heart by telling her I expect him to kill the girl after raping her first? Mind your own business, for God's sake!"

His eyes, their pupils half-hidden by the grey irises, looked me up and down with hostile disdain.

"But Aziz, this *is* my business."

He carried on drying the cup that he had rinsed under the tap, holding my gaze the whole time. I couldn't think of a riposte.

"Leave that," I said, grabbing the tea towel, "I'll wash up the rest."

"If you don't mind, I'd prefer to do it myself. Look at your hands: you must be allergic to something, you haven't stopped scratching yourself since early afternoon. Put some ointment on them."

The Frenchman's voice contained no trace of irony. I plunged my hands into my pockets because I was indeed scratching them just then.

In the bathroom, I washed my face instead of looking for the ointment because I knew what was causing the terrible rash covering my hands as well as my back and lower thighs.

Fear, pure fear. I thought I could feel countless white worms boring their way between my muscles and my skin. Ever since the informer had agreed to meet me, I'd been thinking of how to go about it. In vain: my brain seemed incapable of deciding to murder someone *for real*. I realised that I couldn't count on my brain – not the *logical* part of my brain anyway – because it kept saying that my attempt would go horribly wrong and that at the end of the day the kidnapper wouldn't keep his word.

It was already twenty past six. In the kitchen, I looked for the longest knife we owned – the one Meriem had taken to the mosque. I stuck it in the inside pocket of my jacket. Short of breath, I carefully buttoned up the item of clothing, concentrating hard on every movement. Back in the lounge, I picked up my raincoat on the way past and after giving Meriem a quick kiss on the head as she sat there curled up on her chair, I walked out without looking round.

The car clock showed that I had only twenty minutes at the most to prepare for the murder. "*Help me, Mother, ask your God to give me a hand...*" – this preposterous prayer blossomed on my lips. My poor mother, whom I hadn't seen for over a year and a half at least, and who complained on the phone that I was unfairly keeping her granddaughter from her! Seized by a searing pang of remorse, I swore that if things got back to normal, I would make sure that my mother could see her fill of her granddaughter, even if it meant crossing three-quarters of Algeria to do so.

I had spent a large part of my years at university devouring pile after pile of detective novels. I realised that I was about to act in the crassest possible manner, leaving behind a series of compromising clues, each of them leading to almost certain arrest, the prelude to the death penalty if the victim turned out not to be a mere informer but a fully fledged member of the state security services. On second thoughts I might not be lucky enough, relatively speaking, to attend my own trial: I could end up on the verge of motorway, done in with a couple of bullets in the head after a few good torture sessions.

Despite the chilly dusk, I felt the dampness of sweat on the collar of my shirt. A neighbour greeted me as he walked past. *There goes the first witness – one! You little bastard son of Mother Folly and Father Ineptitude, are you really going to sit here and wait while all your neighbours file past?* squealed the shrill-voiced tenant who never missed a chance to stick his nose into my incompetence. I decided to go away and only come back at the exact time of our appointment so as to avoid any other unwelcome encounters. I had only walked about a hundred yards when I saw him getting out of his own car. From the tense expression on his face, I guessed that the man had been observing me for some time. Pretending to be overjoyed, I signalled to him to meet me in my car. He seemed to hesitate, then a semblance of a smile broke over his face. He strode vigorously across the space separating us and, after a quick glance round, jumped into the car. He held out a condescending hand to me as if he were the one deigning to invite me into his own vehicle.

"Thank you for coming, *Si* Abdou."

My voice had cracked.

"You won't regret it. I mean…"

The weasel-eyed informer cut me off. "We'll see about that, but don't they say that to help one's neighbour is to reserve one's place in paradise? Now, tell me about this business of yours and how it might benefit us both."

I consented with my most gutless smile, feeling how the ridiculousness and the horror of the situation were gradually paralysing me. Only a few inches separated the tip of the knife from my passenger's heart, but it might as well have been the distance between the two shores of the Mediterranean. As if scalded by the acidic hormones of fear, my brain had refused to take part in planning such an insane crime. I had therefore not 'thought' of how events might unfold, in particular to where I would lure the creature presently to my right in order to turn him into a corpse.

"So, shall we talk?" said my passenger with a hint of impatience.

"Actually…"

"*Si* Aziz, I hope you're not messing me around?"

His voice had taken on a threatening undertone.

"Erm, *Si* Abdou, this situation requires trust and confidentiality because the sums at stake are very large… Can… Can I expect both of those from you?"

Stunned by the stupidity of the words that had streamed out of my mouth, I sat there staring into the other man's eyes, which I saw go wide with astonishment and then almost immediately narrow with anger.

"What do you take me for? A thief? You aren't showing me enough respect! It was you who came to see me! I... I..."

One trembling hand on the door handle, he made a move to get out. Covering myself in apologies, I reached out to stop him. My hand touched his, lingering there one or two seconds too long. Then I pulled away from him, as if I had just realised the impudence of my familiarity. Still pouring out a stream of apologies, I hoped with all my might that I had managed to conceal the small surge of joy that threatened to become a smile of triumph.

My passenger's hand was not activating the door-opening mechanism at all.

In fact, the man was just putting on an act of indignation for my benefit. My ever-so-cunning fox had taken the bait, convinced that there was money to be made from some shady administrative dealings...

Abdou magnanimously conceded, "All right, all right, I accept your apologies. But for God's sake don't offend me like that again!"

He raised the palm of his hand to his lips to wipe away a strand of saliva.

"Of course we are all trustworthy people here, dear neighbour," he murmured solemnly with no trace of anger in his voice. "I know quite a few people..."

Lowering his voice: "...Far more than you could imagine... And some of them are very important..."

While his spread fingers mimicked the presence of numerous stars on imaginary epaulettes, he repeated vainly, "Important... Yes, very important..."

With a cigarette in one hand, the informer pushed in the cigarette lighter.

"Let's get down to business. Show me this wonderful building plot of yours first and we'll talk about our arrangement afterwards."

Giving me a faint, knowing wink, he took a long drag on his cigarette. This podgy fifty-year-old man with his receding hairline and teeth that could have done with seeing a dentist suddenly struck me like an ugly, old whore who promised more than she could deliver. I had expected to feel sickened, but I was overcome with pity instead. I bent over the dashboard to hide my strange pain at knowing this individual's likely fate…

So, little man, you're hoping to cheat me out of a few dinars, whereas I'm preparing to cheat you out of your life! I have no idea what horrors you've been involved in before now, but no one deserves to die by the hand of another man, that I grant you!

…And right then I knew that this grief, this hideous compassion, would in no way prevent me from carrying out my plan to murder him!

"Let's go, *Si* Abdou! I'm sorry I expressed any doubts; I am so afraid of greedy people who do not recoil from the dishonour dishonesty brings. But I am convinced that is not the case with you. I often see you on your way to the mosque, and that proves that you fear God and his prophets."

My voice was so soft that my surprised companion shot me a severe, questioning glance.

I smiled, intoxicated with sadness.

"Why are you smiling?"

"Life's funny sometimes. But often at the wrong time!"

The passenger studied me uncomfortably before deciding not to let it show. As I manoeuvred the car, I looked over my shoulder to check that no one had seen me take my passenger on board. The surrounding area was deserted. In passing, my eyes spotted the bag I had thrown on the back seat.

"Let's go."

We drove towards the airport for a good quarter of an hour. Night had fallen and the clouds intensified the darkness. I now knew where I was heading.

The informer and I had struck up a classic Algerian conversation, carefully avoiding the main subject of our meeting. He asked me about my health and that of my family, then about how many children I had. "One," I replied.

"Girl or boy?" he continued.

"Girl."

"Oh, a girl," he sighed with a slight note of compassion. "But you and your wife are still young."

I hastened to pose the question the idiot was waiting for.

"How many do you have?"

"Three boys – and God alone is merciful! They have all left home. Both the elder ones are married; the youngest is doing his military service. I didn't see enough of them! You'd think that time passed only to cause regret…"

The man sighed again. I turned to look at him; he thought I was wondering how old he was.

"In my time people married young and quickly got down to having children. Times were hard, you never knew whether your luck would change or not. I'm a shade over fifty-eight. Maybe God will spare me long enough to see the rottenness around me turn to honey?"

His laughter rang out unpleasantly in the car.

"Top-quality Algerian shit turning to honey; now that would be some miracle! Anyway, that'll soon be your case, if I'm not mistaken?"

"You'll see for yourself," I replied, flicking the right indicator on.

We drove along a track before arriving at a vast, abandoned building site scattered with rusting containers and the skeletons of industrial machinery.

"Is this it?" said Abdou, surprised.

We had got out of the car and were looking out over a desolate landscape of structures and heaps of scrap iron that stood out in the headlights.

"Yes, this is it. But not just this. Follow me."

"But we can't see a thing!"

"I've got everything we need."

I rummaged around in the glove compartment and pulled out an electric torch. Bending forward, I reached out towards the back seat. My hand hesitated between the hammer and the screwdriver before opting for the former. When I stood up again, I had time to slip the hammer into the inside pocket of my raincoat.

Knife on the left, hammer on the right. I felt my hands becoming moist. In contrast, my mouth was so dry it didn't seem to belong to me anymore.

"I've got the torch, *Si* Abdou."

"Why are you shouting? I'm standing next to you."

I turned off the headlights and got out of the car. While my hand smoothed out any bumps in my raincoat, I pretended to struggle with the torch switch.

"Ah, here it is!"

I pointed the beam of light at the informer's face. He blinked, but the mask of mistrust contorting his features had not disappeared.

"Is this your wonderful building plot?"

"Yes, but this is only part of it, *Si* Abdou. I told you it was worth a fortune. Let's go up there and take a look at the other two plots – both farmed – that are also part of the land."

The man snorted.

"But this building site belongs to a state-owned company!"

I adopted a light-hearted tone.

"Belonged… belonged, *Si* Abdou! In actual fact, the land this building site is on belongs to my family. It was nationalised by Boumedienne in the seventies. We pursued the matter through the courts for a long time; my poor father ruined his health doing it. The good news is that the courts have just recognised us as the undisputed owners of this land and some of the plots around it. The state-owned company thought we would win in the end. That's why they abandoned the building work."

"So why do you need me?"

"*Si* Abdou, you know very well that it's not enough for an Algerian court to find in your favour. Its decision still has to be implemented! I need money, but you know all about how troublesome all the bureaucracy can be – it could drag on for years and years. I need someone to 'iron out' some of the problems with the council departments, find a way around the jealous people at the land registry, mollify the jackals at the tax office… you know, that sort of tricky operation. Otherwise I'll only enjoy the benefits of my property in a decade's time, maybe even longer…"

The man's expression was still dubious.

"*Si* Abdou, this used to be farmland. But some of it is going to be serviced. We're not far from the airport here. You know what that means: they could build a hotel, a shopping centre or some other thing! I don't know many people at all in Algiers – but you do. Imagine the price per square foot…"

The word 'airport' had an almost immediate effect on the informer.

"If I help you to… to solve your problems with your land, how much of the sales price would I get?"

His voice quavered slightly. I once more turned the torch on my companion. I would have laughed if I hadn't been so scared; distrust, though it had not entirely disappeared, had given way to good old greed.

"Don't waste any time, do you? Before I answer, I'd rather you got some idea of the size of the plot. At the other end of the building site there's a two-storey building. Let's go up to the top and I'll show you the land we're owed. Don't worry, I know the place well."

That was true; I knew the place because I'd been here once with Meriem! It was in the middle of the terrible nineties. We were supposed to meet some friends at the airport, but their flight from the interior of the country had been cancelled. Pro-FIS staff at the departure airport had walked out on strike, demanding the suspension of the company's flights during the great Friday prayers. In those times of furious hounding by the Islamists, this incident, though minor, had nevertheless dampened our spirits. On the way home we had been seized by a desire for consolation and revenge. The building site was already abandoned, but it didn't seem as ghostly as it did now. Most of the machinery had been looted or, if its weight or volume didn't allow this, meticulously stripped.

It was spring, a beautiful light softened the wounds left by man's plundering, and small yellow and blue flowers had colonised the space between the wrecks. I presented some to Meriem and she had joked that I was trying to buy her favours. I had whispered while I nibbled her ear that I was passionately interested in this transaction but that I was wondering where we might conclude it without ruining our backs and our bums. With a smile, she pointed to the small two-storey structure that used to be offices. The building seemed to approve: come in, lovers, so that the three of us may cheer each other up amid all our country's misery!

A lump of sorrow rose in my throat. To escape the trap of memory, I recalled the kidnapper's phone call. I asked Abdou to follow me. When I reached the entrance, I almost fell into a pothole. Mockingly, but already in a slightly fawning manner, Abdou caught hold of my arm.

"*Si* Aziz, this is no time to go breaking a bone, just when you're about to become rich!"

I muttered gratefully, suddenly panicked by the all-too human touch of his hand on my arm. I felt a vital need to hate this man even more strongly. I went over my reasons in my mind for the umpteenth time since selecting this man: this friendly Abdou had helped to have teenagers imprisoned, he had tortured and raped them, and it was for these crimes that I saw him as the least bad 'solution'.

There was no front door anymore. In the hallway, I had a momentary scare that the staircase might also have vanished. Apart from some litter and shards of wine and beer bottles, the place was less dirty than I had expected.

"Where are you taking me?" the informer enquired at the top of the first flight of stairs with palpable disquiet.

"To the second floor. We'll be overlooking the building site and I'll show you my land. Walk in front of me. I'll light the way for you."

"No, I'd rather you led the way."

His voice had grown suspicious again.

"Worried a rat might jump at your throat?" I sniggered, realising my tactlessness.

"Yes, I'm scared of rats. Aren't you?"

I didn't answer his question, which had an aggressive tone to it. We were already on the threshold of the second floor. The man's breathing was husky, like an asthmatic's. I hoped he hadn't noticed that I was trembling and that my teeth were starting to chatter. The witness I permanently lugged around with me squeaked: *Are you really going to murder this bloke in less than a minute from now?*

I turned to look at Abdou.

"Here we are."

"Almighty God, how did they do that?"

I knew, since I had already been so myself, that he would be impressed by the sight: the second floor was made up of a single large room and in the place where the window must originally have been, an entire wall was missing!

"Did those sons of bitches really make off with a wall? But why take one from the second floor?"

I held out the torch, which he was requesting with impatient gestures. Approaching the drop with careful steps, he shone the light on the wall that used to form an angle with the one that had disappeared. Abdou gave a short chuckle of admiration.

"Seems like those rogues cut through the concrete like butter. The man who pulled this off deserves the Nobel Prize for plunder!"

He turned to face me, shining the beam of light into my face. I blinked, dazzled.

"You're scared of heights by the look of it. Come on, come over here, there's nothing to fear. Look, hold on to me and show me this great building plot of yours that is going to make us rich!

He pointed the torch out at the black horizon. My hand plunged into the inside pocket of my jacket. My heart was beating so fast that I felt quite dizzy, as if too much blood were suddenly rushing to my head. Misreading my hesitation, the man came over to me and put a protective arm around my shoulders.

"Come on," he said, "there's really nothing to fear. After all, it isn't the edge of the Grand Canyon!"

My hand was pinned in my inside pocket by his arm. As I tried to free the knife, I actually made a movement that span me so that my back was pressed against the informer's stomach. He stiffened with surprise, waiting for my reaction. I didn't dare pull away immediately for fear that he would discover the knife before I could get into position to stab him with it. My neighbour misunderstood the reason behind my docility. He moved his pubis closer to my backside and, his voice suddenly shrill, mumbled, "I think you and I will get along just wonderfully. I know how to go about it, I'll do you nothing but good…"

I felt his erect penis rubbing against my behind. Taken aback, I burst out laughing. The man pressed himself further against me, in doing so bringing us closer to the drop. He pulled out his penis with the hand holding the torch while frantically searching for my belt buckle with the other.

"Laughing, eh… You've got a nice backside… Prepare for paradise to enter into you…"

I laughed even harder until tears started to blur my vision. All of a sudden, I pulled away. He didn't spot the knife immediately. I was still laughing.

"So while I'm planning to kill you, all you can think of is screwing me?"

"What? A knife? So you don't like…? What the hell's going on?"

I ripped the torch out of his hand. Making the most of his astonishment, I drove him back with the point of my weapon to within a few inches of the edge. Eyes bulging and penis dangling, the man glanced behind him.

"Hey, stop mucking around, I thought you wanted to… You were the one leading me on, for fuck's sake! Watch out – I'm going to fall off!"

He sized up with his eyes whether he could make it past me. I shook my head, waving the knife about. He scolded me, more in amazement than fear.

"What are you, a terrorist or a queer? Or both at once? Do you realise who I am?"

He continued, his voice grating, his certainty fast evaporating.

"You don't look like a terrorist. You made up all that stuff about the building plot, right? What do you want from me? I'm your neighbour, and neighbours are sacred to us!"

I remained silent. Behind him was the vast darkness of the Algerian night, full of terror and murder, studded with the odd star and, in the distance, the lights of the airport. My stomach was in such knots that I could feel an acidic liquid mounting into my mouth.

"Is that how you went about it with the kids during the riots in October '88?" I whispered. "You tortured them first and then raped them, or was it the other way round?"

Choking, the man barked out, "You're spouting complete rubbish! '88 is ages ago, prehistoric! With everything else that's happened since then, you still have time to think about ancient history like that? It's not true anyway – I never took part in any torture. I'm just an ordinary official in the security services… Hey, don't push me, please, or I'll go crashing to the ground…"

"Don't lie. Tell me the truth!"

"Who the hell are you to judge me, you shitty intellectual! What did you ever do to protect your country?"

I couldn't think of any riposte to my neighbour's ironic grimace. So, taking a quick breath, I stabbed him for the first time, in the shoulder, saving my strength though. Like a child, he yelled out a pointless, high-pitched "You hurt me, you fucker!"

Through my teeth I said, "Shut up or I'll stick this through your eye!"

In a defensive reflex, he put his hands in front of his face as he carried on moaning that he was an honest man and a patriot. But the pain in his shoulder must have been too much for him, for he lowered his arms.

I wasn't scared anymore and a muted anger took hold of me. If this man wasn't guilty, then I was all the more so!

"Tell me the truth now or I'll bleed you dry. If you don't lie to me, then maybe I'll let you live. Did you or did you not rape teenagers in October '88?"

"What's it got to do with you? They were a bunch of young louts! They wanted to set the whole country ablaze. We couldn't let them get away with it. Your wife and you could sleep safely because we did all the dirty work. We just... we just taught those faggots a bit of a lesson!"

His voice petered out.

"Hey, it wasn't just me doing it; I was just an underling! Why don't you go after the ones who gave the orders? Anyway, that mob of rioters deserved everything they got! You've seen how they've ruined the country since '88, with their damn democracy, the bombings and the fucking GIA. You're from a good family – don't tell me you didn't want the best for your country! When all's said and done, I was just doing my duty!"

Abdou tried to put his penis away. Waving my knife, I ordered, "Leave your thing out so it can cool down a bit. And please don't tell me you're shy! You were talking about faggots..."

"Yes, faggots! Real faggots who'd have joined the Islamist resistance, I swear by the face of God!"

His sly manner suggested there was some kind of complicity between us.

"The ones who were scared of the bath or the cloth or electricity presented their arses..."

"You're sure they were the ones wanting it..."

"Why would I lie? You know I fear God and his prophets. They were pissing themselves with fear. A bunch of yellow-bellied thieves and vandals. In any case, they didn't have a choice. It was either that or be forced to sit on the neck of a lemonade bottle. We were just following orders. Don't act as if you didn't know! You know it's always been that way in Algeria!"

"How many of them did you fuck?"

"How many?"

The question appeared to shock him. A malicious smile flickered at the corners of his mouth.

"Why are you asking me? You're not allowed to ask things like that!"

"Answer me. How many did you fuck?"

"I can't remember. Four, five. Some just…" (He pointed to his penis.)

"Did you enjoy it?"

Abdou cleared his throat with an unconvincing little cough that was both embarrassed and thoughtful.

"Looking for a reason to kill me, neighbour? I've got three sons and a wife, don't forget."

"Answer. Did you enjoy it?"

Squinting down at his groin again, he noticed that his penis was still grotesquely tumescent. We both smiled in an unusual moment of male solidarity. For the first time he was scared of me. His voice wavered.

"Forgive me, brother, I am only a man. With a man's weaknesses…"

"So am I, brother. I'm only a man, with a man's weaknesses. I'm not really any better than you, but unfortunately for you I love my daughter…"

"Your daughter? What's she got to do with it?"

And with the point of the knife and with no further explanation, I pushed him over the edge as he shouted, "You promised you'd spare me! We were under orders. You know that… I had to obey!" He tried to grab hold of the sleeve of my raincoat. For a split second, his hand slid along, but couldn't hold on to, the blade of the knife.

There was a dull thud. I had the feeling that it echoed around the valley. I felt a new surge of fear, followed – to my surprise and disgust – by an erection that horrified me almost as much as the sound of the fall. For a second, I spread my arms wide as if to show potential spectators that I wasn't responsible for my member's reaction. A comical piece of self-justification, which I stifled at the very last moment, died on my lips. *No, this isn't me, this filthy pig who's got a hard-on from killing. I do know myself!* I feverishly put the knife away in my raincoat before realising that I shouldn't have done – there was bound to be some blood on the knife that would stain the fabric. I managed to stifle a sob of pity for the man I had just murdered with such ease. He didn't deserve it, even if he did deserve it.

I ran down the stairs. I swept the floor with the torch beam, searching for the body. At last I found it, but not where it ought to have been. Abdou had dragged himself a dozen yards towards the skeleton of a machine. I heard moans mingled with calls for help and snatches of the Shahada, the Muslim profession of faith. I knew then that all my resolve would desert me if the dying man looked me in the eye and begged me to spare him. The man exuded a smell of excrement. Grabbing the hammer, I dealt him a first blow, then a second, to the back of the skull.

An age-old thought (reaching back to the time before I became a killer) tried to surface, but I throttled it in irritation. I wanted whatever the cost to remain in the state of heightened emotions, broken only by the reaction of my member which, like some refractory animal, had stayed as stiff as a minaret. I turned the body over and wedged the head between two stones. I took some photos of the corpse with my mobile by the sulphur-yellow light of the torch. With his hair dishevelled from the fall and the hammer blows, the dead man looked up at me with a shocked expression, as if to exclaim: *Come on, is this some kind of joke?*

I was almost sick when I spotted the traces of blood on my raincoat, some of them dark, others lighter-coloured and fatty-looking. Brain maybe. *Don't be sick here – that'd be another DNA sample you leave behind!* I returned to my car, crumpled my raincoat into a ball and stuffed it into a plastic bag. I had a strange sensation as I put the key in the ignition. I didn't stop to analyse it, but I was struck by a feeling that it was something absolutely crucial. I made it to the motorway in a kind of daze. I drove for a good twenty minutes before I reached the capital's main rubbish tip.

When I left it again, I was coughing so hard my lungs felt as if they were going to burst and my eyes were weeping tears that were sticky with all the dirt in Algiers, but I had got rid of the knife and hammer, and the bloody raincoat was already being reduced to ashes.

I stopped again a little further on. After soaking a piece of shammy leather in detergent from a bottle in my boot, I set about vigorously rubbing the door handles, the dashboard and anything else the rapist might have touched. When I'd taken the wheel again, my phone rang. It was Mathieu asking me curtly to come home as quickly as possible because Meriem was feeling ill. I stammered something before hanging up on him in mid-sentence.

When I reached the foot of our block of flats, a strange shudder ran through me, as if, quite unconsciously, my body was trying vainly to rearrange the load of grief weighing down on its shoulders. My sacrilegious penis participated in its own way in the burial of my soul by curling up between my testicles. The murderer I had become climbed the stairs with a heavy tread, counting them off in a sort of funeral prayer. On the first landing, the idea that had been threatening for a while to clear its way through the sludge in my brain finally showed its snout: *You're horrified because you've discovered you enjoy killing, right?*

The novice murderer didn't attempt to defend himself; that was pointless. The last thing that occurred to him before he opened the door and found the woman he loved again was that he had kept his part of the bargain. A life for a life (*no, two lives for a life*, he corrected himself, *his own, which was now worthless, and Abdou's, in exchange for his daughter's*). It remained to be seen whether the kidnapper would cheat or not.

The latter hadn't rung yet. In the distance, as wistful as the lost happiness of childhood, rose the call to evening prayers, the last of the day. The longer innocent man hung his head, overwhelmed.

"Dear God, whoever You may be, You put my daughter in the hands of this sadist and therefore I beseech You to force Your Satan to keep his word."

When I put my hand on Meriem's shoulder, she mumbled that I ought to have been at her side, that she could feel herself dying and that this was proof to her that her little girl was being harmed. I couldn't come up with any response to this.

Mathieu and his wife were in the kitchen. When she saw me, the latter got up and left the room without a word, too demoralised to show me again how little esteem she held me in. My father-in-law offered me a sandwich. I started nibbling at it with the impression that I was chewing soil.

I said, "I've made some tea. Do you want some?"

Mathieu nodded his head ponderously. He waited for me to serve him some tea before asking me, as if by chance, "Aziz, have you done something for... for *him*?"

"Sorry?"

"You understood the question."

"Nothing, nothing at all. What a strange thought!"

Carefully I set the kettle down. Despite my fears, my hands didn't give me away. I avoided Mathieu's eyes. The old man sat there, concentrating on stirring his tea. From where I was standing, I could see the top of his head with its fine hair like a baby's.

"Yes, it is a strange thought, isn't it," he repeated in the same weary voice. "Unfortunately, it's not mine."

"Oh yes?"

I suddenly felt both cold and headachy at once. Mathieu/Ali was now talking to me in Arabic, as if attempting to force me into confiding in him in my mother tongue.

"Believe it or not, he rang me as well. And he told me he'd... *asked* you – these were his exact words – to do him a *little favour*. He didn't tell me what kind. What 'favour' was it, Aziz?"

I held his gaze.

"Nothing. I haven't done anything for that guy. Who do you really believe in all of this – me or the kidnapper?"

"Aren't you waiting for his call right now?"

"No... Yes, of course I am! I'm waiting for his call, like you, like Meriem..."

I tried to alter my tone of voice, but it had escaped my control, gone all high-pitched and even more false-sounding.

"All of us just sitting here waiting for that damn phone to ring! Why on earth would you think such crazy things?"

Mathieu didn't react to my protests. He carried on stirring his tea nervously as if the sugar wouldn't dissolve.

"In passing, he told me that tomorrow it would be my turn to be invited, to use his expression, to 'please' him."

I gave a start because the man had stifled a retch. He had gone pale and his liver spots stood out more clearly against his pallid skin. My anger dissipated all of a sudden.

"Did he explain what he wanted you... you to do, Mathieu?"

"No."

We were silent for a while, crushed by our misfortune. When I got up from my chair, he called to me in his new voice – broken, older than ever.

"Wipe your feet, Aziz. You've brought... too much mud into the house. Some good detergent will get it off."

My eyes veered down to the floor. My ribcage felt as if it had been seized in an iron grip – my shoes had a generous spattering of mud on them and the right-hand one also had reddish rings on it.

I found the strength to say, "Thanks. I'll go and clean them."

"Hold on, I need to talk to you. Shut the kitchen door and sit down."

"But… what if the phone in the… rings?"

"Don't worry. I'd hear it ring even if I were buried under several layers of concrete. Shut the door and come back over here."

I did as he said with the docility of a child. My father-in-law had at last stopped torturing his spoon.

"I think I know who he is. And then…"

He raised his light-grey eyes clouded with tears to my face.

"…I also have to tell you something about your wife."

Part II

From the way Aziz is looking at me, I can tell that he'd prefer to think of me as a doddering old fool. My son-in-law's aged ten years in less than twenty-four hours. I think I like him, for he's not too stupid (nor too intelligent, mind you) and he looks after his family just about adequately. But there's no doubting that he's not overly fond of me. Sometimes I can read the question clearly in his eyes: who exactly are you and why did you settle in this weird country of mine?

I don't have the time to feel sorry for him anymore. My tired heart feels too constricted for that. It's already bursting with the incredible grief I have felt ever since my granddaughter was kidnapped. *Bursting*: I use the word quite literally, since my chest is relentlessly assaulted by a pain like the onset of a heart attack.

I try to breathe more gently, but it's no use. I just feel all the more keenly the painful fragility, close to breaking point, of the pump that stubbornly continues to supply the oxygen to my bloodstream.

I mustn't die. No: *I forbid myself* to die as long as Shehera is in the hands of that madman.

And after that? After that, I think I'd agree to leave this world with all the gratitude of someone in the last throes of cancer for his final dose of morphine.

After all I've been through, I didn't think that I was capable of feeling anything with such overwhelming intensity anymore. I have already experienced the enormity of other emotions, especially love – or, when I was younger, hate. But nothing comes close to how I have felt since yesterday, particularly since that last phone call.

I would murder God, Jesus and all his brood if that were the price to pay to go back in time and stop my granddaughter from leaving the house.

Such is my prayer.

Two people know, Aziz and I, but neither of us dares open his heart to the other. The two of us are cowards, most likely. Aziz at least has an excuse: he doesn't yet *know* that I *know*.

The kidnapper told me that he'd demanded that Aziz murder someone. "Who?" I'd asked, incredulous and yet knowing from his victorious tone that he was telling the truth. "Anyone, of course! The first person he comes across. Pure chance. A magnificent beast, chance, incidentally!"

I was dumbstruck. Luckily I was on the balcony, out of earshot of Latifa and Meriem. What's more, the driver of a stationary lorry opposite the block of flats was giving his engine a good rev. Before making the phone call, I lit a cigarette, one of the very occasional ones I still allow myself. This one fell from my hand. My interlocutor had adopted an overly affable tone.

"You're wondering how I managed to persuade Aziz?"

I had grabbed hold of the balustrade. The man had insisted, his voice almost friendly.

"Aren't you wondering how I went about it?"

My hand groped along the metal balustrade. I stopped breathing – *for a very long time.*

"Don't worry, I haven't killed her; she's too useful to me. I've just removed two or three of her fingers. I can't remember exactly how many. As you know, we usually have ten fingers, not to mention our toes, but their usefulness is more questionable. So it's not all that bad, even if it does spurt blood everywhere. On the other hand, the knife comes and goes, and I sometimes have trouble controlling it. Especially if people don't do as I say…"

The man gave an involuntary little chuckle.

"But then you know all about that type of *persuasive* argument, don't you? Well, you used to, my friend. Don't be so modest! In the field in which you – how should I put it? – used to *work*, they even said you were something of an ace at your game…"

I didn't immediately grasp the significance of his words. Like my hand on the balustrade, my panic-frozen mind was groping around hopelessly for some new rules for understanding language, unable for an instant to accept that the kidnapper's words about Shehera's fingers might have some acceptable corollary in the *real* world.

"Hey, granddad, are you listening to an old brother who's back from the lands of the past?"

I managed to force a vague *yes* from my dead throat. The stranger sighed in pretend relief.

"Luckily you've got a steady nerve, from your old – how should I call it? – *occupation*. Or would you prefer: *profession, vocation*? Oh, by the way, I don't know whether your Aziz will have the guts to go through with what I've asked of him. Does he love his daughter enough to do it? Well, I'll know more by tomorrow morning. But unfortunately for you, you have even less choice, because here's what you're going to do for me."

Breathlessly, I ventured, "You're not from the GIA, are you?"

"You think I'm stupid enough to belong to a bunch of lunatics like that?"

"Who are you then?"

"You'll find out soon enough. Content yourself with the knowledge that, for the last few years, I've thought about you more often than if you'd been, say, my beloved twin brother! Will that do for... for starters, you fucking shithead son of a bitch?"

A gasp of emotion made him stutter. He had continued, checking his anger badly but jovial nonetheless. "I'm the one asking the questions. I've been waiting for this day for so long. Now, I repeat: here is what you're going to do for me."

I gazed at Aziz with a mixture of disgust and affection. Affection, yes, because, one way or another, the guy was like me now. I don't know whether he faltered at the last, but I know now that he has obeyed the crackpot's orders. I can see it in the lines of his face, in his exhausted posture, in the shifty way he returns my gaze. Too much of an open book, incidentally: he'll be easy game for the police. Maybe he'll withstand the blows, but he'll definitely talk, mainly to justify his actions to himself. All it will take, after a couple of good beatings, is for a clever policeman to whisper to him, "I've asked around and you're a decent man, so tell me why you did it. Tell me, brother, and I'll make sure I explain to the others!" Algerians like the word *brother*, especially in the mouths of people who are beating them up, so Aziz will crack and confess whatever they want him to.

He doesn't yet know that his act won't be enough to satisfy the appetite of the ogre that munches children's fingers.

"So Mathieu, what is it you need to tell me so urgently?"

Aziz crossed his legs in a gesture of fake nonchalance.

I feel like putting my arms around my son-in-law's shoulders and crying all the world's tears with him. I can't, of course; men don't blubber in this bloody country! But how am I supposed to tell Aziz that the kidnapper has now demanded that I kill him too, him, my son-in-law, within a day starting at 8 o'clock tomorrow morning? That the madman has left me no choice, other than to resign myself, should I refuse, to knowing that Shehera will be tortured some more?

I watch, without seeing, a stubborn ant climbing up the waxed cloth towards I know not what ant-sized Jerusalem. Dear God, I should have croaked fifty years ago! Nobody would have batted an eyelid and perhaps even my one-time compatriots, the French in France, would have come to regard me as a hero! A lousy fucking hero, so terrified of the decision he now has to make that he is reduced to waiting for the inevitable moment when his prostate packs in…

I stare at Aziz, taking advantage of the fact that he thinks I'm too old to have all my wits about me. I've never actually had a proper conversation with him apart from the usual commonplaces about our health or the weather and grumbling about rising prices and the corruption of our country's immovable rulers. I try to think what strategy to adopt and realise that I'm not capable of it.

"I don't give a damn whether or not you trust me to release her as soon as your son-in-law's dead!" the man on the telephone chided me, revelling in the terror he sensed in my supplications. "The main thing is that you trust me when I tell you that, if you disobey me, I will prune your granddaughter with a pair of secateurs, twig by twig, taking my time, until she dies!"

Of course I had yelled out, "No, she's just a child!" (but my yells had been drowned out by the driver revving his engine). A nasal snigger had put me in my place. "So you're calling for help from your old friend Allah, eh, like I used to do during my darkest years? As if Allah's ever stopped evil things from happening! Remember what happened to me… Remember what Tahar did…"

I had suddenly felt my lungs compress, as if the oxygen I was breathing had turned toxic. "What are you talking about? Tahar's been dead for ages. What could he have possibly done to you? He was the best of men…"

His voice had jeered at me. "Of course you think he's the best of men! You're bound to; you've shared a wife. Creates a strong bond, a woman's arse does, especially a nice juicy one. Don't tell me there are still things you don't know about your wife's first husband. I bet that whore Latifa told you everything while you were screwing her: how they would do the double-backed beast, she and her dog Tahar, about her husband's little moans of ecstasy when she sucked him off, and all the other dirty secrets of his oh-so-heroic life he boasted about as pillow-talk after a good shag... Ah... Oh... bastard...!"

He was overcome with rage. I had objected feebly, "I've never done you any harm..." He had whistled, before bursting into a succession of very high-pitched cheeps. "Ah, but you have too, you bastard! A long time ago, it's true, but – ah – to me it feels like it was yesterday! Rack your brains, trawl through your cesspit of memories and I'm there, up to my neck in it, and I'm not the only one..."

I had heard a very distinct sob as he repeated, "...And I'm not the only one..." Before hanging up, still spluttering, he spat out, "Now it's payback time. Cash down. For everyone."

He had referred to the war. To my war. To Tahar's war, and therefore to mine. I had seen black dots moving about in front of my eyes. Over fifty years had passed, but to me – and to this kidnapper, it seemed – it was more like a handful of days.

An obscure aphorism popped into my mind, one my fisherman father had used and I had never really understood: "Time, when you give it time, runs quicker than a hare chased by a ravenous hound." A surly man, exhausted by endless trips out to sea, he would repeat it over and over again to me when I complained about his long absences. As I looked at him in incomprehension, my father would finish his sentence, his voice turning all mysterious, with his characteristic dry humour: "...especially since, for us humans, time is both the running hare and the hound chasing it."

Oh, my poor father, capable of punishing me for some stupid prank with a slap that would have felled a bear, as well as watching over me several nights running when I was struck down with fever... We loved each other as many people on this planet love their parents: a great deal of love mixed in with a touch of unchanging resentment. I was twenty when I left home after a violent and of course trivial argument. The hound of time had set about savaging the frightened hares we had become, and neither of us had been smart enough to patch things up before it was too late.

No longer bothering to hide his exasperation, my son-in-law got to his feet.

"Mathieu, I don't know quite what you're brooding about, but as for me I'm knackered. I'm going to have a lie-down, unless you tell me what's going on right now."

I thought: "Yes, you future corpse, I've been ordered to kill you. So I'd like to have a chat with you about how best to go about it without causing too much anxiety to the rest of the family…" and to my alarm I spoke the words I dreaded with all my soul because they implicated me: "Aziz, I think I've… I've got something to do with… with your daughter's kidnapping. I mean, somehow…"

My diction was disjointed with panic. I must have gone bright red. Aziz looked at me as he might have looked at a raving madman. Finally he shrugged his shoulders in contempt. With my index finger I chased away the ant, which, with great effort, had made it to the edge of my cup.

"Don't worry, son, I've still got all my wits about me. But it's a long story… a complicated one… a family matter…"

Irritated, my son-in-law made a gesture with his hand that meant both '*Stop taking the piss!*' and '*Fancy a punch in the face?*'

"I'm not kidding, Aziz. Especially not at a time like this."

His lower lip trembled. There was some hatred – and some loathing – in his voice.

"Do you think there's not enough suffering in this house without you adding to it with your ramblings?"

Aziz had started off muttering in French but finished – from *suffering* onwards – in Arabic. He had gone stiff. He clenched his fists, raising them slightly in front of him. I sensed that he was close to hitting me. I felt a surge of anger of my own. We squared up to each other like two stupid apes, an old ape and a young ape that hadn't come to earth to suffer like this.

I hesitated just long enough for one last warning from my inner martinet (*Don't jump off the cliff, Mathieu. It's too high and, at the bottom, there's no sea, only rocks! What if you were wrong all down the line? You've been wrong so often and about so many things in the past.*) before saying, "I'm going to try and explain, Aziz. But first make sure the door's shut properly."

"Listen, Aziz. However long we live, when all's said and done, we live little. I have therefore lived little. And, incidentally, you too will live little, even if you live till you're a hundred."

My voice trickled to a ridiculous, husky halt. His face closed, Aziz hesitated, rubbing one shoe with the end of the other, before electing to sit down again.

"…And during this short existence, among those I have loved the most have been Tahar and then Latifa…"

The old man, lost, looks with great pity at the individual sitting opposite him. But he can't avoid feeling this heartrending pity for himself too or, at least, for the young man he was when, decades earlier, he had first set foot in Algeria. He would like to stroke the head of this other him, so innocent and so full of enthusiasm, so stupid too, who would have screamed in horror had he known one-tenth of the crimes that awaited him, stacked carefully on the shelves of his future life. Of course, back then Mathieu was a handsome twenty-eight year old and he thought himself truly happy for the first time in his life because he had met a girl in Paris. She was pretty, a minor council employee, and so shy to begin with. But things had gone quickly and efficiently; after three weeks of sustained courting, he had kissed her. One month later (which was remarkably quick for the time!), he made love to her. And in early autumn, he had brought up their future plans together, admittedly in the usual roundabout way, but leaving no doubts as to his intentions.

What was her name again, the girl who would take his penis in both hands and slide it inside her but then bite the cushion when she had her orgasm out of fear that her nosy neighbours might hear her and, through the concierge, inform her parents who had stayed in the provinces? Françoise, that was it... Joy had sparkled deep in her eyes when she understood the muddled declaration he had taken days to piece together in the loneliness of his hotel room. He had been overwhelmed with gratitude at his ability to spark such rapture in a woman. He felt that she deserved to be loved even more. The next day she had taken three days off to travel down with him to the famous docks at Port-Vendres, which at the time were buzzing with maritime traffic between France and the Algerian colony. The two lovers' promises had been even more explicit when they separated. They did not know that their kisses on that Mediterranean quayside, moist with the spray of the unknown, would be their last and that, despite the letters they exchanged for a year with their share of ardent promises and recriminations, they would never see each other again.

Mathieu shudders. It feels as if he is recalling a time several million years ago and that, like the enormous saurians of old, this Françoise of such sweet memory is no more than a fossil buried under the debris of time. Maybe she really is dead? All of a sudden, he hopes against hope that, if that were to be the case, at least his pretty Parisienne with the cheerful eyes and the then firm buttocks and breasts might have been lucky enough to glean a few moments of happiness here and there.

He sighs. The silence draws on. Aziz gives a little cough and the man takes up his tale again. He starts to tell Aziz – who occasionally nibbles his lip in alarm – how the events leading up to this cursed day fit together. But Mathieu has already vaguely decided that he will skirt whole sections of the truth. For one never tells everything, not even to oneself.

Basically, it had all begun with him playing a trick on his own destiny. He'd never envisaged enlisting in the French army again, let alone the French Algerian army. After some scratchy and shortened studies, he had done his military service in barracks in the depths of his native Brittany; then, half out of spite, half out of a desire to disappoint his father, he had stayed on in the army. His memory of it now was of a hazy period, solid boredom during the week, solid drunkenness at the weekend, surrounded by non-commissioned officers and officers doing their utmost to deserve the reputation for pig-ignorance associated with their function.

Like most of the men, he had spent a few days in the military jail following more or less drunken fights. Every time he came out again feeling that he had done his level best to become even more like any other man of his age. Although he was surprised by the fact, he didn't like himself; and not liking himself, he didn't feel the need to 'improve' the image and social status of the imbecile doing such a bad impression of him before the eyes of the world.

The garrison commander had finally taken umbrage at this grumpy and notoriously incompetent non-commissioned officer and had decided to get rid of him as quickly as possible. By one of those odd quirks that are not uncommon in army administration, Mathieu had been summoned to Paris and then forgotten for months in an office at the ministry. He had used the time to scour Paris and meet the young woman who would occupy his heart and body for the rest of his stay.

His disciplinary posting to Algeria had, at first sight, come at the worst possible moment, but he consoled himself with the thought that his contract would expire less than six months later and that *real life* would then begin, with that Françoise, for example, or a different one, even prettier and even more in love, if fortune really swung his way. Up to that point, he hadn't had to make any real choices, having been happy to follow, at every stage in his life, the path of least resistance in his decision-making. He had found himself in Algiers the summer before the endless war against the FLN, the National Liberation Front, started.

He hated the country from the very first day. Too hot, too much cheeriness and too much chattering among the Europeans, *too many* Arabs in the streets with their dark looks and this language that was a personal attack due to his ignorance of it and whose guttural sounds conveyed something other than the apparent submissiveness. When his contract ended, driven by the very same process of self-contempt and spineless acquiescence to events that had already pushed him into the army's arms once, he span a coin in front of colleagues as tipsy as he was to decide whether he should re-enlist. The army chiefs of staff were starting to take the 'troubles' seriously. There were whisperings among the rank-and-file that this wasn't just an umpteenth Arab uprising, but that an organised movement seemed to be coordinating actions by men whom the local newspapers would continue for a long time, seemingly to reassure themselves, to call a bunch of highwaymen.

Mathieu had bet a quarter of his wages that he would leave the army if it came up heads and that he would then choose, well, a career as a… or, even better, a… but, sitting in this kitchen in Algiers opposite a son-in-law who is staring at him with a mixture of animosity and fear, he can no longer remember the professions that had seemed so attractive at the time.

He lost his bet of course and without any regrets signed up for five more years, this time to serve the strange tribe of the Algerian French. It should be said that in the meantime his love for the council employee – and, indeed, for any other subject – had withered like a cut flower in the Mitidja sun. He'd had flings with a few French women. On evenings when his depression was darkest, he satisfied himself by giving an Arab prostitute a good seeing-to in a squalid room in a seedy hotel in Bab-el Oued, before drinking himself senseless in one of the bars along the coast as part of what he called his 'minimum political programme for friendship between peoples': French cock in a *fatma*'s pussy, washed down with a few patriotic *pastis*.

It was incidentally during one of these single-man's pub-crawls, as he was coming out of a little restaurant, that he came across a customer who was drunker than he was, a noisy pimp who'd been thrown out by the owner and lay face down on the ground. Moved by the drunkard's instinctive compassion for his fellows, Mathieu, who was none too steady on his feet himself, pulled the stranger onto the pavement just before a goods lorry sped past, thus saving his life. Between two fits of vomiting, the man – an Arab of around fifty in a magnificent suit – insisted on seeing him again to express his thanks. The man's conception of gratitude was fairly unusual because the next day, after a few drinks, he provided him with no more, no less, than the name and address of the head of an FLN cell in the Casbah. "If it weren't for you, brother, I'd be in the morgue, so we're friends for life now! This free piece of information is my gift to you. It'll give your captain a massive hard-on, just you wait and see! Maybe with time you'll make it to general, who knows? To make sure you get even more credit, don't say it was me who gave you the information but that you just kept your ears pricked while you were chatting to people here and there, if you see what I mean?"

Of course, Mathieu didn't tell Aziz all of this and especially not in this fashion. He just said: *I served in the French army and I was sent to an army base in eastern Algeria.*

He didn't specify that his superiors had appreciated enormously the surprise tip-off about the head of one of the nationalist cells in the Casbah and had credited the Breton with it. "How did you pull it off? You don't even speak Arabic. Hmm, you sure have a way with the natives!" an officer exclaimed by way of congratulations. Following the arrest of the minor rebel leader, an officer had ordered Mathieu to take part in the interrogation, reasoning that his knowledge of Arab psychology might be invaluable to help break the prisoner and maybe even to get him to change sides. Mathieu almost retorted that he knew almost as much about the psychology of Tasmanian aborigines, and that the pimp informer (about whom he hadn't breathed a word) was in fact the first native he'd talked to since he'd been sent to bloody Algeria – apart, of course, from Arab hookers. Noting his NCO's reticence, the officer cajoled him, "Don't be modest. It's obvious you've got a knack for this kind of thing and the army needs people of your calibre!"

And thus everything – *everything!* – had been triggered by a stupid misunderstanding: his supposed knowledge of the workings of the Arab soul (often Kabyle, actually) compounded by the crude flattery of an officer short of personnel. Less than twenty months later – and with unexpected zeal on his side – Mathieu was posted to a French army base not far from Sétif, officially at first as an ordinary secretary but in a very particular unit – a DOP, one of the eighteen formidable and deliberately innocuous-sounding Operational Protection Units stationed throughout Algeria whose existence the military authorities would stubbornly deny for years.

Mathieu can't remember which clever thinker it was who asserted that history was an abattoir in which individuals and whole peoples were sacrificed. In his case, he knows it was his *soul* (he sniggers at the solemn word his memory has had the nerve to use) that he deliberately murdered while serving in that damn DOP. When his feet first trod Algerian soil, he was nothing more than a poorly rated, lazy and boozy soldier. His dishonour was not yet sealed. A part of him hoped that some day, for no particular reason, the beautiful butterfly within him would extricate itself and fly away fast from the disgusting caterpillar he'd resigned himself to being up to that point.

He had once been a child himself and so excitable in his admiration for the great privateers of Saint-Malo that he had secretly nicknamed himself 'Li'l Robert' after the illustrious Robert Surcouf. This little Breton would revisit him, ticking him off in his sleep, utterly exasperated but not yet despairing: *Hey, arsehole, drunkard, you shitty little wino, when are you going to* really *look out for me?* Mathieu sometimes dreamt that he shouted back across time at his alter ego for using such totally inappropriate language for his age, only to wake up on the verge of tears and realise that it was actually him who was the embodiment of obscenity compared to the innocence of the boy he'd once been.

In that god-awful DOP, the poisonous miracle of abjection that lies in wait for all men had taken hold of him; if opportunity makes the thief, it also produces swine by the cartload. Mathieu had become an efficient and reasonably respected NCO, whose drunken weekend binges were forgiven because he achieved his objectives of making the captured *fells* talk at any cost, combining persuasion, insults and, naturally, torture with the single-minded goal of filling in the local rebel organisation's chain of command. The screams – every one atrociously *individual* – of each broken man (another 'box' ticked…) could only be forgotten by substituting them with others, like glasses of alcohol replaced by new glasses of alcohol.

How had he come to this? He'd never totally understood, and even today, years later, he wouldn't have known how to explain, not to this Algerian, crushed by grief, – it was impossible, he would rather tell him barefaced lies – but at least to himself (dear God, *to himself!*) how he had graduated so quickly – in two or three weeks – from insults and punches in the back to his first real beating, then kicks in the stomach, water-boarding and electric shocks. He couldn't even cite greed as an excuse – the wages were terrible; nor conviction – like a *pied noir*, for example, losing control at the thought that these sub-human Arab rats who were so dirty, so ignorant and until now so submissive should have the cheek to contest the ownership of this land that his parents and grandparents had seized in fierce fighting in 1830 and brought to fruition ever since.

Sometimes, after *work*, in a moment of alcoholic abandon, he would catch a glimpse in the eyes of his colleagues, even the worst ones, those who abused female prisoners before torturing them, of a similar stunned question: *Hey, my Man, ruling everything from Your immaculate paradise, is this all I was born for? To be worth less than a mangy dog's turd? When exactly did I become 'unhinged'?*

No one would have put it that baldly: he would have been called a sentimental chicken happy to offer up his Vaseline-free anus to a Muslim prick or, worse, sent to a different unit for defeatism and aiding the enemy through such Communist propaganda. Of course, most of the time they were only too happy to cling to the general clamour surrounding the 'question': patriotic oompah-pah about defending France and Christendom, fighting Bolshevism and Nas-serism, the barbarity of their rat-like adversary who massacred one hostile village after another without a second thought, drawing ear-to-ear 'Kabyle smiles' as a matter of course or chopping off French squaddies' dicks and stuffing them in their mouths… When they felt like it, they believed so firmly in these self-protecting justifications that they would enjoy the sleep of the just for weeks until the yelps of pain of a new suspect – even if this one wasn't tortured much more than his brothers before him – pierced the bottom of the raft that kept them from sinking into their own filth.

Sergeant Mathieu had fought off drowning by repeating that there would be an end to all this – either the end of the war against the *fells* or at least the end of his contract with the army. He could imagine returning to his native Brittany and getting absolutely blind-drunk for a week, no, more like a month or, better still, taking a year's sabbatical dedicated exclusively to getting plastered in settlement of Algeria, before making a fresh start, memory purged and mind purified, to take care of that damn kid, the admirer of privateers who once dreamed of glory and honour.

The second decisive words he spoke to Aziz were these: *Then I met Tahar.*

And he fell silent again, not knowing how to continue, despite his son-in-law's obvious impatience. How was he supposed to confess that, a few days before meeting Tahar, he had been involved in some 'work' on a particularly tough *fell* who had been captured in a remote *douar* in the Constantine area after being denounced. Rumours from informers suggested that preparations were underway for a meeting of resistance leaders in the east of Algeria, and the local DOP staff hoped that the prisoner would eventually reveal the date and the place. Overexcited at this prospect, the chiefs of staff in Algiers had ordered them to extract the precious information from the man as fast as possible, since it would naturally only be of any use if the meeting had not already taken place. The forty-year-old man, a certain Hassan, had been tortured at length. His face swollen, his body reduced to one large bleeding wound, shitting himself with fear every time the soldiers fetched him from his cell, he hadn't give a single scrap of useful information, persisting in playing the fool and swearing by Allah and His Prophet that he loved France and the three colours on its flag and that, if the lieutenant so wished, he would be delighted to spit on the

FLN and its leaders, including Amirouche and his stooges, as many times as they wanted him to.

"We can't even find out if he's a big fish, some kind of political commissar," complained a colleague, chain-smoking to drive away the smell of shit. "If we can't find out, then he must be one!" the lieutenant had decided.

Mathieu had water-boarded the prisoner himself, before sending electricity through the rebel. The glans of his penis, black from electric burns, had been almost completely severed. Several times the Arab had passed out. Once they thought he was dead and the lieutenant panicked, having received clear orders not to kill him without having first extracted the information the top brass in Algiers were waiting for. The team in charge of dealing with him had hardly ever seen anyone resist for so long and their uneasy admiration for the *fell* was tinged with rage as time ticked remorselessly away.

"He's going to die without talking, the bastard. And we'll get shat on from so fucking high we'll be up to our eyeballs in it. They'll accuse us of being a bunch of useless wets!" the intelligence officer had groaned, summing up the general feeling of frustration. It was Mathieu who had come up with the miracle solution. He had asked if the man was married; the colleague who updated the files on the people they arrested had confirmed that, according to his sources, his wife had been killed in a coach accident three years previously. It wouldn't be possible, he remarked with a rueful expression, to use the *fatma* as a means of pressurising the man into giving in. "How about children? The bloke must have some. All wogs have kids, they love it..." Mathieu insisted. His colleague had shrugged and conceded that he didn't have a clue; the suspect's house had been empty when the soldiers searched it. As he nibbled away at a bar of chocolate as usual, the lieutenant gave Mathieu a strange look. "You've got something in mind, haven't you..."

A faint voice in his mind called out: *No, Mathieu, leave children out of this, leave them out of this shit – it's too despicable even for someone like you. Think of your mother – she loved you so much when you were a boy!* "Tough luck, schmuck!" Mathieu had retorted in his mind, "my bitch of a mother didn't love me and the feeling was mutual."

Then as if in thrall to his own ignominy, he explained that if the prisoner had any kids, they must have been taken in by their uncles and aunts. All they had to do was to pay a visit to their relatives, round up all the kids and threaten them with the worst kind of torture if they didn't immediately point out which of them was Hassan's son or daughter. "At least one of them will crack, I promise you. It's as old as time: force someone to choose between their own children and their nieces and nephews, and they'll always choose their children!" he concluded with great solemnity.

Everything happened exactly as Mathieu had predicted. The panic-stricken parents handed over the *fell*'s son almost straight away, a small eight-year-old boy half-dead with fear, who stammered amid much sobbing that he had lost both his father and his mother and then, as soon as he caught sight of the man naked and trussed up on the table, ran towards him whimpering in Arabic, "Daddy, Daddy, what did they do to you?"

As his son tried to kiss him, the father, his face blank, looked away and muttered something. The intelligence officer made a sign to the *harki* who served them as interpreter and on occasions as a zealous helper during interrogations. "He's angry. He's telling him that he's not his father and ordering him to get away from him," said the auxiliary soldier, "but I think the prisoner really is this little bastard's father!"

"We've got the *fell* faggot now!" the lieutenant smiled triumphantly. "Tie the kid up next to his father. We'll give him some volts straight off – there's no time to fuss about! We'll see if this guy loves his son more than his bosses in the FLN."

Mathieu thinks of Shehera being tortured by her kidnapper. He is no better than the madman who has kidnapped the teenage girl. He has known that ever since that day when, at his suggestion, a child was tortured to extract secrets from his father that the end of war a few years later would render so horribly meaningless. As soon as the electrodes were placed on his ears, the child urinated on the floor below him in terror; and the father started to shake. His eyes, swollen from the blows he'd received, stared incredulously at the soldier about to crank up the magneto. At the little prisoner's first scream, the *fell* struggled violently as if he thought he could break his bonds, but his lips stayed tightly shut. When the second came, the man shut his eyes as the child choked and spluttered out a growling noise, which the *harki* said meant something like "Daddy, help me… hurts, it hurts, they're hurting me…"

He caved in at the kid's third high-pitched yelp. Then, in one breath, without looking at his son, the cause of his weakness, he gave the names, the place and the date of the meeting. The lieutenant was so happy he gave Mathieu a slap on the back. "Well, well, you really got us out of a hole there! I owe you one, my friend. The colonel'll come as if he was fucking his wife for the very first time. We've killed two birds with one stone – getting the tip-off and recruiting an influential rebel. This *fell* has become a traitor to his FLN mates, so he and his son don't have a choice anymore; they're going to have to work for us now. If he doesn't agree, we'll do the *son* trick again. By the way, go and see the cook in a moment and bring back something nice for the kid; the lad's earned it, after all! Before that, wipe his face and get him some clean clothes. And don't forget: no one's *to know about this…*"

The lieutenant had a knowing look on his face. Still tied up, the kid followed the soldiers' movements with his eyes. His face was stained with tears and snot; drops of blood were forming on one of his ears. Mathieu saw from his terrified look that he expected to be murdered at any moment.

It was then that the man who was to be Aziz's father-in-law heard, very distinctly, the soft, fluty voice of the boy who loved Robert Surcouf and Jean Bart beating on the walls of his skull. *You can give him all the sweets you want, you're still going to hell, Mathieu. You've tortured a kid… but you're going to fry all alone like a rancid sausage.* The voice was weeping uncontrollably and repeating over and over again: *I haven't said anything up till now, but you've gone too far… I don't want to go to hell with you, I haven't committed any atrocities, I'm not guilty of anything, I don't want…*

Never before had it criticised him for torturing people and belonging – without so much as a grumble – to an army that carried out large-scale operations in which they combed and bombed villages under suspicion, napalmed fields and forests, displaced the population and worse still. It criticised him – incessantly, it's true – for his lack of ambition and the sickening sordidness of his life. Mathieu knew he was despicable, but he couldn't work out why he had become like this and especially why he had grown accustomed to it so easily. However, to his amazement, that hadn't stopped him from drinking, fucking, joking and even – albeit infrequently – trekking heroically around the *jebel* when his superiors ordered him to.

At the end of the day, he had decided, he didn't owe anyone any explanations since he despised *himself*. What's more, all that stuff about heaven and hell bored him to tears. He thought he'd sorted out the 'problem' by deciding that he was both the one who vomited and the vomit itself: when he found a part of himself unbearable, he would quite literally *expel* it by drinking continuously until every nook and cranny of his stomach rebelled. Without a hint of irony, he deduced from this that his failing organism would one day have nothing more to regurgitate and that the unfathomable metaphysical mystery of his potential guilt would thus be resolved, like some conjuring trick, by the prosaic capitulation of his liver to a good old cirrhosis.

He spent the rest of that cursed day looking after the child, taking him first to the shower and then to the sickbay, clothing him from head to toe and later stuffing him with the best things he could dig up in the canteen. But the kid obviously couldn't understand this change in treatment, and a shiver of fear ran through him every time Mathieu came too close. From time to time, he moaned in Arabic: "My ears hurt… I want to see my father!"

When evening came and he had got rid of the kid by putting him back in sickbay, Mathieu had fallen back on his tried-and-tested method of getting completely plastered. He woke up the next morning with a migraine the size of Algeria but afflicted nonetheless by a new itch more unforgiving than the worst parasite: *shame*.

Only once that day had he tried to defend himself. *Come on, you're exaggerating. I'm only torturing to get information; I'd never abuse anyone just for kicks. You know, I've never helped rip off a rebel's ear, for example, to earn a round of pastis from a beaming barman! I'm a soldier; I'm fighting for my country and the free world…*

He heard his answer – and there was mocking pity in the retort from the scoundrel crouching somewhere deep inside his brain: *And that's your excuse for the kid?*

It was as if the entire moral circuit that he thought no longer existed inside him had suddenly been activated again, its needle stuck at maximum voltage, the tortured boy flicking a wall switch with a potential accomplice in the little sniffling Breton boy fighting not to spend eternity in hell. No matter how often Mathieu sniggered and repeated to himself, "Listen up, you three fucking policemen in my life – father, mother and You, you incomprehensible clown spying on me from up there in Your clouds! When I interrogate someone, I'm like a septic tank: I stink to high heaven, I disgust anyone who approaches me. But who'd dare claim that a septic tank isn't useful?" that which he had almost instantly baptised the *moral magneto* had not loosened its grip.

Hunched on the kitchen chair, Mathieu coughs. Half a century later, that damned shame is still alive and well, polluting his nightmares, clinging to what is left of his soul like incurable ringworm. He has never told anyone any of this in detail, not even the person he has loved – and loves – more than anything in the world: Latifa. No love could survive the proximity to such filth. So it is out of the question that Aziz here, whose sole attribute is to be Latifa's daughter's husband, should hear it from his lips.

Time is short, so all he says to the father of his granddaughter is: *We carried out a large-scale operation after a tip-off.*

However, the informer had been wrong on two counts. Firstly, about the basics: there was no meeting of high-ranking FLN officials, but rather a movement by six platoons of rebel troops preparing to carry out a huge wave of reprisals, ordered by local FLN chiefs and completely out of proportion to earlier operations, against villages in a region suspected of supporting a rival movement called the Algerian National Movement, the MNA. And, secondly, about the date: the event – the massacre – had taken place two days before the date the prisoner had given.

The old soldier sighs; he is, as they say in this country, eaten away by sadness and regret. He shifts on his chair before relieving his aching stomach with a discreet fart.

Mathieu looks at his watch – how fast time flies, as fast as the kidnapper's knife on the girl's fingers! – and whispers a silent entreaty: "Li'l Robert, my failed privateer who used to have so much tenderness to spare, if you're going to stir up the muck in my heart some more, please help me to speak about Tahar in front of this Algerian bastard…"

He brings his hands together and rubs his phalanges, all the while praying intensely: "…Without betraying my friend, please, without betraying him."

God must be hooked on luck, for Mathieu had only come across 'his' rebel by accident around the side of an earthen bank several hours' march north of the huge peak. The exhausted patrol had given up the hunt and he was merely looking for a sheltered spot, firstly to relieve himself and then to take off his boots and rest his aching feet a bit.

That day the new captain had decided that every available soldier, including the DOP staff and the pen-pushers, had to take part in the hunt. "We've got to take advantage of what's happened in the villages in the Béni Ilemane area and then, I can assure you, the battle with those FLN criminals will be as good as won. Or at least the one we're fighting to win over public opinion back home and around the world, which has been a fiasco until now. Those sand niggers have done us a real favour this time, gentlemen!"

The officer's eyes were shining with excitement and he pointed a threatening finger at the soldiers. "This place is going to be crawling with journalists in under twenty-four hours. So get out there and hunt, and make sure you bring me back some of those responsible for this slaughter alive – and I mean *alive*. If you catch one, take care not to rough him up too much. We need those vermin so we can show them off left, right and centre. It'll be headline news around the world, I swear, and those rags back home that spit on our army will be forced to admit that they've been misled by these FLN murderers ever since this trouble began!"

Someone objected that the *fells* had a day's march on them. The officer barked at him that he didn't need reminding of that and that he was counting on them to pull off a miracle. "You DOP blokes have got a free rein! Interrogate anyone you want – Kabyles, Arabs, their donkeys, their dogs. There's been so much bad blood between Kabyle and Arab *douars* around here for so long, there's a good chance some bloke'll cough up some useful information!"

Curled up tight, his boots brown with coagulated blood and his old English .303 rifle thrown down at his feet, the fighter in ALN fatigues hadn't lifted a finger in self-defence when the Frenchman pointed his weapon at him.

Something was wrong; the catch had been too easy! The man shouldn't have been there, he'd had all the time in the world to melt away into the jumble of ridges, passes and thick undergrowth. There was no reason for fortune to smile on Mathieu and his fellow soldiers like this, but it had: the Breton, short of breath, was immediately convinced that the guy in his sights had taken part in the massacre.

The man, as though oblivious to everything around him, still didn't react to the shouted order to stand up and put his hands in the air. It was only after he'd received several furious kicks in the back and sides that he obeyed with some short whimpers that sounded more like mechanical reflexes from his body than real complaints. His face, half hidden behind several days' stubble, was drawn and his wide-open eyes appeared not to take in any of the landscape of stunted olive trees. After retrieving his prisoner's rifle with the usual precautions, Mathieu had yelled, in a voice filled with a strangely revengeful joy that he could only explain to himself much later, "Come on, you bastard. Walk ahead of me – it'll be dark soon! One move and I'll kill you, and you can ask at that Allah of yours' reception desk which basement of hell he plans to send you to!"

The man seemed to rouse from his torpor as if pricked by a needle. His pupils were bright with hope.

"You'll shoot me if I try to run away?"

The stranger had spoken with a harsh accent, rolling his 'r's, but his French sounded decent. Mathieu had knitted his brow in satisfaction: his catch was all the more special because the resistance fighter was probably an 'intellectual', a cadre, not just some illiterate peasant. He had responded with a chuckle.

"You bet – and twice rather than once. Bastards like you deserve to be shot without warning and then thrown to the jackals as an appetizer!"

"Kill me then. I'm going to try and run away..."

He had then repeated the words in a strange tone of voice – a beseeching tone – but his whole body was trembling with fear. ("So why didn't you make a run for it earlier, you fucker?" Mathieu thought, taken aback.)

"Please kill me."

Then, pointing to a sort of hole on the side of the bank: "Over there in the thistles... end of story. I deserve no better."

Mathieu was speechless. The man was addressing him as though he were begging him for a favour! The French soldier had been overcome with anger. He had hit the *fell* on the temple with the barrel first, then pushed him to the ground and then smashed him repeatedly with the butt, avoiding the head this time so as not to disobey the captain's orders.

"Huh? You think... hem... you can get out of it like that, do you? After everything you and your mates did up there... A bullet... um... in the head and it's all over? A little patience, mate... um... you'll see, we'll take care of you back at the barracks all right..."

They brought the prisoner back in an army lorry trussed up by his ankles and wrists like a sheep, having first notified their superiors by field telephone. The soldiers took it in turns to smack the *fell* on the backside while shouting at the top of their voices "*A mile on foot wears out your boots, a mile in a Jeep wears out your arse...*" but, heeding their officer's warnings, they didn't hit him very hard. Worn out from the hours spent trekking in the sun, some of them were annoyed that they couldn't take it out more on the Arab at their feet and from time to time a sly boot would come down on his coccyx. A beaming Mathieu protested but watched the rebel's face eagerly for a sign of supplication – which still didn't come, even though the corner of the man's mouth was twisted with terror.

Mathieu had started the day in the horrifying lanes of Mechta Kasbah and had ended it here in this lorry, his heart flooded with a feeling of relief, as if God himself, by allowing him to arrest a murderer like this, had decided to wipe away the shame that had ruined his life since they had tortured the little Arab boy.

In the military lorry taking them and the bound prisoner back to HQ, he had been very careful not to dwell too long on why he was so excited. Was he not, he thought, trying to sum things up for himself, responsible for an arrest that would probably earn him the captain's congratulations and maybe a promotion to Constantine, whose brothel, just behind the municipal theatre, was famed throughout Algeria?

Even as he was yelling with his comrades, he had tried to re-establish contact with 'Li'l Robert'. But the boy had refused to answer and the man had been scared that he might have fallen silent for good since that bloody carry-on with the kid.

That morning, long before he had captured the *fell*, when Mathieu had seen the dozens of mutilated corpses piled up like rotting meat in the town square, their throats slit, battered to death with axes and picks or shot, he had felt sullied by having witnessed such a spectacle…

…and at the same time secretly delighted that he'd been given this chance to assure himself that there were "*of course*" people far worse than him in the rebels' ranks "*and* (he added, aware of how important this observation might prove on those depressing evenings) *by a long way, mate, by a long way!*"

A few feet from the corpses, he caught himself mumbling the opening words of his defence speech in front of judge 'Li'l Robert'. *You see, you idiot, we were right to torture that* fell *shit and his brat! Maybe we could have saved these fucking* fells *that bring tears to your eyes if we'd got down to it earlier? Answer me – these lazy good-for-nothings are bigger savages than us, eh?*

'Li'l Robert' hadn't reacted. Suffocating with the almost liquid smell of putrefaction, Mathieu had covered his nostrils with one hand and beaten away the thick clouds of flies swirling around the dead with the other. He had wandered around the wretched stone huts where women were scratching at their faces and wailing in grief while their terrified children clung to their multicoloured dresses and soldiers were busy either dragging together corpses or nosing around for clues. Scattered objects – cooking pots, kanouns, shoes, burnous – obstructed the steep lanes, which were slippery with trails of blood. A spade or a fork here and a hammer or kitchen utensil there had spots of a greasy, whitey-grey substance on them, and Mathieu did not immediately realise that it was human brains. When the crows grew bolder and picked at an obscenely undressed body, he kicked out angrily at them and, a couple of times, hit the birds, weighed down by their revolting feast, in the head. Several Sikorsky helicopters landed, each disgorging a bunch of top brass and feverish officers flanked by their bodyguards.

A young soldier, who had been given the task of counting the victims and had reached the figure of three hundred, started shouting,

"What the fuck are we doing in this country? This is a slaughter-house... Let's just kill them, kill all these Arabs! This can't be real..." before receiving a resounding slap from a sergeant and breaking out in sobs.

"Shit, it's lucky they're not French!" a journalist cried out after slipping over in a pool of blood. Having clambered to his feet again, the potbellied maniac examined his stained raincoat with disgust. Then, a cigarette dangling from his lips, he resumed his casual stroll around a group of teenagers who had had their throats slit and their penises and scrotums cut off. Their faces were frozen in their final horror-filled expression. Only the youngest among them, twelve or thirteen years old, his head nestling in the arms of some other poor devil, seemed asleep. It looked as if all it would take was a gentle tap on the shoulder to startle him awake.

There was something strangely beautiful about his sulky expression. Suddenly captivated, the photographer snapped several shots of him. The scar on his throat was barely visible, as if his murderer had been affected in spite of himself and couldn't bring himself to disfigure the fine-featured boy's face. Trying not to look at him too much, Mathieu was nonetheless struck by his vague resemblance to the boy they had tortured. He shrugged his shoulders, deciding with a confused sense of panic that this was no surprise given that Arabs, like Blacks, all looked pretty much the same.

He almost broke into a run when a dishevelled old woman, her face scarred with wrinkles and traditional tattoos, suddenly walked up to the heap and, her shoulders convulsed with sobs, attempted to move aside one body after another, slowly at first, then forcibly. Mathieu only looked round when he was already fifty yards down the road; the woman, her arms and dress red with blood, seemed to have finally found what she was looking for. Sitting on her backside, she had grabbed the hand of a corpse and, letting out a series of unbearably sorrowful guttural moans, she showered it with kisses.

It was the first time Mathieu had seen so many massacred civilians in one place. Of course, he had taken part in some skirmishes that had ended in losses, sometimes considerable ones, on both sides. But he had seen little of the real war on the ground, even if he had his fair share of stories, from hearsay or the files that passed through his hands, of Arab villages razed to the ground by mortar shelling or burnt down with napalm (the pilots called them halal meat barbe-cues!), of suspects tortured by amateurs and then strung up on trees in retaliation for FLN operations during which French soldiers had had their throats slit and been castrated. Up until that point, his work in Algeria had involved being cooped up in a room or cellar with prisoners his superiors had labelled dangerous outlaws. It was his duty to break them quickly so that their even more harmful associates could be neutralised.

Little by little, Mathieu had reached the conclusion that it was down to their own (incidentally stupid) stubbornness that certain suspects died after an overly intensive interrogation session, since everyone eventually spilt the beans. Wherever they now found them-selves, roasting in the flames of hell or polishing their cocks between a *houri*'s thighs, those fanatical mujahideen only had their own lack of judgment to blame. "If, once we've started tearing out your nails, you think you can still resist us, you're wrong, mate, you're wrong…" he would sing to the tune of *Saint-Germain-des-Prés*, with a certain soft spot for the most unyielding – who all gave in, the poor fools, when he got started on the second hand. He was against pointless violence and could not remember having tortured anyone more than he needed to. That was maybe why he had a reputation for reliability among his superiors.

Basically he didn't have anything to reproach himself for as he had always been just a humble and *le-gi-ti-mate* helper (he had begun to love the latter adjective passionately) in a large-scale law and order operation that was beyond him. All the rest – the fate of Algeria's Europeans, the future of the country's institutions, the patriotism on both sides, the atrocious situation of the natives, the discussions with an alleged 'third force', autonomy or independence, etc. – left him utterly cold. In any case, he hadn't read a newspaper for ages. One of his colleagues from the DOP, a hard case from Alsace with a Resistance medal, theorised about their attitude, stating that when you were up to your neck in crap, you weren't going to start devour-ing the tabloids that told you what the shit was made of! "Nothing but short-sighted policies for a land full of Arabs. Ever since cherries had stems, we soldiers have had to obey. In other words: we're there to wipe the Republic's arse when it's shat its laws and decrees. Full stop! So, gentlemen, we'll just get on with our work and all those lying politician clowns in Paris can go fuck themselves, as can all these *pieds noirs* who pretend not to notice that they're only in charge in Algeria and their *Oh-what-a-lovely-French-cottage-I-have-in-Africa* attitude can only last because of the work we do on their behalf in stinking cellars!"

As he left the village, the Breton had started walking faster to escape for a moment from the horror behind him. At the end of a long path stood a house that was a little less crude than the others, its front still smoking. A group of soldiers were poking around inside. One of them told him that an entire family had been massacred there – the village constable, a teenage boy, two women and a girl about three years old. "It's the only house where they killed a child this small. They must have had quite a grudge against the policeman. They tortured him for a long time. Maybe they thought he was an informer... Want to go inside? It's not a pretty sight..." Mathieu excused himself saying he had orders and beat a swift retreat.

He stopped halfway between the *douar* and the policeman's house. The scenery was magnificent and kindly; on one side was a eucalyptus wood hemmed in by two hills and, on the other, plots of land dotted with a delicate mix of daisies and poppies. The hedges of prickly pears indicated that there were native *douars* close by. As always, the spectator noticed, nature could not give a damn about clashes between humans; in less than twenty-four hours most of the bodies would have already been buried under the ground, the smell of sun-scorched grass would have replaced that of decaying carcasses, and a single rain shower would suffice to wash away the last spots of blood and brain. A wave of resentment rose up inside him: why couldn't these people have been decimated while he was on leave last month? Why did they think they were allowed to lodge themselves, uninvited, among his jumbled thoughts with their hideous faces craving explanations?

His heart was pounding away in his chest, his lungs felt more like crumpled waterskins, and his legs were threatening to give way.

(After all, he hadn't killed that fell's *fucking brat, had he! Just... how should he put it...)*

"What a load of crap!" he swore in a voice that sounded ridiculously hoarse to him.

Nervously he scratched his testicles – and was shaken by the thought that someone might well have chopped them off. He imagined himself with no balls and decided without laughing that the grand visit to the brothel in Constantine he had promised himself wouldn't really be worth it anymore...

"If I carry on thinking like this, I'll end up handing in my notice," he reckoned, without daring to pursue the thought. He leaned against the trunk of an olive tree and took an unfiltered cigarette out of his battledress. He had the impression as he put it to his lips that it too stank of decaying corpses. He crushed it between his fingers and scattered the scraps of paper and tobacco, forcing himself all the while to concentrate on the beautiful scenery. A gust of wind blew the terrible scent of death into his nostrils again; the soldier bent over and threw up.

The cheeky and strangely familiar voice called out harshly to him: *Hey Mathieu, you're not going to get rid of it that easily this time... Between you and me, if* this *is bothering you so much, maybe that's because you're partly to blame?*

"You what, you fucking..."

Insult at the ready, he span round with his fist raised to hit whoever had dared to fling such an accusation at him.

There was no one there.

No one at all.

Latifa came into the kitchen without knocking, as if she wanted to overhear their conversation. As she filled a glass from the tap, she gave the two men a suspicious look. Mathieu felt his heart stop beating; it seemed worn out, grown so old. A new wave of panic washed through him: no one would come out of this unscathed.

Overwhelmed by his own helplessness, he glanced at his watch. Less than a quarter of an hour had passed since he had decided to tell Aziz at least half the story. These few minutes might have proved awfully long to Shehera, exposed to the boundless imagination of the madman who was holding her.

Suddenly Mathieu was gripped by a familiar, intense longing for one never-ending swig of gin that would slide down his throat into his stomach before exploding in a merciful apocalypse at the centre of his brain, in the exact spot where love, hate, all those kind of things are born.

It had been so long since he had got absolutely blind drunk! The last time was at Tahar's funeral, he seemed to remember.

Running his fingers through his hair, he sighed and every molecule of air was a concentrate of bitterness and regret. No, the time had not yet come for the shroud of drunkenness; no, the Algerian war was not yet over and he had told Aziz nothing of note apart from that, one day, by chance, he had captured an exhausted maquisard called Tahar not far from the mixed community of Melouza, a large village on the High Plateaux on the border between Kabylie and Constantine.

"When you've finished your drink, Mathieu, come and join us in the living room. That monster hasn't phoned yet and Meriem isn't feeling too well."

A shadow passed across Aziz's face and his fingers fidgeted nervously with the mobile phone lying in front of him.

Once Latifa had left the room, Aziz asked bitterly, making no attempt to conceal his annoyance: "So what happened to the rebel after that?"

"Just the normal routine in such situations, as you can imagine."

"*The routine*? You mean you…"

The words ("*tortured him?*") were written all over the Algerian's stunned face, the words Mathieu feared and which Aziz, probably out of what little respect he still had for his father-in-law, was reluctant to pronounce.

Mathieu defended himself. "What are you suggesting? We threw him in a cell with a few regulation kicks up the backside, that's all!"

The old man avoided his son-in-law's suspicious gaze.

"But that's not the main thing, Aziz. My prisoner had nothing to do with what had just happened at Melouza."

"And what really did happen at Melouza?" his son-in-law asked him, his sugary tone indicating that he wasn't fooled by this ploy.

"Some farmers were killed… Lots of them… A terrible settling of political scores with civilians paying the price…"

"And you say Tahar played no part in it?"

"That's right… But someone else convinced themselves of the opposite…"

"And that someone was Algerian?"

The routine. That was the first of several misleading words, repellent

140

as a turd, which he had used to describe to Aziz the treatment meted out to this strange prisoner – at first sight the worst kind of coward – who screamed and cried out in pain as much, if not more, than other men when they burnt his penis with electricity from the magneto, but not once begged for mercy – just to be killed.

To begin with, Mathieu, whom the DOP unit regarded as their 'classifications' specialist, had thought that this prisoner was a chicken who would pour out a torrent of confessions after just one 'roasting'.

"Put your hand here," he had said to his superior. "What can you feel?"

The officer had touched the man's chin as he lay naked on the work surface.

"Well, he's trembling, but that's normal, isn't it? They all tremble…"

"No, this one's trembling all over. Look: his stomach, his legs and his butt-cheeks are all trembling – even his dick's trembling!" he exclaimed as his colleagues looked on, giving the prisoner's penis a pinch. "He's a right poofter, his skin's softer than a lamb's. He'll talk faster than I can piss, with all due respect, sir!"

However, the man hadn't talked. The colonel had flown into a rage (because his own superiors were growing impatient…), accusing the members of the DOP unit in the harshest terms of bragging and of a lack of professionalism in dealing with these bleeding terrorists, repeating that every man, no matter how obstinate, had a breaking point and ordering them to find it as quickly as possible.

"But don't spoil any 'visible meat'!" he enjoined them. "I absolutely have to have a presentable witness to tell the whole story at the press conference. What we have here, gentleman, is a nice little massacre perpetrated by the enemy and I fully intend to use it to show that the French army is fighting not a resistance army but a pack of knife-wielding maniacs who deserve no respect! Don't fuck this job up, boys, or believe me you'll regret it!"

The more the DOP's group of specialists went to work on the prisoner, the more obvious it became that not only would he not yield any information, but also that he was determined to find any possible means of taking his own life. He had been subjected to water-boarding. The session had taken up a good part of the afternoon, the only result being to plunge the interrogators into a horrid mood. The team were used to this kind of delicate operation, which involved pulling their customer's head out of the water just before he drowned, taking care not to let the man pass out underwater because in that case he would lose all vital reflexes and be unable to struggle hard enough to survive. There was always one man nicknamed 'the nurse' who kept a close eye on this sort of thing if for some reason they didn't want to 'wear out' the interrogation suspect too fast.

By the end of the afternoon, not only did Tahar no longer show any resistance when they re-immersed him in the dirty water, he had to be yanked out when they realised, a fraction of a second before he suffocated, that it was now he – and no longer they – who was intent on keeping his head in the putrid liquid. Mathieu had to ask a colleague to help him prise apart the fingers clutching the sides of the tub. The head of their unit – the man from Alsace who wept with emotion when, after his fifth or sixth Pils, he talked about the village on the Rhine where he was born – was so afraid of the dressing-down they were certain to receive from their commanding officer at headquarters that he whipped the prisoner with his own belt, although he did avoid touching the future witness's face or arms. In his characteristic accent, he yelled, "You towel-headed Kraut, we're not impressed by your stupid bloody show of bravery. You want to commit suicide without chickening out, but we're not going to let you, you dirty little throat-slitter. You don't deserve a favour like that! Now it's personal between you and me, and boy, are you going to suffer, believe you me. You'll end up telling us who organised the massacre and where your mates from your unit are hiding! And don't bother imploring heaven for help. If God hadn't wanted men to be tortured, He wouldn't have put their balls on the outside!"

The prisoner was taken to a makeshift cell in the barracks. A nurse – a real one this time – gave him some medical care. To avoid any further risks (the Alsatian had realised a little late that he might have been a bit heavy-handed), a member of the DOP team was given the task of watching over the Arab while he was asleep and, if necessary, alerting the nurse if the man's health deteriorated dangerously or if he tried to escape them again by committing suicide. "We might get further if one of us mollycoddles him and plays the good cop surrounded by baddies. Hey Mathieu, would you like to have a go, since you're meant to know so much about Arab psychology?" his superior chortled without quite managing to hide his disquiet.

That night Mathieu resigned himself to his chore, even if he would not stop cursing that he was neither a priest taking confession from weirdo criminals nor a faggot into young lads, let alone young Muslim lads. Someone spluttered, "Ask the *fell* to give you a fellatio. *Fell* and fellatio – that rhymes backwards. He's trembling so much, you'd come in a flash!" and Mathieu snapped back that he'd prefer his colleague's sister's cunt or wife's mouth.

The two men, one handcuffed to his bed, the other slumped on an old chair, spent most of the night without exchanging a word. Apart from the prisoner's moans of pain as he searched for a better position, the only sound was the cicadas in the surrounding countryside rubbing their wings together with a frenetic energy unusual for the season. About four o'clock in the morning, Mathieu woke with a start from a restless sleep during which a soldier from the ALN, the National Liberation Army, who resembled his prisoner like two peas in a pod, suggested with friendly compassion that he check whether his crown jewels were still safely nestled between his legs. He heard himself roar in rage that he wouldn't talk to criminals, that he was a soldier and not a murderer of civilians. The muddled dream ended with his imaginary interlocutor flashing a broad, surprised grin.

Mathieu's first, ridiculous gesture was to put his hand to his testicles. Then, still thrown by his dream, he lit a cigarette and forced himself to think of a nice cold beer. The prisoner shifted on his makeshift bed, stifling a groan. Telling himself that professional conscientiousness required him to have at least one go at the famous good cop trick, Mathieu tapped him on the shoulder to pass him his cigarette. His eyes half shut, the man gave no reaction. Mathieu stuffed the cigarette firmly into his mouth, then lit himself one. The bound man coughed and then pushed the cigarette out with the tip of his tongue.

"Hey, don't waste tobacco."

"I don't smoke," the prisoner answered curtly.

"Scared the FLN'll cut your nose off, are you? Or of dying of lung disease?"

"That must be it."

"You're right. Got to look after your health if you want to live nice and long, don't you? Life's beautiful and you've got to make the most of it. By the way, are you thirsty?"

"No."

"That's normal," Mathieu said mockingly. "Almost drank a whole bathtub by yourself."

Silence fell again, heavier than before, because now the two men were sizing each other up. The Frenchman furiously stubbed out his half-smoked cigarette, exasperated by his own confusion. *Who did this fucking throat-slitter think he was? To hell with pretending to be the good cop...*

"So what's it like being a child murderer?"

The man kept silent, his eyes riveted to the opposite wall. It looked as if he had sunk slightly further into himself.

"I'm talking to you, wank-stain!" Mathieu chided.

Faced with his detainee's immobility, the guard stood up, deliberately knocking his chair over.

"Answer when a French soldier speaks to you! Otherwise, what use does jabbering our language do you? I'll ask you again: what did it feel like in your guts to slit open so many of your little Arab brothers' throats? You Arabs will stop at nothing, eh?"

The man span round. With quivering nostrils, he stared at his guard through bloated eyelids. The general expression on his face still betrayed that disturbing mixture of intense, almost palpable fear that should have made him cave in long ago and even an greater stubbornness, drawn from some bottomless reservoir that allowed this shitty prisoner to hold his tongue.

"All right, so they're all curly on top, but don't go telling me you thought they were sheep for Eid? Kids make a different sound when you kill them! Is that what liberating Algeria is all about?"

Mathieu thought he glimpsed a flash of sorrow – or was it disdain? – in the Arab's eyes, but the light from the bulb hanging from the ceiling was too dim for him to be sure. He was gripped by anger nonetheless, as if the man had insulted him by daring to feel emotions to which a murderer like him was not entitled.

"Why are you staring at me like that, you lump of shite?"

He wasn't supposed to succumb to rage and his superior would definitely not appreciate the result, but the perverse blow rang out anyway. Despite the chirping of the cicadas, Mathieu heard the tiny cracking of cartilage. The *fell* made a sound like a muffled yelp and his nose immediately started to bleed. Mathieu repeated his question in a less confident tone of voice.

"So what does it really feel like deep down, eh, to murder so many people?"

The man, whose nostrils and lips were slowly becoming covered in blood and snot, screwed up his eyes, which were clouded with tears.

"You would know... euh..."

"What are you mumbling about, you bastard?"

"You..."

His voice had turned whiny, probably because of his fractured nasal septum. He needed a gulp of air before he managed to speak, with bitter mockery: "You torture, *so* (he had stressed the word) you know... *brother*..."

"Fucking... I'm not your brother!"

The Frenchman had raised his fist. The handcuffed man's face tensed in expectation of the punch.

But, probably to the great surprise of them both, the punch did not come.

The next morning Mathieu left the room and came back with a bucket of water and a sponge. Face closed and eyes avoiding the prisoner's, he set about washing away the scabs crusting his mouth and nose.

"Thanks," the prisoner said once the job was finished.

"It's not for your sake," the guard objected sourly, "it's for my superior's. He doesn't want us roughing your face up. You've got to look presentable."

With a resigned sigh, the rebel said, a little quieter this time, "Thanks anyway."

The soldier threw the sponge angrily into the water. "I don't need your thanks. Remember I'm the one who smacked your face in, you son of a bitch." Then, grabbing the bucket, he headed towards the cell door.

"Why do you want to die," he asked him without looking round, as though the question and the possible reply were of no importance. "You're shit-scared and yet you still want to die... Do you want to die for your country, Algeria? Want to go down in patriotic folklore, be called a freedom fighter or some bullshit?"

The prisoner sniggered faintly, then said to himself, "How easy that would be – to die for Algeria. I'd be a hero and everyone would mourn me... and..."

A gasp cut him off.

"So why do you want to die?"

Caught off-guard by his guard's neutral tone of voice, the prisoner answered with the same indifference. "Because… because I don't deserve to live anymore."

"Why don't you deserve to live anymore?"

The man remained silent and Mathieu thought that he wouldn't open his mouth again, like in a 'real' interrogation. He was turning the door handle when the man whispered, "One day, when you've become human again, you too will try anything you can to die…"

He coughed and Mathieu, filled with inexplicable anxiety, listened out for the rest of the husky words.

"…Until then, make the most of your luck. You'll see – it's unbear-able when you find out you're worthless."

Mathieu still hadn't said anything when the telephone on the kitchen table rang. Aziz and he looked at each other, paralysed.

"That's your phone. Take the call," the old man ordered. "He might get angry if you hang about."

Aziz cautiously picked up his mobile. His hands were shaking.

"It's a message. Just a message."

Aziz's ashen face had fallen as the disappointment hit home.

"What does it say?"

The Algerian pushed a few buttons, then his eyebrows arched in surprise.

"Nothing. It's incomprehensible."

His voice rang false. His complexion had gone even pastier. He flicked the lid of the phone shut.

"Show me, Aziz."

Mathieu was too quick for his son-in-law and assertively grabbed the phone. He blinked at the tiny screen.

```
put fone on vibrate
be alone when I phone in morning
number to follow
```

"Did he write the text?"

"Who else do you think it could be?"

Mathieu handed the phone back to his son-in-law. His tic had returned and was more febrile than ever. He pushed the unruly eyelid down hard.

"Have you done anything for his guy, Aziz?"

The grief-stricken father appeared to hesitate before protesting.

"No, of course not. What do you think he'd ask me to do for him?"

"That's for you to tell me."

"Go to hell! Firstly, I don't owe you any explanations. And secondly, I haven't done anything for him, all right? Where did you get that idea? Did he ask you to do something perhaps?"

"Why me?"

They looked each other up and down for a few seconds, resentfully mingling their silent lies. Mathieu was just opening his mouth when Latifa appeared, terrified.

"The phone rang, didn't it?"

She stared at her son-in-law as if she held him responsible in advance for any coming disaster.

"Yes," her husband replied in his son-in-law's stead, "but it was a wrong number."

The old man stood up and put his arms very tenderly around his wife's shoulders.

"Go on, I'll be with you in a few minutes."

She groaned.

"Oh, this is all so awful, Mathieu."

"Yes," he replied simply, struggling not to cry.

He whispered a couple of words in his wife's ear before closing the door behind her. He poured himself a glass of water while Aziz tapped away on the buttons of his mobile, probably setting it to vibrate.

The man who had once been a soldier sat down on his chair again. With the exhausted acquiescence of his companion in misfortune, he resumed the pathetic process of dissimulation from which he hoped at least some truth would emerge.

Otherwise, all he had to do was to kill his son-in-law. Pointless – but did he have a choice? – other than to earn a little more time for Shehera, a few bubbles of oxygen before she drowned.

It was that night, the night when he broke Tahar's nose – although he didn't know his first name yet – that his 'conversion' began.

Even now, as he sat opposite Shehera's father beating about the bush, dreading having to announce to him that he has probably found out who the kidnapper is, he can think of no other word than the ridiculous 'conversion'.

He hadn't fallen suddenly to his knees with imploring words to a new God. No, he hadn't needed to address any novel prayers to some brand new avatar of Yahwe or Allah, like the slippery formulas whispered by a child's toy.

Yet overnight Mathieu had become incapable of torturing.

Later, when he rediscovered a little of his irony to fight off his despair at having betrayed his country, he distinguished two stages in this transmutation, which he described – to himself, of course, for he didn't breathe a word of this to anyone else – using the Sunday school images of his childhood.

Instead of the Angel Gabriel, he received a visit from a weak-bladdered little boy who warned him, just by his screams, that he would soon be carrying a shame that would grow endlessly inside him like some ravenous embryo he would never be able to get rid of.

As for the bearer of these 'good tidings', it was no longer a bearded Jesus dying on the cross to save the human rabble but Tahar, tortured in a stinking room belonging to the DOP, a criminal among criminals who was trying, despite his terror, to kill himself in atonement for sins greater than his own life.

Mathieu became utterly disgusted with himself in the space of twenty-four hours. Years later, as he emerged noisily from a cheap restaurant, he found an amusing explanation for this complete turnaround. He'd been very hungry that day and the dish the waiter had brought him looked absolutely perfect in every respect: appearance, aroma, quantity… Anyway, he was getting ready to stuff his face when a tiny bit of snot dripped off the waiter's nose and immediately sank into the delicious sauce that filled his plate. This was all it took for the meal to become instantly vile to Mathieu and impossible to swallow without throwing up.

That summed up his life in his own caricature of it until that fateful morning. At some stage in his childhood, some damned angel that was dying of boredom on the plains of paradise had squirted a long flow of snot into the pot where what should have been a fairly honourable future had been simmering for the little Breton lad. The contrast between the absolute innocence of the one and the limitless guilt of the other – the child and the *fell* – had, to his misfortune, allowed him to smell the 'revolting dish' he'd become. Since then, Mathieu, the wringer of bodies who had been indifferent to such considerations up to this point, could no longer stand himself. Worse: *he disgusted himself*.

When his Alsatian unit commander saw the prisoner's broken nose, he tore a strip off him. Mathieu got out of it somewhat by stating that he had had a long and extremely informative conversation with the rebel.

"Your method works, sir. People tell their torturers all kinds of things when they start mollycoddling them!"

His superior's blotchy jowls had twitched. The officer loosened the collar of his shirt by running a finger around his neck. He must have shaved a bit too close, Mathieu noticed, because there were some raw patches on the skin on his throat.

"What did he tell you?"

"Nothing particularly useful for the moment. Some vague stories about his childhood, the Koranic school he went to, his mother – that sort of thing. But give me one more night and I'll winkle some information about his *katiba* out of him…"

"Why would he grass on his mates? Does he fancy you that much, sergeant?"

Mathieu had shrugged his shoulders, as if to say slyly: "*I couldn't give a damn – you're the boss! There's a real chance of extracting the information the colonel's been longing for and it'll be your fault if we fail…*" The suspicious Alsatian had come round to his subordinate's suggestion, but only reluctantly.

"Type me up a complete report of everything he told you last night, especially any details that could help us locate his home *douar*. If that helps us track down one of his relatives, who knows, maybe there'll be some way of putting pressure on the bloke. We've got copies of the survivors' statements. They all claim they don't know who attacked them. Have a look through the papers again, just to check we haven't missed anything important by mistake. The rest of the team and I'll work hard on the guy and if we haven't made any progress by this evening, you can take over for another night. Hey, don't go falling in love with him though!" the Alsatian said in an attempt at a ribald joke. "There are more than enough women in Constantine or Sétif, not to mention all the *fatmas* around, if you're into that kind of creature."

"Witty one, sir!" Mathieu hissed as he turned on his heel, his stomach churning with fear at the decision he had just taken in the depths of his soul. A minute earlier it would have seemed not only insane, but also contrary to any moral sense he had left.

"One last thing!" the officer shouted. "Make him understand that our patience has just about run out. If he persists, explain to him that soon, as if by chance, he'll try and escape and, obedient soldiers that we are, we will be forced, as the law provides, to shoot him dead after the customary warnings! The colonel gave us a week to get as much out of this *zouave* as we can, and we've wasted five days already."

He guffawed, but his eyes, which had an unfamiliar glitter of distrust in them, did not join in with his mirth.

"Oh and by the way, you're going to be on 'fire' duty. Some time since you last did it, eh? You've already broken your mate's nose so you might as well finish the job."

Mathieu saluted without bothering to point out the contradiction in threatening with death a man whose sole wish was to die.

The morning passed in a kind of terror that he had never experienced before. While he laboured over a report describing an imaginary conversation, he could hear Tahar's screams through the breezeblock walls. In this army post in the open countryside, there was no record player to cover the prisoners' howls of pain.

He sighed, bursting with anger at himself. The gods were real gamblers: they weren't satisfied with his self-contempt; now he was turning all queer, no longer able to stand the screams that had until now formed the background noise to life in the DOP! He was tormented for much of the morning by the urge to have a stiff drink, but he resisted it, unwilling to face his superior's bad mood.

Mathieu recognised every note of what was known as the 'scale' of screams. The most harrowing screams weren't necessarily caused by the most extreme pain. On the contrary; suspects yelled more at the beginning of their interrogation, when they not only still had the strength but were expressing above all their terror at the suffering to come. He could recall a prisoner who had squealed like a pig having its throat slit when he received the first blows and kicks, but who a few days later could only wail imperceptibly when they held a soldering iron to the soles of his feet. A good interrogator had to have a keen ear to pick up quickly the *kind* of pain that his suspect could endure before talking. That particular *fell*, who'd spilled the beans after having both feet burnt with a soldering iron, had withstood the field magneto turned up to maximum voltage without flinching.

Tahar, to whom Mathieu had listened attentively during their 'work' on him, had reached the stage of whining punctuated by barks, panting and wheezing – signs of atrocious pain, which, apart from a miracle, still wouldn't break him if his behaviour during the previous sessions was anything to go by. He must gradually be losing control of his sphincters; by now, he had probably, if not defecated, then at least urinated on himself.

Towards eleven o'clock the Alsatian came in to have a look at Mathieu's report.

"You're losing your touch, sergeant! This is bullshit – there's nothing concrete in here!" he said after flicking through the two-page summary of Tahar's supposed confidences. "That son of a bitch has been having you on. Apparently our mate lives in a little village surrounded by mountains, his mother loves her only son, and the head of the Koranic school was terribly strict… Well I never! Are you taking the piss, sergeant? Think there's a shortage of mountain villages in Algeria, do you?"

However, all of a sudden, the officer's anger subsided. Dropping the sheets of paper on the desk, he pulled a strange face.

"An Arab came by this morning and swore to the sentry that he was pretty sure he could identify our prisoner. Rumours spread fast around here and he thinks he knows who our captive is. Come with me – this could be our lucky day, who knows?"

In the room adjoining the interrogation room, which was nick-named the 'golden cage', Mathieu caught sight of a white-faced young man, and it was clear from his frantically bobbing Adam's apple that he was in a state of extreme agitation. The paleness of his features was accentuated by frizzy hair of the brightest ginger that Mathieu had ever seen. A soldier whispered in his ear, "Living proof that the Vikings squeezed a few cuddles out of the local women…" Mathieu thought bad-temperedly: *There weren't any Vikings in Algeria, you stupid prick – those were Vandals!*

"Bring me a hood for the witness!" the officer ordered.

"There aren't any, sir! We left them at headquarters."

"Well, fix one up quick," he spewed.

A few minutes later a soldier came back with a cement bag he'd just emptied of its contents. He cut two rough parallel holes in it with scissors and a third one for the mouth a little lower down.

"Come on, walk ahead of me," the lieutenant ordered the man whose head had been covered with the dusty bag. "Don't speak to the prisoner, say the bare minimum, and preferably answer yes or no when I ask you a question. If you've got any comments, wait until we're out of the *fell*'s sight. I don't want any stories or tricks, is that clear? You don't need an interpreter, right?"

"No..." the redhead said, suddenly doubling over with coughing.

"Are you OK in there?" the Alsatian enquired almost kindly, patting the civilian on the back, but the muscles standing out on his neck showed how tense the soldier was.

"It's nothing, it's nothing, major," the other man continued, "just some cement dust."

The lieutenant smiled at his 'promotion', delighted by the witness's servility. Ill at ease but curious, Mathieu followed the procession formed by the officer, the witness and two privates as reinforcements in case anything unforeseen happened.

"Yes, that's him," the Alsatian said in response to the man in the makeshift hood's questioning gesture. "But you said you knew him?"

The man said nothing. He walked towards the naked prisoner trussed up on the plank. Mathieu hadn't been wrong: the near-unconscious rebel stank of shit and urine. He wrinkled his nose in disgust as he remembered a military intelligence officer's motto that had made him laugh the first time: "The shit of the prisoners we interrogate is like the smell of fresh bread to a baker – proof of a job well done. Can you imagine a baker feeling sick at the smell of his own bread?"

"Hey, hands off, you peasant!"

The witness had put his hand on the prisoner's chin and was trying to wake him up. When the man didn't obey, the furious lieutenant punched the witness in the back. The rebel opened his blurred eyes, uttering some indistinct '*Yemma yemmas*'. Drops of blood were trickling from his penis and there were some fresh purple belt marks on his chest. The team had worked long and hard on him by the look of it.

The man had taken off his bag and was screaming something at the prone man.

"What's he jabbering on about? Is the fucker speaking in Arabic or Kabyle?" the lieutenant roared. "Get the interpreter in here right now. And keep him away from the prisoner!"

The 'witness' was shouting angrily and from time to time his voice broke down into splutters. His cheeks were grey with cement, which his tears turned black in places. The two privates stepped in between the two men, while Mathieu, overwhelmed by the newcomer's grief, rushed outside to fetch the *harki* who usually served as their interpreter.

"He's telling the prisoner that he's seen his face now and one day he'll kill him; one way or another he'll pay for the others. He swears this by…"

The back-up soldier, a middle-aged man in fatigues wearing a traditional *chèche* rather than an army helmet, was fiddling with one end of his moustache to hide his emotion. This chap was no softie. He regularly attended suspects' interrogations as an interpreter and wasn't averse to lending a hand if permitted. Even though the lieutenant didn't respect him (a *harki* was, according to him, disloyal by nature as he had betrayed once and was therefore likely to betray again), he appreciated his clear translations and his willing explanations that helped to disentangle the customs of the region.

"Sir, he also says that his father and mother, his brother, his wife and his three-year-old girl were all killed by this bloke and his *fellagha* accomplices. He says his father was the village constable… He says they had their throats slit like… burned like… This guy's face, he'll never… He says… he'll never forget it… He says that… his daughter was called… I can't understand everything he's saying, sir…"

"So," the Alsatian growled, "he didn't know our *fell* at all before he saw him here?"

In the face of the lieutenant's anger, the interpreter stammered, as if he'd been caught out: "Well… I don't think so, sir…"

"So he was just having us on with that pack of lies that he knows something about this bloke here? What are you waiting for? Ask him."

The disconcerted *harki* nibbled at his lower lip, as if he were caught in the crossfire between his superior's rage, whose consequences were unpredictable, and this other, near-sacred rage of a human being deprived in one fell swoop of both his families, the family that had seen him being born and the other he had founded himself.

"Hey, I'm talking to you, you lousy interpreter! Are you going to translate?"

"He's talking about his daughter again… She was three years old, she was called…"

He pronounced the first name, commenting to himself emotionally, "It's a beautiful name."

"What's all this crap about a name? I can't understand what you're muttering…"

The interpreter repeated the dead girl's name, making sure he articulated it more carefully, like a schoolboy. Chilled by the strange scene taking place before his eyes, Mathieu rubbed his temple nervously. He recognised in his unsettled stomach the signs of the nauseating pity that sometimes overcame him by surprise, like an enemy waiting in ambush, when he was tormenting a suspect, so that he had to slink pathetically out of the interrogation room at the first excuse. He would have liked to have been brave enough to step forward, in a selfish, protective reaction, and put his arms around the shoulders of the man who was raging and lamenting the loss of his two families. Maybe – the idea seemed obscene at first because this man was an Arab, and then not so obscene after all – maybe if he shared the man's mourning for his family, he might mourn his own family that he had loved so little, to the point of cutting his mother to the quick and falling out with his father for good… For the first time in a long while he felt an intense pain in his chest and a nostalgia for the world before he went into the army, before the torture and its base works, before this system of military obedience that was so handy for escaping individual infamy.

"Come on, you idiot, I couldn't care less what the girl's name is! Ask this arsehole," the head of the unit screamed, "why he's come and stuck his oar in if he hasn't got any information for us!"

In his rage, the lieutenant had forgotten that the visitor could speak French. No longer able to keep quiet, Mathieu whispered as neutrally as he could: "Sir, the witness isn't a witness. He's made up a story just so he could get close enough to identify one of his family's murderers."

The officer's small, blue eyes looked daggers at him, as if to say: "*What's this got to do with you?*" before, wide with frustration, they turned to the so-called informer.

"I… I… How dare you? You bastard, you think the army's got time to waste on your personal quest for vengeance! I don't give a damn if someone bumped off your father and mother, or how many hairs you've got on your arse. What I expected was information about the rebels, you son of a…"

Crimson-faced by now, the lieutenant advanced towards the young man and threw a punch at him, followed by a kick when the man collapsed to the floor. Slightly put out by having lost his cool in front of the privates, the lieutenant wiped his brow with a handkerchief.

"Consider yourself lucky just to get punched, you little shit, because it might have crossed my mind that you were – who knows? – an informer sent by the *fells* to see if their man had caved in or not! Now get this liar out of here!"

Then, turning to the prisoner as if he was telling him a secret, he said, "So, my lovely little faggot, seen what you've gone and done? Now you've really got it coming. You're not a prisoner of war, just some second-rate murderer who's cost us a lot of time. I'm sick and tired of you, so now the fun's really going to start and if you haven't talked by the time the fun's stopped, well, too bad, I'll make sure I shut you up for good, with or without orders from HQ!"

And, pointing his index finger upwards, he enjoined them to hang the rebel from one of the hooks on the ceiling.

Before dawn the next day, having asked the prisoner if he still wanted to die (and the man, incapable of speaking, nodded almost incredulously at this godsend), Mathieu dressed him and then led him out of the camp in full view. The courtyard was still empty and the stunned sentry asked him where he was going this early with the battered Arab prisoner who had to lean on his shoulder.

"To the wadi," replied Mathieu, casually readjusting the strap of a haversack containing civilian clothes. "The lieutenant hasn't got enough fuel for his morning coffee. He ordered me to fetch some with a little help from... our old friend here."

"Fuel, sergeant?"

"Come on, soldier. What do you make a fire with in the countryside?"

"Oh!" said the sentry in embarrassment, finally grasping the allusion to 'fire' duty. "Erm... Watch out for yourself, sergeant, it's still dark and there's some dangerous cover here."

The young squaddie's tone was hesitant and perhaps even slightly disapproving.

"Thanks," Mathieu replied simply, suddenly brimming with affection for the last French soldier in whose eyes he wasn't yet a traitor.

He fought a stupid temptation to explain himself, then just said, "Watch out for yourself too, soldier. Think of your loved ones; there's no point dying too soon."

Aziz gazes wide-eyed at the man who is suggesting that he knows his daughter's kidnapper and that all this horror might be somehow connected to the distant past.

He is about to get up and grab the old man by the collar to make him cough up more than the scraps he has revealed until now when his phone starts to vibrate.

Mathieu sees him tense up and reach for his pocket.

"The phone?" he whispers in a very old voice.

Aziz rushes to the bathroom. He shuts the door carefully before opening his mobile phone and at the same time turning on the cold tap.

"Is that you, Aziz?"

"Yes."

"Are you all right?"

Aziz feels the same icy pick driving into his chest. He feels like sinking to his knees and begging; he feels his whole body turning into a mountain that is suddenly about to crumble.

"So have you done my little errand?"

"Errand? Um… yes."

"You took the photo?"

"Yes."

"Send it to me now."

"But I don't have a telephone number…"

The voice burst into a high-pitched laugh – ridiculous, thinks the father in terror.

"Oh yes you do, my boy. Take a look at your screen."

Aziz holds the telephone up to look at the luminous rectangle. On it, instead of the 'Caller unknown' message he was expecting to find, are displayed the nine figures of an Algerian telephone number.

"Don't get too excited, my friend. I'll only use this number once. I've already told you: there's no shortage of anonymous chips in this country. Anyway, if you tip the police off in any way, your daughter will go straight to the paradise reserved for murder victims after some, let's say, *special* treatment in this hell on earth of which I am a humble servant."

"I want to talk to my daughter," said Aziz.

His throat is so tight that he is afraid the other man didn't hear him.

"Send me that fucking photo first!" the latter snapped back. "And stay where you are!"

"My daughter... my..."

The line went dead and Shehera's father had the very precise sensation that a vein, an artery or some vital organ had burst inside him, like an overstretched elastic band made of flesh.

After several unsuccessful attempts (Aziz realises that he has never done this operation before, since sending files from a mobile telephone is ruinously expensive in Algeria), he sees the flashing icon appear and then go out, signalling that the photograph has been successfully sent.

He only has to wait a couple of minutes – interminable though they are, as he now has a stomach ache, unbearable colic pains – until his telephone vibrates again. This time the screen displays the usual 'Caller unknown'.

"Nice photo, very expressive. Who is it?"

"A neighbour."

"Can you be more specific?"

"I think he was working for the army. An informer, or a hired man, something like that."

"So you've performed a good deed there and certainly done society a favour. One small criticism, though: I would have preferred an innocent person. The sacrifice is so much more precious when the person's thoroughly innocent, the genuine article. Can you imagine for a second sacrificing a depraved pig at Eid rather than an angelic sheep? Having said that, I do like the photo of your victim a lot, *but... but...*"

Aziz can sense the man savouring the feel of the word *but* on his tongue, first holding it up against his palate like a sweet, before turning it to spit.

"*But* nothing tells me that you were the one who carried out the job... that this photo hasn't been taken from the Internet, for example.

Eh? In all seriousness, what proof do I have that you are really the creator of this, let's say, work of art?"

The kidnapper let out a short, amused laugh. In his terror, Aziz hears himself – but it's so obscene it can't possibly be him! – protesting in a profoundly shocked voice: "*But I'm honest, I am! I swear that I killed that man! I fulfilled my part of the deal…*"

Silence followed. Aziz crushed the sweaty phone against his ear, hoping to make out the man's breathing – and maybe his mood. In vain. He turned the tap to halt the sound of running water.

"If I say I did it, then I did it!" Aziz implores. "You're not going to tell me I've murdered a man for nothing? I want my daughter…"

He is struggling not to cry.

"I," the cursed voice suddenly intones, "am not *honest*. I do not have to keep my word, I can lie if I feel like it. Or churn out little slices of truth and boil them in acid before forcing every last one of them down your throat, if I so wish."

Aziz is bent over the washbasin. The man's cheerfulness terrifies him.

"You claim that you've obeyed me, and I'm not saying that you've disobeyed me. It's just that that's no longer enough. There is no deal between us, my friend, only obligations for you. I am your God and you are my subject. Maybe it's a whim, but then God is whimsical."

Aziz feels like lumps of flesh are sticking to his tongue, weighing it down as it attempts the curious exercise of trying to convince a total nutter to see a little sense.

"Silence gives consent, my dear Aziz. So get ready to make me another gift."

"Another gift?"

"Yes. Now that you've got a taste for it, you're going to kill someone else for me."

"Kill someone else? But that's impossible! No way… I don't want to go through something that awful ever again… Money – do you want money? We'll sell everything we have. Even my parents-in-law are ready to sell their flat."

"Money? You think I'd have gone to these lengths to get your wretched money? You insult me and now you're grumbling too. No way you'll kill someone else? Oh well… oh well…"

He puffed.

"Don't hang up whatever you do!" he ordered. "Give me just a few seconds, my shitty old friend who refuses to make me a tiny little gift!"

Aziz feels as if he is experiencing a series of nightmares stacked in the opposite order to Russian nesting dolls, each matryoshka giving birth to a worse nightmare than the one before.

"Can you hear me?"

He feels his hair suddenly stand on end, like a multitude of needles stabbing into his skull.

"Da… Da… ow… are… you li… ste… ahh… ning?"

It is Shehera, her voice almost unrecognisable, spitting out her words like splinters.

"…He's hol… ding a kni… fe… oww… to my thro… at… Dad… he… lp… He's go… ing to… kill… me…"

"I can hear you, my love, but not very well. (He is trying to convince himself that his good-for-nothing brain is misinterpreting his daughter's moans!) How are you? Are your fingers…?"

"Funny questions you're asking!" the man shouts into the phone. "Allow me to describe the situation to you. Your daughter is lying tied up on the floor, and I'm kneeling on her belly holding a knife to her throat. The knife is as sharp as can be and it's already made a mark. My word, I can see a few droplets of blood peeking through. If your sweet kid were to move or even so much as fart, my knife would plunge into her throat like sliding into a pat of butter. So, if you choose not to say *yes, yes, yes* immediately to all my demands, your daughter's life will cease this very instant, my fucking moron friend. Is that clear?"

"Yes, yes, yes," Aziz whispers, floundering in the horror of it all. "Take the knife away, for the love of all that is most sacred to you, I beg you… Sorry, sorry… She's only a child…"

He clings to the washbasin, choking on his sobs.

"Stop snivelling. You sound like a barrel of tears. And don't talk about sacred – nothing is sacred on this planet! You're checkmate, matey, checkmate like no one has ever been before, and even God, the greatest chess player in the universe, can't do anything about that. So, are we agreed? You do as I say and your daughter's life will be saved."

"Yes."

"Here we go then. You will kill someone for me by tomorrow morning."

"Another stranger? I can't do it! It's... it's so hard... And I'll never have time to find someone!... It's dark and..."

"Who said this one's going to be hard to find? The first one was so you'd get the hang of it, in a word so you'd learn to dirty your hands with another man's blood. I wanted to initiate you, like they initiated novice maquisards who wanted to join the FLN during the war. This time I'll make your job easy for you, so you won't have to go on a random hunt. I want you to kill your father-in-law."

"What? My father-in-law? Mathieu? He's never done anything to me..."

"Are you refusing to do it?"

The man must have pressed down on the blade, for Shehera let out a high-pitched whine.

"No!" moaned her father. "Stop!"

"Will you do it? Say *yes* clearly!"

"Yes... yes... But why... why my father-in-law? He's so *old*, so *useless*..."

"Ask him... before you do away with him, of course. If his memory's as good as mine, maybe he'll explain."

"He knows you?"

"Ha ha, would you like to know? Torture him – he'll tell you everything eventually."

"What are you gibbering on about? Torture him? You're... you're..."

"Hey, shut that sewer mouth of yours before your daughter pays the price! But before that, apologise – fast."

"Sorry... sorry."

He clicked his tongue against the roof of his mouth in satisfaction.

"Actually, we're having some fun, you and me. One day you'll tell me how you went about killing your first victim. Did he cry for mercy? Did he lie dying for long? Were you really scared? And did remorse come crashing down on you like a mountain of garbage? I'm dying to hear you hold forth on the subject of the torments of remorse now you're a specialist! Unfortunately, neither you nor I are really in the mood for talking right now. Work comes first, eh? Talk to you tomorrow morning then, Aziz. But take care not to get nicked by the police. A guy like you would need to keep a stock of Ventolin in one of our jails..."

"Ventolin?" squeaked the father. "But I'm not asthmatic."

"I know, my boy. Asthmatics use Ventolin because it dilates the vessels in the lungs. In jail, Ventolin is used to enlarge the anus of rebellious types like you to make them more *hospitable*, if you see what I mean. So don't get yourself nabbed by the cops, especially as it would also spell death for missie here. It's one of the basic laws of nature: you can carry on living with your fingers cut off; you can't if your throat is in the same state. OK?… *OK?*"

"OK," Aziz agreed in his most servile voice. "Just don't touch Shehera."

"I'm not bluffing, young man. I even bet you'd be horrified to learn how little I actually have to lose in this. Do you want me to prove it?"

"No… please."

"Good, so you've seen reason."

In the mirror in front of him the father contemplates a grey, diabolically ugly face that is petrified by his fear of the kidnapper's mad verbal outpourings. *This is the face I will have when I am just a corpse*, he has time to remark before his interlocutor utters some strange words that, this time, bear no trace of boastfulness or mockery: "I like you, brother, I really like you. You've brought meaning back to my life."

"Pass me my daughter, please. Just one word."

"No. All that would do is unsettle you even more and waste our time. Well, I'll be off. Keep your spirits up, my friend."

The father stands there motionlessly with the phone stuck to his ear. The line has been dead for several seconds already. The connections between his neurones seem to have gone dead too; there is not the slightest twitch of the slightest emotion…

…apart, that is, from the germ of a question. A black swirl of a question approaching from the distant horizon of his closed eyes…

And afterwards? What else will you demand of me?

He raises his hand to his forehead; he has fallen into his own ambush. *And meanwhile*, the monstrous wormlike thing introducing the idea of killing his father-in-law is set in motion, crawling and sniffing its way through the winding passages of his brain, surprised, though not unduly, at the new task being asked of it!

"My daughter," he now groans, "my daughter."

Tipsy without having drunk, the man tries to take a step forward before toppling over, just managing to catch hold of the tap in time. Someone knocks on the bathroom door and implores him: "Open the door, Aziz. Open up."

"Aziz, your wife needs you. She's in a complete panic."

Mathieu pretends not to notice the red eyes of the man who opens the bathroom door to him.

"Wash your face, put a comb through your hair, and come and join us."

Aziz takes his wife in his arms. Meriem's whole body is trembling. Her breasts touch Aziz's chest, transmitting some of her warmth to him. He reflects that this woman is the most wonderful thing in his life. Then, as though his heart had been fitted with a pain gauge, he wonders which gradation the needle of suffering would reach were he to lose Meriem.

She stares her husband straight in the eye, but her overly dilated pupils do not appear to see him. It looks as if a vital part of her soul were escaping through these dark holes.

She stammers, "I'm sure he's killing her at the moment... Dead... our daughter..."

Barely able to choke back his tears, Aziz pats her on the back.

"No, she's alive... You'll see, she'll come through this... she's alive..."

She tries to struggle free.

"Don't treat me like a half-wit! You don't know a thing about it... You... you... my God... I can't believe what's happening to us... And you... you've done nothing... for our daughter..."

Pushing Aziz away as if he were giving off some pestilential stench, she moans, "You're twiddling your thumbs in the kitchen while our daughter is being... is being..."

With a stifled gasp, she breaks free of her husband's embrace. She throws him one last hostile, disgusted glance. For a few seconds he stands there stupidly, his arms stretched out in front of him, his brows knit in disbelief, gradually overwhelmed by anger and a fresh wave of utter despair.

Mathieu holds out a glass to his daughter-in-law.

"Drink it. It's just a sedative," her mother insists, "it'll help you cope. I'm going to take some as well."

Meriem shrugs, muttering that she doesn't need a sedative before finally giving in to her mother's request. Draining her glass, she bursts into tears.

"Come here, my love," the old woman implores her, "you're shattered, you haven't slept since yesterday. Mathieu will wake us up if there's any news."

"We need to have a chat, you and me. But first of all, forgive your wife, Aziz. She doesn't know, she can't imagine for a second what you've had to do to save her daughter." Mathieu has taken him decisively by the arm and leads him back into the kitchen. The older man watches the younger man with a certain indifference. "So you, my lad, are the instrument of fate?" he thinks with dark irony that triggers a shooting pain in his ribcage. He lights a cigarette, inhales a first drag, then a second, before deciding that it is time to finish things off and that the end of the world might as well begin in an ordinary kitchen with Formica fittings.

"It was really tough, wasn't it?" he whispers as he stubs out his cigarette in the ashtray.

"What? What was tough?" retorts an exhausted and bad-tempered Aziz. "You mean my daughter's kidnapping? Or my wife's grief? Think it could've been easy, do you?"

"No, of course not. I'm talking about the person… you were forced to kill…"

Aziz started as if he'd been bitten by a dog.

"What are you talking about, you old fool? I… I… Is it old age? Couldn't find any better time to come out with such tripe?"

His son-in-law's surprise is pretty well acted, but his facial expression, once the initial stupefaction – and the very real contraction of fear – has faded, is so false that Mathieu knows he isn't mistaken. Exhausted from guessing correctly, he sighs, "There's no point denying it, Aziz. Don't worry, I'm not the police. And keep your voice down too – the women might hear us."

"But I… I haven't killed anyone… How dare you accuse me? In my own home, as well!"

With a somewhat disdainful smile, Mathieu waits for his son-in-law's protests to cease.

"In any case, Aziz, he's asked me to do the same."

"What? He asked you to… to kill someone too?"

Mathieu would cry with laughter if he didn't feel instead like drowning in a lake of tears instead – his son-in-law's amazement is so comical! What's more, he's completely given himself away with that *too*.

"Why stop when things are going so well? As it so happens, he's ordered me to kill someone you know well."

"Who?"

"You."

"Oh?"

Aziz no longer bothers to fake surprise. Slumping down into a chair, he pulls Mathieu's cigarette packet towards him and fiddles with it for a few seconds.

"He demands that I kill you by tomorrow morning, Mathieu."

"Oh?" the father-in-law simply says, unwittingly adopting the Algerian's tone of voice and exclamation.

"I'll stab you, then you kill me before breathing your last. Or the other way round? Or should we arrange it so we stick our knives in each other's bellies at exactly the same time? That lunatic must be having a whale of a time."

He takes out a cigarette and studies the end of it far too closely.

"I've got to kill you, Mathieu, and of course I can't kill you. But if I don't carry out his orders, he'll cut my daughter's head off. He's already amputated several of her fingers."

"I know, Aziz. He told me over the phone… to put me off disobeying him. I've got to kill you too, Aziz. I'm much fonder of Shehera than you think. She's my granddaughter, even if you won't accept that."

"Can you imagine the horror of it, Mathieu? Cutting off a teenage girl's fingers as she screams in terror and pain? No child is born to go through an ordeal like that."

The father studies the old man as if he were short-sighted.

"He suggested that you'd be able to explain why he's attacking us. According to him, you only needed not to have completely lost your memory. I'm convinced now that he's nothing to do with those GIA killers. It looks as if he's operating on his own and he doesn't act like a kidnapper who's in this for a ransom. Just now you let slip that you might have something to do with the kidnapping, but you've been beating around the bush ever since. Out with it: is there any truth to his ramblings? But please, nothing melodramatic about the Algerian war. Right now, I don't give a fuck about the Algerian war and its atrocities, its litany of bloody heroes and traitors. Get straight to the point: is there some connection between you and this criminal?"

He insisted sarcastically, "Cut to the chase, no mucking about. Maybe it'll make things clearer? You and I have some decisions to take. Before tomorrow morning, if you recollect."

Mathieu feels his chest contract once more. The old pump for circulating the blood is obviously complaining. With one hand resting tensely on his leg, the ex-soldier holds his breath until the biting pain in his plexus has faded.

"Well, this bastard is convinced that Tahar killed his whole family... I mean, not on his own, but along with other FLN maquisards when they took Melouza in 1957 and massacred most of the villagers."

The Algerian opens his eyes wide in astonishment.

"Tahar, Meriem's father, was a murderer? Were there any children among the victims?"

"No... yes... no... yes..."

Mathieu beseeches him – he would lie face down on the floor if he dared: "Just give me a little time to explain."

Aziz cuts him off in the same ghostly voice. "And why's he after you?"

"I saved Tahar's life..."

"The life of a murderer, right? Didn't you have anything better to do?"

"Listen to me, please. I promise you it's not that simple."

The whining inflexion of the words that come out of his mouth strikes him as grotesque, but another inner voice makes the stupid objection: *But Aziz, if I hadn't saved Tahar, you wouldn't have married his daughter!*

The father gets up from his chair with a look of total defeat.

"The kidnapper lost his whole family. He has the life of my daughter in his hands, but that probably isn't enough for him. How many of his people were killed? I guess that's all he's being doing for the last fifty years, counting and recounting his dead! And you want me to listen to you? So you can explain what? That the rest of my family could well die because of some fucking atrocity half a century ago?"

The old man grabs his son-in-law's arm.

"Hang on, Aziz. I am… *ready*."

The Algerian shakes off his arm brusquely.

"Ready for what?"

Listen first, boy. The eagle of ultimate misery swoops down on the Breton fisherman's son, who now knows that the thread of his life will definitely be severed before morning. *Listen to me, the Tahar you knew was no murderer. Or, if he was, then he paid a high price for it. I, however, was – a murderer or worse – and I have yet to pay for it.*

The father turns to Mathieu and the malicious expression on his lips shows fairly clearly that he is exasperated by the hangdog look on the face of the man who has claimed to be 'ready' and has since been silent. A magnificent grey moth that has somehow got into the kitchen flutters about between the two men for an instant. For the briefest of moments Aziz's thoughts are taken up with the zigzagging of the moth, before returning to his father-in-law.

Right now he feels intense hatred for this man who has, in one way or another, brought misfortune upon their home.

"Ready for what, Mathieu?"

Mathieu can still feel the scalding tears lodged in the back of his eye-sockets. Shehera's father wouldn't understand. Maybe it would be better not to tell him anything? After all, tomorrow it will all be over for Mathieu, and whatever he might or might not have been fifty years ago will no longer matter. The old man is convinced that the game is up, that the end of the world – his little world, the only one that counts – is nigh.

So what is the point of all this? He has read somewhere that knowing the meaning of life does not at all help human beings to survive and that evolution, with faultless internal logic, has wasted no time making up for this flaw. Maybe it even sensibly gave up after a few trials revealed the self-destructive force of such knowledge? The old man feels like sniggering at his philosophical pretensions even as fear is swelling his prostate painfully once more, but he manages only to emit a sorry sigh.

"Aziz, listen to me. In a former life I tortured people. And one of them was Tahar."

He nibbles at his lower lip, preparing himself for his humiliating confession.

"My friend Tahar."

His son-in-law stares at him, as he expected, in amazement tinged with repugnance. Then, as if this surprising idea had only just crossed his mind, Mathieu sticks his hand in his jacket pocket and takes out an object wrapped carefully in a handkerchief.

"It's a pistol. A 9 millimetre, loaded. It's ancient; the trigger's stiff, the hammer's even stiffer, but otherwise it works fine. I'll show you how to use it, but listen to me first, please…"

And the old ape finally told the young ape the truth.

At first Tahar was scared, thinking that the walk would be nothing but the inevitable and classic 'fire' duty. Could it be anything else, when the soldier ordering him to dive into the bushes was the very same that had tortured him in every possible fashion? Mathieu had understood from his prisoner's submissive attitude that the man was preparing to die, although that didn't stop him feeling terrified.

"Get a move on or they'll catch us! We've got to make it to the wadi and into the forest before they sound the alarm."

Despite his chattering teeth, Tahar had reacted angrily.

"You think I'm falling for that one? Not satisfied with shooting me like a dog, you want the Arab to put on a funny act for you as well? Do your duty as a soldier and let's get it over with."

The headquarters was still in sight. Mathieu's heart was beating so hard that black dots appeared in front of his eyes. He too was scared to death.

"You stupid idiot! I'm not going to kill you, I'm trying to save your life!"

The emaciated and bruised face tautened with contempt.

"Why would you do that for me? I didn't talk when you shoved a bottle up my arse and crushed my balls in a vice. And now you're hoping that I'm going to spill the beans because of lies so ridiculous even a child would spit in your face? I'm not moving. I'll die here – this is as good a place as any."

The man hurled an Arabic insult at him, then, indifferent to the thorns, sat down in the bushes.

"Shoot, arsehole! I'm tired and anyway you won't be killing much of a man."

Eyes closed and shoulders hunched, he waited for the shot to come. The soldier's panic grew. If this Arab prick didn't get up straight away, the soldiers would find them in no time. He was under no illusions as to what would happen to him. His boss's rage at one of his best men's treachery would be so great that he would dish him up everything in his arsenal: electricity, water-boarding, the bottle in the anus, and finally, if the DOP didn't finish him off, there'd be a military tribunal, prison and doubtless execution for going over to the enemy.

He wasn't an Arab! He wasn't supposed to be tortured!

A taste of limitless despair welled up in his throat. For a few seconds he considered killing the Arab; he could always pretend there had been an attempt to intimidate him, a sham execution gone wrong. His officer would be furious, obviously, and would discipline a subordinate who had shown such disastrous independence of mind, but the matter would probably stop there.

What was he doing freeing this prisoner? This guy was the worst kind of murderer. He himself, as a well-regarded soldier, had never been on the receiving end; was he now going to risk his career because of a few spasms of a guilty conscience?

Get a grip on yourself, ordered a voice stationed on the threshold of his conscience, *you've already made up your mind!* A part of Mathieu objected that his conscience could go to hell. Another, just as horrified, claimed that it was too late to turn back and that, even if he put a bullet in the *fell*'s head, the Alsatian would suspect treachery; and having electrodes attached to your balls must hurt like hell…

The soldier wavered between these two thoughts. Then, as arbitrarily as though he'd decided on the toss of a coin, he put the barrel of the gun to the Arab's temple.

I'm going to kill this man? Mathieu wondered in astonishment. The prisoner curled up on himself. He was breathing noisily, like a diver preparing to suck in as much oxygen as possible before going down.

What do we swim in when we're dead? a stunned Mathieu asked himself.

"Hey, do you hear me? he said, tapping the prisoner softly on the temple with the gun barrel as if knocking on a door. "Hey matey, look at me!"

The intrigued Arab opened his eyelids. He was panting with the effort of controlling his fear. His haggard cheeks aged him, but he was probably not much older than himself, the soldier guessed. *Deep down, I must be just as much of a bloody yellowbelly as this wog,* he acknowledged, sickened at finding a resemblance with a creature he so disdained. *And I mean to redeem myself by saving this bastard? What if all he does in return is cut my throat?*

No, he couldn't be making such a stupid mistake! He turned his gaze towards the forest, then back towards HQ. Dawn was already daubing the sky with an orange glow.

"Fuck it!" he muttered, once again changing his mind. Dry-mouthed, he stared into the Arab's flickering pupils, which said both *"Kill me, I entreat you!"* and *"Don't kill me, for the love of…"*

Resignedly he removed the magazine from its housing and held it out to the prisoner.

"Why?"

"So you trust me…"

"I don't trust you or anyone else."

"You don't have any choice. Either that or they recapture you. You heard the officer, so you know what to expect."

The man tried a mocking smile, but pain transformed it into a grimace.

"What about you? Do you have any choice?"

Mathieu got angry.

"Are you going to take the magazine or not?"

"Give me your pistol instead!" the prisoner suggested with the same incredulous scorn.

The Frenchman glanced towards headquarters, then handed over his gun.

"But I'm keeping the magazine. In the meantime…"

"You've got another gun? I bet you're hiding another gun."

"No," Mathieu retorted, too quickly.

The man clambered awkwardly to his feet. He weighed the gun in his hand before muttering, his voice full of regret: "You don't want to kill me anymore?"

"No. I almost did just now. I changed my mind."

"Why? Did the Archangel Gabriel order you to love Arabs?"

"That's none of your business, wanker. Now get moving or they'll catch us."

"Where are we going?" scoffed the Algerian. "I'm in a bad state. I won't be able to run or even walk for long. My balls have swollen to the size of watermelons. I feel like screaming whenever I move, my cock is falling apart and the soles of my feet aren't much better. You are aware… erm… of all the kindnesses you and your friends showered on me."

"We get out of here, then we'll see."

"You want me to lead the Frenchman who tortured me to our men?"

"You mean the *fells* from your *katiba*?"

"I think you mean the *FLN fighters*," the prisoner suggested, stressing every syllable, his face suddenly bare of all expression.

"No, I definitely don't want you leading me to your… to *them*," cried the deserter, unable to conceal his fear. "We get away from HQ, we reach the road under cover and then, when the time's right, good day, goodbye, we separate and clear off in different directions."

"You're setting me free only to split up so soon?" the prisoner said sarcastically, his face still every bit as closed. "Arabs may be thick, but even a donkey might start wondering about you! You need me in order to quit the army, is that what you'd have me believe?"

He spoke calmly, rolling his 'r's a lot and rubbing his wrists where the rope he'd been hung up by had left deep, ugly weals.

"Look at these wounds – you almost took my arms off! Your offer makes no sense. Why would you run the slightest risk for me when you've tortured me for days on end? Where's the catch? Are you trying to obtain through cunning what you couldn't through beating?"

The man eyed him with quiet hatred. The sergeant's voice was supposed to sound scathing, but started to quaver as the insult hit home.

"You're like the plague victim's turd laughing at the pool of piss under the guy who caught cholera! After what you did in Mechta Kasbah, a shit like you isn't really in any position to lecture people, wouldn't you say?"

The *fell* shook his head sombrely, but it wasn't clear whether he was agreeing or not. Then he uttered an unexpected sound – a kind of furious "Heuh!" – before spitting on the ground. For a couple of seconds, Mathieu was about to hit this native who was making fun of him with impunity; he had beaten him so often that it felt almost unfair not to be able to thrash him anymore.

"Watch it, mate. You think too much for someone who deserves to be flushed down the toilets of a brothel."

Still holding the empty pistol in his right hand, the prisoner unwittingly puckered up his lips as if tasting the spice of the strange fate his former torturer had presented him with.

Mathieu lost his temper. "There is no catch – I swear on my mother's life! I've brought along some civilian clothes. If you want to be free, you should put them on…"

He had sworn on his mother's life for the first time ever! *I'm going nuts!* he thought. Trembling with anger and incomprehension at himself, Mathieu opened his haversack to get out the clothes. He just had time to notice his ex-prisoner's raised arm. Something exploded in his skull and he fell, first to his knees and then face down on the ground.

A cracking of branches roused him abruptly from unconsciousness. He spat out the dirt and small stones soiling his mouth.

"Ow!" he went, putting one hand to his temple, but stifled a second cry of pain. How long had he been unconscious? The soldiers sent out from HQ to look for them must be hiding in the bushes; they would have heard him shout out!

How am I going to explain myself? God, they're going to tear me to pieces! he screamed silently, curling up in terror. His head was aching horribly. Mathieu cursed with all his soul the strange outbreak of scruples that had driven him to release an inmate he had tortured for so long. Now it was his turn to shit his pants!

"Hey?"

The voice behind the bush called out to him in a chillingly ironic tone: "Get up, idiot! And just so you know, I've put *your* magazine in *your* pistol! Come on, hurry up, your friends will be here any moment…"

"I… It's…"

Eyes still wide, the soldier brought up the sleeve of his jacket to wipe his lips without thinking.

"Yes, it's me, the disfigured freak! Biting the dust, are we? Ah, I almost forgot that you loved Algeria so much now you'd like to eat it! Come on, let's get going. Actually, the good thing about having a hostage is – that you could come in useful if the patrol catches up with us."

The words spilled out of Mathieu's mouth. "They'll… they'll kill us both."

Then, as if embarrassed by such a spontaneous expression of his fear, he said, "The captain must have realised – he's not a jerk like me. He'll definitely ask for a commando party to be sent out."

For a short moment a hint of uncertainty veiled the Algerian's gaze.

"All right then, you'll be my justification for my own people."

"Meaning?"

"I… I left them in a bit of a hurry, without having really received permission."

"You're a traitor to the FLN?"

"No, but the tendency is to regard you as one until there's proof of the contrary! You're my ticket home – coming back with a *gaouri* from the colonial intelligence services can't do me any harm. You must know a few things, eh? At least the names of traitors from our side…"

"But then I… they'll…"

"I very much hope they'll…"

The *fell* let out a long, apparently gleeful chuckle, but his eyes took no part in it. He mimicked several instruments: a whip, a nail wrench, a soldering iron.

"Yes, they'll… you, then they'll… you and even… you…. If need be I'll give them a few ideas about how an experienced French army torturer goes about making someone talk. And then, when the fun is over, we'll post your bollocks to that fine DOP captain you admire so much."

"But you can't… I set you free…"

"Set me free, did you? After making me drink bucketfuls of water mixed with disinfectant and urine? Get walking, you son of a bitch. One wrong move and I'll put a bullet up your arse. Wouldn't make a pretty sight, comrade. Your shit would mix in with your blood, infect your intestine or your stomach, and you'd suffer for many long hours, days even, of agony before dying of gangrene. By that time, you'd have been stripped to the bone by jackals or wild boar. Because they are allowed to eat pig!"

The farcical flight of the battered torturer and the murderer twisted by this land of distrust is how Mathieu would describe, much later, their several days of wandering through a landscape of thorny undergrowth furrowed by almost waterless wadis where, without admitting it, they hid from both the French military and the local peasants. The latter might just as easily have turned out to be allies of the FLN maquisards as relatives of the victims of Melouza hell-bent on vengeance. Not to mention the zealous *harkis* or the even more numerous and unpredictable 'neutrals', who were quite capable of turning you in to someone, anyone… Any of these had excellent reasons for eliminating them in a way that was par for this war – in other words: as hideously as possible.

Mathieu very soon realised that Tahar didn't know the area any better than he did. They passed some shepherds who didn't see them – or pretended not to see them, which was very much the role of a lookout. They were very fortunate when some French soldiers just missed them. A helicopter passed overhead, but they hid under some jujube trees in time. The Frenchman, still in his fatigues, walked in front of the Algerian.

Tahar was showing signs of exhaustion towards the end of the first day. Mathieu guessed that they were probably deep in rebel territory where the army only deployed commando parties and air support. His companion's eyes kept falling shut with fatigue and pain before opening again to search around haggardly for his prisoner. They rested as best they could (Tahar balanced the gun on his knees with his finger on the trigger!) in the shade of a copse of ash trees lost in thorny scrubland that announced the sheltering forest they could make out on the horizon. They hadn't eaten since dawn, and the little water they had found in a wadi crevice was but a maddening memory. Running his tongue over his desperately parched lips, Mathieu cursed himself for not having brought either a canteen or any food with him, even though he knew that kind of clobber would have aroused the sentry's suspicion. The old and new prisoners exchanged very few words, the former contenting himself with a waggle of his chin to convey his orders. Only once did Mathieu beg him, "Take me back to the road; I saved your life!" All his guard granted him was an indifferent glance.

In late afternoon they ran into a cork harvester perched on his donkey. As if it were a normal occurrence to meet a swollen-faced native with his gun trained on a French soldier with a bloody forehead, the peasant greeted them ceremoniously and went on his way without looking round.

"Hey, call him back. Maybe that bloke has something to eat or drink in his bag. I've got some money on me, remember?" Mathieu asked, raising his voice, driven to distraction by his companion's silence. "This can't go on. We're dying of hunger and thirst!"

"We're carrying on. He'll report us!"

They upped the pace heading west, only stopping when they reached the cover of some cork oaks at dusk. Finding their way by the croaking of the frogs, they came to a pool which, despite the vile-looking water, struck them as a miracle of nature. They gathered together some mealy acorns, which Mathieu reluctantly swallowed for want of anything better. Busy chomping on the large seeds with his back against a tree trunk and the pistol flung down at his feet, Tahar didn't seem to be watching his hostage as closely as before. The bucolic, almost fraternal nature of the scene, beneath an unreal moon, plunged the Frenchman into a stupor. Had he really tortured the man who was now nibbling away just as melancholically as he at these acorns, which were bound to give them both diarrhoea before long? And this Arab, whose expression occasionally segued into utter despondency, and who was deep in thought at that moment, twiddling a blade of grass between his fingers; could he really have murdered teenagers? Were they not like Robinson Crusoe and Man Friday on a virgin island, miraculously deprived of everything and especially of the memory of their crimes?

"Own up to something for once," Mathieu exclaimed, spitting out the fibrous bits to escape this feeling that was seriously bothering him, "you're just as scared that there might be some maquisards around, aren't you? What kind of filth have you been up to make you so afraid of your brothers from the ALN?"

Tahar studied him maliciously.

"You've made a fair bit of progress since this morning, my boy; you're saying ALN now instead of *fellagha*! Another blow with a rifle butt and you'll forget those '*sand niggers*' and '*rats*' you've showered me with… Maybe the mountain air will go to your head and you'll forget that you even tortured me?"

The brown eyes stared intently at him – different eyes from those that had blinked in terror when he was in the DOP's hands. (*More intelligent*, Mathieu realised with horror before thinking, unaware of his own irony: *You little wog, you speak French far too well to be completely trustworthy!*)

"What do you expect? That I'm going to forget that you wrecked my body and soul, all because you helped me escape? You fucked me with bottles, made me swallow my own shit and piss, and now you want to chat to me as if we were in some Moorish café in Constantine? Or maybe you think you're some kind of inverse Christ figure? You beat someone and then forgive the person you've beaten. But I haven't asked you for anything!"

He stood up, clenching his fists. Close by, perched in the upper branches like some sinister bystander, a crow croaked away like a saw.

"Why did you set me free anyway? You think I'm just a child-killer, a barbarian. Since when does anyone help someone like me? Since when does a shit like you help a shit like me? What do you expect of me? That I'm going to thank you for it as well? *Eh*? That you'll get off that lightly, *eh*?"

He had uttered these two "*ehs*" like the groan of a very old man, several tones lower than the rest of his outburst, and all the more menacing for it. The two men sized each other up for a few seconds, then Mathieu suddenly dived forwards, reaching for the pistol on the ground.

The soldier felt as if his jaw was going to explode, because Tahar had jammed his knee between the gun and his chin. Before he could even check whether it was broken, another blow, this one aimed at his lower back, sent him sprawling face down for the second time that day.

"Move so much as a finger and you're dead. Watch out: this isn't the Arab son of a bitch you demolished back at the DOP talking to you; this is the barrel of your pistol. And it's in great shape…"

He sniggered. "A real pistol from your mother country."

Tahar ordered the prisoner to take the laces out of his big army boots and then, at gunpoint, to tie his feet together.

"Pull it tight, no cheating. Now, lie down and stretch your arms out well behind you. Further."

He tied his wrists together with the second bootlace. Then he doubled the bonds around his ankles with Mathieu's belt.

It was now completely dark. The moonlight barely filtered through the thick branches. The man contemplated the figure lying at his feet and his face displayed only immense despair. He turned the captive's body over with the toe of his shoe. Neither of them could see the other's eyes.

"You and I have a problem of vocabulary, my friend."

And tearing a branch off the cork oak, he lashed Mathieu with it. The latter screamed, more in surprise than pain.

"No bawling, dickhead. Sound carries a long way round here and those ALN guys have sharp ears."

The second blow was even harder.

"The vocabulary problem is the following: I know what torture is like; you don't. You have practised it on others, but it remains – how should I say? – theoretical. I thought you needed to gain a deeper knowledge of your profession by crossing that boundary. I've decided to generously share some of my past experience with you. You'll find out that no experience is more personal. We'll make do with what we've got here – some branches and maybe some stones. When you've learnt your lesson well, we'll be on a roughly equal footing to talk about it."

After a pause, he added, "If you're still alive, of course."

He beat him all night, carefully seeking out the most tender areas, pulling down the prisoner's trousers to lash his buttocks, then his genitals. When Mathieu, unable to stand the pain any longer, started screaming in a voice that was so distorted it could have been a woman's, Tahar gagged him.

"Answer my question," panted the Algerian with tear-soaked spite. "Is my beating worse than the ones you and those DOP fuckers of yours dealt me? If you don't tell me the exact truth, I promise that I will break open your skull here and now and piss on the brains spilling out of it! So answer by nodding your goddamn fucking head: Is this blow… (Mathieu had huddled up, but the branch caught him on the testicles)… Hurts, does it?… But do you think it hurts more than electrodes on your ears or having your nails ripped out with pliers? Don't be selfish. Don't just think about your own pain; think about what my pain was like when you really let yourselves go. If you're not truthful, that's too bad for you – I'll crush your head with a stone!"

A vile terror gripped Mathieu when he forced himself to nod his head in denial.

"I'll carry on then!"

Stifling his sobs, Tahar went back to his methodical work, letting out *Hah!* and *Heh!* noises like a lumberjack and moans of pain when too sudden a movement revived the injuries the DOP had inflicted on him.

Blows rained down on the prisoner, and Mathieu, haggard now and urinating under him without even noticing it, had the impression that an unbelievable multitude of creatures were screaming inside his head, each of them voicing a different version of his pain and his fear. The focus of this fear was the *fell*'s sorrow, which seemed to worsen with every blow he administered. Between two grunts that drowned out his sobs, the maquisard hurled insults, most of them in Arabic, others probably in French but rendered unintelligible by rage.

An entreaty swept through Mathieu: "Dear God, I'm not a hero, prevent this murderer from killing me – I don't want to die like this! Console him; make him stop. I'm sorry, don't abandon me!"

The beating ceased at dawn. But Mathieu didn't know it. He had lost consciousness and only came to because something was tickling his face. The rodent that was sniffing at him – a kind of small field-mouse – ran off at the sight of his furiously blinking eyes. Flies were buzzing around his lips, attracted by the clots of blood.

His guard had removed his gag. *I'm going to die in a stupid bid for freedom,* he thought. *Or maybe like some low-down, rabid dog instead. I'm already laid out like a corpse and no one will ever lift me up again. Or maybe I'm already dead and this is…*

From the moisture on his cheeks he knew that it was raining. He took little superstitious sniffs to curb his own morbid prophecies: deciding that he was dead was likely to 'tempt' reality. His eyes sought out the person who had reduced him to this state. His heart skipped a beat when he caught sight of the man's legs above his head.

"Now tell me why you made me escape."

A slight breeze had got up. Leaning against a tree trunk, his voice hoarse with fatigue, the man spoke calmly.

"Are you going to finish me off?" the Frenchman asked resignedly.

"I don't know. You already stink like a corpse, but have I smashed your skull to a pulp? Have I driven a stake into your heart or up your arse? No… at least, not yet… So why are you in such a hurry to find out the future? Answer my question instead. And remember: I'm the one leading the interrogation this time, not you."

Mathieu knows that time is growing short and that these details are of no use to Aziz. But he has an almost physiological need for these confessions – the first he's ever accorded to an Algerian, with the obvious exception of his friend Tahar. As great a need, he senses, as for the pills he's been taking against heart trouble for some years.

He told the man who had beaten him everything, and that 'everything' could be summed up in one word: *shame* – irresistible, corrosive, poisonous shame.

"I realise that it's ridiculous, that it's hard to swallow, but that's how it is. Forgive me. I…"

He had stopped talking, unable to offer any reasons. A blush had come over his face, but luckily it was invisible in the darkness of the undergrowth. Tahar had listened to him in silence, with a thin, incredulous smile on his swollen face.

"So one day," he sighed, scratching his nose, "there was a *knock! knock! knock!* on the door of that torturer's head of yours. You said: *Who's there!* and someone or something answered: *It's me – morality! Can I come into your life?*"

He dissolved into a deeply insulting burst of laughter.

"You think a single good deed is enough to wipe out all the dirty things you did to those men who passed through your hands? Sounds like you know a thing or two about bookkeeping!"

A gasp of indignation shook Mathieu – and for a brief moment a mixture of anger and scorn overcame his fear.

"And you really think you're in a position to give me lessons on morals, do you, fucker? That fake informer's little girl – what was her name again?"

The man started. His face tensed instantly, as though he'd been slapped. He staggered to his feet, looked around for the pistol that had fallen from his lap, seized it and levelled it at the prisoner.

"You… you…"

His eyes raging, Tahar cocked the gun, bent a finger around the trigger and… burst out crying.

Mathieu lay there stunned. The fellow who, one minute earlier, had been prepared to shoot him without any ceremony had brought his hands up to his face to hide the tears that were streaming down his drawn cheeks.

"Hey, what's got into you?"

Tahar dried his eyes with the sleeve of what remained of his shirt, muttering something that sounded like "Leave me alone, you idiot!"

"I ne… never… wan… ted to kill anyone… I… Never… I'm not a… a…"

Mathieu felt a strange sensation – a wish to console him? – spread insidiously through him at the sight of this man who had withstood so much torture and was falling to pieces now that he seemed to be in control of the situation. He left him to cry ugly great adult tears – and realised that his own eyes were growing moist.

"That girl… I never laid eyes on her… I didn't kill any children… That's not what I joined the rebels for…"

He wiped his nose on the back of his hand. He had hung his head, keeping his finger on the trigger of the pistol.

"So who killed everyone in that *mechta* then?" muttered the Frenchman, choosing to ignore the pistol.

"That wasn't how it was supposed to turn out."

He gazed at his gun with an expression of such hatred, at once stubborn and lost, that Mathieu thought he was actually going to use it.

"The villagers were pro-MNA. Some of them refused to feed FLN fighters or wouldn't pay their dues. Others were informing the French army of our whereabouts; that kind of thing. We only meant to teach them a lesson… not kill them! That's what our leaders had assured us – that we were only going to cure them of their taste for treachery, and give them a good thrashing if need be…"

He picked up a stone and flung it at a tree.

"In any case, that's what I thought when we arrived in the *douar*."

The scene, as the old man would remember several decades later, was pretty unreal; tragic, because a human being was speaking about his part in a massacre; ridiculous, for the man who was greedily soaking up the other's confidences was lying at his feet trussed up like a sausage. Lost in the middle of a forest of cork oaks, the two associates didn't look good. One of them had tortured the other; the other had taken his revenge by beating him to a pulp all through the night. If some divine director exists, he must take great pleasure in such an unlikely reversal.

"I was a novice teacher in a hamlet on the High Plateaux. I'd been lucky for an Arab growing up in the countryside; I'd been able to go to school and then study with the white priests. I was hoping that fortune would continue to smile on me, that I could cobble together a nice future for myself, a nice house, a nice wife. The schools inspector despised Arabs and didn't have much time for me – nor I for him for that matter. I didn't show it, of course; I satisfied myself with liking my pupils and my job."

Tahar gave a sad smile.

"You see, it wasn't much. But for me, coming from where I came from, it was enormous."

He sighed, as if apologising.

"My parents' village was about sixty miles from my school. Everything was wretched there. I hated its degrading misery and even if I loved my family, I only went back to my *douar* for special occasions. That particular time, it was for my nephew's circumcision, my elder brother's first son. The day after the festivities, a group of soldiers led by a captain entered the village. They were chasing some maquisards and claimed we had sheltered them. They questioned us one by one. As we all kept silent, they undressed several men and beat them with sticks and wet rope. Then they forced them to drink salted water. The captain ordered his men to hang up the man he thought was the village chief from a beam by his foot and wrist."

Gently he stroked the bruise turning blue on his cheek.

"That chief was my father. For the first time in my life I saw this austere, white-haired, intransigent man weeping with pain and humiliation like a kid. The soldiers were laughing and I didn't have the courage to take a strong stand against it. As for my elder brother, he leapt at the captain, but a soldier stopped him in his tracks with a bullet in the thigh. The officer, mad with rage, had my brother dragged off to a rocky outcrop and pushed him over the edge."

Again his voice broke. He looked coyly in the direction of his prisoner.

"Do you have any brothers?"

"No."

"Then you certainly won't understand. That brother had protected me throughout my childhood; he turned himself in instead of me whenever I did something stupid because my father ruled us with an iron hand. How many thrashings did my brother get because of me! It was simple: I revered him; he made the sun rise for me. Up until that damned morning I was sure that I would lay down my life for him."

A cuckoo made its characteristic *coo-coo* call. The dawn had long since melted into morning.

"What did the soldiers do next?"

"Nothing, apart from dealing out a few punches and disappearing as quickly as they had appeared with threats of the same treatment the next time they patrolled."

"And you weren't maltreated by the soldiers?"

"No, probably because I was the only one in the *douar* who spoke French. Maybe, to their minds, a native schoolteacher who spoke their language was necessarily on the side of the French army…"

Tahar broke off a blade of grass and stuck it in his mouth.

"We made a formal complaint. Well… I complained, because no one in the *douar* trusted in French justice. I quickly realised that people were whispering behind my back that I was turning to the courts to make people forget my cowardliness. Hadn't they stripped and flogged my father, then killed my brother before my eyes without any sign of revolt from me? My poor mother didn't accuse me of anything, but I saw that she more or less shared their opinion. She still loved me – I had been her favourite… – but she also began to despise me a little."

Pulling the blade of grass out of his mouth, he crushed it between his fingers and then threw it away.

"Actually, they weren't wrong. I'd been paralysed with fear in front of those soldiers. And also I didn't want to lose everything – my brother, my teaching job and the minute ambitions I had devised for myself – in one go. A few months later, notwithstanding our statements and the lawyer who had relieved us of all our savings, the judges acquitted the soldiers and their captain. The worst thing was that they finally confessed, but the court didn't take that into account. According to the judges, the accused had been doing their duty."

The Algerian turned to the soldier, a bitter grimace twisting the corners of his mouth.

"That doesn't really come as a surprise to you, does it, such indulgence towards your mates?

Mathieu forced himself to keep a neutral expression. The rebel shrugged his shoulders.

"After the acquittal, I took to the *jebel*. I didn't have any choice."

His voice was full of resentment.

"Yes… neither the village nor the French left me any choice. It wasn't that I couldn't care less about liberating Algeria back then, but, well, the humiliation had been going on for over a century and independence could wait a few more years, just long enough for me to feather my little nest! Until you captured me, I'd been wading around in mud for six months, dying of hunger, cold and fear, scared the whole time that a plane might bomb us or, worse still, burn us to a crisp with napalm. Looking back, I feel like eternity itself would have trouble matching those six fucking months for length!"

The pistol span one way on his finger, then the other.

"You see, at the end of the day, it's not very difficult to become what you call a terrorist. How would you have reacted in my shoes?"

And realising the absurdity of his question the man fell silent for several minutes. Mathieu thought the other man would never speak again. He started to shift his legs into a less painful position but gave up, called to order by the pins and needles numbing his limbs.

"Then came the events in Melouza."

"At the camp, I didn't understand or get involved in any political discussions. I was too busy with my own rancour and remorse at having done nothing for my father and my brother while there was still time. Oh, such remorse! It was like a poisoned fruit that I just kept peeling. The more bitter it tasted, the harder I chewed. The leaders had decided to put several *mechtas* in the Melouza area that were casting sidelong glances at Messali Hadj and the MNA back on the right track. It was true that the war veteran had fought all his life for Algeria, but they kept telling us that he was past it, that his inflated personal ambition was harming the common cause and that his MNA, the *Mouvement National Algérien*, was gradually turning into a pack of traitors in the pay of the French army. The political commissars hammered it into us: if you want to fight for Algerian independence, there is only one party capable of this historic enterprise, the FLN and its military wing, the ALN, the *Armée de Libération Nationale;* everyone else are just fledgling renegades and *harkis.* For my comrades and me, that had become an article of faith as incontrovertible as the Koran! I had no reason to doubt my leaders' word, all of them tough, courageous men who were always in the front line risking their lives when we clashed with enemy soldiers. One night we set out with six platoons totalling several hundred *djounoud.* Our commander had told us that the aim was to put the local MNA out of action and punish the recalcitrant *douars.* According to them our mission was simple: a show of strength, arrest some traitors, stiff fines and assorted threats for the future should the villages not come over to our side."

He nibbled at his lip.

"I realise now that I wasn't very smart. Not a doubt crossed my mind when the commander recruited back-up troops in rival villages: the FLN officers must know what they're doing! The area around Melouza is a patchwork of Kabyle and Arab *douars*, and the two populations have never got on. I didn't like the look of these civilians armed with knives and axes one bit, but we were assured that their presence would inspire even greater awe in the refractory villages."

Mathieu saw him dig around in one of his pockets with the reflex of a smoker searching for a packet of cigarettes that wasn't there. A wrinkle creased his brow. An additional concern knotted the Frenchman's stomach: *Why was the* fell *telling him all this now, and in such detail, when he hadn't admitted it under torture? Did he already regard him as a simple pair of quivering ears on top of a 'nice ripe corpse', as their platoon referred to suspects due for elimination?*

"After the first night and a skirmish with an armed group from the MNA, we headed for a *douar* a few miles from Melouza. We surrounded the rebellious *douar* of Béni Ilemane. I was just a novice *mujahid* in the midst of hardened fighters and I didn't feel I had any right to comment on my leaders' orders. So when, early on, I saw houses on fire I didn't like it, but I didn't say anything. That was maybe when the village constable and his family were slaughtered. I didn't know anything about it at the time. Our troops were spread around the five *mechtas* and each of us had only a very partial view of events. Basically I felt that the brutality was inevitable; we had just been involved in a bloody skirmish, the region was turning out to be very hostile to the FLN and, naturally enough, the French army was playing on that to pursue and kill our men. The local people had made the wrong choice and they had to be taught a lesson to remember… Next, our leaders ordered us to take all the men over fifteen up onto the rocky peak above Mechta Kasbah. The local dignitaries had been gathered in a mosque with the aim of forcing them to rally to our cause. The discussions had dragged on all through the night. At dawn, despite the threats, the village leaders still refused to disown their old messiah Messali and his damn MNA. That was the moment the order was given to massacre all the men and teenagers assembled on the peak."

Tahar clutched one hand with the other and a look of extreme bewilderment came over his battered face.

"I couldn't believe what I was hearing… I asked the man next to me, 'What? What did the lieutenant and the captain say? For God's sake, it can't be true! We're not going to kill them all? They're just like us – I don't believe this!' And I added the following stupid question: 'Brother, what will they say about me back in my village?'"

The horrified man ran the back of his hand over his chin.

"Yes… what will she say about me?"

Intrigued, Mathieu muttered, "Who are you talking about? Your mother?"

The Algerian flew into a fit of anger.

"No. I'm talking about a different woman… The woman I love… That I want to marry… I… I… And the devil take you!"

The Algerian's clay-coloured cheeks had turned scarlet. Despite the gravity of the moment, Mathieu suppressed a smile.

"And shit too!"

His eyes were riveted to the ground; the man seemed to be reliving a scene he couldn't tear himself away from.

"I think I killed two people up on that peak… The first was a peasant, whom I shot in panic because my platoon commander was furious at my hesitation and thumped me on the shoulder with an order to fire into the crowd. All I could see of that poor civilian was his *chèche*. I was taken aback by the bland, warm smell of the blood running past our feet, the axes, the flames from the burning shacks, the screams of pain, the cries for mercy from women lacerating their faces, the insults from officers as they yelled in our ears that traitors were worse than the French soldiers. It was horrible; I noticed how incredibly enthusiastic some of my companions were…"

He pinched his bottom lip between two fingers for a long time, as if punishing it for the horrors he was uttering.

"I asked God for help, but around me some were shouting 'Allah, save us!' and others 'Allah, help us kill them!' My prayer was grotesque; God seemed to me like a spectator who wouldn't dream of helping anyone. I fell silent and carried on shaking. My second victim was an old man my father's age. One of our back-up men chased after a young boy and sent him sprawling with a kick in the backside. Lying on the ground, the teenager started to yell in terror at the sight of the pickaxe raised above him. His father, the old man, had managed to escape from the main group of prisoners. Amid the hail of bullets and the unbearable moans of men having their throats slit he was yelping, 'Don't kill my son, he's too young, he knows nothing about politics. Oh mercy – God will reward you!' The guy with the pickaxe hadn't heard or seen him approaching. The old man was getting ready to batter him to death with an iron bar. I reacted without thinking: I fired a shot, killing the old man instantly. Our man turned round, scared out of his wits. He was a kid of about twenty whose good humour and helpfulness had caught my attention. Throughout the negotiations with the dignitaries from the mosque, he hadn't stopped serving tea and biscuits to our group of *djounoud*. The bloke caught sight of the body stretched out behind him first, then me with my rifle still pointing at the dead man. A broad relieved smile spread across his face. A second later, just as cheerfully, he stove in the kid's skull with a single blow of his pickaxe. A mixture of blood and brain spurted as far as my boots."

Tahar hunched up, as though this memory had struck him dumb.

"That pickaxe blew the boy's head apart and shattered my heart into a thousand pieces. I wanted independence – but not at that price. Since then I've been like a dead man. I didn't join the rebels to kill a father defending his son… My brother had been killed for trying to protect an old man. So I disobeyed and ran away. I roamed like a madman, but I knew I never wanted to go back to the mujahideen. I thought of suicide, but I wasn't brave enough."

He cackled with a kind of wicked delight.

"I let myself be captured by the French military because I was convinced you would execute me on the spot. It would have all been over in one go: my cowardice, my stain, this war I no longer understand… Seems I was wrong. I hadn't reckoned with people like you…"

"Just to get this straight," Aziz interrupted him with a contemptuous gesture, "you became friends because you were like each other: one tortured rebels, the other killed civilians."

"No, please don't say that about Tahar!" Mathieu protested in a cracked voice. "I'm a real bastard, but he was just a killer. Or, in any case, a reluctant killer... Listen to me, Aziz..."

"No, you listen to me, Mathieu. And you'd better open your ears wide."

Mathieu thought that Aziz would have less trouble agreeing to the kidnapper's demands after hearing these revelations.

"I couldn't give a damn how you justify your vile stories from half a century ago. All I can think of is my daughter being cut up into bits. Tell me one thing: what did the man who swore to take revenge on Tahar look like? Can you describe him? His face? Anything particular that might help us recognise him?"

Mathieu shrugged. A far-off commentator at the back of his mind replied exasperatedly: "How's a muttonhead like me supposed to remember an Arab I glimpsed for a few minutes over fifty years ago? You all looked the same to me back then..."

"No, nothing specific," the old man finally sighed, "...except that he was a redhead... So damn red it was a shock and you forgot his face."

"Great clue, that! The nutter must be so old now that his hair's had all the time in the world to go white. Look at yours. Who knows, he might even be bald!"

His voice grew ever more high-pitched, both beseeching and menacing at the same time.

"Nothing else comes to mind? What language did he speak in, Arabic or Kabyle? Think harder: some detail... a scar... I don't know... a name? Something that slipped out during his confrontation with Tahar?"

The old man gazed at the utterly distraught individual as he searched vainly for some meaning in the disaster engulfing him. *How alike all sufferers look!* he thought. He recalled the frantic pupils of Tahar's eyes, the same futile revolt.

He moved his hand and placed it over Aziz's. The father was startled by this unexpected familiarity – and then his body froze, suddenly alert.

"You remember something?"

"The first name, Aziz."

"His first name… *his*?" the Algerian managed, his voice quivering with hope, however tiny.

"No. Not *his*."

Mathieu felt like an icy stone was swelling up in his stomach. And that soon, by some terrible miracle, it would crush his exhausted heart.

"I never agreed with Tahar on this. I begged him not to do it. But he was as stubborn as a mule when he decided to be."

Aziz didn't give him time to explain why he loved Tahar more than the brother he never had. There is too little time left until the fateful dawn. Will no one ever know? Mathieu entwines and untwines his fingers again and again, as if picking apart the strands of the tragedy. For the first time in a very long while, he asks for help from 'L'il Robert'. A tiny part of his soul manages a smile. *That pigheaded Tahar loved you, maybe not as much as the brother he lost, but for you it was something at least! And then, don't forget, he saved you; not your life – yours wasn't worth a curse – but something more precious than that…*

When the mujahideen appeared in the clearing at the end of that morning, they found the two men sitting facing each other in silence, Mathieu still shocked at his release. A moment earlier, Tahar had climbed a tree after a bird alerted them by suddenly taking flight. He had come back down looking tense and unsure of what action to take. Then, aiming one last passing kick at his prisoner, he set him free.

"Put your belt on and your laces back in. Tell them you're a deserter who's been tortured by your own side because they suspected you of treachery. They're distrustful and they'll give you a hard time, so make sure your story's credible. They'll kill you if they think you might have belonged to the DOP. Pray that none of them passed through your hands."

He concluded with a snigger: "You can add that you helped me to escape. With a little luck, the maquisards will soon think you're a hero."

"Why are you saving my life?"

"You saved mine, didn't you?"

"Yes, but first I…"

"Tortured me, you mean?"

He made only a vague gesture by way of reply.

Mathieu insisted. "Why?"

"Do you really want to know?"

"Yes."

The Arab bent down to him, his eyes narrowing with grim anger.

"Because I'm a bastard and because you're a bastard, both of us of the very worst kind. We're pretty much as bad as each other, you and me. One shit lending another shit a hand – that's the secret of our association. God has gone off on a trip to see some happier people and he's taken all His morals with Him, so we make do with what we've got. There's nothing attractive about it – pure filth."

The sorrowing figure stood up straight again.

"If the mujahideen don't believe us, well, at the very worst they'll put a bullet in our brains and then throw us to the jackals. But I was hoping for something better from life…"

He didn't complete his sentence, but his hand kept beating the air like some large, indignant butterfly. Mathieu sat there aghast; his fellow fugitive was saving him for the same dodgy reasons that had made him desert. Furious at the large lump in his throat, he lowered his eyelids and tried to concentrate on knotting his shoelaces.

The maquisards were indeed more than a little distrustful. They took them to the FLN's regional HQ, where they were initially treated as suspects. Not as declared enemies, obviously, for if that had been the case, Tahar would not have lived a day longer; as for Mathieu, he would have been used as a bargaining chip with the French military, or killed in response to the guillotining of pro-independence activists at Barberousse prison in Algiers. The heads of the region imprisoned the two men after interrogations that left them sceptical. They shared the cave that served as a cell with other Algerians and some French soldiers. Some of the Algerians, most of whom were *harkis* or alleged traitors, were in just as bad a state as Tahar having quite obviously been beaten up by their jailers.

One reached the cells, which were plunged in constant darkness, via a maze hewn out of the solid rock. Mathieu would long remember, with a sense of affectionate disgust, the crunch of sun-dried grasshoppers between the teeth of their jailers who were as famished as they were and sometimes added these 'Saharan shrimps' to their one daily meal. During the three weeks they spent in captivity, they shared the same obsessions as their companions in misfortune: hunger, thirst and, above all, keeping their cell clean to avoid rats appearing. It was claimed that these filthy animals anaesthetised their victims' muscles with their urine, enabling them to devour them without waking them up. A *harki* prisoner swore that one of his cattle had been found one morning with half of its lower leg shredded by rodents!

A tacit rule, and a result of their mutual suspicion, forbade anyone from bringing up the subject of the war or the circumstances that might have led to them all rotting several yards underground deep in the Algerian *jebel* as they awaited for an arbitrary verdict that, for reasons of secrecy, could only be one of two extreme outcomes: release, or death. What they talked about, when their mood did not lapse either into despair or racism, were their fond memories of the time before the troubles or, preferably, the gastronomic and sexual excesses they promised themselves once released. This did not prevent nightmares and fits of terror from striking the youngest inmates, who were unable to cope with the uncertain nature of their sentence in this eternal night, broken only by latrine duty.

Another moment of unspeakable fear was when an aircraft flew over the area. More than bombs, it was napalm the prisoners were most afraid of. It found its way into the deepest cracks and, if it didn't kill you on the spot, burnt your skin beyond healing. Ignoring the rule of silence, a French conscript said that he had seen, in the middle of a *mechta* gutted by incendiary bombs dropped by a plane that was combing the area, a child whose face was intact but whose body was burnt all over; the child was in such pain that even its eyes could shed no tears.

By some freak occurrence that he could never fully explain to himself, Mathieu very soon felt a compulsive need to tell his life story to his former victim. Although he couldn't see Tahar in the darkness of the cave, he knew he was listening closely by his astonished or even shocked 'huhs' when too crude a secret offended his peasant's conservative sensibilities. "Stop talking like that – it defiles my ears to hear such rubbish!" he murmured in exasperation. These monologues imposed by life at such close quarters ("Confessions to a kind of Muslim 'priest', from whom I unconsciously expected some kind of absolution," he later admitted to Tahar) became as essential to him as the very occasional cigarettes their jailers allowed those inmates who smoked. Repelled by the strange familiarity between tortured and torturer that prison dictated, Tahar pondered his profound confusion in silence, only accidentally giving in to the bitter consolation of pouring his heart out. "You have no shame, Frenchman. You're lucky to be so naïve!" he grumbled when the ex-DOP serviceman's awkward and intrusive camaraderie became too brazen for him to bear.

Mathieu succeeded in cheering the maquisard up only once when a tick had burrowed deep into one of the other man's testicles. Tahar was in such searing pain that he resigned himself to asking his annoying neighbour for help. Due to his introverted character, the teacher had not managed to strike up any kind of relations with the Arab or Kabyle prisoners and had convinced himself, as a last resort, that there was no cause for prudery with this accursed Christian because the man had already been in the position of 'handling' him stark naked… Using a tin can, some oil skimmed off the soup and a strip of blanket, Mathieu managed to build a rudimentary lamp to shine on his fellow inmate's scrotum and then, with much patience and little bits of matches, to remove the clawed parasite. The operation was painful, but after a great many more or less blasphemous swearwords Tahar burst out laughing: "You mongrel son of a hyena and I don't know what, you used to try to bust my balls – now you fondle them!"

After days of prevarication, the local FLN leaders decided to accept the two men's version of events. People explained to Tahar later that the carnage at Mechta Kasbah had shaken many combatants, who protested vehemently that they had taken to the *jebel* to free Algeria, not to reproduce the large-scale massacres committed by French settlers in May 1945. Luckily for Tahar, the camp commander was one such protester. It was therefore decided, although he hadn't argued his case very persuasively, that Tahar would not be accused of deserting his detachment. They preferred the story of the fighter who had got lost and was captured and then tortured by the enemy. It was even decided that he had never been involved in the massacres at Mechta Kasbah, since the official party line now was that they should be attributed to French troops.

"The brothers are so ashamed of what happened in Mechta Kasbah that they're trying to make themselves believe in their own yarns! We're not even independent yet, but history is already being blighted by lies!" Tahar sighed as he told Mathieu about his conversation with the political commissar. As for the Frenchman, his decision to come over to the Algerian side was greeted with something like resignation. "Couldn't you have deserted in a town? What are we going to do with you now?" the irritated camp commander said reproachfully, but nevertheless thanked him for having risked his life to help a *mujahid* escape.

"So you're going back?" Mathieu asked Tahar when, barely recovered, the latter was preparing to set off with a group of *djounoud* for another rebel area.

"Of course. What else am I supposed to do?"

"*In spite of…*"

"In spite of."

A stern expression was written on his face.

"Doesn't what brought me here (he pointed to the mountains, his boots and his cobbled-together uniform) mean anything anymore? Am I… am I no longer a wog to your compatriots and now they'll call me *Monsieur*? Will my brother's murderers be brought to trial again? You can be sure of one thing: I still want independence. Maybe more than ever, precisely *because* of…"

He stroked his moustache nervously.

"My head is full of pitch-black birds. Sometime I feel as if a dead man is crawling around in my brain ordering me to join him, but I resist because I have unfinished business. Don't be mistaken, Mathieu. I'm not fighting for the FLN; I'm fighting for my brother and my father…"

The maquisard added, after a pause: "…And also for those two blokes in the *mechta* who'd done me no harm and whom I shot like dogs."

The top corner of his lip twitched.

"Aren't you afraid... of being caught by the army... and finding yourself back in the hands of the DOP?"

A smile softened his face, still marked by pain.

"You know me, Mathieu. I'm a chicken, but I'll cope. Maybe there'll be another remorse-ridden bastard like you to lend me a hand... after using me as a punch bag first, of course."

Mathieu tried to smile too, in vain.

"Will you forgive me some day?"

"Me?"

"Yes, you."

The Arab threw him a surprised and disapproving sideways glance.

"That doesn't matter anymore. I was incredibly lucky to get to repay you a tiny fraction of what you inflicted on me. Ask those people you didn't free for forgiveness instead. Because they..."

He blushed at his show of emotion and tried to work himself up into a rage.

"That's enough useless chat! My brothers are waiting for me! So long and look after yourself, Mathieu."

The Frenchman and the Algerian parted without much fuss, unaware that they would soon be following the same route. The Frenchman was first packed off by the FLN to Bône and then to Tunis with false papers, whereas the Algerian, most likely in a disguised disciplinary measure, was sent in one of the convoys that crossed the Tunisian border to bring back weapons and ALN soldiers from the so-called 'exterior'. Work was only just starting on the electric barrier, but the crossing still had a dangerous reputation – and this would only increase when the Morice Line was reinforced with two huge electrified barbed-wire fences, separated by a no man's land several miles wide in places that was liberally sprinkled with mines and patrolled day and night by armoured vehicles to do any 'mopping up'.

It was during one of these crossings, less than a year from the end of the war, that Tahar suffered a serious leg wound and was taken to hospital in Tunisia by the FLN. And it was the week after his hospital-ization, in an unprepossessing building in the suburbs of Tunis, that chance – which sometimes arranges human destinies while bursting its sides with laughter – brought the men face to face once more.

Imagine my astonishment, Aziz. I'd been hanging around in the

Tunisian capital for months, making a living from lousy jobs and poring over the wreckage of my life again and again in my mind. Everything in me stank of mediocrity and even the remorse I occasionally felt never got the upper hand over my boredom! One desperate day, after a huge drinking binge, I had a car accident. Some Algerian exiles remembered that I'd helped one of their own out of a sticky situation, so they sent me for treatment at a clinic directed by a sympathizer. There were about twenty rooms and it just so happened that I ended up in Tahar's.

It was a miracle! You'd have thought that the idiotic, blind, deaf and dumb deity that elaborates the poisonous concoctions of our lives had picked up the wrong test-tube and dripped a droplet of luck on my head.

I wormed my way in there, clung on like a leech; I swallowed my pride, I persisted. You cannot imagine how happy I was to meet up with this filthy-tempered Arab again, so shy that he came across as having no manners, impatient and awkward towards the admiring nurses who'd been told that he had fought heroically, that he had never known fear in the face of the enemy, crap like that. I prayed that his convalescence might last as long as possible. You didn't have to be a strategic genius to work out that hostilities would soon come to an end and on no account did I want the man I already considered my friend to be pointlessly killed by the final bullet of the final machine-gun burst of this bitch of a war.

If he died, who would vindicate me? By the very fact of Tahar's death, I would slip back into my cesspit, into my private desert.

My friend, my best friend... Well, when I say best... talk about boasting! In truth, the only friend fate ever gave me.

Eventually, he no longer turned me away. I told him about my childhood, my parents and, thanks to him – to his silence above all – I managed to more or less make my peace with them.

Three months later, Latifa, the woman who was to become his wife, turned up.

The next day Tahar, still limping slightly, asked me as an aside during a conversation about a book (we seldom talked about the war, of course), with his usual up-tight sense of humour, if I would do him the honour of being his witness.

I bawled my eyes out, of course, because it took me completely by surprise. Not in front of him, but I spent a good while sniffling gratefully in the clinic's stinking toilets.

Part III

"What's all this about a name for God's sake?"

"When his daughter was born he wanted to give her that first name, but I was against it. I was terrified. I had no right to beseech him, but I did. I loved them so much, that guy and his wife, that I thought of their daughter a little as my own. He had no right to burden a baby, even symbolically, with a crime for which it wasn't responsible. He shouted out that I had a nerve to meddle in the choice of the first name for the fruit of his balls; I had tortured them enough. His private parts had ached for ages and he was convinced, until the birth of his daughter, that we had made him sterile. Tahar and I had almost fallen out for good. Latifa wasn't aware of our argument, but I imagine that she too would have been dead against her husband's choice with all her heart."

Aziz tries to interrupt him.

"Let me go on… He backed down and they called their daughter Meriem. The years kept passing; their child grew up and became a woman. I had no idea, I swear, that Tahar hadn't given up on his idea and that he had made Meriem promise to name the daughter she bore Sheherazade. It was your wife herself who told me; she was convinced that the name belonged to your father's beloved grandmother. She didn't have any problem with it, especially since she liked the name, even if it did sound 'archaic' and a little conceited. Moreover, Tahar was very ill at the time and you don't refuse a dying father anything. He had taken some medicine by mistake and it hadn't done him a lot of good."

Mathieu observes Aziz's face. The man is obviously sifting through his memories, wondering whether he ever discussed the name with Meriem.

"It wasn't you who chose it, was it?"

"No," the son-in-law says shaking his head, taut as a steel wire. "I had no reason to oppose my wife's wish. I didn't know it was a promise she'd made to her father, but what does it matter? At any rate, I wouldn't have been against it. Malika was my first choice, but either way," he adds with an emotion that made his voice go hoarse, "I already thought of my daughter as a little princess who was destined to grow up to be a legendary queen."

Mathieu sees his own hands begin to shake – and he is angry with himself for being so worn-out and so incapable of controlling his own body.

"Tahar never forgot what had happened at Mechta Kasbah. The more years passed, the guiltier he felt. He said that he should have rebelled and cried out to stop the butchery. 'Don't be stupid, it wouldn't have been any use,' I retorted, 'you'd have been shot right there. They cut off your nose for a cigarette, so for mutiny…!' 'Maybe that would have been the way out?' he returned; he hadn't been born to swell the murderers' ranks. 'And, Mathieu,' he insisted, 'look how generously fate dispenses luck to those who don't need it: after we split up, I volunteered for the most dangerous missions, the ones from which no *djoundi* came back alive. I was scared to death each time, but actual death always carefully evaded me, the bitch!'"

A long sigh wrings the distraught man's chest.

"Oh how he suffered! He was the taciturn type. Latifa never knew. Sometimes he opened up to me – I had followed the couple to Algeria after independence. He said that that night in Mechta Kasbah, a monster had closed its hands around his throat and it had not stopped strangling him since. 'I can't breathe, Mathieu,' he complained, 'even when I'm making love to my wife.'"

The old Frenchman feels the red flush of shame flooding his crumpled cheeks. He shrugs his shoulders to avoid thinking about the rogue sob galloping in his throat.

"Do you remember the village constable's little daughter?"

"Where are you going with this, Mathieu? Which little girl?"

"And the redhead who claimed he could identify Tahar to get close to him at the DOP? Is it coming back to you? Well… He had a three-year-old daughter. She was with her grandfather when the whole family was killed. Can you guess what the unfortunate kid's name was now?"

Aziz recoils on his chair as if a snake had reared up in front of him. In a frightened voice, he hisses, "Sheherazade?"

"Poor Tahar believed that if he gave his own daughter's daughter that name, he would be offering a kind of borrowed life to the girl he had helped to kill."

The ex-soldier itches his brow distractedly in an embarrassed and puzzled gesture.

"He once asked me: 'Mathieu, *who* will save me from damnation?' He firmly believed in such things as damnation, hell... He had the occasional drink and he hadn't been to the mosque since the war, but he admitted that he was powerless against that stupid thing, eternal malediction; that it was his own blood, which was incapable of scrubbing clean the sewers of his memory, that threatened him with it every night. Deep down, the brave *djoundi* he had become in his despair was still a great big coward when it came to that sort of thing."

Aziz tries to sit up, but his insides have turned to jelly. He no longer has the strength to interrupt his father-in-law.

"The kidnapper must have convinced himself that Meriem's father was poking fun at him."

Aziz's face falls. Mathieu lowers his head.

"Forgive him, Aziz. Tahar was good man, but his times were not."

Aziz feels like lying down in an icy pit that would freeze all sensation inside him and banish the agitation of billions of suddenly freewheeling neurones: one finger, two fingers, three fingers... Rather than a thousand and one nights, his little Sheherazade has only the fingers of her two hands as an hourglass measuring the time she has left to live.

The father feels alone on earth. And then he corrects himself, full of self-contempt: it is his daughter who is *alone* on earth, prisoner of a different loneliness, the loneliness of a madman ruined by fifty years of sorrow.

If Shehera dies, Aziz would willingly kill the whole world. Like the village constable's son. Then a little voice whispers to him: *Well now, you're making quick progress along the path of understanding – isn't that precisely what the kidnapper wants you to do in memory of his child?*

Aziz almost knocks the sugar dispenser over when the mobile phone rings next to him. Almost immediately there is a second, more smothered ring. Aziz forces himself not to look at Mathieu, who suddenly rummages in his pockets. The Algerian's hand grips the small device just as it and Mathieu's mobile, which he has pulled feverishly out of his jacket, both stop ringing.

"A message," Mathieu says dully.

"A message," repeats Aziz in a choked echo.

"*Time passes, but my anger is like a mountain. Fear and obey,*" the father reads out.

"*Time passes, but my anger is like a mountain. Fear and obey,*" Mathieu reads in turn.

"Why has he sent us the same message? Does he know we're together?" Aziz asks, feeling his hair stand up on end in horror at the message's almost Koranic solemnity.

"That's what he suspects. He's watching us. Maybe he even lives on the estate?"

"…and that now we both know what he requires us to do?"

Mathieu gets up, leaning heavily on the back of the chair nearest to him.

"It's time, Aziz. I'm ready."

"Time for what?" his interlocutor stammers in panic. "I'm not really going to ki…"

"You've already killed, so don't make such a fuss about it."

"But I didn't know the other guy. And he was a shit too."

"Oh yeah, because you know me, do you? Did you have the slightest idea about what I was like before today's conversation? I'm a shit too, as well as being a rotten deserter who lost one country without gaining another. Even so, I've had my fair share of luck."

Mathieu's voice is almost jaunty. A smile flickers in his eyes.

"Tahar… Then Latifa… A wife who loves me after having loved the person who showed himself more brotherly to me than a brother… How many so-called decent people have enjoyed such blessings? After all the harm I caused, I admit I didn't deserve it. But since when has justice ever shuffled the cards of life fairly? So if fate gives me a chance to pay back a part of what Tahar and Latifa have so generously offered me…"

The old man pats his companion softly on the shoulder.

"Your daughter is their granddaughter, a part of them. So it's less difficult if…"

The figure crumples into an awkward, dislocated pose.

"Now get a move on, Aziz. I'm going on a bit; I'm scared. Help me to go through with it. Latifa mustn't suspect anything. If I see her, all my courage will leak out of me like piss from a newborn baby. The great cowardice of love will be all I have left."

While my father-in-law was conversing with me about his fear, I felt as jittery as if my own fear had turned into a vindictive mutt snapping at my calves. The stark reality colonised my mind and almost immediately darkened it – this man with the service record of a jackal was agreeing to die for my daughter and had made me responsible for executing him!

"Mathieu, I…"

"Let's go before the women wake up."

From the corridor we heard the sound of a muffled conversation coming from Shehera's bedroom. Mathieu pushed me towards the front door of the flat.

"Don't make a sound," he whispered in my ear. "Or they'll guess we're up to something."

We went down the stairs without exchanging a word, with him preceding me despite his laboured step. I felt like touching this strange individual on the shoulder and expressing both my anger and my gratitude. I didn't dare.

We were just leaving the unusually deserted pavement in front of the block of flats when my phone rang again. I opened my mobile, my eyes surveying the innumerable openings in the estate's peeling façades, some of which were still lit despite how late it was.

"Aziz, put it on loudspeaker so your father-in-law can hear."

I jumped, before spinning round as if someone had tapped me on the back.

"Are you on the estate? Are you watching us?"

"You'll have to answer your own question. How many buildings and windows are there in front of you? Then again, I might be sitting in a car or on a flying carpet (he burst out laughing) with a pair of binoculars. Have you put it on loudspeaker?"

"Yes," I murmured. "Please, how is my daughter?"

The voice on the telephone snickered.

"You mean, is she still alive?"

I swallowed with difficulty while Mathieu strained to hear the loudspeaker.

"Yes."

"*Still* – that's the right word! Don't worry, I *still* need her."

"Have…"

I stopped, unable to ask my question.

"No, I haven't… hmm… cut off anything else."

The same mocking cackle escaped him.

"Not yet… Unless you and the old man choose not to obey me anymore. In which case…"

I interrupted him.

"We will obey you."

"Then one of you must die before dawn. Work it out between yourselves, but only one of you will return to the flat alive. Otherwise the little girl will feel the full force of my anger."

"We'll work it out."

I had the impression that I'd been thrown back to ancient times and was speaking to a man-eating divinity demanding a human sacrifice. I felt like prostrating myself on the pavement and begging at the top of my voice for mercy from this evil, fantastical god making his mad utterances over a mobile telephone.

"Listen, we'll do whatever you ask, but will you release the girl?"

"Huh, is that old Mathieu prattling on? Are you ready for the great leap into the unknown, you little shitbag?"

Mathieu took the mobile from my hand. Lit by the feeble light of a functioning streetlamp, his face appeared waxy and incapable of expressing the slightest emotion.

"I think I know who you are…"

"Oh really? So the old fart's suddenly become clever overnight, has he? And who do you reckon I am?"

"Melouza…"

A silence followed, such a long silence that I grabbed the telephone from Mathieu's hands and stuck it to my ear to check that the line hadn't been cut off. The kidnapper was still there; his breathing was still audible despite the crackling.

"Check out the turd the beast has just deposited!" the stranger resumed. "But it doesn't really matter who I am now. What does matter, hmm, hmm, is that I'm the one who decides."

"Why do you want to take revenge on the girl? She hasn't done anything to you, has she? Her grandfather died long ago…"

A scream saturated the loudspeaker.

"Don't interrupt me, motherfucker! Another word out of you two and you'll hear the little whore squeal. You are only here to obey, and that's all. Understood?"

"Understood," I articulated, then bit my lip. Mathieu stood there motionless, his face blank. *Already dead*, I thought fleetingly.

"Don't even think about looking for me on the estate. The slightest doubt and I'll cut the girl to ribbons. I've got a whole set of knives, some of which, alas, are not very sharp. The knife-grinder doesn't come round here that often, you see…"

He lowered his voice, 'compacting' it as if he himself feared that he might start shouting.

"I'm going to tell you a secret: I'm not scared of dying. Quite the opposite. I'm old now. It's exhausting; life ends up like a canker in the middle of your arse – whether you scratch it or not, it just makes things worse, right up until the day when you shit your insides out through your own arsehole as you scream with pain. So, if you really push me by acting smart, you'll find out how I long for death!"

I nodded hurriedly in a sign of submission, as if he could see me through the mobile phone. *But the fucker really could see me* – with the omniscience of God and his little pal, the devil!

"Only one of you has the right to live, the other will have to die before morning. And I want irrefutable proof, my lambs! I'll call you later."

I shut the lid of my phone, avoiding looking Mathieu in the eye. My father-in-law touched me on the shoulder.

"Let's go to my car, please."

We got into his car, which was parked in a dark corner out of sight of any binoculars the kidnapper might have. I couldn't open my mouth for fear that I might puke up my guts and my bile.

"Here you go."

Mathieu thrust the pistol wrapped in the large handkerchief into my hands. I dropped it in surprise. The object fell at my feet.

"Hide it," my father-in-law ordered. "Take your car and follow me at a fair distance. We'll finish off this… chore a few miles away, in a field or something like that. Then you'll go home without arousing any suspicions."

Mathieu's voice reached me in distorted form, as though I was at the bottom of a lake where sound had changed speed and consistency. I didn't understand the rest of what he said. He gave me a furious thump.

"Do you hear me, Aziz? Now is not the time to waver."

I turned my head slowly towards the driver.

"Do I... really have to shoot you?"

"There's no other solution."

I walked over to my car in a fog of unfinished emotions. We drove along the motorway, one behind the other, until Mathieu decided on an exit leading to an orchard.

We parked behind the orange trees. The old man hurried over to meet me. He asked me for the pistol and cocked it before handing it back.

"Aim at my head. Now, without thinking... And then take a photo... Good luck with your daughter."

In the moonlight I saw the wrinkled face and the fine white hair. The frail torso was bent forwards in readiness for the impact of the bullet. Mathieu moaned timidly, with a grimace that might have been a smile.

"Son, my Algerian war is well and truly over this time. And none too soon, believe me."

I stretched out my arm. A slight breeze set the leaves of the fruit trees swaying. A heartrending fragrance of ordinary happiness tickled my nostrils. I took a deep breath, thinking of my daughter. I started to pull the trigger. We looked at each other. The future dead man's face had tensed, eyes popping. I fired.

There was no report. I glanced at my index finger, which had refused to move, and at Mathieu who had raised his elbow in a final attempt to shield himself.

My arm fell back to my side.

"I can't, Mathieu. I'm too much of a coward."

His throat hoarse and a little angry, Mathieu retorted, "It doesn't matter. I understand. But it doesn't make things any easier. If you start to feel pity, then your daughter is shafted."

Running a weary hand through his hair, he sighed before waving me towards my car in a dismissive gesture as though I were a valet who couldn't be trusted.

"Go back home. Keep the pistol – you might need it against that nutter."

"And you?"

"I'll deal with the rest… and the evidence."

I got into my car, weighed down by shame and despair. Just as I was moving the gear stick, Mathieu tapped on the window. I leaned towards him. I would have liked to say one last word to him, that I was sorry that circumstances hadn't allowed us to get to know each other better and to become – who knows – friends. I kept quiet, since such words no longer meant anything after the scene with the pistol. Stiffly, his face closed, Mathieu said, "Try to watch over your family."

Then, his voice trailing gently away: "Watch over Latifa. She's part of your family too. Promise me that."

I got back to my flat, fighting off my relief at the thought that someone else was about to pay the price for my daughter's life. Meriem and Latifa were waiting for me on the landing. Holding her phone in one hand, my mother-in-law called to me bitterly, "Where's Mathieu?"

"I don't know. I walked with him to his car. He couldn't stand the tension, so he's gone for a little drive."

"A drive? In the middle of the night? It's after three in the morning! How stupid is that? And why isn't he answering his phone?"

While trying to calm her mother down, Meriem cast an inquisitorial glance at me. Her exhausted face creased with worry; she obviously knew that her husband was lying to her.

"Why didn't you let us know beforehand? Things are bad enough without whims like this. Have you had any news about Shehera? Has he rung?"

She tapped on her mother's arm as if she were calming a small child, studying me unkindly all the while. I felt myself turn pale as I explained that neither Mathieu nor I had thought it worth waking them.

"Mathieu would never have gone off without telling me!" Latifa protested. "Especially as late as this! What are you hiding from us, Aziz?"

Then, her voice going up in pitch: "Something's happened to him, hasn't it? Did he take his heart tablets at least?"

"I…"

My telephone rang. We glanced at each other, suddenly silent, once again reduced to our condition of boundlessly terrified beings.

"Answer it," Meriem whispered in a voice I didn't recognise.

She sucked her lips against her teeth. I felt like begging her not to clench them so hard, for I could see her teeth's imprint on the flesh of her lips. As I took the accursed device out of my pocket, I mused that the devil no longer had to have recourse to the services of messenger demons, as he did in ancient legends. A simple, bottom-of-the-range mobile was more efficient.

"It's me – Mathieu."

"Who? I thought…"

"It's really me (my interlocutor was talking in a low voice). Be quiet and listen: nothing has changed for the time being. But we need some proof for… For you too, by the way. I mean: you need an alibi. Pass me Latifa."

I obeyed automatically; my brain span in search of a rational explanation and then just crashed like an ordinary computer overwhelmed by a programme. My mother-in-law's physical transformation was miraculous. Behind the withering of old age, I caught a glimpse of the pretty young girl she must have been whenever a smile lit up her face.

"Is that you, Mathieu? I was so scared…"

She gave a little nervous laugh.

"You love me? I know you love me… But why are you telling me at three in the morning? Come on, come home quick. You know it's dangerous for a Frenchman to be out and about in Algiers in the middle of the night…"

A furrow between her eyes like an exclamation mark joined the smile that still had not left her lips.

"You're so odd, Mathieu… You don't feel well? Don't hang about on your way home, OK? We need you here… No, no news about the little one… Your heart isn't hurting you? OK, I won't worry… But you've never told me you loved me over the phone before… All right, all right, don't get impatient, I'll pass you Aziz… But why are you saying you love me again?"

The exclamation mark on her brow was now a gash. I sensed that my mother-in-law was trying hard to ignore the alarm signals sent by her intuition. Ashen-faced, her smile transformed into a snarl, she turned to her daughter to beg her for support. But her daughter was staring obstinately at me. The old woman stood there with her arms hanging by her sides, shrivelling up before my eyes with the shock of her discovery: it was no longer *one* but *two* fears that had sunk their claws into her, and neither her heart nor her head knew which to combat first.

"Is that you, Aziz?"

"Yes."

"There's no one listening?"

I raised my bleary eyes to the two women.

"No."

"The kidnapper rang me just after you left... To make up for the change of plan, he demanded that... it all takes place in front of him... Well, on the estate... at about six or seven in the morning, so..."

"Yes?"

"When there are people around... Otherwise he'll dump Shehera's body outside your block of flats."

Caught in Meriem's suspicious gaze, I found nothing to say apart from a fake-sounding *Oh?* accompanied by a feeling like I was vomiting inside.

"Our chap intends to have some fun. He says I fully deserve my fate; I shouldn't have saved people who didn't deserve to be... See, he admits it... without admitting it. He swore that he's hiding so close by that he could count the hairs on our arses if it took his fancy."

He broke off, overwhelmed by dejection rendered all the more terrible by the obscenity of these last words.

"He'll tell me the objective in the next hour or two. In the meantime I've got to stay in my car... There's definitely a method to this bastard's thinking – if you can call it thinking!"

"And what is it, erm... do you think?"

"The objective? I don't know. He repeated several times that everyone has to pay."

My father-in-law let out a strange chuckle.

"I'll soon find out what lies beyond the rainbow."

"What?"

He adopted a more sententious tone of voice.

"*It's a nice day to die...*"

The mobile resonated with the beginnings of a timid laugh that was so unexpectedly light-hearted that I felt a sob throbbing inside my chest.

A question almost slipped out of my mouth: *What's up with you, you old cretin? Been drinking?* His breathing died away, rattled by another couple of bursts of that disconcerting laughter.

"Even so, Aziz, I'm still shuddering with fright at the thought of..."

He ended with a quick side-step: "...of cleansing my soul after all the crimes I've committed, huh, isn't that what I'm supposed to say?"

I heard a slow exhalation, a kind of *Pffeuh!* followed by a barely audible "My God, I'm talking such bollocks!" Then nothing more, apart from the sound of my own blood pounding in my temples.

I choked back a swelling of pity. *Of course you're scared witless, Mathieu, you're not some heroic Indian chief. You're just a fallen Frenchman – and a failed Algerian to boot. And to cap it all, you ran into me, a man with all the balls of a rabbit!*

I kept the phone pressed to my ear for a couple of needless seconds, then put it away with a lingering look out of the gaping window – which supposedly led to my daughter's prison – and then at Meriem. The woman who had long ago taken possession of my soul looked as if she wanted to annihilate me with a single question: *Had I really done* everything *a father is duty bound to do to save the flesh of his flesh?*

I had failed from start to finish. I had killed a man for nothing, Mathieu had pipped me at the post by electing to die in my stead, and my daughter was still a lunatic's plaything.

It was a perfect trap: if we alerted the police, the girl was lost; if we didn't, the result would be the same. With one small difference: in the first scenario, the killer *alone* decided on her passing; in the second, it was *we* who decided on the timing of Shehera's execution.

When I was younger, I had been unlucky enough to witness a man commit suicide by throwing himself off the suspension bridge in Constantine. The man had bumped into me by accident just before he climbed up the bridge and had been polite enough to turn round and apologise. It took several seconds for him to hit the bottom of the canyon. Throughout his entire fall, he let out a bloodcurdling scream. For several nights afterwards I kept waking up with a start, imagining the terror of the man as he saw the ground approaching at breakneck speed. For him, that fear had come to a swift end. I had no such luck. Ever since Shehera's kidnapping, I felt myself falling at an ever more breathtaking velocity down the sides of a canyon infinitely deeper than the one in Constantine.

I suddenly realised that the bulge of the pistol in my pocket was far too visible. I evaded Meriem's accusing gaze. Once again I wondered whether I had been wrong to lie to her. The mere thought of the words I might use to tell the truth caused my tongue to sag down against the bottom of my mouth.

When he lowers his eyes, Meriem thinks with bitter surprise that she would have laid down her life for this man who 'stole her soul', as the old cassette they played over and over again in Aziz's car in the early days of their relationship proclaimed so prettily. The song swore that "*I won't stop loving you until the Good Lord starts to grow old.*" The tune had been playing by chance on the radio the first time they made love in the car. Over the years the little ditty had become a sort of anthem celebrating this event.

How long should you love? the wife ponders, stirring the broth of grief that is poisoning her heart and mind. *Before*, this gently blasphemous chorus had had a joyous meaning without any ambiguity.

God had all at once grown old and that had made our daughter's death possible. Shall I continue to cherish this dillydallying husband, who buzzes around, goes out and comes back in like a fly, but doesn't bring our little girl home in his arms?

The broken woman supporting another grief-stricken woman guesses – knows – that she is being unfair. She senses that the love she still feels for this man is beginning to be contaminated by something resembling, yes, contempt; a *real* father has a duty to protect his family, whereas this one has got bogged down in lamentations with his doddering old father-in-law…

You imbecile, a voice rebuffs her, *it isn't your husband's fault if a maniac has kidnapped your daughter. For God's sake, don't act like some silly little Arab goose who's always blaming someone for her misfortunes!*

Deep down, Meriem agrees, but at the mention of her daughter's disappearance and the glacial desert she will have to face for the rest of her life, she clings to this resentment for her companion in life.

Dad, why did you have to die so young? she thinks in a rage. She observes her mother with suppressed anger. A strange jealousy grips her heart: her mother is no longer grieving only for her kidnapped granddaughter, but also for her… her… Meriem can't bring herself to speak the usurper's name in her mind.

And yet she used to like him, this 'uncle' who spent all his evenings at their house when her father was still alive! Spoiling her silly, bringing her countless toys at first, then books, telling her interminable and wonderful stories about his native Brittany.

She had never understood the origins of the friendship that

bound her father so strongly to this Frenchman who'd appeared from nowhere and of whom she knew only that he had 'helped the Revolution' and that he wouldn't allow himself, despite the nostalgia gnawing away at him, to go back to France. He had always managed to find work not far from them. That wasn't very hard with his job as a post office counter clerk. There were post offices in even the remotest parts of the country! Every time Tahar was posted somewhere, Mathieu managed to follow him, sometimes needing a year or two before he obtained a transfer. Not really understanding the reasons for these constant changes, his superiors at the post office grudgingly satisfied what they viewed as a *gaouri's* whims and finally buckled in the face of their strange compatriot's obstinacy.

Mathieu had Algerian identity papers, but he didn't seem to hold his adoptive country in great esteem. Meriem had often caught him grumbling about these Arab layabouts who spent their time complaining about the entire world while they shamelessly frittered away the fabulous riches that nature had bestowed on them. Meriem was shocked to hear these criticisms verging on racism coming from the mouth of a European, but she was forced to acknowledge that all he was doing was repeating, sometimes word for word, the diatribes of her own widely admired father.

They were living at the time in a small town in the east of the country, where her father exercised the post of headmaster. When she mentioned the rumours about his heroism, the former *mujahid* curled his lips in disgust: "What do those meatheads know about courage and the evil of war? The only thing they're interested in is whether I'll agree to be their candidate for mayor to cover up for their dodgy real estate schemes and their swindling with *my heroism!*" He had always refused to tell her about the deeds that had earned him his reputation as a rebel, once objecting scathingly when she pressed him: "Everyone always lies when they talk about the war. So don't ever force me to lie to you!"

Dad, you would have known how to bring back our little girl... Whereas this useless twit doesn't even know how to look after the monkeys entrusted to him!

She takes her mother by the arm and pulls her into Shehera's bedroom.

"Have a rest, Mum. Mathieu will be home soon."

"You think so? I know him like the back of my hand, my Mathieu. His voice was odd, as if he were afraid…"

After tucking her mother in like a child, Meriem goes back into the living room. All she can see of Aziz is an exhausted profile so ravaged by despair that it makes her heart melt with both grief and anger. She puts both hands on her man's shoulders, finding nothing to say to him. He grasps them. He too remains silent. He is afraid of starting to speak, afraid that he won't be able to stop.

The ringtone kills off the sigh rising in Meriem's lungs. It is her mobile that is tinkling with those ghastly cheerful musical chimes her daughter installed for her because she thought the old ringtone was too bland.

"So then, has he confessed everything to you, your nice little husband?"

She feels a shooting pain. She raises her hand to her breast, but manages to stammer: "What was he meant to confess?"

"Oh, always keeping secrets! That's no good… You should tell the woman of your life everything! Tut, tut, that's not the behaviour of a faithful husband…"

"Which secrets do you mean?"

The man doesn't answer right away. Meriem feels a new pang biting into a different corner of her heart. What if the kidnapper hangs up? Without giving any news of her daughter? Plunging them once more into the horror of ignorance?

"Pass me your husband," the awfully familiar voice resumes, adding, "please, ma… *madam* (he stumbles deliberately, with mocking disdain, over *madam*)… Is that you, Aziz?"

"No, it's still me, his wife. Please, I…"

"Come on, you slag!" the stranger yells. "Why don't you do as I tell you?"

She holds the mobile out to Aziz. Her face is so bloodless and so devoid of emotion that Aziz believes for an instant that she has just learnt of their daughter's death…

"You… you've…"

He gasps for the air he needs to release the cry that has already taken control of his brain.

"If you scream, I'll kill her. Right now."

The part of Aziz's brain that is still functioning retains only one element of the kidnapper's threat: *If he's threatening to kill her, then he hasn't killed her!*

Suppressing the mixture of relief and rage then and there throws Aziz into a state verging on nauseous dizziness.

"OK, I'll be quiet, I swear… (Then, to his wife.) She's alive… (To the stranger again.) I beseech you, let us speak to our daughter…"

"Don't give me orders, if you please."

"No, no – never!"

Aziz has adopted the most servile tone possible.

"Well now, tell your wife everything. Or would you rather I did? Come on, put it on loudspeaker!"

"Right now?"

"Right now."

Aziz does as he's told, focusing his gaze on the small buttons to avoid his wife's eyes.

"So, what are you waiting for?"

Panting with excitement, the kidnapper's voice is like a perverted little boy's as he awaits the outcome of some naughty prank.

"I…"

Aziz's lips are as swollen as if they had been plunged into crushed ice.

"Speak, you idiot, or it'll be your daughter yelling instead!"

"I… I murdered a man and…"

The final whispered words hiss out of him like a punctured tyre.

"…And Mathieu is going to kill himself before dawn…"

"Why are you telling me these fibs, Aziz?"

Meriem shakes her husband's arm in disbelief.

"Why?" she puffs out in a halting, almost inaudible breath.

"He's cut off three of Shehera's fingers. He threatened to cut off some more if we didn't obey him."

Meriem half-closes her eyes and gropes around for help as if the floor had turned to quicksand. She is in terrible pain; a monstrous animal is sinking its claws and its fangs into her breast. She articulates painfully, carefully – she *has* to rescue her daughter – by clutching with all her might to the tiny shaft of intelligence she has left: "My daughter… Give me back my daughter… Take my life instead of hers… Right now, if you want… I'll leave the house at once… Look, I don't even need to put a coat on…"

She gulps in spite of the sickening bitterness of her saliva. The man takes his time.

"You're suffering, eh? It's tough, I know. I'm not guessing – *I know*. You tell yourself the pain can't get any bigger, that it's already bigger than the universe, and yet it carries on getting bigger... I won't say I pity you, but I understand you, you can be sure of that."

The voice is not sarcastic and seems to show a genuine concern for his interlocutor's mental state. Then, as though the man had cast a glance at his watch:

"Here I am, nattering away! I have to go or else I won't have any minutes left for our conversation tomorrow morning."

"My daughter... Just a little word with my daughter," Meriem implores him. "I beg you... just one tiny second..."

A burst of laughter crackles over the loudspeaker. Then the man rebuffs Meriem with almost fatherly irritation.

"Now, now, my poor foolish woman, you'll have to do more than beg for your wishes to come true. Even if you behaved like an Inca priest and piled every living being in the world on top of each other for sacrifice, it would still be far from enough. That would be too easy, woman. Anyway, talk to you tomorrow... well, as long as your father-in-law doesn't shy away at the last minute... He's made one hell of a wager, your father-in-law: his life for his granddaughter's, who might already be dead. I can cheat too, sometimes... No, I'm kidding! Who knows..."

The kidnapper clicks his tongue against his palate in a sign of derision, before speaking again, with something like envy. "Does he really love you all this much, that fucking *gaouri*?"

The question catches the woman off-guard. She opens her mouth, but nothing comes out.

"You don't know? Well, you will tomorrow..."

"Stop blubbering!"

She is berating him violently. She doesn't want to sit down for fear that her body might not obey her now. Moreover, she feels like her brain is only working in fits and starts: one moment, extremely sharp; the next, incapable of understanding what had appeared obvious.

"Tell me everything," she ordered before interrupting him: "This stuff about Mathieu committing suicide before dawn, is it true?"

Aziz nods, ashen-faced.

"Yes. Otherwise Shehera will have her throat slit."

The words have lost all their modesty. The beast whines and sinks its teeth into another part of his belly.

"Will he do it?"

"Do you mean Mathieu or the…"

"Mathieu."

Her heart is cold. She speaks in a low voice to avoid her mother eavesdropping on their conversation. She'll have all the time she needs, later, to share his grief. She can think only of her daughter; she'd be prepared to sacrifice the whole world to save her child.

"You never really liked your father-in-law, did you?"

Her husband studies her in fearful astonishment.

"And you're not going to ask me about the guy I killed?"

Yes, how come she hasn't questioned him about… Oh, my God! The pieces of news slam into each other so hard that some, even the most appalling, temporarily disappear beneath the horizon of her understanding. Aziz tries to give her a hug; she pushes him away. If she lets herself dissolve into tears, Shehera will die of abandonment. Right now, she feels something close to revulsion at Aziz's betrayal. How could he have kept such alarming information about her daughter secret from her?

She digs deep into her lungs to bring a breath of calm to her voice.

"Tell me everything. And please don't leave anything out."

She learns successively of their neighbour's murder, her father's past, her father-in-law's too, his planned suicide at dawn, and the likely reason for her daughter's kidnapping.

If she has understood correctly, her daughter is going to die because of a massacre during the Algerian war. One of her hands is shaking.

"No, she's not going to die, I promise you that. He wants revenge? Well, he can have revenge! He'll take Mathieu's life and I'll offer him mine if he so desires, but he won't kill Shehera."

She notices that he is searching for reassurance in her eyes. She refuses him any such aid; the kidnapper had no second thoughts about cutting off her daughter's fingers. This man's thirst for vengeance is impossible to satisfy. In his mathematics about an exchange of corpses – those of his family in return for Shehera's – he still comes out a heavy loser.

She knows that Aziz is ready to throw down his life at the kidnapper's feet like a mere potato peeling. He had the courage to commit a murder, he who had never been in a fight in his life. He tried to kill his father-in-law. She feels her chest tighten with love for this indecisive man who gave her so much joy in the early days of their marriage, and more and more regrets in recent years. She recalls the happiness that had washed over them when the little one came into the world and they began, despite the bombings and the butchery, to hatch marvellous plans for the future of their little family: leave this squalid place, buy a small flat, have some 'normal' neighbours, go to the cinema and the theatre, no longer fear the hate-filled looks due to uncovered hair or too short a dress…

She decides to twist the cruel tap of memories tight shut because otherwise a chasm of despair will open beneath her feet. To quell her trembling she goes off the kitchen to make herself a coffee. She tries to think of a possible way out – *necessarily* possible. She catches herself murmuring a snatch of a prayer, before a sniggering thought stings her mind: *"Even Eve, close as she was to God, lost her son. So you, my girl…"* With tears in her eyes, she tastes the scalding liquid and suddenly recalls the cursed day her father died.

…She is coming home happily from the university. Her linguistics test went well, she enjoys her studies, even if she knows in advance that they won't be worth a great deal when the time comes to transform this knowledge into a job. She knocks on the door of her family's flat. She left home early that morning because of the erratic timetable of the bus that takes her to the university. She didn't kiss either her father or her mother as they were both still asleep.

Her mum opens the door immediately, as if she were on the lookout for her return and tells her bluntly, her face impenetrable: "Your father is dead."

She breaks down in tears and stammers, "Ho… how… come? He… he was fine yesterday."

Her mother stares at her. In her eyes she can read grief and anger in equal measure, both of them vast.

"Your father committed suicide."

"What?"

"Sleeping tablets."

Her mother claps her palms together. For one ridiculous second, Meriem thinks she's applauding. In reality, her mother is doing her best to keep her hands busy and stop them from scratching at her cheeks until the blood comes, as the ancient Arab mourning custom requires.

"Yes, he's done this to us… I loved him though… Oh Tahar…"

She eyes her up and down brusquely, almost accusingly.

"You loved him too, didn't you?"

"Of course I loved him, Mum."

And again Meriem collapses, overwhelmed this time, in addition to her sorrow, by an unbearable sense of guilt.

She gasps, "Why did he do it, Mum? He hasn't been in a good mood recently, but to go and… He was fine…"

"No," she said pointing to her temple, "your father was never well."

"Why, Mum?"

Large tears well up in the corners of her mother's eyes, without any change in her facial expression.

"The past, my girl, the damned past drove a rusty nail into his soul that was impossible to pull out again."

She doesn't say another word. Meriem rushes into the bedroom where her father is resting. Her mother has lovingly combed his hair and dressed him in a suit. He appears to be sleeping, a vague pout of protest pulling his lips downwards, like some tearaway who has sunk into sleep leaving some quarrel unresolved. He is the first dead person she has ever seen close up. She feels like touching him to check that her mother isn't mistaken. Maybe he's just fainted? People don't commit suicide for no reason, even at her father's age. A squall of tears, dark with rancour, beats down inside her head. The preposterous thought occurs to her to tickle her father like when she was small: he used to scream with laughter when she slid her hand under his armpit. It was so good to hear him laugh, this father with his black moods! If you help a dead man to laugh at the state he's in, perhaps he will eventually agree to wake up?

Mathieu comes into the room just as, despite being eighteen years old, the young girl is shaking her father by the shoulder to attempt the impossible. Her old 'uncle', whom she now calls by his first name, is distraught, his eyes red from crying. He holds her tight, asks her not to be angry with her father and, in the same breath, makes her swear on the soul of the man lying in front of her that she won't breathe a word about his suicide. Cornered, she promises. Some day, he insists, she will understand. He asks her to leave the room and bustles about on his own for a while before calling her mother. Although she is grateful for his support, she is shocked at how he has taken control of *her* family's affairs. She stays by the door. She hears snatches of conversation: "…Cleaned everything… taken all the boxes… A doctor… a friend of mine… He owes me one… Don't worry about it, Latifa… No one will know…"

An hour later the doctor Mathieu has fetched solemnly confirms death by sudden cardiac arrest after a speedy examination and issues the burial certificate…

…Fairly soon she began to detest him. He came round to their house too often. She would have liked to do her mourning face to face with her mother, to savour alone with her the bitterness of recounting the little, insignificant facts that make up the heartbreaking memories one has of a loved one after his death. Like, for example, the comedy surrounding the sugar lump for his coffee, which he wheedled out of her unbeknownst to her mother. Something to do with a high diabetes level, if she remembers rightly.

Or another day when he had tucked into some asparagus, which had then triggered a spectacular allergic reaction on his face. Her horrified mother had cried, "Tahar, you've got great big spots on your face!"

"Really? This asparagus is delicious, though!"

He got up from the table and went off to gaze at himself in the mirror in the corridor. Without turning round, he called out phlegmatically to his wife: "I can't really say I'm better-looking than King Kong! You, however, are still a thousand times prettier than the blonde in the film!"

She had seen her mother blush with pleasure at this unexpected compliment. For a long time afterwards, Meriem teased them with the joint nickname of 'Beauty and the Gorilla'.

Mathieu was very fond of Meriem, but the opposite was no longer true because it had become all too apparent that he had begun to fall in love with his friend's wife. Sacrilegious love according to Meriem, a betrayal of the friendship that bound him to her deceased father. For her part, her mother had been devastated by her husband's suicide, which she initially felt as a defilement of their love. For several months she refused to pronounce his name. By a strange paradox, the attentive presence of her late husband's friend eventually restored, little by little, her ability to talk lovingly about the man whose life she had shared.

Mathieu probably suffered from Meriem's enmity, although it didn't stop him from asking her mother for her hand two years after his friend had passed away. By that time, Meriem had already got wind of the rumours and slander being peddled around the neighbourhood, things like: "The widow of a former *mujahid* doesn't spend time with a Frenchman, not unless she's a shameless whore!" She also held it against her mother that she had not resisted the clumsy advances of a man who should only have aspired to the title of 'best friend of the family'. Partly due to Meriem's bad mood, the mother stalled for a further two years before agreeing to marry Mathieu. They moved to Algiers, as their neighbours' hostile looks were becoming too hard to put up with. For the wedding to be able take place in Algiers, Mathieu agreed to go along with a sham conversion to Islam and it was under his new forename, Ali, that he officially became her stepfather. She should have been as happy for her mother as her mother was – as completely as with her previous husband. Deep down, the daughter was perhaps jealous of her mother for having managed to find her smile again in a country that was so ill-suited to joy. Meriem left the table when conversation turned to her father and she heard the two rogues talk about him with a quiver of emotion in their voices, as if he had died only the day before. Yes, she was sure – and she was sometimes beside herself, it seemed so inexplicable and even indecent – that Mathieu and her mother still cherished the friend and husband as much as ever. Deep down, she found it unjust that her father's suicide, though profoundly distressing for them, also allowed them to experience the joy of consoling each other.

She feels like yelling at her mother, "Hurry up, stop snoring, your husband is going to commit suicide just like the first!" But an observer perched somewhere in her mind grips her by one of the arteries of the heart: *If you have a conscience, switch it off fast if you really want to save your daughter!*

She tries to swallow, but her mouth is but a dry orifice. If she were to lose her daughter, she would no longer be able to name things. Like an incision in her brain, she remembers, with unbearable tenderness, the scent of her daughter as a small girl, just waking up and rubbing her eyes. The child reaches out to her and snuggles her head up against her chest.

Three fingers! An absurd question bites her without warning: What has the devil done with the three fingers? Has he thrown them in the bin?

Oh, this is too unbearable!

Does her mother know that Mathieu tortured Algerians? Tortured her father? And that her father was mixed up in some sordid crime? Have their whole lives been lies?

Aziz comes into the kitchen, walks over to her and hugs her. She forbids herself to sob; she chases away the desire to throw herself down the deep well of tears, as one kicks a cur up the backside to chase it away.

She slips free of his embrace. They stare at each other, he standing there motionless, arms dangling, lips clenched, as pitiful as his wife. The fear of losing their daughter is slowly draining away all love between them. It's not his fault; she has nothing to reproach Aziz with, at least since his confession. She believed him to be more faint-hearted, not to say cowardly in certain circumstances, but he didn't hesitate to kill in order to save Shehera. She should be thankful to him for that...

(Two little mental mice are engaged in a mad dialogue on the fringes of her main stream of thought: "*Grateful because he killed someone? He's a murderer now...*" "*I hope he didn't leave any clues. If the police catch him, they won't let him off lightly; they'll start off by beating him black and blue...*" "*Yes, Aziz is always so careless...*")

Yet she knows that if she does not recover her daughter, she will never love anyone ever again. Not even this man whom she had once cherished more than anything in the world...

(One of the mice lies down flat, as if it were resigned to being eaten by the cat whose scent it can already smell: *You were solid gold to me, Aziz. For a long time, if you happened to be away and I found myself alone in my bed, I only had to speak your name to conjure up in my mind the fragrance of the lemon trees in the park where we first kissed. For years and years I always hungered for your saliva. Why do we always change for the worse?*)

She stands in front of the window, Aziz's silence weighing on her from behind like an iceberg. She wipes the misted-up windowpane with her hand. The openings in the blocks of flats resemble great, gouged-out eyes. According to the kidnapper's boastful insinuations, her daughter might be being held prisoner in one of those matchboxes.

She stares down at the dimly lit street. An idiotic part of her implores her to put all the intensity she can muster into this gaze, because that will help her little girl – *her little, little girl* – to escape and find her way home.

When the telephone rang, the muezzin was shouting himself hoarse over the mosque's loudspeakers, exhorting the faithful to rise and accomplish the first of the five prayers. Dawn, with careless brushstrokes, had begun to brighten the blackness of the sky with striated splashes of yellow and red.

Meriem gives a start, dazzled by the light from the ceiling lamp; it is nearly six in the morning by the wall clock.

"It's your phone, Aziz."

She doesn't recognise her own discordant voice. Aziz is slumped in his chair. Despite everything he addresses her a comforting grimace. She tries unsuccessfully to return his faint smile.

"Yes?… Is that you, Mathieu?"

Her husband's puffy eyes start to blink. He runs his fingers through his hair in a curious manner, as if he were going to tear the skin off his skull.

"…Your wife?… She's still asleep, the sleeping pills seem to have knocked her out… Meriem? Yes, she's right beside me…"

He hands her the mobile. Panicking, she shakes her head, but Aziz insists.

"He'd like to talk to you."

She gives in and takes the device.

"Is that you, Meriem?"

"Yes, it's me."

She perceives a slight hesitation due to her overly flat tone.

"You know now?"

"Yes, I know."

"You know everything?"

"He rang and ordered Aziz to tell me everything. The past, the present."

"Will you forgive me?"

Her throat tightens. She is on the verge of tears.

"Forgive you? What do I forgive a man who's about to lay down his life for my daughter?"

She breaks off with a gasp.

"It doesn't matter, Meriem. My carcass is no longer listed in the directory of human beings. I won't be a great loss."

"To my mother you will, Mathieu."

"Apart from to your mother... I'm sorry to cause her so much grief."

The Frenchman's voice has become dreamy. With her sleeve Meriem wipes away the tear that is blurring her vision.

"All the good things I've experienced since the war have been a bonus to me. And what's actually going to happen: just the end of a lout who is paying off his debts, nothing more. I haven't been a very commendable person. Long ago I did a lot of harm to your father, you know that now."

"Mathieu, don't say that..."

The old man lets slip a little chuckle.

"I loved it so much when you still used to call me Uncle Mathieu."

She is crying her eyes out now, crying so hard that she doesn't speak the sole sentence that is yapping away in her head: *Don't kill yourself, Mathieu, maybe there's another way of saving Shehera.*

"I don't have any more time. I've got to go."

He has a frog in his throat. The fine hairs on the back of Meriem's neck stand up on end. She wants to ask: *Where have you got to go?* but the words won't cross her lips. A little, insolent gatekeeper mutters: *Hey, slut, don't insist too much or else fright will make short work of the courage he has mustered and your daughter will take the rap.*

"Promise me one last thing, Meriem. If your daughter gets out of this alive, make sure you explain to your mother that I barely had a choice, that none of us had a choice. But, please, tell her as often as you can that I loved her. That's maybe not consolation enough, but it's all I can offer her."

Then the weary voice goes quiet. It is replaced by a crackling noise – and then silence. The telephone is just an inanimate object in her palm. Meriem looks at it incredulously with the feeling that she is holding Mathieu's corpse in her hand.

They didn't wait for long. In the meantime, the husband and wife didn't dare look at or speak to each other, gripped by the same sensation of being slaves to some barbarian cult, reduced to hoping against hope that this fresh oblation of human flesh will appease once and for all the raging hunger of the divinity holding their daughter.

They heard a loud noise, followed by a clamour of voices. They rushed over to the window. The square in front of their building was still deserted, but lights quickly went on in the neighbouring flats and people appeared at the windows. One of them was pointing somewhere with an outstretched arm.

"Maybe we'll see better from the balcony?" Meriem whispered.

"It's the mosque," yelled their neighbour from the foot of their block. "An attack, I think!"

The father and mother turned their heads towards the religious building. The neighbour ran off, shouting frantically, "My son, my son... My son went to morning prayers... Dear God, save my son!"

"What can you see?" asked Meriem.

"Not much. Looks like..."

The already considerable crowd in front of the building concealed the entrance. Aziz's mother-in-law's voice rang out from Shehera's bedroom: "What's happening?" Aziz dashed down the stairs, with Meriem close behind.

The crowd didn't make a sound. Some were in pyjamas, others in their underwear; all of them were listening to a man in a burnous.

"I was about to go home when this damned car appeared. It drove into the courtyard of the mosque, heading straight for us. In God's name, I thought our final hour had come. At the last second..."

Still in shock, he stressed, "He swerved at the last second!"

Eyes bulging, he gestured towards the vehicle embedded in one of the wings of the building. Only the boot was visible in the light shed by the lampposts, protruding from between breezeblocks. A wheel was lying on the ground a few yards from the vehicle.

"The mihrab wall has been reduced to dust. God saved us, believe me! Let us give thanks to Him, brothers!"

Several "*Let us give thanks to the Merciful One. Amen!*" echoed in reply.

"Is the son of a bitch dead?"

"Probably... Unless his head is harder than bricks..."

"He was probably a drunkard..."

"Or one of those bastard drug addicts..."

"Have pity on him, after all he's a son of Adam!"

"You're right, brother… But there's loads of damage…"

"Have you seen? The steering wheel has crushed his ribcage…"

"Hey, don't smoke. It stinks of petrol…"

"Have you called an ambulance? The police?"

"Yes, but they won't come until it's light…"

"Yeah, those poofs are worried about their arses…"

"Aren't you ashamed of uttering such coarse remarks so early in the morning? You are outside a mosque!"

"Sorry… It is Satan speaking through our mouths…"

"Are we going to pull him out?"

"Steady on. This side of the building's collapsed and the beam's only staying up by a miracle… What if it catches fire, eh? Would you risk your life for a dead man?"

"Not for a stranger, no."

The neighbour who'd been worrying about his son was now hugging a tall, bearded beanpole. Catching sight of Aziz and Meriem, he smiled at them misty-eyed.

"See, God protected him for me! I'm going to throw a great party in thanks and you'll come, I hope?"

Aziz ignored him and walked over to what remained of the automobile. The colour and the make matched; he deciphered the number plate merely to save time.

"Is it him?" Meriem asked with a quavering voice, joining him as the bystanders looked on with a mixture of curiosity and disapproval. She was only wearing a housecoat and her arms were bare.

"Is he dead?"

Aziz nodded. They stood there motionless and stunned. The imam recognised them. He knitted his brows in displeasure at the sight of an uncovered woman in the courtyard of the mosque. Muttering through his teeth, he strode over to the couple with the intention of reminding them publicly of the rules of decency. Then, perhaps because of the haggard fixedness of their faces, he stopped.

"By Allah, I hope it's not a relative."

"What did you say, imam?"

Aziz stared wide-eyed. A stabbing pain shot through his temples; it felt as if he'd been hit on the head but that only now was the blow producing its effect.

"Do you know the dead man inside the car?"

"It's my father-in-law," he croaked back.

He swallowed, moistening his lips as he did so, but not managing to rid himself of the lump in his stomach.

"The father of your…"

The imam hesitated, then with the customary and excessive prudishness of peasants and clerics, he opted for 'mother of your children' rather than 'spouse', motioning with his chin at the woman accompanying him. Aziz thought: 'At least you didn't add *with all due respect*, you bastard!'

"Yes, it's my wife's stepfather."

The imam was surprised. "The old *gaouri* who went by the name of Ali? Whatever got into him? Had he been drinking?"

A murmur ran through the small crowd. Aziz felt like laying his hand on his wife's shoulder, but decided against it because the people were now examining them with an increasingly unfriendly interest.

"Erm… No, he didn't drink… He had heart trouble… Maybe a heart attack?"

The man muttered dubiously, "Poor man… May God grant him His mercy… But why was he driving then? We'd just finished the main building work…"

The imam gestured sorrowfully at the ruined wall. Aziz saw the moment coming when the man would start complaining about the cost of the damage. Someone groaned, "A mosque damaged by a Christian – that was all we needed in such miserable times! We'll have to see if someone can pay for it…"

Show some pity, Aziz almost screamed, *we don't even know if he's actually dead yet!* but some unrest in the crowd cut his anger short. He couldn't make out what was happening in the half-light of dawn.

When she suddenly appeared in her dressing gown, forcibly pushing aside the people blocking her path, Aziz thought to himself that her appearance was in the order of things: there was no reason that either their misfortune or the absurd play they were forced to act should cease when everything was going so well. Latifa, her hair unkempt, contemplated the scene of destruction with an incredulous look. Then an ululation formed in her throat. Stretching her arms out towards the crashed car, she keened, "My little one… My little one… My little one…", then slumped to the ground.

Terror-stricken, Meriem tried to pull her mother to her feet, but she shoved her away. On all fours, panting between sobs – "Oh, what are you going to do there without your dear wife… My liver is bleeding for you as if it was I who nursed you…" – she headed towards the car. As the mesmerised crowd watched the indecency of this old madwoman proclaiming her love for a foreigner in the midst of believers, she reached the car. With Meriem still in hot pursuit, she swept aside the brick and breezeblock rubble that was preventing her from reaching the door. One of the girders swayed. Latifa pulled on the handle to no avail. Bending down to the window and cupping her hands round her eyes, she surveyed the inside of the car.

"There he is… There's my husband… Oh, there you are, Mathieu… My whole life crushed in this rotten car… And I told him not to drive at night… Is he dead? Really dead?"

"Yes, Mum."

"Why are you so sure? You're like everyone else, you don't like him, eh?"

"I'm telling you he's dead."

"We have to get him out of there, my girl. Iron defiles the body."

"It's dangerous, Mum, the wall's going to collapse! There's petrol everywhere – look at the bottom of your gown!"

"Well, let me burn! That'll be the end of me too."

And, turning away from Meriem, she called out to the gathering: "You are not men… Not one of you is helping him… And yet he loved this country… You're leaving him to die like vermin… You lie to God, you lie to one another…"

A man shouted, "Someone shut this loony up! We nearly died too!"

Followed by another protest: "She married a heathen and now she thinks she can lecture us about religion!"

"You're all cowards!"

A murmur of anger rose up, punctuated by cries of "Frenchman's trollop!" and "Shameless slut!" Trapping her mother with both arms, Meriem begged her to be quiet. As she struggled to escape from her daughter, Latifa eructated, "…A man is dying before your eyes and you don't even lift a finger, you damn…"

Meriem placed a hand over her mother's mouth and called to Aziz to help bring her under control before her explosion of grief caused irreparable damage. Aziz reacted late. His empty head throbbed with just one ambition, as piercing as toothache: to lock himself away for a whole day and drink, drink, drink until he could no longer remember having ever been capable of a single rational thought, and thereby to escape from this mob of humans – of which he was such an intimate part – caught up in their wickedness, their repressed sorrows and their grotesque certainties.

"Bloody believers my vagina! Satan will grind your bones!"

Latifa was shouting herself hoarse with a vulgarity unimaginable of a stickler for proprieties.

"Everyone's screwing you – the GIA, the government, the cops, the army – and you take revenge on someone weaker than you: a dead man!"

The stone just missed Aziz and crashed down on the bonnet of the car. The next ones hit their target: Latifa. Hiding her head in her hands, she muttered a final insult before dropping at her daughter's feet.

Spotting the blood that was already stickying her mother's temple, Meriem yelped at the top of her voice: "Help me, neighbours. They're killing my mother… Help!" Meriem was shouting in the same angry and simultaneously shrill tone as her mother. Aziz focused for a second on this strange observation, gaining a moment's respite from the horror of the scene around him. From a window a man cried, "What's going on? Can't we sleep in peace?"

Frightened by the course events were taking, the imam interposed himself between the crowd and the two women.

"Brothers, curse the Devil. She has lost her mind, the old woman is not responsible for what she's saying. For the love of the Beloved, listen to me! Regain your calm, I be…"

A last stone hit his shoulder. A voice apologised: "Excuse us, imam, that wasn't meant for you!" The cleric called to Aziz in a brusque tone: "Neighbour, take your women away. There's already one dead and one wounded; that's enough for today!"

The man who held forth five times a day on the grandeur of Creation and the ultimate purposes of existence was spluttering with fear and impatience at his interlocutor's slowness.

"Have you been drinking too, or don't you understand Arabic anymore? A fire might break out at any moment. By the face of the Prophet, go. Take your old woman to casualty. Don't wait for the ambulance, it'll take an hour to get here. I'll take care of the dead man and the cops. Come back and see me when everything's calmed down. I don't want any trouble, not with the locals nor with the authorities!"

The husband whispered, "Meriem, wait here for me. I'll get my car."

Curling her lip, Meriem avoided looking at him. Turning on his heel, he noticed the reflection of the streetlight in a puddle of petrol that had leaked out of the tank. He spared a final thought for the corpse with the staved-in chest: *You dirty bastard, you made one hell of an exit!* and a wave of hideous love for Mathieu swept through him.

Admission to the casualty department went as messily as usual at the Mustapha Pacha Hospital. The duty house doctor palpated the half-unconscious old woman in a slovenly manner in the main waiting room, as visitors and inquisitive people looked on. Other patients waited resignedly for someone to come and take care of them. A chap with an arm immobilised in a bloody scarf was openly smoking.

Meriem was entitled only to some indistinct grumblings from the house doctor as a response to her questions.

"Your mother's head has suffered a serious injury. It's the end of my call and you can discuss everything in a little while with the doctor who takes over from me. In the meantime, a nurse will clean her head, but she'll have to be hospitalised."

Upon which he turned on his heel.

"Aziz, we can't sit on our hands waiting for a doctor. Do something," Meriem begged tearfully. "It's my mother, after all! This can't be happening, so many disasters all at once!"

A middle-aged woman wearing a *haik* came up to the couple.

"Don't cry, my girl. But don't trust these shit doctors; they have no heart and no conscience! Don't leave your mother without anyone to look after her. My husband was unlucky – he didn't know anyone here."

Without waiting for an answer, the stranger began telling them, with a kind of angry eagerness, about her husband's misadventures since his hospitalisation.

"The sheets – can you imagine, we had to bribe the nurse to get some clean ones! If you can't pull any strings here, you're done for. Anyone God loves never goes near an Algerian hospital! Even the bread they give the patients is stale in this rotten hospital! Little one, what does your mother have on her temple? You should wash your hands: you've got blood all over you and that won't do. The blood of others, even a close relative's, is poison, believe me."

Aziz left Meriem to deal with the gossip and her clingy concern. "If you do have to leave her here, make sure you buy her a private toiletries kit as soon as possible, with all due respect, something for when she has to..." was the last sentence he heard before he found himself out in the open air again.

During the drive to the hospital, with him at the wheel, and Meriem and her mother in the back seat, they hadn't exchanged a single word about the stepfather's death. When the traffic conditions happened to bring their eyes into contact – but only in the rear-view mirror – they saw that their relationship had withered, perhaps irretrievably, through their all too easy consent to this proxy murder.

What now? was the only question that floated between them at present, harshly filling in the hollows and little by little sucking away the oxygen of love that had nourished their relationship for so many years.

"Do you think he'll let her go?" she had asked all of a sudden, in a voice that she had forced herself to keep under control, but shot through with a plea that he answer as she wished. Her mother's head, wrapped in a bandage, was resting on her lap. From time to time, the still-unconscious, injured woman would emit a garbled sound, and Meriem patted her reassuringly on the shoulder.

"He's got what he wanted, hasn't he? Now he just has to let our Shehera go."

Then she had uttered some fairly crazed words, doubtless forgetting her mother's presence: "That's what I'd do if I were him; he didn't get my father, the chief instigator, but he got the stepfather, his accomplice in a sense. Throw in the man you... that ought to be enough, hey, Aziz? Two souls for crimes committed over fifty years ago, plus three of our daughter's fingers, that should make up for it now."

Aziz hadn't opened his mouth out of superstition. But he couldn't help but think: "If we're talking about the number of deaths, you're forgetting the woman lying on your lap. And then, you see, the bloke is an ogre, his sorrow is insatiable, and none of your sums will satisfy him!"

Perhaps Meriem had suspected the significance of his silence, for she added, still just as feverishly, "What do you think he's done with our daughter's fingers? Has he thrown them away? Has he kept them?"

Faced with his speechlessness, she had cast him another glance in the rear-view mirror that was full of fear and hatred. He felt as if he had taken an axe blow to the heart. His legs started trembling; the engine had stalled on a hill and, once again, an urge to vomit out of terror for his daughter had tortured his guts.

His passenger had bent over her mother, whispering in near hysteria, "Mum, I haven't got time to look after you right now. Don't die, please... Put it off till later if you like, but first we have to find your granddaughter!"

He recalled that at that moment, in a final defensive reflex, a phrase had sparkled like a neon sign in the night of his soul: *I love you, Shehera, tell your mother that I'll love her too; I love you, Shehera, tell...*

He rings his friend the vet from the hospital courtyard. The man grumbles at first – "Hey, do you know what time it is? I hope your question's a lot more urgent than the re-election of our dear life president now you've dragged me out of bed this early. Unless, that is, our most handsome male bonobo has run away with the chief's wife, or that little monkey Lucy has suddenly converted to Islam and volunteered for a suicide attack on the Ministry of Agriculture!" – before giving up this exuberant demonstration of bad-temperedness on hearing his friend's distraught voice.

"Are you all right, Aziz?"

"I need you, Lounes. Do you know a doctor in a good position at the Mustapha Pacha Hospital? My mother-in-law has had an accident."

"Is it serious?"

"Maybe."

The vet hesitated momentarily.

"I'll see what I can do. I've got a relative who's a consultant at Mustapha Pacha. Where are you?"

"At the casualty department."

"We'll meet there. Hey, don't hang up! A man phoned the zoo administration yesterday. He said that you wouldn't be coming in all week. Urgent family matters to see to, he said. The bloke didn't seem all that trustworthy. According to the receptionist, he was much too cheerful, and he repeated that you were thinking about changing jobs. He presented himself as a close relative of yours. You can imagine that the director didn't appreciate the fact that you got a stranger to announce you'd be off. He's furious with you and he's talking about sacking you, especially as you made him lose face in front of the delegation from the ministry. Hey man, what's going on? You disappear overnight, you skive off work... Got a problem?"

Aziz gulped, barely withstanding the temptation to confide everything to his friend.

"No... Well, not really. I'll explain. Please come as fast as you can."

He went back into the waiting room. A nurse with her hackles up was explaining sourly to Meriem that it wasn't her fault if the doctors were late every morning. Voices began to be raised. Aziz laid a hand on his wife's arm to calm her down. Just then a telephone ringtone went off. His.

"Is it him?" whispered Meriem.

"Yes... I think so... Hidden number... I'm going outside to speak to him. Lounes will be here any minute. He knows a well-placed guy at the hospital."

"Oh my God, rescue her..." she groaned as she put her hands together, in a wounded tone that caused the exasperated nurse to spin round. The latter furrowed her brow at a demonstration of such trivial despair in this place, before walking off dragging her feet.

Aziz slipped out of the building like a thief. A guard watched him suspiciously as he passed. He took refuge behind a wall. With the phone pressed to his ear, he tried to form a "Hello", but no sound crossed his lips.

"Let's talk about your mother-in-law. Has she died?"

"No..."

"But she's going to, isn't she?"

The voice was hopeful. Aziz's armpits were suddenly moist. He sensed that it was dangerous to annoy the kidnapper.

"Probably. Her head injuries seem to be serious. She's in a coma. The doctor was very doubtful about her chances of coming through."

"Guess I'm a good shot: the old man crashed and the old woman made sure she followed him! But I've still got a few balls to pot. And I'm ahead, right?"

Aziz was dumbstruck, overcome by an irrepressible urge to kill. He leaned against a wall, sucking in a great gulp of air to bring himself under control. The effort brought tears to his eyes.

"Don't have any comment?"

"You're going to kill my whole family, right?"

A long silence. Then the sounds of a chair moving.

"No more cheating: your aim is to kill us one by one, whatever we do. Am I wrong?"

"I haven't killed anyone, my boy. That is the plain truth."

"Stop all this play-acting. According to Mathieu, you've kidnapped my daughter because of Melouza. Why would my daughter be responsible for the crimes of her grandfather or Mathieu? How would her death console you for your daughter's death?"

Then, in a sudden burst of fury: "She was called Sheherazade, right?"

More chilled than if the polar icecaps had lodged inside him, Aziz waited for the reaction from his daughter's executioner with the curiosity of the condemned man waiting for the blade to come down on his neck. Maybe the maniac was going to slit Shehera's throat the next moment? If so, the father decided with a realisation that his action would be but a minor blip in the man's plan, he would immediately bring his own existence to an end, without even taking the trouble to warn Meriem.

"Do not vainly desecrate the past, Aziz. It bears enough grudges against you already; you couldn't imagine how many."

There wasn't the feared explosion of anger.

Aziz took up his futile pleading again.

"Listen… Today's children are not guilty of crimes of the previous generation… I beg you…"

"No, the past does not turn into the past without a helping hand. With goodwill, with tenderness, with the respect due to those who have suffered. As far as I'm concerned, the past is a gigantic bone stuck in my throat. In Algeria, you have spat on it, you keep on spitting on it and you will continue to spit on it… No, no, *my* past is far from passing, there is a price to pay for that… I shall be in touch in an hour's time to set a meeting place. It's in your bird's and your interest to come running when I signal. Your daughter has lost a lot of blood, so no dawdling. Rejoice, partners, your impatience will soon be at an end."

"What? She's losing a lot of blood? I beseech you, let her go – we have to look after her, she's innocent!" Aziz begged, panic-stricken at not finding the magic words that would breach his interlocutor's monstrous logic. "Are you really the man Mathieu talked about? Please answer me… Is my daughter on the estate? Have mercy… Why us? No, don't hang up! For the love of…"

White-faced, the father put the telephone away in his pocket before walking stiffly back towards the waiting room. From time to time, he pressed on his chest, for he was having trouble breathing. Ten yards or so away, the hospital security guard was picking his nose and following the man with his eyes who had spent over ten minutes on the other side of the wall shouting into his mobile. "Must be some dirty story turned sour. Half the people in this country are looking for a shag and the other half are barricading their arses!" he ventured and decided not to call the guardroom.

The little boy was making a lot of noise in the waiting room. His worn-out mother gave him a clip around the ear. The child burst into tears. Overcome with remorse, the woman in the *haik* gave him a hug before plastering his nose with kisses. Smiling again while still snivelling, the child snuggled his head into his mother's lap and pretended to doze off.

Aziz was overwhelmed with an unbearable sense of jealousy as he watched the scene. He had overheard while the woman was chatting with her neighbour that her husband had been a victim of an accident on a building site. The child was wearing shoes with worn-out soles. Their day was going to be full to the brim with the humiliation that the administrative officials reserve for those with no social influence. Yet Aziz felt his throat desiccate with lust for this banal exchange of tenderness: would he ever be able to place another kiss on his Shehera's forehead?

The madman had mentioned a considerable loss of blood…

To Meriem he first of all explained that Lounes had promised to meet up with them to put them in touch with someone important at the hospital. Then, as if there were no way of postponing the moment, he allowed her no respite and announced the kidnapper's latest demand – without mentioning, however, his allusion to their daughter's critical state.

"He wants to meet us? We'll see Shehera? When?"

"Any time now. I don't know anything else."

"But what are we going to do about my mother?"

Hearing a stifled cry, a middle-aged man sitting next to them turned to look at this haphazardly dressed woman who was watching over another older lady lying unconscious on a stretcher. The visitor was himself accompanying a young man as thin as a rake, whose features were drawn with suffering, and he sighed with a trace of irritation, as if to say: "This country is an unbelievable bloody shambles, so be patient, we're all in the same leaking boat." Then, pulling some prayer beads out of his *kachabia* cloak, he fell into a silent invocation, his free hand patting the boy's back at regular intervals – his son, by all appearances.

Aziz begged Meriem with a glance to keep her composure.

"If necessary, I'll ask Lounes to take care of your mother."

"But she's not his mother, he won't know how to look after her," she protested, wringing her hands.

The vet arrived out of breath. Lounes gave his colleague's wife a kiss, putting on the appropriate pitying expression. He assured them that his relative had already been promised by the head of the trauma unit that the woman he had officially presented as 'the mother-in-law of a favourite nephew' would receive VIP treatment.

"Was it a car accident?"

"Well… yes, sort of," Aziz retorted, getting in ahead of his wife.

Intrigued, Lounes opened his mouth to ask for more details. Grabbing him by the sleeve of his raincoat, Meriem broke into a stream of excessive and garbled thanks. Lounes, impressed by her grief and the two scratches on her chin, stammered a few words about the compassion of God, who never neglected good people. Then, as if ashamed of having spoken in such conventional terms, he tried to relax the atmosphere.

"The head of the unit will be here in ten minutes or so. He's got a reputation as an excellent specialist. I'm convinced that everything will go perfectly and your mother will be up and running again in no time… and chasing after this bonobo-lover, who deserves it from time to time, eh Meriem?"

The attempted joke fell flat. Embarrassed by the couple's gloomy attitude, Lounes tried again, his tone still too cheerful.

"How's Shehera doing? She's just turned 14, that's what you said, isn't it, Aziz? If she were capable, our little Lucette would probably have sent her a text message to congratulate her *Homo sapiens* godmother!"

Confronted with the married couple's helpless looks, the vet ran a hand through his unruly hair, some new wrinkles at variance with his forced joviality.

"Let's go outside for a smoke, if you don't mind," Aziz suggested, leading his friend towards the exit.

"But I don't smoke!"

"Well, I'll smoke then."

Outside, Aziz made some nonsensical comment about the din of the traffic and winter pollution in Algiers, before taking a half-empty packet of cigarettes out of his pocket. He smiled miserably.

"I won't offer you one."

"This accident's really got to you, hasn't it?" Lounes remarked with concern.

"How can you tell?"

"Your fingers are shaking – anyone would swear you'd got Parkinson's. It's true that your mother-in-law's in a bad way. I can understand too that your wife is terrified of this shithole Mustapha hospital. By the way, I didn't see your father-in-law. Has he been informed?"

Incapable of improvising a reply, Aziz stared straight ahead, wide-eyed. As if driven by some unconscious inverse imitation, Lounes creased up his own eyes and stared with puzzlement into his friend's tired and vaguely guilty-looking face. Aziz was tempted to rebel at this: *Hey, no point examining me with that concentrated, condescending look you use on your sick animals at the zoo!* before biting his lip, aware that that was *exactly* what he had been since his daughter was kidnapped.

"Don't tell me…" the vet suddenly whispered, as if struck by the obvious.

Aziz went bright red. The vet interpreted his colleague's reaction as a sign of assent.

"…That he was driving? Oh, please don't tell me that on top of that…"

Lounes tapped his forehead.

"…That he died in the accident… Am I right?"

Aziz nodded without thinking, suffocated by how close the lie was to the truth. Lounes let out a curse before reaching for the packet of cigarettes.

"That's a tough blow for your wife. I really feel for her. Come on, give me a fag, please. Might just as well poison your lungs as pollute your ears with such bad news."

They smoked in silence. Aziz pretended to be lost in thought so that Lounes would think twice about pursuing his questioning about the circumstances of the 'accident'.

"Why are you looking at your watch?"

"Erm... what?"

"You're looking at your watch every minute."

"I... What are you talking about?"

"Aziz, you're so on edge, you'd make a blind goldfish nervous!"

"Why 'blind'?"

"So you'd ask me that question, you venerable fool. By the way, where did the accident happen?"

To gain a bit of time Aziz took a long, deep breath, praying that his lie would appear credible.

"My parents-in-law were driving to our house this morning. He had a heart attack at the wheel. The accident happened on the way into the estate. Some neighbours let us know."

"What a disaster! Your father-in-law's at the morgue?"

"I... Yes... Sorry... Phone? Is it mine?"

"Yes, in your pocket, Aziz... There... Don't you feel well? You're white as a sheet..."

Aziz made a vague gesture to signal to Lounes that someone was already talking to him over the telephone.

"Hello. Is it you?"

"Are you missing me, my friend?"

Controlling his voice so he didn't start shaking in front of his colleague, Aziz replied in an overly detached manner: "If you only knew how much..."

There was a snigger at the other end of the line.

"Is there someone with you who knows nothing about our little secret, my friend?"

Every time that 'my friend' felt like a sticky lick from a venomous animal's tongue.

"I'm not your friend. Let's get down to business, if you don't mind?"

"In that case, get in your car with your wife. You must be at the hospital, if my deductions are correct. Be at the entrance of the Central Post Office in twenty minutes from now. Exactly twenty minutes. You don't have a second to lose, lad."

"Are you joking?"

"Joking am I? Is *this* enough proof that I'm not joking?"

A scream of pain reached him through the tiny earpiece. His heart flagged, as though it was refusing to carry on beating.

"Recognise the voice? Want more details? So, you pathetic father, you will follow my instructions to the letter. Incidentally, you only have 19 minutes and… 45 seconds, 44 seconds… left. See you right away…. Run, run, if your brat means anything to you!"

"I… I don't believe this!"

Lounes was startled by Aziz's distraught face – an automatic smile jarred with his glassy pupils.

"More bad news, Aziz?"

"Lounes… Please don't ask any questions. Follow me – you'll find out more later."

"Why are you running like a madman? What's going on? Hey, wait for me!"

They burst into the waiting room. A nurse threatened to call a guard if they didn't stop their racket. As several heads nodded in agreement, she complained that Arabs only ever respected the stick. Aziz whispered something in Meriem's ear. She put her hand to her mouth as though she were about to scream and her fingers should prevent her from doing so at all costs.

"Neither of us has a choice. Give him your mother's papers. Quick, quick, quick."

"I've got her identity card… The family record book too? Should I leave him my card?"

"Hurry up. We've got quarter of an hour at the most."

The people in the room watched the man and the woman fidgeting around the stretcher. Curiosity could not mask their disapproval. Even Lounes almost made a rude remark, but Meriem thrust an envelope decisively into his hands.

"I'm handing over my mother to you – please treat her like your own!" she whispered with a sob caught in her throat, "I only have one mother."

She stroked the inanimate old woman's cheek before rushing towards the exit. She wavered as she touched the handle of the main entrance.

"Are you out of your minds?" Lounes protested, waving the envelope.

"I'll explain everything over the phone," Aziz implored him from the other side of the door. "Don't let us down – you're the only one who can help us!"

The stunned vet pulled an angry face as the rushing footsteps died away down the corridor. "I've already got a mother… You're nuts… What terrible manners. I'm working today, I am… Several meetings… A tiger with colic… The Director's going to be furious…"

Then, turning crimson with the sudden attention focused on him, he lowered his head towards the stretcher, puffing nervously through his teeth: "Oh well, beautiful lady, your own family has abandoned you. I'm not your son and my mother wouldn't appreciate having you as a rival! So there's no question of us signing a love contract, but, all right, I'll see what I can do for you…"

They drove along at full speed, ignoring the red lights. Meriem asked her husband if he'd been able to talk to Shehera. No, he replied.

"So how can you be sure she's alive?" she fired back as her knee moved as if it had a life of its own.

"I heard her shout 'Dad'," he lied.

A spasm ran through Meriem's chest and she gave up asking for further explanations. Aziz's phone rang; the name of Lounes the vet appeared on the screen. Aziz didn't answer, postponing till later the time when he would have to face up to his friend's questions.

A policeman whistled at them after a dangerous overtaking manoeuvre, but they didn't stop. The traffic jam they feared had started to form in rue Didouche. As soon as the Central Post Office was in sight, they parked the car quickly on a patch of pavement. A shopkeeper sitting in front of his store warned them: "The police come round here a lot. Trust me, they'll clamp you!"

Paying him no heed, Aziz and Meriem set off at a run, bumping into pedestrians who showered them with insults. Aziz shouted to Meriem, "We're five minutes late!" On the square above the underground, they dashed across the sloping street leading to the esplanade in front of the post office, attracting beeping horns and obscenities from drivers. "Go fuck your mother, you whore's brood, instead of haring around like that!" yelled one taxi driver after almost piling into the vehicle in front of him.

"What time is it, Aziz?"

"We're over ten minutes late… My God… my God… Protect her!"

"I… I'm going to be sick."

He gave his wife a tissue. She covered her mouth with it just before another convulsion shook her. Aziz got out his telephone and stared at it, imploring it: "Ring, I beg you, ring, you bastard!" A policeman coming out of the post office glanced suspiciously at the sweating couple and sidled up to them shiftily. Aziz pretended to interpret his mistrust as an offer of assistance.

"Don't worry – my wife's pregnant. She hasn't been feeling very well for the last few days. Thanks for your help."

The husband's smile was so false that the policeman shrugged his shoulders before continuing on his way.

Aziz jumped when the ringtone finally sounded. The small device slipped out of his sweaty hands. A plaintive yelp escaped him when he thought that the telephone had broken.

"You're late, lovebirds!"

Meriem clung tightly to her husband's shoulder, straining towards the earpiece. She was still clasping the dirty tissue to her mouth.

"No, no, we've been waiting for your phone call for several minutes."

The voice turned menacing.

"Are you calling me a liar?"

"Pardon me. No need to get angry."

"Incidentally," the voice resumed in an ironic tone, "my – how shall I say? – my associate is watching you and he just rang to tell me you were late."

Aziz had a quick glance all round him. Crowds of people were going in and out of the large neo-Moorish building. The old man with the cigarette staring grim-eyed at him; might he be this accomplice? Or that other, younger but bearded man selling peanuts? Or the woman in a hijab waiting at the pedestrian crossing even though the light had turned green?

"There's no point trying to recognise him. I've hired competent people."

"What do we have to do now?"

Aziz was having trouble forming his words. His chest was beating so violently that he had the impression it was spilling into his mouth. Paler than ever, Meriem shouted out, so that the kidnapper could hear, "Listen to my prayer, man, that God may show you the path of righteousness and protect you! He will bless you if you take pity on our daughter. Take us in her place."

"Be quiet!" the father yelped. "Don't give him any more ideas!"

The man chuckled gleefully at his exasperation.

"It's not out of the question, this exchange thing. Maybe I'll agree to it, but there are two or three formalities to see to first. I intend to make sure no one has followed you. Go and see the bookseller…"

"You're messing us about!"

"Shut up! From the steps of the Central Post Office you'll see a bookshop on the corner of rue Ben-Mhidi. You'll tell the bookseller your first name and then thank him on behalf of your uncle. You will buy the *El Watan* newspaper. From there, still with your wife, you will go to the Sanctuary of the Martyrs. You will wait for my instructions at the base of the three concrete palm fronds. You have half an hour starting now. The traffic jams heading up onto the heights of Algiers are a damn nuisance at this time of day. Get a move on. I hope that you know Algiers and its shortcuts well."

"But why the newspaper?"

"I've published a classified ad in it for you. If you're smart, you'll work out what it's about. It will, let's say, facilitate our negotiations. You're both graduates, so I trust in your intelligence. No dillydallying on the way – I've a knife waiting to be sharpened. Enjoy the race!"

The bookshop owner soon lost his business smile.

"OK, your name's Aziz. So what?"

"My uncle sends you his thanks."

"What uncle?"

"My uncle," the father replied, "*whom you know well.*"

"I don't know your uncle, especially if you won't tell me what he's called, mate. All right, you can see that whole queue of people behind you – what do you actually want?"

The bookshop owner threw a hostile look at the woman whose hair was glued to her sweat-streaked temples.

"I'd like today's *El Watan.*"

"Because you're scared I'm going to sell you yesterday's, are you?" the bookseller objected bad-temperedly, pulling a copy out of the revolving stand.

When they were outside again, Aziz heard the shopkeeper

remarking to the other customers, "What are things coming to if they let mad people go around in couples!"

The nightmare began all over again: a gallop in the opposite direction back to the car – where a butterfly awaited them on the windscreen – uphill towards Pasteur, boulevard Mohamed V, Télemly, Clos-Salembier... Meriem read the classified ads out loud: job offers, situations wanted, unfinished villas and computer equipment for sale, and so on. His head full of fog, Aziz listened to her run through the marriage proposals from spinsters spelling out that they owned a flat and a car or from men noting a preference for a candidate who had emigrated to Europe. Nothing seemed to bear any resemblance to a message from the lunatic.

"I can't make head nor tail of this," she groaned. "How about you?"

He shook his head to signal 'no'.

"Read some more, please."

Meriem put a hand between her legs like a little girl trying to stop herself peeing, before resuming the absurd litany.

"...*Minibus for rent... Home repairs of electrical appliances... Urgent, flat to rent... The Doha family is looking for their son Nasreddine, who left home on... Young woman, practising Muslim, good-looking, 30, would like... Shell of two-storey house for sale... Hairdressing diploma for rent...*"

From time to time, Aziz rubbed his eyes with his arm to wipe away the sweat that was blinding him. His brain was wearing itself out searching for some clue among the mush of information reaching him. Why had the kidnapper referred to an accomplice operating openly? Was that portly bookseller really involved in his daughter's kidnapping? He seemed too young to have been caught up in Melouza, didn't really have the look and the arrogance of an Islamist terrorist... What then? Some thug who'd risk the death sentence for kidnapping without taking any precautions of anonymity? But why? For money? And what about this ordeal of decrypting the classifieds, which was turning the search for their daughter into some unbearable parody of a televised treasure hunt?

Something wasn't quite right. He scratched his head in rage, as if to crush the cloud of unanswerable questions.

"Watch out!" Meriem screamed, when a car that Aziz had tried to overtake on the wrong side swerved towards them.

"I can't concentrate anymore," he said by way of an excuse, smacking the steering wheel in anger. "There's nothing odd about those bloody ads. Maybe his goal is just to stop us thinking!"

"What did you say? You can't think?"

There was a glimmer of disdain in Meriem's hollow eyes, which said, in substance: *My daughter is being tortured by a maniac, my mother is dying because of him, and you dare to complain about being too tired to think?*

"Nothing. Carry on, please. We've still got another ten minutes or so."

Driving down a one-way street the wrong way (*...villa in Hydra at a fair price...*) enabled Aziz to avoid a crossroads (*...looking for work as a chef...*), which he knew to be very busy. A driver stuck two fingers up at him. As luck would have it, the traffic (*...3-room flat for rent to a foreign company...*) wasn't very dense. The Sanctuary of the Martyrs was already showing off (*...2005 Mercedes, price to be discussed...*) its enormous concrete palm leaves (*...looking for partner with financial contribution, significant yield guaranteed...*) which were meant to represent the three revolutions (*...pretty, well-educated, God-fearing...*) of modern Algeria: industrial, agrarian and cultural.

They parked alongside the run-down housing of Diar-el-Mahçoul, then, newspaper in hand, climbed the flight of steps leading up to the sanctuary square. One of the soldiers keeping watch over the surroundings of the flame of the unknown martyr favoured them with a suspicious frown; usually only lovers, school groups and families in their Sunday best came for a walk on this esplanade, not some dazed rogue accompanied by an untidily turned-out tart, both of them panting as if their heels were on fire!

"Shall I carry on reading?" Meriem asked.

Then, switching abruptly, with the neutral tone of someone who has actually had her mind on one thing: "I really hope it wasn't a mistake to keep the police out of this."

They had stopped on the other side from the shopping centre, in the shadow of an immense statue of a fighter with a Kalashnikov. On the horizon before them rose the bulk of Mount Chréa.

"Yes," he agreed, taking out his telephone, without indicating whether this was 'yes' to reading the ads or to keeping the police out of things.

The wind was blowing, making it difficult to unfold and read the newspaper. Meriem's voice cracked at regular intervals. It sounded as if she were chanting the prayer of the dead, the one the imams pronounce over the coffins of the dead just before they are lowered into the grave, but here the surahs had been perverted to mock the survivors' grief.

It was only after ten interminable minutes or so that the telephone rang. Aziz activated the loudspeaker.

"Oh, now it's me that's late! Do I have to apologise? (He cleared his throat.) Excuse me, I must have caught a cold."

His cough was merry.

"Hey, fine weather today. Is the flame of the martyr burning?"

"Yes, I think so. Where are we supposed to meet?"

"Not so fast. Did you understand my message?"

"No."

"I'm not happy with you. Are you and your wife that stupid? You know that nature abhors an idiot? And that I respect nature's tastes? You're forcing me to take action."

"Listen…"

"Shh!"

The spring sunshine toned down the bronze of the statues. They awaited the stranger's verdict without exchanging glances. Aziz put his arm round his wife's shoulders. Her whole body was trembling, while he could no longer feel his limbs. The stranger coughed again. His coughing fit was so everyday that Aziz dared to break the silence.

"Why all the complications? Tell us the meeting-place and we'll go there."

"And how do I make sure that no policemen are following you?"

"I swear it by all that is most precious to me."

"I've already got what is most precious to you. But I'll give you another chance. Lucky I've thought it all through! Go to the cigarette seller's on the first floor of the shopping centre. You will present yourself as the mayor's brother and you will ask him for the address. If he doesn't find anything suspicious, he'll give it to you. On the other hand…"

"Which address?"

"The address, that's all."

"Will our daughter be there?"

"Probably, if you continue to knuckle under. And I did say *knuckle*…"

He burst out laughing.

"Keep your phone on," he ordered. "I want to follow your conversation with the tobacconist. Off you go!"

They raced across the esplanade to get to the shopping centre, he with his ear glued to the phone, she like a robot. When she turned her head, drops of sweat flew off her face. The kidnapper hustled Aziz along with extraordinarily cheerful cries of "Faster, faster!".

"Have you found the tobacconist's?"

"The one next to the bookshop?"

"The very same, sonny. He's ready and waiting for you. Let me warn you again: no sneaky tricks!"

The young salesman smiled at him. He was sipping his tea as he listened to the radio.

"What would you like, brother? Some cigarettes? Algerian or foreign ones?"

Aziz stared at the accomplice in disbelief. The man displayed a nonchalance incompatible with the role he was supposed to fill. His telephone was still on.

"Hello," he said, forcing himself to return the man's smile – and feeling his face wrinkling with the effort. "Erm… I'm the mayor's brother."

"Ooh, aren't you a lucky man! And I'm the president's son!"

The salesman guffawed – even though, with a wary sidelong glance, he had taken in the woman's ravaged features.

"Anyway, the president's waiting for me because we're going out clubbing tonight. So, brother, do you want cigarettes from here or from abroad?"

"Give me the address."

His voice had gone husky. He held out the telephone, still on, in front of him. The salesman studied him with burgeoning irritation.

"I didn't get you, brother."

"Give me the address, by the face of God. Nobody has followed us."

"What address?"

"I was told to ask you for the address."

"The address?"

"Yes, the address. You're meant to give me the address."

The smile had disappeared, hardening into a grimace.

"Hey, mate, you haven't been smoking something a bit stronger than a cigarette, have you?"

Then, more aggressively: "Are you going to buy some cigarettes off me or not? If not, just let me get on with earning my children's keep. As for the addresses, look in the directory. Gonna buy something then? Hey, are you listening to me?"

The worried seller had a surreptitious look under the counter, probably searching for something to defend himself with, just in case. Aziz tried one last beseeching look before turning away.

The seller watched them walk off, the man with his mobile stuck to his ear and the sickly-looking woman following stiffly on his heels. He suddenly felt sorry for this creature. If he didn't beat her, the weirdly behaved husband must, at the very least, give her a hard time. OK, so that was his right, but he shouldn't overdo it!

"Honestly, Algeria's in a bad way. I tell you, mother: Algeria's in a bad way."

The laughter coming from the phone sounded like a whinny. They were standing in the middle of the vast esplanade bordered by the Sanctuary of the Martyrs and the shopping centre.

The father said, "It's a joke, is it? The classified ads, the bookshop, the tobacconist – all a big joke? Just to stamp us down a bit further? And so you can laugh your guts out more than ever?"

"I wanted to take off those American films... You know, the ones where the hero gets sent all over the place by a guy who doesn't want the cops to find him... ha, ha, ha... I'd have given anything to see the bookseller's and the tobacconist's faces... The uncle's nephew and the mayor's brother! Oh dear, that's so funny!"

His spluttering laughter continued to fill the small loudspeaker. Meriem nodded, as if she'd guessed it from the start but had refused to listen to the warnings from her brain.

"Why? Aren't you doing us enough harm already?"

"This devil knows his craft: even the greatest pain can be significantly increased if you scoff at it too."

This was Meriem answering Aziz, her voice monotonous, expressionless, almost sterile; then, speaking directly into the mobile: "I think that's what happened to you. When you told your family's story, not only did no one take pity on you, but they made a clown of you, they ridiculed your misfortune. Am I right?"

The laughter abruptly cracked – as if the stranger had been caught off guard by this calm 'diagnosis'.

"You've got some gumption, little lady, and some guts too," he eventually mocked, imitating the woman's tone of voice, "especially after what happened to your mother and your stepfather this morning. Aziz, you're lucky to have such a smart wife. The slut would've been better off keeping quiet, though. I don't like people spoiling my good mood. For that, we'll get straight down to the serious business."

Aziz hung his head. Meriem's eyes remained vacant, lending her features a new, almost mineral aspect.

"Go straight home. Don't leave your flat whatever you do and get ready for the big day. This must all end today. And that, I promise you, is not a joke."

A seagull landed close to the couple, hoping against all logic to be given some leftover food. Maybe it had mistaken the telephone held out between the two human beings for a sandwich?

"Come on," said Meriem, "our daughter's waiting for us."

The woman looked as if she was in shock and, at the same time, seemed to be greeting events with total indifference. Aziz almost yelped: *I'm frightened, Meriem!* He put his phone away and followed her.

Here and there, people were walking across the vast concrete area, some of them hurrying, others strolling, each of them caught up in the small world of his two or three joys, his worries and, perhaps, his tragedies. He didn't envy any of these passers-by, not even the luckiest amongst them. He just wanted to be like the greedy seagull, entirely devoted to its own hunger, a blessed creature devoid of love and of the despair that always ensues.

I gave her the phone. The text message was from Lounes:

`Mother room 24 in traumatology critical`
`Come quick Good luck`

She read it and sniffed angrily before kissing the screen with a ludicrous show of tenderness that I nevertheless immediately deciphered: she had just chosen between her mother and her daughter.

"Hurry up," was all she said, her voice hoarse, "our girl is hurt. She's lived too little for me to wrap her up in a shroud."

She turned her head away and perhaps afraid of breaking down, didn't address another word to me until we reached our flat. When we walked in, the telephone had been ringing for several seconds.

"Hello?"

"What's the idea, Aziz, not answering my calls?"

Lounes didn't hide his displeasure.

"You ran off and left me with the old lady, even though I'm snowed under with work. Luckily, I managed to get her looked after pretty fast! She's lucky in her misfortune because the boss has a good reputation. He didn't seem very optimistic, though. The injuries are fairly strange, he said, for a road accident and he'd like a bit more information about the circumstances of the crash. The secretary wants some other healthcare papers. Hello? You've got nothing to say? What's wrong with you? I can understand you at a pinch, but your wife? That injured woman's her mother, for God's sake!"

"I'll explain…"

"You'll explain what? That looking after her mother in casualty is such a pain for your wife… Hey, let me talk to your wife!"

I held the receiver out to Meriem who shook her head.

"She's… she's on the toilet…"

"That's the only excuse she can come up with to wriggle out of this. It's… it's a scandal… There you go, you disgust me!"

He hung up. Then almost immediately – just as I expected – he rang back, less angry and more worried this time.

"You're really weird, Aziz. You don't come to work anymore, your wife and you seemed in a daze this morning, you drop her comatose mother, your mother-in-law, without warning like a dirty sock. It's not like you to behave this way. Something's the matter. I'm your friend, you can tell me."

Before my exhausted mind could think up a plausible response, the vet went back on the attack, a little embarrassed about going out on a limb like this, but unable to stave off his curiosity.

"I only know one thing that can distress a couple, or rather parents, like this: their kids… Sorry for poking my nose into your family affairs. Is your daughter in trouble? School? No, you wouldn't make such a fuss about that, especially not you anyway… Is… Is she ill? Shehera's a teenager… maybe she's…? She's run away? A crush that's got out of hand? Hello? Can you hear me?"

I bent double, winded as if someone had thumped me flush in the chest. This clever snoop would end up finding out the truth if I let him talk! Meriem gesticulated wildly at me to get off the line. I stammered, "Sorry, Lounes, I'm expecting an urgent phone call on the landline. I'll… I'll explain later…" before putting down the receiver on its base like someone getting rid of a dangerous object.

Meriem went into the bathroom. A little later she came back out after a refreshing shower, her hair done and a hint of make-up under her eyes. She carefully selected a sober, dark dress from the wardrobe in the bedroom and slipped it on, all without saying a word. She added the finishing touch with her raincoat and had a last look round the kitchen before coming back to sit down on the couch with the attitude of someone preparing for a long journey. Except that there was no suitcase at her feet.

"What did you take from the kitchen, Meriem?"

Only a twitch of the chin betrayed how tense she was.

"We're going to meet the devil, Aziz. The devil in person. He laughs and does evil. We can't afford for our brains to be foggy when we confront him. He might want to kill us. And if I have to die, I want to die clean."

"What did you take from the kitchen, Meriem?"

She held up the long knife she had hidden in the inside pocket of her raincoat.

"Wash your face, Aziz. You've got to have a clear mind too. And get yourself some kind of weapon."

I did as she said: soap, razor, comb. When I sat down next to her, she asked to see my weapon.

"Do you recognise it?"

"Mathieu's old pistol. Is it loaded?"

"Yes, several bullets. But I don't know if it works. No one's used it in a long time."

She checked a tearless sob.

"Poor Mathieu. I loved him, then I hated him. Now it's too late – he died like a dog. Forgive or be forgiven – there's no more you can do when it's too late. At least he loved my mother. As for the rest…"

In an almost inaudible whisper, she said, "My mother…" before sinking into a silence that I didn't dare interrupt.

She roused herself with a moan of pain. And at that moment she performed the most surprising gesture of the whole day: she caught hold of my hand and plunged it between her thighs until it touched flesh, then knelt down, opened my flies and took my penis in her mouth before standing up again.

She wiped her lips. The whole thing had only lasted for about ten seconds. I watched her in amazement. Her features were harsh, her voice strangled – in utter contrast to that violent burst of intimacy.

"I have no idea what is going to happen to us in a little while, Aziz. If the worst were to happen, that is the final worldly proof that we were husband and wife and that we had a child. If there are any witnesses in this room, then they will bear witness for us."

"What witnesses?" I almost objected to the woman I loved more than anything on earth. She evaded my gaze. On each cheek, a red stain like a drop of blood stood out against the white of her skin. Meriem straightened her dress and her raincoat. I wanted to stand up too and take her in my arms, whether there were any 'witnesses' or not. I felt like weeping. She pushed me away with a brusque hand movement and set about flicking imaginary specks of dust off her raincoat.

I did my flies up and we waited together, husband and wife, mother and father, for the demon to call.

His voice was almost shy, the demon's, even though he was striving to hide his emotion behind fake cheer.

"Well, not a minute too soon!"

My heart was beating so hard that I had the same trouble breathing as if I'd run as far as my legs could carry me.

"Where do we have to meet you? With our daughter, of course."

"Now, little lady, and with your daughter, most certainly."

The tone of their exchange, normal and very polite, made me even more frightened. Could she be as scared as I was, with this taste of poison in my mouth?

"Well, let's go then," she replied without the slightest emotion. She made one furtive movement (as if her interlocutor could see her) towards her raincoat pocket to check that the knife was well hidden. I did likewise, with the peculiar sensation that my wife was better armed with her kitchen knife than I with my army pistol.

"Go out of your flat. Walk down to the bus stop directly opposite your block."

Before stepping over the threshold, I clasped my wife in my arms. I smiled inwardly, but my face muscles refused to obey me. I caressed Meriem's cheeks, incapable of finding any other way of expressing the flood of love coursing through me.

"Wait," she said when we reached the top of the stairs. She rushed into the flat and came back out less than a minute later carrying a plastic bag.

"It's to give Shehera some first aid," she whispered, showing me the medical kit we used to treat the bumps and scratches of everyday life. "We could do with a surgeon instead," I thought without daring to say it out loud.

We waited at the bus stop for about ten minutes. The driver, roughly on time for once, waved to us to get in. When we declined, he shouted that it was worth him putting himself out for people who lazed about rather than working.

I saw Meriem's eyes become blurred when a beaming neighbour drew up beside us in his car.

"I bet your old banger's finally given up the ghost. I'm going into the centre of Algiers. I can drop you off, if that's any help."

I turned down our helpful neighbour's offer, explaining that we were waiting for a friend. As soon as he had driven off, I turned to Meriem. The tear she had been holding back for some time was running down her nose. I let her deal with her tear; I had enough trouble stopping myself crying out for help as 'everyday' life carried on around us.

The kidnapper's phone call was, in a sense, welcome.

"Go to Block 4; Entrance C, the one that…"

"…is directly opposite us. That's where it is?" I exclaimed in amazement.

"Yes," he assured me, with gaiety in his voice. "Wait for my instructions in the entrance hall. No tricks – I'm watching you through binoculars."

"Is my daughter with you?"

"You'll find out when you get there. In the meantime, get out your mobiles and smash them. Be careful; don't forget I've got my eye on you. Hey, what are you waiting for to obey me?"

"How are we going to keep in touch?"

"I'll find a way. Obey me this minute or I'll order my – how should I call him? – my colleague to take care of your daughter!"

"Is Shehera with you, yes or no?"

"Shit! Are you going to obey me, you cockroach spawn!"

We did as he said, certain that we were committing a terrible mistake that was as awfully inevitable as the condemned man's march towards the rope that will hang him. We contemplated the plastic and electronic debris at our feet. I spotted a kid who was playing with a ball on the other side of the street looking aghast at us. Meriem murmured, "I'm scared, oh I'm so scared…"

It took us a few seconds to make it to the entrance hall of Block 4, which was every bit as seedy-looking as ours with its peeling paint, vandalised letterboxes and broken-down lift. A sentence that I'd read somewhere came to my mind: 'Abandon hope all ye who enter here.'

"What now?"

"Look by your feet."

Lying openly on the floor was a sheet of paper folded in two. An elderly man came in just at that moment. Wrapped up in a coat, his head covered by a forage cap, he called out a loud "Hello!" before noticing the piece of paper himself. He bent down to examine it. A sudden intuition made me protest: "That sheet's mine – I just dropped it."

The newcomer pulled an ironic face at us and made a vague gesture that said "Well, take it then, if it's so precious!"

I picked up the sheet as the man, still racked with coughing, reached the stairs. I read, "Count to 200 and go up to the top floor, right-hand door." The writing was perfectly legible. A postscript had been added at the bottom of the page: "200 is two times 100, so count to 100 twice!"

I swallowed uncomfortably. It was the first 'physical' contact with the man who had kidnapped our daughter. Meriem began to count out loud, probably as a way of controlling the terror that threatened to relieve us of all capacity for thought. Paradoxically, the seemingly schoolboy humour of the postscript chilled me more than the message itself.

"…199, 200. Shall we go?"

We climbed, slowly at first, then almost at a run. The building was a perfect replica of our own. We passed an old lady in a traditional white *haik*. She tried to strike up a conversation, but we put a quick stop to her lengthy greetings. One floor higher up, two boys were arguing. The elder asked us where we were going, but received no answer.

After a further three flights of stairs, we reached the top floor. There were two flats opposite each other. Between them, a staircase leading to the laundry room had been blocked off with a metal door. "This is it. Oh my God…"

A chant from the Koran was coming from the right-hand door. Aziz recognised the reader of a sacred text, a very famous Egyptian called Abdou Samed. The volume of the cantillation was turned up almost to full volume. The passageway between the two flats was relatively clean and the tenants had even made a point of arranging a few potted flowering plants.

Was it possible that Shehera was being held in this unremarkable flat, suffering violence and mutilation whilst all around 'normal' people went about their 'normal' business?

Aziz felt himself torn between two options, the first suggesting that the place was *Too – what would you call it? – inoffensive, that's it! for horrible events to take place there*, and the other murmuring *Remember the young conscript in the bus who had his throat cut; neither the trees nor the wind speed, nothing changed! Remember when you murdered the informer: did the scenery rebel? Did a comet appear in the sky?*

And the 'reasonable' voice flung back: *Come on, man. Your daughter might already be dead, even as a wonderful aroma of coriander soup tickles your nostrils!*

Ever since his daughter had been kidnapped, Aziz had been prey to all kinds of fears, each viler than the other. The one that immobilised him now in front of this door surprised him by the form it took: a diffuse cramp like the effects of an electric shock spreading through his body – kidneys, stomach, testicles, anus, brain, not to mention his damn legs, from which all motor muscle memory seemed to have disappeared.

His wife stepped forward unhesitatingly. With keen admiration, he mused that *mothers are stronger than fathers; that's why humanity has survived.* She knocked. Once. A second time, harder, because of the racket of the chanting.

The door was flung open. In the doorway, a thin, very old man fixed them with a kindly stare. Aziz recoiled as he recognised the man wrapped in his coat who had let him pick up the sheet of paper.

"Sorry... We got the wrong flat."

"No, you didn't get the wrong one. Please come in," before adding to the stunned couple, "Don't you recognise my voice? It's true that the telephone distorts one's voice. Even I don't recognise myself when I hear myself on the answerphone."

He forced himself to cough a couple of times – and it was by this slightly rough cough that Aziz recognised him.

"I caught a cold," the man explained uncritically. "Can you place me now? I allowed myself a little trick on you just now."

They followed him into the flat, still dumbfounded.

"Sit down," he offered in a slightly more authoritarian voice. "Coffee? I've prepared some for you; it's still hot."

The voice of the teller of the Koran filled the entire room. Meriem almost shouted, "You're the..."

"Your little Shehera's new 'uncle'? Yes, otherwise we wouldn't be gathered here in this grotty flat in a grotty neighbourhood in a grotty city, would we?"

The bald-headed man with almost non-existent eyebrows suddenly extinguished his pretence of a smile.

"So you don't understand why I'm asking you to take a seat? If you don't want me to get vulgar, lady, put your plastic bag down so I can check what you've brought with you."

The enthralled couple did as they were told and perched on the edge of a couch facing the television. With the sound turned off, it was showing a report about the President of the Republic's activities. As he examined the contents of the bag, the old man remarked, "He's got everything perfectly worked out, that dear President of ours. Chief only of himself yesterday, chief of us all today until death carries him off to tamper with some other elections somewhere in hell! Do you like our little master?" he asked as he set down two cups of coffee on the low table. "Now, if he'd had a daughter..." he continued, with the same cheerful grin on his face.

He sniggered.

"He wouldn't have called her Sheherazade, though! The guy's too smart, even if his life resembles the Arabian Nights; I mean the caliph of caliphs with lots of courtiers competing to lick his boots... Anyway, the bloke isn't married and doesn't have a daughter, so the matter is closed!"

When he served the coffee, his shirtsleeve rode up slightly to reveal white hairs, some of whose roots had an ochre tinge.

Mathieu had described the man who threatened Tahar as a flaming redhead.

So ghosts did exist. The man opposite them was indeed the same father whose soul had exploded during the Algerian war and who was bent on taking revenge by burning them, half a century later, as an offering to his grief!

He studied the stranger's face again – an ordinary face, no sooner seen than forgotten, a few wrinkles, a smoker's neglected teeth; nothing that indicated that the man had suffered exceptional sorrow and that he was preparing to pay fate back in its own coin. To bring his breathing under control Aziz forced himself to take a furtive look at the décor around him, which was just as bland as the occupant of the flat: unshowy furniture, a cheap carpet, doilies on top of the television set and on the table. Closed doors at the end of the corridor. His gaze swung back to the living room: on the far wall from the window, a rod held up a black curtain that covered a large part of the wall. A chair had been set down facing the strange curtain.

"Why?"

"Why is our President so smart?"

"Why have you made us responsible for your misfortune? You're well aware that we are innocent of what happened to you fifty years ago."

The man shrugged, seemingly finding the question stupid.

"Do you know this surah? It is about God's bounty. God is obliged to keep repeating that He is good, otherwise no one would believe Him seeing what goes on in the world! I've turned the volume up for two reasons: so that no one hears us should, let's say, our conversation get a bit heated; and secondly so that you absorb the implacable irony of our Creator. I would like…"

"I couldn't care less about your mad meanderings. Just give me back my daughter."

Meriem's voice had dwindled to a trickle, but it didn't quaver. *Your cheeks are ashen, my sweetheart. You should put on a bit of rouge once this is all over.* This outrageous observation had crossed Aziz's mind like a highwayman. To his amazement, he pondered that the hormones released by his fear were gradually unsettling his thoughts.

The thin man made a show of reprobation, wagging his finger at the mother.

"In my day, people didn't use to interrupt their elders when they broached important subjects."

"Give me back my daughter," Meriem repeated, raising her voice. Her lips were blue, and the hand she had rested on her knees was shaking like a small animal. The rest of her body had stiffened with a considerable effort of will.

Ignoring the mother's interjections, the kidnapper continued his mockery of a sermon.

"My dear friends, I would like to remind you that there is only one day that counts – and that's the day you die. In a sense, it is the happiest day of all the ones our birth condemns us to suffer. You will agree with me on that: no more cares, no more grief to rend our guts, no more hopes that are as cruel as they are futile. It's such heartbreak to come into the world and such a relief to disappear forever from this damn universe. Life is like leaving behind a repulsive turd that the merciful void will clear away forever."

Aziz felt certain that the man was declaiming a carefully prepared text. An itch was tickling the back of his throat. He was scared of coughing; maybe his body would react by unleashing a terrible scream that would transform the nightmare Meriem and he were living into reality. For it could not be possible that this skinny old shortie with the look of a peaceful grocer was the sadist who had coldly chopped off his daughter's fingers…

"I can tell you that two of us, maybe three, will know the happiest day of their lives today."

He sipped his coffee, watching for his visitors' reaction.

"Naturally, I'm not talking about the accomplice who's guarding your daughter. He's an amnestied Islamist terrorist, an unscrupulous brute who'll do anything I order him to. He's got quite a number of slightly twisted libidinous instincts, but he tries to curb them… well, as long as I'm around to control him. And so he should; I pay him enough money to obey me. He's scared of me too; the idiot thinks I'm a top dog in the GIA or some other bunch of nutters like that. I persuaded him that you were anti-God and that you deserved the most severe punishment. He's spent time with the rebels himself and he is still fascinated by cruel leaders who are afraid of nothing. So as long as I shower him with money and verses that absolve him of each and every filthy crime he commits for me…"

He plunged his lips into the cup again.

"I think this coffee's delicious, don't you? Just so things are clear, I need to add that I count myself among the blessed who will no longer be alive (he glanced at his watch, pretending to calculate)… in half an hour, three-quarters of an hour's time if we chat for too long. Oh and while we're on the subject, hand over anything that might, let's say, cause harm to any of us in any, erm… unforeseen manner. I'm sure you're hiding at least a knife, maybe a hammer or an axe?"

Meriem and Aziz kept an enthralled eye on every move of the madman holding forth in front of them. He furrowed his brow bad-temperedly.

"It looks like you don't take me seriously. Well, watch this."

Picking up his telephone, he pressed a few buttons before showing them the screen of the device.

"Come closer, it's a small screen. I shall receive an updated message like this every fifteen minutes. Hey, stay calm – don't get hysterical, it'll just make things worse!"

The tiny photograph was under-exposed. Scrunching up his eyes as if he were short-sighted, Aziz made out the figure of a teenage girl – his daughter. She had her hands behind her back and was standing on some kind of platform. Her mouth was gagged with a piece of material or some sticky tape. He only spotted the rope around her neck as he was about to look up.

"What the heck is she doing on that crate?" he asked, fearing the answer with all his soul.

His wife, who was still peering at the screen, grabbed his wrist and let out a single, hoarse sound, maybe the word *no*.

The man shut the lid of his phone.

"Aziz, I think your wife's sight is better than yours. So I'm going to describe your daughter's precise position to you. She is standing on a stack of tins the height of a chair. Those tins contain tomato puree. I like my soup nice and red, and these last few years I've been worried about a shortage of tomato sauce in the run-up to Ramadan. The pile is obviously unsteady, as you can guess. The girl has her hands tied behind her back and her mouth is gagged. So far, nothing too serious. But your wife has seen the… 'hitch.'"

The man laughed scornfully. Meriem's nails had pierced Aziz's wrist. Some blood welled out of the scratches. The husband passionately wished the scratches might tear his muscles and nerves, and that intense physical pain might prevent his brain from understanding the kidnapper's reasoning.

"That photo was taken just now. Accounting for the fatigue and cramps that will soon set in, quarter of an hour, twenty minutes would seem to be the maximum time before one unfortunate movement by your daughter will cause those tins to collapse. It doesn't matter too much for the tomato sauce, but the crash will immediately tighten the slipknot around your loved one's neck. She won't be able to scream in terror because of the gag, although she might be able to twitch her feet for a few seconds – then croak!"

He lit a cigarette and took a long drag on it. He probably didn't realise that he was jigging around nervously on the spot.

"There is a chance, though, that she won't suffer too much. Her neck might decide to snap straight away and, in that case, your little frog will cross over from life to death without even noticing it. You saw Saddam Hussein's hanging on the television. The bastard was so heavy that he almost had his head ripped off, with the result that he died instantaneously. I imagine that right now he's plotting with the devil and a couple of fallen prophets on the quickest way to annex some emirate in paradise."

After greedily sucking in a second drag, he threw the cigarette down on the rug and stamped it out. Aziz followed the movements of the foot crushing the cigarette butt. He set out in search of his own brain in order to react to what had just been revealed to them – and couldn't find it.

"Your daughter's real problem isn't death; it's her fear of moving a hair's breadth and bringing the tins tumbling down as we sit here chatting. Compared to that, her severed fingers are nothing."

His hand stretched out towards them.

"Give me your weapons. They're no use to you. If my partner doesn't get a phone call ten minutes from now, his orders are to give the tins a big kick. And the girl will be off to join Saddam Hussein, the imbecile friend of every Arab."

He let out a cawing jeer when he saw the knife ("Ooh, ooh, now that's scary!"). He studied the husband's weapon with interest.

"This is a French army peashooter, isn't it?"

"It belonged to my father-in-law. It's… it's loaded."

"That swine Mathieu," he hissed through his teeth. "He's not very kind – he could've given you a more modern gun. I would gladly have skinned that man alive, one piece of skin after another, one piece of flesh after another. Then I would have thrown his meat to the dogs with a warning that it wasn't edible. Oh, I would have enjoyed that, I can tell you! But the trick with the car accident wasn't badly thought-out. By the way, you said the gun's loaded?"

"Yes," said Aziz, his eyes bulging as his interlocutor pointed the pistol first at him and then, suddenly, at his wife. He was terrorised and incredulous at once, because the old man's gesticulating was so over the top that it seemed as if he wanted to make them laugh.

"So which one of you shall I take out first?"

He exaggerated his grimace of indecision.

"I scare you, eh? You don't know what I'm up to? You're saying to yourselves: he doesn't have a hair on his head – is that what drove him mad? Is he kidding, with his absurd story about killing one, two or three of the people in this room?"

"Stop the CD of the Koran, please! I can't understand a thing with all this noise," Meriem suddenly begged, putting her hands over her ears.

"Sorry, I need the noise. Firstly, because my neighbours are the nosy kind. And then because it doesn't do any harm, a little Koran here and there; it appeases the soul, it's better than Prozac and we really should listen to a bit before leaving for the other world. Who knows what awaits us there? There's no question about it: a nice chant adds a certain solemnity to any event. One other advantage – and no trifling one – of playing surahs over and over is that no one dares ask you to turn the volume down. Your neighbours tend to think that if someone listens to the Koran all day long he must be friends with hard-core Islamists and therefore likely to give them some serious bother if they annoy him. In a nutshell: holy scripture as a deterrent weapon! Do you really want some different music? Some rai? Oum Kalsoum? I've got them in my collection, you only have to choose."

With her hair covering her eyes, Meriem kept her hands on her temples in a strange pose like an obstinate child shouting *I'm not playing!*

"…On the other hand, if you promise me you'll stay calm, I'll turn it off. OK?"

Silence fell on them like a cold shower. Aziz felt an urge to rub his eyes, but didn't. The old man placed the knife and then Mathieu's gun on the coffee table within reach of the couple. A faint smile played on his lips when he saw them exchange astonished glances. Casually opening a chest of drawers, he took out a revolver that was smaller than the Frenchman's weapon.

"I'd never thought you'd get your hands on a pistol by yourselves. I intended to give you mine. This one's brand new; it's all shiny. I keep it polished, as you can see."

He clicked his tongue against his palate.

"My plan is very simple. There is a gun in front of you. One of you will grab hold of it and shoot the other. The survivor will then kill me. Before he shoots, I promise to tell him where the girl is. He will then have a tiny but real chance of saving her."

"Really, that can't be what you want!"

The mother had reached out with both hands towards the elderly gentleman in a prayer-like gesture.

"You were probably a loving father. You can't really want a child and her parents to die!"

The man took a step back, his eyes sparkling with anger when Meriem touched him.

"Don't come near me, you slut! How would you know if I was a loving father? I cut off three of your daughter's fingers – don't forget that before you try the weeping harlot act to soften me up."

"But…" she attempted, "see some sense… What you're demanding… is horrible…"

"Sense? Another word and I'll kill you both before hanging your beloved tadpole."

The kidnapper was spluttering with rage. He clenched his fists, took a deep breath and suddenly resumed the conversation as if nothing had happened. Only a swollen vein on his forehead showed how extremely tense he was.

"You have a choice between two options. One of them is radical: you all die – father, mother, daughter – and I survive. The second is, by comparison, more moderate: there are two deaths, for sure, one of you two and me. In this case, your daughter has some chance of survival, either with her father or with her mother. This option has two advantages. First of all, it puts your love for each other to the test; secondly, it's fairer because I, the cause of all your troubles, disappear forever."

He ran his tongue over his bottom lip.

"There is a flaw in the second option, you'll say: trust. If you choose the second option, I categorically commit myself to tell you where your daughter is being held and maybe even how to overpower her guard. The bloke's a real moron."

The old man sniggered.

"Just imagine – he uses his real phone number to talk to me!"

His expression changed to that of a second-hand car salesman vaunting the qualities of an old banger to a customer.

"Go for the moderate option, it's the best offer I can make you. Non-negotiable, sir and madam!"

A covetous grin twisted his lips.

"Yes, I know. I've seen too many weird films in my life, the kind where a mother is forced to choose between her two children. So, which of you will make up your mind first?"

Meriem's face had remained frozen in an intensely questioning expression. Aziz's face looked stupid.

"Do you think you've got divine power over us?" muttered Aziz, more in astonishment than anger.

"Yes," exclaimed the old man in a sudden spurt of resentment, "I do have that power over you."

"By what you're saying, you want to spare two out of the three members of my family?"

The kidnapper eyed Aziz distrustfully, obviously wondering whether he was addressing him in the crafty manner one uses with dangerous lunatics.

"I need an heir, my boy," he finally whispered with a tired look.

"An heir?"

The man walked towards the black curtain and pulled it back in one movement. Surrounded by a black wooden frame was a photograph: a pretty young woman in a traditional, embroidered dress was holding hands with a little girl of three at the most. Both of them were smiling faintly at the lens. The black-and-white picture had been so magnified that the outlines of the faces had become blurred, as if they had been drawn with a silver charcoal pencil.

"My life stopped then. I loved them. I was the happiest…"

A spasm choked him.

"It's the only photo I have of them. I've had dozens of copies made because I'm so scared of losing it. I hadn't thought of taking photos of the rest of my family at the time. My father, my mother, my brother… You always think you've got time for those things."

"Why are you talking about an heir?"

The man seemed surprised at the interruption.

"For years, I tried to make myself heard in Algeria. People couldn't have massacred an entire village without ever repenting. My compatriots had snatched independence for the country and there was no longer any need to spit on the victims of Melouza. My little girl, my wife – what had they done to deserve being cut up like cattle at the butcher's? People sniggered and told me to my face that it was a village of traitors that had sold out to France, that one could only piss on the memory of renegades like them. My daughter a traitor, a renegade, at her age?

Aziz sensed an immense, devastating fury spreading gradually through the old man. It had probably never left him since the massacre. Pity as bitter as bile blended in with the hatred that Aziz felt for this creature.

"Once I was kidnapped by military security. I spent a week being beaten in a cellar. According to them I was a disruptive element. Talking about Melouza and Béni Ilemane was regarded as siding with Algeria's enemies. Can you imagine? I just wanted some recognition that my daughter and my wife had been wrongly killed. I was even prepared to forget about my poor mother and my brother, and to admit that that my father, the village constable, might have been punished for his alleged links to the French military…"

He gave a muffled scream. "But my poor Sheherazade had nothing to do with the French army services or with some so-called general arsehole allied to some political leader prick! We are precocious in Algeria when it comes to treachery, but she was only three years old, my little girl."

A nervous twitch ran through his body.

"My heir will be one of you. I'm going to die soon anyway. In three months or six months. Testicular cancer that's spread to anything it can get its teeth into!"

"Heir to what?"

"To my pain, of course! I need someone who will suffer as much as I have suffered and who will speak everywhere and forever about the cause of his misery: Melouza. Infinite pain is an effective prod to the memory!"

The little man pulled the curtain back into place. The slight genuflection he made did not escape the couple. He wiped his lips, then his brow, with a large handkerchief.

"We never feel someone else's pain; we only feel our own. For many years I contemplated the best way to perpetuate the memory of this atrocity. The Algerians didn't want to talk about it anymore. At best, they advised you to shut up, their argument being that there had been so many unjust deaths during and after the war that they weren't going to favour some people over others. The disease struck and I began to fear that I'd be six feet under before I found someone to take over from me... And then I found the answer... Or rather the answer found me!"

His face lit up with pride. All his limbs were trembling.

"For years and years I looked for Tahar, the only man I was sure had taken part in the massacre. That son of a bitch didn't half move around a lot. The first time, I wasn't brave enough. It was in the centre of Constantine. He was walking calmly along the pavement, completely unsuspecting. I was driving a car – I wanted to run him over. At the last moment I couldn't do it. I was scared I'd get arrested; there were witnesses, I'd have been tried and maybe sentenced to death. A policeman asked me for my papers because I'd caused a traffic jam. I explained that I'd had some engine trouble and that I'd be more careful next time. I wasn't worthy of my daughter's misery, nor my wife's, that day. I wept with shame, then I consoled myself with the thought that Tahar's death, on its own, would not offset my family's. For half a century I have lived with this intolerable contradiction: dying of desire to take revenge, yet lacking the balls to go through with it!"

"Why only my father? He wasn't the guiltiest; he was just a simple soldier then. There were loads of officers above him who'd given the orders, people who were colonels and majors, who became ministers, deputies and who knows what else after independence? Why didn't you go after his superiors?"

The man scratched the top of his nose in bemusement.

"You're right. Human beings are stupid. Unfortunately for your father, his was the mug I'd seen. The others – the colonels, the political commissars – were abstract to me. You may consider that unjust, but isn't most of our business on earth about suffering and creating injustice?"

A sly glint flashed across his pupils.

"Do you know that you almost found yourself in your daughter's position? I told you I'd been looking for you all for years before I gave up. I'm sure that it was the inconsolable hatred that gave me this cancer of the bollocks. About two years ago a sort of miracle occurred. I had gone to a town in the Aurès for business purposes. You know the kind of place: just one tarmacked road, a seedy hotel, a single restaurant as dirty and sordid as the inhabitants. It was only the day before I left after a four-day stay that I realised that the street my hotel was in was named after your father. Your father! The half-rusted plaque proclaimed in no uncertain terms that Tahar, a hero of the Revolution, had been dead for over a decade having earned the eternal gratitude of the Algerian people! Chance, my girl, is the universe's only true comedy director, with a real flair for taking the piss out of us! I couldn't stand such a coincidence. I banged my head against the wall in rage – your father had managed to slip cosily into his grave before receiving his rightful punishment! I was already sapped by my illness. I had a heart attack; they took me to the hospital where the doctors thought I was a goner. I almost died without having avenged my family. I was hospitalised for a month, and it was in a hospital bed, full of tubes and on a drip, that I swore to myself that I would devote the remainder of my life to finding Tahar's family. They would pay for him, and that was that. Hatred helped me to recover, they repaired my heart somehow, I bribed whoever I had to for a visa and to have my cancer treated abroad. I had to hang on for a year or two more, enough time to finally claim my dues."

Overwhelmed, the man dabbed his face with his handkerchief.

"I'd saved up a fair amount of money over the course of my life and it was of no use to me anymore because I had no family left. So I put it towards the only cause that mattered to me before being devoured by worms – to find you, every last one of you, and present you with the bill! To begin my hunt, I turned to the organisation for veteran mujahideen. Before she remarried, your mother had received a pension as the widow of a war veteran. I obtained a first address – money, as usual! A year ago, I located your mother's flat. At first I wanted to kill Latifa and that damn Mathieu who lived with her. I didn't immediately recognise the Frenchman who went by the name of Ali. I made enquiries, with lots of baksheesh. I was stunned by what I discovered; while he was a soldier, Mathieu had helped his prisoner, Tahar, to escape from a French army prison! That was when I clearly realised that the hand of God was guiding my steps towards you, perhaps to make up for what He had inflicted on me in the past. By poking around a little more, I found out about you. By killing you first, I wanted to cause as much grief as possible to your mother before I went after her and that thug Mathieu. I followed you one afternoon with a pistol in my pocket to liquidate you. And then I almost went crazy: a teenager as pretty as springtime came to meet you. You called her Shehera, she ran up to you and hugged you, laughing…"

He shook his revolver violently.

"That was the day I decided that I would start with the youngest; she, of course, was to set Tahar's family's labour of grief in motion! For weeks I gathered information about each of you: telephone numbers, jobs, habits… Then I planned my operation, sparing no expense to buy this shitty flat on your shitty estate, hiring the services of a hard-up, amnestied terrorist, kidnapping the girl on her birthday, black-mailing you with her death, etc."

A bad-tempered groan escaped him.

"How dare you give your daughter the name of the poor girl that your father and his kind had murdered! That was utter sacrilege for me! I had the impression that my daughter was dying even more. One Sheherazade replaces another and Bob's your uncle! Your father recommended the name to you, didn't he?"

"Yes," Meriem conceded in a neutral voice, her face marbled with blotches of colour. "My father isn't the murderer you describe. I believe all he wanted was to perpetuate your daughter's memory."

"You disgusting sow! You hope I'll be satisfied with a trick like that? That my daughter isn't dead because your daughter's lucky enough to be alive? Yet every moment your daughter lives is an insult to the memory of my own!"

He had advanced towards Meriem, arm raised, and Aziz had in turn started to move sideways to protect his wife. The old man bit his lip before lowering his hand, which was still holding the revolver.

"Do you want to show me that you love your wife – to the point of risking your life for her? That's easy, son. What I want, though, is for one of you to kill the other out of love. So, who's going to go for the pistol? No volunteer?"

He opened his mobile, dialled a number and waited, favouring them with a mocking pout. A voice, a young one, crackled over the loudspeaker.

"Who is it? Is it you?"

"Yes. Give me the girl."

"Shall I take her down?"

"No, just take the sticky tape off her mouth. For a few seconds, just for a chat."

"OK. Hey, when do we get rid of her?"

"The plan hasn't changed – you act in half an hour. For the moment you wait, is that understood?"

"Understood! If we take too long, they'll find us in the end. I'm fed up of being locked up indoors…"

"Not another word. The loudspeaker's on and I've got visitors. The girl – quick!"

Aziz knew that what he was going through was real. Nevertheless, despite the evidence of his senses, part of him kept repeating that this was so absurd that it couldn't be part of reality. A little to reassure himself, he gazed lovingly at his shattered wife, her frame crumpled, her eyes red.

Reality…

The old man still had the mobile in his hand. The loudspeaker initially transmitted some muffled sound, maybe footsteps, then faint breathing, followed almost immediately by a grunt, from the accomplice, threatening her: "Scream and I kick the tins over! Understand?"

A female voice – which chilled the couple – agreed with difficulty.

"All right, I'm going to hold the telephone up to your ear and you talk. Don't move or it's all over…"

"Who do I have to talk to?" asked the small, exhausted voice.

"**W**ith Mummy," Meriem answered, eyeing the telephone intently. "With your mummy."

"Is that you, Mummy?"

"Yes, my darling, it's me, your mummy who loves you so much."

Tears were running down Meriem's cheeks, but Aziz noted, with pain and admiration, that she maintained a virtually normal intonation. Parents should never show their children that they are scared, she had once told him; it just terrorises them even more.

"Have they hurt you, baby?"

"Yes, Mummy, a lot. And now…"

Shehera started sobbing and her sniffing prevented her from regaining her breath.

"And now… now… they… wa… want to hang me… at my age… I haven't done… anything…"

"Daddy and me won't let it happen, baby…"

The strangled cry rang out: "Help, Mummy, don't let them, don't…" before being consigned to the void by the phone lid snapping shut.

The woman walked towards the man. With one hand she brushed aside the revolver pointing at her. She poked the old man hard in the chest with her index finger.

"You can't do this, you madman… You can't do this… You can't…"

Even as he retreated, the old man spat out furiously, "Now you understand! It hurts, eh? I shouted like you at the time: those nutters couldn't have done something like that – they couldn't have done *that*! But they did it… They did it!"

He spat on the floor – probably to stop himself crying.

"They did it… So now it's my turn to be mad! You will pay for everyone in Algeria…"

Aziz now spoke, his tone shrill, although he tried to strengthen it by coughing.

"What is your deal exactly?"

Meriem started. Knitting her brows, it looked as if she was about to protest. The kidnapper gave a knowing wink before bending down to pick up the old pistol and throwing it to her husband.

"Finally a serious conversation. You kill your wife, then you kill me and, with a bit of luck, you free your daughter."

"How can I be sure that you'll tell me where she is?"

"You don't really have a choice. Hurry up, you've only got 25 minutes left. After that, everyone, without exception, will be dead."

"I want something more concrete than just idle talk. Your price is high," Aziz retorted, forcing himself to talk as if he were in a business negotiation, "and you don't offer any guarantees about the rest of the contract."

The man Meriem had called the devil let out a snigger.

"Some keys – would that be acceptable?"

"Keys?"

"The keys to her prison, for example."

The man rummaged around in a drawer and pulled out a bunch of keys.

Aziz didn't reach out for them.

"First you have to swear to me on the soul of your dead daughter that those keys really do unlock my daughter's prison."

The man scowled. He thought hard for a few seconds, fiddling with the bunch of keys. Then, shrugging his shoulders, he threw the keys into the open drawer. He took two other keys out of his pocket, one small, one big, the two tied together with a piece of string.

"Fine. I swear on my daughter's soul that *these* keys really do unlock your daughter's prison."

"What if you're still lying?"

"Don't ever say that word again when I swear by my daughter, please, otherwise I'll kill you here and now, one after the other."

Aziz searched for his wife's eyes, but her head was hanging and she refused him any sight of her face. The old man became impatient.

"I'm not going to wait for the coming of the Messiah with you. Are you ready to kill your wife now?"

"First give me the keys. What's more, for *all this* (he gestured towards the old pistol and then his wife) to mean anything, I have to be certain that the cell is accessible in under two minutes – on foot of course – and that the survivor will have a good chance of freeing Shehera. Can you guarantee that?"

The old man sucked on the inside of his cheek before blurting out, "It can be done… if you're quick."

"Will you swear on…"

"On my daughter's soul I swear. Here are the keys. Are you satisfied?"

The kidnapper's eyes now exhibited an almost childish excitement.

"Well, let's get it over and done with! Your wife has gone all pale; she can't stand waiting at the abattoir door any longer. And I'm in a hurry to meet up with my family again."

Meriem had sat down again. Keeping her eyes obstinately lowered, she had put both hands on her lap after straightening her dress. Apart from one of her legs vibrating, she betrayed none of her emotions.

Aziz cocked the pistol. He was amazed that he was so calm. Were their lives destined to be shattered in such ignominious fashion? Was there nothing to be done to avoid this unimaginable gunshot?

Her breathing shallow, Meriem held her arms across her chest, hunching over as if trying to reduce the area of flesh exposed to death. The old man's eyes lit up with eagerness.

"Still hesitating, son?" he whispered in slight disappointment. "Abraham hesitated too, but when he had to do it, he did it!"

"You take me for Abraham? And yourself for God?"

Aziz's tone was one of amused astonishment.

"But I'm not Abraham," he murmured to himself. "You can both piss off, you and your Abraham!"

He looked longingly at his wife, who had pulled her head down into her shoulders and was waiting for the deathblow. Her raincoat was open; the dress suited her particularly well and Aziz regretted not having complimented his wife on it.

Aziz's heart melted with pain. He thought, with the ridiculous hope that she might hear him: "Sweetheart, how could you think for one moment that I would put my life above yours?"

Meriem raised her head, surprised at the silence that reigned in the room. For a second, Aziz allowed himself a smile at her, before pulling himself together.

He held out the gun to the slumped woman.

"Here you are, Meriem… It was my job to defend you… Come on, get up… Take the gun and the keys… Shoot quickly, don't think… Don't laze around like that… Stand up and turn towards me. Aim at my forehead. Afterwards, ask him for the place and run there to free our daughter…"

He took Meriem by the shoulders, manhandling her roughly.

"Hurry up. You haven't got much time left…"

The woman tottered on her feet and she had to catch hold of her husband's arm. She threw a horrified glance at the weapon that had been placed decisively in her hand. She beseeched him silently. Aziz shook his head, still wearing the same smile that chilled one part of her soul and warmed another.

"Meriem, you have honoured me by living with me and by giving me a child. That's sufficient for my life not to have been a failure."

The old man said sarcastically, "Maybe I ought to apologise for being here, but the clock is ticking, lovebirds."

Frightened and angry, Aziz yelled, "Shoot, for God's sake, shoot. Otherwise, our daughter will be hanged. You can't let that happen. Mathieu would have died for nothing, and your mother too!"

She levelled her arm at him. But the trembling of her lips showed that she hadn't yet made her mind up to shoot. A tear welled up in her eye, then a second. She wagged her head in a gesture of helplessness.

Aziz started cursing her – and night the colour of pitch invaded his heart.

"I can't," she whimpered. "You're my husband…"

"Are you going to shoot or not, you slut? Shoot, you idiot, you bitch! Do you want our daughter to die?"

A furrow appeared on Meriem's forehead. He noticed a small crease of anger between her eyebrows, so he heaped even more insults on her.

"You whore… you dirty louse…"

He heard a first *click*, then a second.

She had fired. And he wasn't dead.

With feverish eyes, she pulled the trigger again. The same sinister click. He read utter shame in her eyes: *I've killed my husband and yet he's still here staring at me!*

Their host's laughter rang out thunderously.

"The old peashooter is jammed… That bloody Mathieu! A damned nuisance even from beyond the grave!"

Meriem muttered, "Oh, jeering at us, are you…"

She dropped the useless gun. She was breathing spasmodically, as if she'd just surfaced after a long time underwater.

"You devil! I kill my husband and you burst out laughing…"

She bent down over the table, her back hiding her hands. She leaped forward with a grunt.

The knife plunged into the madman's chest while he was still shaking with laughter. Even under the impact, the man didn't lose his balance. Grabbing Meriem by the hair, he twisted her neck round and, with no hesitation, shot her in her exposed temple at point-blank range.

The sound was strangely quiet, little more than the *pop* of a cork from a champagne bottle. Meriem fell to her knees in a strange position as if she were praying to her murderer. Then the body slid over to one side.

"Ah…"

Aziz pushed the man over backwards with one violent kick.

"Ah…" he growled, his whole being reduced to this single sound.

He was holding his wife in his arms. Blood was running down her temple onto her chest, splashing on the husband's hands and raincoat. Without any hesitation, for his wife's precious life was for one more tiny moment beating within her, Aziz kissed the spots of bright red liquid.

Meriem's face had taken on the obscene rubbery look of a sleeping drunkard, a twisted grin deforming her features. The husband ran his hand over her lips to wipe away the grimace.

"You don't look your best, sweetheart."

Then the sob came, the first of a ghastly horde – which he stifled, exasperated by the futility of his own grief.

"You're dead, and the last words I spoke to you were insults. I am the lowest of the low, Meriem. It should have been me instead of you. I didn't manage to protect my family."

He coughed. The small, pointed stones of sorrow would not come out. And they announced their intention to grow and become even sharper.

"You're lucky, son."

"What?" Aziz grumbled, awaking from a thousand-year absence.

"You're lucky to be surrounded by people who love you so much."

The husband jumped (and part of him, to the great scorn of the rest of his soul, took the opportunity to gripe: *She loves me? But she shot at me!*)

"Aren't you dead yet, you rat?"

"It's not going to be long, I don't think. I don't know what the knife hit, maybe a lung, maybe my heart, but it'll be suffocation or a heart attack. Even if the blade only went halfway in, it still hurts like hell. Your wife was a brave woman, boy."

The murderer was sprawled out on the floor with his back leaning against the wall with the black curtain. He was still holding the revolver that had pierced Meriem's temple. Surrounded by a scarlet halo, the kitchen knife was sticking out of the man's chest like some strange, evil plant.

"About to kill me?" Aziz enquired indifferently.

"No, no, son. I need an heir, I've already told you that. In this business between us, pain is a relay race. We're on the same team and you're the next runner. I've just passed you the baton."

"Give me the address then. You swore by your daughter."

A gasp ran through the man. A frothy liquid, like red-stained sick, appeared at the corners of his mouth.

"Of course I'll keep my word."

A smile joined the bubbles springing from his mouth.

"The City of Joy, Block 4C."

The father creased his brow before turning red: "But that's here!"

The wounded man's sardonic pout didn't fade. Laying Meriem's head on the floor, Aziz rushed out into the corridor, opening the doors to every room, from bathroom to bedroom, one after another.

Foaming with rage, he came back into the living room.

"You lied, you lied, you swine! Where is she? I'm going to... I'm going to..."

He shook the wounded man by the shoulders. Between two hoarse coughs, the old man managed a snigger.

"You're going to... you're going to kill me before I can speak. Look at the knife. Life is flowing out of me like a washbasin, you stupid little shit! Stop and listen... First of all, I didn't lie to you, and secondly we're going to do each other a favour. For the last time..."

Aziz let go of the kidnapper's shoulders. The latter handed him the revolver that had put a hole in Meriem's temple.

"Here is proof of my good faith. Answer a question first, just one, before I specify where in the building the cell is. Hurry up, because the guy must be losing patience. He's the cowardly, irascible type who's a bit keen on young flesh; you know the kind. With the rebels, he raped a whole load of kidnapped women. That was before he was granted an amnesty, but I'm not so sure that his dick has changed much since. So, do you agree?"

Incapable of uttering a single word, the father nodded. He seized the weapon he was offered and thrust it into his pocket. He resisted the desire to tidy his wife's hair: her curls were hanging in her eyes, giving a neglected look to a woman who was the personification of elegance. A pool of blood was spreading over the floor around the body.

"What's it like being surrounded by people who love you so much? I mean: Mathieu, your wife, all of them ready to give their lives, maybe not for you, but at least for Shehera?"

"Well…"

The horde of sobs once again came knocking at the top of his throat. Once again, Aziz decided to ignore them, while surprising himself by how diligently he could answer his wife's murderer.

"I could have died at any time in my life for Meriem and Shehera – and my life would still have been complete."

He whispered 'complete' with a feeling that the innumerable mountains of sadness that he would have to scale one by one for the rest of his days were already rearing up inside him.

The waxy-cheeked old man observed him greedily. The bloody foam had now formed a crude beard around his chin. In a rasping voice, he articulated with difficulty, "I wasn't so lucky. My wife and daughter had only just begun to love me. They weren't given any time to cherish me more than that. But unfortunately for me, I had all the time in the world to love them. The longer I lived, the more I loved my vanished ones. That ever-growing love, which churned my entrails, was worse that any disease; it was a cancer of the soul that no morphine could soothe."

Aziz sighed with a shrug.

"Your deal?"

"You saw the frame behind the curtain. Promise me that once a year you will publish the photo in the newspaper, in the 'Birthdays' section. Until your death."

"I don't know either your daughter's or your wife's birthday."

"It's simple: it'll be the anniversary of Melouza. Now take an oath that you will respect your promise and I'll tell you where your daughter is."

"I swear."

"...On the soul of... the deceased woman."

"...On the soul of my wife..."

The wounded man gave a grimace of satisfaction while pointing to the ceiling with his index finger.

"So... where did you hide my daughter?"

"Look where my finger's pointing."

"Yes?"

"I had a laundry put in up there. I made sure I bought it at the same time as the flat. You have two keys on you: one of them opens the door to the staircase leading up to the roof, the other is for the laundry room. You've got a chance of making it."

Aziz stood up at once, but the man was clinging to his trousers.

"Hey, you've got one last chore to see to – to help me depart this planet."

"Fuck off!" Aziz barked, breaking free from the old man's grip. "You can die by yourself!"

"No, I'm too... soft to stand hours of agony," the wounded man protested, stretching out his arm to grab hold of Aziz's leg again. "And also I might feel like yelling out of the window or, better still, phoning my accomplice to warn him of your arrival. I wouldn't hesitate for a second; you've seen for yourself that I sometimes keep my promises. Ah, there goes the phone. I bet that rogue of mine's getting impatient... Please, if you've killed someone already, it's not that hard! So, push the knife in up to the hilt and then it's bye-bye to the Algerian war, bye-bye to this dump called Earth! With a bit of luck, God will be a sport and acknowledge the validity of my actions. If so, I will see my family again in paradise; if not, I will find myself in the company of Satan and I'll ruin his eternal life with my story."

A snigger shook his shoulders as if he'd heard a good joke.

"The funniest thing about all of this is that I spent my entire adolescence dreaming of just one thing: that Algeria would one day be free and independent. Seems like we got far more than we bargained for with our new masters!"

Laughing made him vomit up more blood. Shehera's father contemplated with an air of bewilderment the incomprehensible creature

imploring him with a whore's simpering airs to put an end to his
ordeal. Without further thought, he shoved the old man over backwards and, as one might crush an insect, put his shoe on the knife
before pushing down on it with all his strength. The dying man urged
him on with his eyes until the death rattle came.

Then, grabbing the mobile that had started vibrating again, Aziz
dashed for the front door.

The larger key opened the metal door. He tiptoed up the twenty or so steps.
A second door, wooden this time, blocked off the access to the terrace. He
wiggled the large key in the lock, then the small one, to no avail. A rush of
despair deprived him of his mental faculties until he thought of touching
the handle: the door swung open without further effort.

Wiping away the sweat streaming into his eyes, he had a look
outside through the half-open door.

The crook who had somehow or other sold the utility room to the
kidnapper had done things properly. Not satisfied with extending the
laundry with an extra room, he had also added a little garden of sorts,
made up of a host of potted flowers. To top things off, the building
was surrounded by a wooden palisade so that the whole arrangement
rather called to mind a suburban house that had been whisked away
to the top of a block of flats.

Aziz eyed the weapon that the kidnapper had given him; his hand
was shaking and he had the impression that the revolver was still hot
from the gunshot that had killed his wife. He checked for a second
time that the safety catch was off. The gun's range must be very short
judging by the ridiculous noise made by the bullet that had killed
Meriem. He decided to only shoot at his target point-blank.

Crouching down, he crossed the space between him and the palisade. Straddling the fence on the blind side, he kept tight to the wall
until he reached the door. The laundry room door also had an extra
locked metal covering, but this one was made of wire mesh. The sole
shutter was closed. Aziz put his ear up to the wire mesh. There was not a
sound coming from inside the laundry room. He rubbed his ear with his
coat sleeve and held it to the metal again. A distant rumbling gave him
renewed hope, before he realised that it was the beating of his own heart.

He stood up, defeated. The kidnapper had lied to him. His daughter was probably already dead. A dark shroud replaced the daylight.

He opened his eyes wide, at the same time emptying his chest: in front of him, less than ten yards away, yawned the void.

The void, with its promise of permanent peace, stripped of remorse. Still clutching the pistol, he took a step towards deliverance.

See, it isn't hard, chuntered a corner of his brain.

The telephone rang. He didn't recognise the ringtone. He shuddered and looked around him before realising that the device was stowed in his pocket. He flicked it open. Displayed on the screen were two letters, initials perhaps.

"Is it you?" enquired a voice when he pushed the call button. "Do we do as planned? First, though, I'm going to have a bit of fun…"

The voice let out a coarse guffaw.

"It's halal because it's war booty… And I'll get rid of the body at the dump tonight. No one will be any the wiser. Hey, old man, have you lost your tongue or something? Hang on… It is you? Where are you?"

The line went dead. A few seconds later, the same ringtone went off again. Once more, Aziz took the call in a daze.

"What the hell's going on? I can hear your ringtone… You're out on the terrace, right? You're not the old man, eh? How did you make it up here? Hey, butt-face, I'm talking to you!"

The inside door of the laundry room had opened. From behind the wire mesh of the second door, an unshaven man in his early thirties armed with a sawn-off shotgun was shouting at him.

"What's that in your hand? Answer me or I'll blow your balls off!"

"Nothing – just a telephone."

"Are you taking the mickey? I'm talking about the other hand. It's the old man's gun, isn't it?"

The accomplice pointed his gun at him.

"What old man?"

Just then, a voice called out from inside.

"Is that you, Dad? Dad, he wants to kill me!"

The fellow turned round and yelled, "Shut up, tart! I'd have been better off fucking you, with a rag in your gob!"

The thug went down in two movements, initially sprawling down the side of the wire mesh door with the first shot to the stomach, then onto his back after the second bullet, fired point-blank into the mouth that had insulted the girl. A spurt of blood and some pieces of flesh soiled the father's fist, but he didn't even notice.

"Help, Dad!"

He thought that the key would refuse to open the wire mesh door. It didn't. The oxygen that his lungs were forcing themselves to gulp down had congealed to a thick substance.

Stepping over the body, Aziz saw nothing of the first room, apart from a camp bed and a chair. The air smelled foul, musty with mould and excrement. The door to the second room was open.

His daughter let out a high-pitched whine. He caught her just as the stack of tins collapsed. He almost passed out; he didn't remember his child's body being so heavy. The teenager choked on her tears. As nothing else came to mind, Aziz whispered, "Daddy's here, Daddy's here…"

"He wanted to… then kill me… there's an old man as well… he's cruel… he's going to come… Kill them, Dad, kill them…"

He hugged her tightly to him with her feet a good foot off the ground, lifting her up to leave some slack in the rope encircling her neck. Shehera's arms were tied behind her back, but he spotted the bloody bandage wrapped around her left hand.

"Try not to move – I'll take the rope off first."

His daughter carried on sobbing, haemorrhaging fat tears, and he had no tourniquet to stem them. Despite the surrounding stench, he smelt Shehera's heartrending child's scent through her sweater and he struggled to stop himself weeping too. "She hasn't got a lisp anymore, my princess! As soon as possible, I'll take her to the zoo to see Lucette. Will she remember Lucette, though?" he forced himself to think, horrified by the absurdity of the dykes his mind was erecting against the infinite sorrow that threatened to swamp him. Moving his foot forward to shift his daughter's weight onto his right arm, the father began, with his left hand, to loosen the knot in the rope. A new fit of panic gripped him at the sound of breathing. The revolver was lying on the floor and he was defenceless! It took him one more breath to realise that it was his own breathing.

"He took the tape off my mouth… He said he wanted to hear my fear… that it gave him pleasure… Daddy, oh Daddy, if you knew how much they hurt me… The knife…"

Then, suddenly, before he had been able to take her down, the teenage girl asked, "Daddy, where's Mummy? I want Mummy… Daddy, I want to show Mummy my hand! Mummy…"

Epilogue

"**D**ad! A stork!"

Shehera points to the beautiful, slender bird flying off towards the Ouanougha mountains across the Hodna plain. This June is already hot and the summer promises to be like a furnace. I had pulled the old car up in a wooded grove, its engine grumbling after a good half-an-hour's climb. I smile at my daughter.

"They say storks bring good luck."

"Yes," she replies, slightly surprised. "We could certainly do with some," she adds after a pause.

I try to think up a suitable riposte, but I lack inspiration. I look away. I've felt that strangling feeling in my throat. Maybe Shehera has noticed this because she opens the door.

"I'm going to stretch my legs a bit."

My daughter gets out of the car. She takes a few steps before freezing and contemplating the barren countryside that has witnessed so many crimes. I join her. She has taken off the glove she usually puts on to hide her stumps and massages her fingers distractedly.

My daughter's face is so hard it pains my heart. She looks up at the summit before sighing, "I thought I could do it, but I think I was wrong, Dad. Everything's too real here! I feel like I'm about to meet some almost living ghosts. What should I say to them?"

"We'll be in Béni Ilemane in quarter of an hour. But no one's forcing you to, my girl. We'll go back to M'sila if you want."

A faint, apologetic look comes over Shehera's face. Without answering, she returns to the car and comes back with the bouquet of flowers we bought in M'sila.

Her chin is quivering. I've known this symptom of imminent tears since she was very small. I'd like to put a hand on her shoulder, but I don't dare.

She walks over to the side of the road. She doesn't seem to know what to do with the bouquet to begin with, but then she starts pulling out the flowers one by one and throwing them out into the void. Once she is halfway through, she gives up and, with an enraged gesture, chucks the remaining flowers away.

"There's no point in remembering. This is stupid!"

I put my arms round my teenage daughter. She rests her head on my chest and thinks about rebelling before being racked by sobs.

"Dad, I miss Mum… Mummy…"

"Me too, sweetheart. You can't imagine how much…"

And as I had feared, I too begin to cry.

Today's newspaper is lying on the back seat of my car. The photograph of the woman and the child is there in the births column accompanied by the two words *Happy Birthday*, without any surnames or first names. The employee at the newspaper's advertising department had been surprised by this when I placed my order. I had said it was for discretion's sake, but the man had commented: "If you're trying to be discreet then you shouldn't publish the photo! And anyway, whose birthday is it, the woman's or the girl's?" I had muttered that it was both of theirs. As he filled out the form, the employee said in delight, "The mother and the daughter were born on the same day? A happy coincidence like that will bring you luck, mate – there's an old proverb says so!" I stood there speechless, offering only a stupid grin by way of thanks.

I do actually think that a good part of my intelligence abandoned me the day Meriem died. I use what little I have left to look after Shehera. Whenever I think of my wife, memories float up to the surface like water-swollen corpses. I am torn apart by sadness as well as anger – because Meriem deserved better than these grim memories. None of her beauty and none of what we once were have survived in my memory. I see only the two days following my daughter's kidnapping. I keep going over and over those final hours leading up to Meriem's death, asking myself with an awful sense of guilt at what moment I might have changed the course of events. Deep down inside me remains the confused but extremely powerful intuition that there was some such moment, and that I was unable to grasp it.

At the funeral someone said to me (and I don't know how he dared) that no one should boast of having been lucky enough not to have lived. I did hear some words of condolence after that, but that little phrase about the misfortune of existing is the only one that has stuck in my mind from that sunny morning when I lowered my wife into the ground. Up till now, all it takes is to close my eyes to prove him right and then open them again – to the sight of my poor daughter... – to prove him partly wrong.

Shehera is here next to me, lost in her own thoughts. A muscle twitches by her cheekbone. She has become almost totally speechless, my little queen. Yet she was the one who insisted on conducting this short ceremony at Béni Ilemane. Less than ten days ago, she stated that she wanted to lay a bouquet of flowers on the spot where the people from the *douar* had been gathered to be tortured. That was when she told me that, during her imprisonment, the kidnapper's recriminations and threats revolved around the family he had lost at Béni Ilemane. And above all around the tiny girl who bore the same name she did.

"That man is the person I hate most in the whole world. I cannot possibly imagine hating another human being more than him. And yet when he talked about his love for the child that had been cut to bits, I sometimes felt pity for him. And for her. Even after he..."

She went pale, as if to apologise for her compassion for her torturer and her mother's murderer.

"...you know, cut my fingers off. And then my grandfather's also partly to blame for all of that. I can't pretend he isn't. Do you understand?"

I said, "Yes, I understand' although I didn't.

For over two months she refused to say anything about her imprisonment. The first time I tried to press her clumsily into confiding in me, she flung in my face, almost bristling with hate, that three fingers was nothing compared to her mother's murder and that she would be ashamed to complain after all her mother had gone through.

That was on the day after the particularly painful operation she had had to undergo. The surgeons had cut back her stumps due to the first signs of gangrene, warning me that she would suffer from her missing fingers for a long time to come.

I had almost turned down my daughter's strange request to go and commemorate the victims of Melouza with the objection that I had inherited the old madman's grief, not she, her sole task being to repair her soul and forget her appalling ordeal. She suffers from long periods of insomnia and when she does manage to fall asleep, she frequently wakes up with a start in the middle of nightmares of which she reveals nothing to me. Her marks at school are disastrous and I was called in by the headteacher because she had behaved unusually insolently towards one of her teachers.

I had resigned myself to this trip, hoping that it might give my daughter and me an opportunity to share our burdensome secrets. I had taken only one precaution, that of phoning the town hall beforehand pretending to be a journalist preparing an article about the area. I had been swiftly passed to the deputy mayor, since I was supposedly the special correspondent of one of the country's most influential newspapers. The voluble man had expressed how pleased he was to see the capital's press finally showing an interest in small municipalities like his. To gain his trust I had let him chatter on about the ostracism he felt Béni Ilemane suffered from, the lack of interest shown by the prefecture in his municipality's basic needs, the drinking water that only flowed from the taps once every month and a half, about unemployment, stillborn social housing projects, etc. I had finally got a word in edgeways to say that my planned article was more wide-ranging, since I wanted to look at the part history played in his municipality's current difficulties.

"The part what plays?" he had asked, suddenly on the alert.

"The... the events... you know, Melouza... Are people still suffering from it? Have they forgiven?"

"Oh, is that the main focus of your article? I should have guessed. The anniversary is in less than a week."

His tone had hardened.

"Yes," I agreed a little too quickly. "I'd like to visit the spot where the victims were buried."

"Is that all you're interested in," he complained. "Stirring up muck from the past. What good will it do to re-open the scars of the war? It's so long ago, all of that! And isn't the main thing that we're independent now? Independence is essential, right, unless you have a slave in your mind?"

Interrupting my laborious attempt to argue for the importance of the past in order to construct the future, my interlocutor jeered, "Admit that it's because a nice smutty article about these *harkis*-who-weren't-*harkis* will sell a lot of papers! You couldn't care less about us really. You think of us as peasants still, even if we have been to school!"

The council official spoke with a bitterness that no longer had anything administrative about it.

"Everyone is connected to everyone else here. Everyone has a relative who was somehow involved in that disaster. My grandfather had a brother who was much younger than him. Before they killed the brother that night, they first cut off his legs."

"What about your grandfather?"

"Let's say that he was a bit luckier – he was guillotined later by the French. He'd shot one of their soldiers."

The deputy mayor breathed in.

"So, do you think my father knows how to go about mourning for his own father and his beloved uncle?"

I heard another sigh. Then the man exclaimed, "But why I am telling you all this? To hell with your article!" and hung up.

We returned to Algiers the same day. We now live in my mother-in-law's flat, as the mere thought of setting foot in the City of Joy again made our hair stand on end. Latifa has spent most of the time since emerging from her coma at a clinic specialised in brain injuries. I often go to visit her, firstly because Mathieu made me promise that I would and maybe also because, deep down, I see something of Meriem in this patient whose gaze wanders unfathomable depths of panic.

My mother-in-law occasionally recognises me and recovers the darkly ironic tone of our conversations from before the disaster. More often, when she has all her wits about her, she is overcome with despair. Since she cannot stand the thought that her daughter and her husband are dead, her mind eventually turns to pulp. She will ask me all of a sudden if I'm a new doctor. Not convinced by my answer, she begs me bitterly to phone her daughter and ask her to visit her. "You only have one mother on this earth and you don't just drop her like a dirty dishcloth. I didn't bring her up to behave this selfishly!" she laments. "And Mathieu went out to get some bread and he isn't back yet! What's he hanging about outside for? I hope he's remembered that Tahar's eating with us this evening. Oh my God, how are we going to organise things? Where's he going to sleep? My telephone – where's my telephone? Did someone really come and ask for Meriem's hand even though nothing's ready? What's going on in this house?" she cries out in an anguished voice until a nurse, infuriated by the din, orders her to swallow a sedative. I take my leave of Latifa with a kiss, before hastily closing the door behind me to escape from the half-embarrassed, half-frightened reproach of an old lady worried that a perfect stranger – what's more claiming to be her son-in-law – is treating her with such familiarity. When she is in this state, Latifa only ever mentions Shehera as a baby tucked up in her pregnant mother's tummy, as if by not letting her be born yet, she were trying to bring back her dear granddaughter's luck (and all her fingers).

A fresh police summons awaits me in the letterbox. They don't scare me anymore... Well, not much anyway. At first, the detectives had shown a great deal of mistrust. I hadn't reported the matter to the police until well after I'd taken Shehera to the hospital. I had gone back into the kidnapper's flat to look for the recording of the murder plans that he had forced me to make at the zoo. Apart from the phone I already had in my possession, I had found three other mobiles and about ten chips hidden under a wardrobe, some of them still in their packaging. One of the devices did indeed contain the photo of the informer I had pushed over the edge, but no trace of the compromising recording.

That was the moment in my life when I felt the most disgusted with myself. I rummaged through the various rooms like a maniac for a few minutes, returned to the living room to place kisses all over Meriem's face, one of whose cheeks little more than a mass of coagulated blood by now, and resumed my fruitless search. From time to time, I aimed a furious kick at the corpse of the kidnapper, whose paradoxical name I would only find out later: Zahi, *the Joyous One*.

Weary of the struggle, I armed myself with a hammer and smashed the chips and the mobiles into tiny pieces – apart from the one I had used to communicate with the accomplice – before throwing the whole lot in the toilet. I urinated for a long time, in fear, grief and rage.

Next I phoned the police. Having identified myself, I briefly explained that three dead bodies were waiting for them at such-and-such an address and that I would be at their disposal at the emergency department of Mustapha Pacha Hospital as my daughter had suffered mutilations after being abducted. I hung up when the policeman spluttered that he wanted more details. During the subsequent questioning, I was 'pressurised' but I stuck as closely as possible to the truth, leaving out only the murder of the informer. One of the detectives kept coming back to the time I had taken to alert the police after I first got back from the hospital. The excuse of complete confusion didn't seem to wash with them entirely. I spent three long days in prison (like a terrorist suspect!) before being released, as Shehera's statement was difficult to impugn.

"No Melouza and no uncalled-for comments about the war of independence to the press!" was the sole but *emphatic* piece of advice from the superintendent after my release. "We have had – and *you* have had – enough problems already. Why go and tarnish the memory of a hero like your daughter's grandfather? If some muckraker turns up looking for news, just tell him that your family were victims of a mentally disturbed person. As for the Frenchman, the official version is an ordinary car accident."

He eyed me up and down with a look that was both dreamy and hostile at once.

"What else could your daughter's kidnapper have been apart from deranged? How can someone store up such a desire for revenge for half a century without going rotten inside? If that nutter had been bitten by a rat, I'm sure the rodent would've dropped down dead."

I still jump sometimes when someone knocks on the door too hard. For a few seconds I'm convinced that this is it, this time the police have come to announce that they have found the recording and that I can look forward, if not to the firing squad, then at least to many years in prison. And then utter desolation overcomes me because I imagine my daughter's life as a complete orphan, trapped forever in misery, with no money and nobody to help her. Luckily – up till now – this lasts only until I realise that the person knocking on my door is but a travelling crockery salesman or a beggar asking for a little money.

Tomorrow I'll take her to the zoo to see her beloved Lucette. It's the only place where she feels anything like safe. Midweek, when the weather is good enough, Shehera takes the bus on her own to come and meet me after school. She goes for a walk before reading or doing her homework in front of the bonobo enclosure. Despite it being forbidden to feed the animals, she always has a titbit for her favourites: the little female and her mum, Lucy.

"They and I share a common fate," she retorted one afternoon when I was teasing her about her affection for the two female bonobos. "They and I have been kidnapped, Dad. My abduction is over; theirs still goes on."

And seeing my stunned look, she added with the same earnest expression, keeping her lisp under control as much as possible: "I come to give them moral support. If I could, believe me, I'd help them escape and make it back to their forest."

I had returned to my office with my heart empty. On the way I had bumped into Lounes, who had become an even closer friend – and far less of a chatterer – since he had found out the circumstances of the disaster that had befallen us. I had jokingly related my daughter's words. But my pallid face must have given me away, because the vet had put his hand on my shoulder with a hoarse, mumbled "Mate… mate…" before, to my great surprise, slipping away without further comment.

Three weeks later I handed Hajji Sadok the report he had requested from me. Hajji Sadok, now permanent Director, had flicked through the ten-page document with a worried look on his face. My superior seems constantly ill at ease in my company since my return. He had, it is true, demanded – and obtained – disciplinary action against me for what had been interpreted as my wilfully offensive behaviour towards the delegation from the ministerial supervisory committee. What's more, the incident had almost cost him his appointment. He had attended Meriem's funeral and apologised several times for not having imagined the tragedy my family was trying to cope with. Sick with guilt, he had subsequently used every possible means to have my reprimand revoked, and this had also been very badly received by his superiors. Nonetheless, for some time he avoided walking past the new bonobo enclosure when my daughter was there.

"You should learn to be more conciliatory, Aziz," he flung back at me, throwing the report on the table. "What would it cost you to write that it's an excellent idea to present some Saharan gazelles to our Congolese counterparts? In any case, it's already been decided by people more important than you and me. The Algerian President is absolutely determined to present these symbolic animals of Algeria to the President of the Congo by way of thanks for his bonobos."

"I merely highlighted that the Congolese climate is very humid and not suitable for..."

The Director interrupted me with some irritation.

"Rewrite the report for me. I want it by tomorrow, with the opposite conclusion. As for this one..."

And adding gesture to word, he tore up the sheets of paper and threw them in the bin. Resignedly, I made for the door.

"Hey, our conversation isn't over yet, Aziz! I've decided that Lounes will lead the delegation that will escort the eight gazelles presented to the Congo..."

I laid my hand on the door handle with an imperceptible shrug of the shoulders.

"...And that you will accompany him to supervise the administrative aspects of the trip."

I didn't hide my displeasure.

"That's impossible. There's my daughter, school... My daughter's not very well, you know..."

"Will you let your boss finish his instructions? Lounes has informed me that two of the bonobos are in a bad way."

"Which ones?" I jibbed with rising irritation. "I saw them just now and they were all in the best of health!"

Hajji Sadok pretended to be fascinated by the tip of his pen.

"Our vet knows his job. In his view, it's the two female apes, Lucy and Lucette."

I stood there dumbfounded because the Director had used the two names my daughter had given them.

"Lounes suggested repatriating them to the Congo to have them examined by specialists, for example those at the station on the Kasai River... Nor should we underestimate the chances of losing them on the way..."

"The Kasai River? Where the mother was captured?" I remarked in surprise. "Is this some kind of joke? You say yourself that we might lose them?"

The Director's expression turned crafty. "I didn't say that we *should*; I said that we *might* lose them. What's more, you'll need a secretary for the trip... a secretary the monkeys know well... who can reassure them if they get scared."

He coughed while I waited with a faint sense of anxiety to find out what his true intentions were.

"I thought of your daughter."

"What? This is madness! I…"

Breaking off my protests, he added hastily, "I know she's still young, but I'll deal with the paperwork… And the tickets. The president's office has granted me a line of credit for operation 'Present for the Congo' to manage as I see fit. It seems as if there are some important contracts at stake between the two countries. I'll make sure everything's in order. And anyway it's not really cheating – your daughter isn't completely illiterate; she can string a couple of sentences together."

Stunned with emotion, I stammered, "What about school?"

"A good medical certificate should do the trick for ten days or so. In any case, I suppose school isn't really your daughter's number one concern at the moment. The girl's had more than her fair share of trouble and a journey outside Algeria will give her a bit of breathing space."

Faced with my suddenly misty eyes, Hajji Sadok looked down at his file. Only his crimson ears showed that he was just as emotional as I was. I managed to stop my voice from quavering.

"Hajji Sadok, you could end up in really hot water if the ministry's financial controller gets wind of your little scheme."

"Lounes reported your girl's remark about the monkeys' being kidnapped. So I don't want her to spend the whole year sighing in front of *my* zoo's cages thinking badly of me. This animal brothel is no place for a kid."

His voice turned husky. To allay suspicion he guffawed a bit too loudly. "I only became a grandfather two years ago. You have to earn the title of grandfather! And to hide nothing from you, I've received some more complaints from some uptight sods at the ministry who think that the new enclosure is still too visible to the public. So losing one or two sex-crazed specimens won't bother several bearded officials of my acquaintance. Now get out of here and write me an extremely optimistic report about how happy our gazelles will be to leave Algeria behind!"

I talked to Shehera about it the very same evening. She was so surprised that she almost felt a stabbing pain in her heart. She raised her hand to her chest, began to smile but then froze. I realised that my little girl had felt guilty for her burst of joy. With a lump in my throat, I assured her that her mother would have been happy about this trip and that releasing Lucy and her baby was a way of paying tribute to Meriem. Silently trembling, Shehera went to her room.

Two hours later I opened her door softly. The bedside lamp was on, lighting up Meriem's photograph like an icon. I studied my daughter before turning the light off.

She was sleeping curled up on her side, her chin stern but both hands clutched tightly to her body, as if she were protecting two precious creatures, the great black bird of her sorrow and the fragile little bird of her new joy.

I went back into the room that served me as a temporary bedroom. For a second I felt boundless gratitude to that old fart Hajji Sadok before sleep – more salutary than a bottle of alcohol – took me off on another visit to my cemeteries – the only places, paradoxically, where I could still think of Meriem as a living woman rather than a bloody corpse.

...I circled her grave, like every evening, until my pain became more or less bearable. I was grateful for the flowers growing thickly around the little mound. It needed flowers for me to tell Meriem the story of the miraculous journey that had come out of the blue. For the first few nights the earth around my wife's grave had remained bare. I felt my chest swell with contentment and part of my despair took on their fragrance.

I sat down and, after a moment's reflection to recall where I'd left off the night before, I took up the thread of our conversation. For the time being I couldn't see her and I was the only one chatting, of course, but I carried within me the hope that that the night would eventually come when she would decide to answer.

Having finished my account of the day's events, I stood up. I hesitated a little before paying a visit to Mathieu. His grave was near the edge, yet visible from Meriem's tomb. Sometimes I wasn't sleeping deeply enough to recognise the place where my father-in-law lay straight away. He didn't speak either, maybe because he was too preoccupied with his troubled conscience? But I guessed that he was probably happy enough about my presence, even if I only spoke a few words to him. I gave him some news of Latifa and Shehera, lying a little of course, as you lie to a friend of whom you have grown fond.

Once, early on, I made it as far as the informer's grave, which was located, as if by design, in the middle of a field of rubbish. I wanted to apologise to the man I had killed, but I didn't have the courage to go through with it. Even in my sleep, I was afraid I wouldn't be able to justify myself to a rapist.

I could almost end up calling the Other Man my companion, however, as he is never far from me. I felt his presence again that night.

"Is that you, Zahi?"

I didn't look at him. I couldn't have borne it. I merely perceived that the old man had crouched down on a grave a few yards away.

Perhaps because of our trip I asked him, "Did you recover your peace of mind after taking your revenge?"

He let out a little wry laugh that still sounded menacing even though I knew he was harmless now. For some reason that escapes me, I realised that he had not found his family and that even here in this cemetery of sleep, he remained dreadfully unhappy.

I 'heard' him sigh, then get up and go back to his searching. I didn't look round. I whispered, "What about us, Meriem? Will we recover our peace of mind one day?"

And tenderly I caressed the smooth stone with her name engraved on it.

Glossary

ALN (Armée de libération nationale)	Armed wing of the FLN
djoundi (pl. *djounoud*)	ALN fighter
douar	Mountain village
fatma	Pejorative word for Algerian woman
fellagha/fell	Pejorative French army term for ALN fighters
FLN (Front de libération nationale)	Revolutionary party that led the war against France
GIA (Groupe islamique armé)	Islamist terrorist organisation aiming to overthrow the Algerian government
haik	Large outer wrap, usu. white, worn by both sexes
harki	Algerian back-up soldier fighting for the French
houri	Virgins of the Muslim paradise promised as wives to believers
jebel	Mountains
katiba	ALN company
mechta	Small hamlet
MNA (Mouvement national algérien)	Rival nationalist movement to the FLN